A FORBIDD[...]
BOOK [...]

by
John Williams

© 2025 John Williams. All rights reserved.

Acknowledgements
This book is dedicated to every gay man who has faced persecution, prosecution or even death because of who they chose to love.

Coat of Arms of the Earls of Grafton

CONTENTS:

1. REUNION IN MAYFAIR — 5
2. TENSIONS RISING — 23
3. ESCAPE TO NORFOLK — 35
4. A SAILING ADVENTURE — 51
5. UNSPOKEN FEELINGS — 65
6. THE STORM'S EMBRACE — 73
7. A WORLD TURNED UPSIDE DOWN — 79
8. ONE LAST NIGHT — 87
9. CHRISTIAN'S DEPARTURE — 99
10. LETTERS ACROSS ENEMY LINES — 107
11. THE BATTLE OF JUTLAND, 1916 — 119
12. INTO THE TRENCHES — 123
13. BONDS OF WAR — 133
14. ARMISTICE AND AFTERMATH — 151
15. REUNITED — 159
16. INHERITANCE AND DUTY — 169
17. THE RETURN OF WAR — 181
18. NORFOLK RECOLLECTIONS — 211
19. THE LAST SPRING — 221
20. EPILOGUE — 231
HISTORICAL NOTES: — 238
ABOUT THE AUTHOR — 239

A FORBIDDEN LOVE

CHAPTER ONE:
REUNION IN MAYFAIR

June 1914

The hiss of steam and the groan of metal announced the train's arrival, its engine exhaling a cloud of white that mingled with the already sooty London air. As the carriages juddered to a halt at Victoria Station, Lord John Langley stepped down onto the platform, a figure of slight build among the boisterous throng of Eton College pupils. His blond hair, a stark contrast against the dark wool of his uniform, caught the weak sunlight as he scanned the crowd. He clutched his cricket bat a touch more tightly, the rubber grip familiar and reassuring under his fingers.

John's blue eyes swept over the sea of uniforms and sporting equipment until they landed on Thomas Cooper. The valet's presence was like the quiet amid chaos, his sandy brown hair and hazel eyes setting him apart from the rambunctious youths jostling past. An understanding passed between them, unspoken but clear; here stood his anchor in the shifting tides of aristocratic life.

"Welcome back, my lord," Thomas said, his voice steady but carrying the faintest trace of warmth that went unnoticed by the others.

"Thank you, Thomas," John replied, his words measured but his relief palpable.

He handed over his luggage, and together they navigated the press of bodies toward the exit, leaving behind the cacophony of excited chatter and the resonant clatter of trains.

The journey through London's congested arteries felt both interminable and fleeting as John absorbed the sights and sounds of the city he had not seen for months.

They arrived at Langley House where the white stucco facade loomed, a silent sentinel guarding generations of aristocratic legacy. The household staff stood arrayed before the grand entrance, a tableau vivant of servitude and hierarchy that brought a sharp awareness of the social order that John sometimes found so suffocating.

Thomas, along with other servants, moved swiftly to unload John's luggage from the carriage. Their movements were choreographed with an efficiency that spoke of long practice. Each trunk and case were ferried inside with care, though none of the servants would dare peek within at the cricket gear and personal effects it contained. John could feel the weight of their deference, a cloak woven from threads of expectation and propriety, settling around his shoulders.

Bolton, the butler of Langley House, approached the carriage and opened the door for John. As he stepped onto the gravel pavement, he could not help but hear the crunching sound under his feet, mirroring the chaotic thoughts in his head.

"Welcome back, my lord," Bolton greeted him with natural authority and a respectful nod of the head.

"Thank you, Bolton. It's good to be home," John replied before pausing, flashing a broad smile, and playfully tapping his old servant on the arm. "Oh, and I heard from Papa that he has moved me out of the nursery."

"Yes, my lord. A proper room befits a young gentleman such as yourself. We have packed all your childhood belongings away in the nursery, and we have moved your clothes into the late Princess Victoria's room," Bolton's tone was now that of a mentor to his pupil. "I hope this arrangement is to your satisfaction?"

"Yes, thank you Bolton," John responded as he took a step towards the house. However, just before he could completely turn away, he spotted a faint smile on the butler's face. "I'm going to miss my toys."

"Of course, my lord," Bolton said with a thin smile returning to his lips.

As he continued to ascend the steps, each footfall was a whisper against the stone, a soft counterpoint to the creaking oak floors that awaited him inside. The line of servants bowed their heads or curtsied as he passed. John lingered on the steps, a thoughtful expression etched onto his youthful features, the anticipation of reunion with his cousin, Prince Christian, a subtle tremble in the air around him.

These familiar rituals, comforting though they were, also underscored inherent social barriers. Briefly, Lord John Langley pondered discarding his noble title, becoming Jonny. He briefly considered it, then dismissed the idea; expectations and his circumstances overrode it.

And so, with the doors of the Georgian mansion closing behind him, sealing him within its grandeur and history, John prepared to confront the life laid out before him, a life that promised as much constraint as privilege.

The setting sun cast its amber light across the spacious bedroom, the shadows elongating on the richly papered walls where vibrant birds seemed to take flight among exotic foliage.

Lord John Langley stepped through the threshold of his new adult quarters, the space still unfamiliar, echoing with the promise of autonomy and unseen thrills. He paused by the towering mahogany wardrobe, fingertips brushing the cool brass handles before turning to Thomas, who stood a respectful distance away.

"Cricket was the same tedious affair," John murmured, his blue eyes reflecting a glint of nostalgia as he recounted the matches at Eton. "Though I must say, I've improved my spin bowling considerably."

"Your father would be proud, my lord," Thomas replied, his voice carrying the soft lilt of Norfolk, a soothing reminder of simpler times amidst the grandeur. The hint of pride in Thomas' tone was not lost on John, who managed a small, grateful smile.

"During my absence, how has the earl been?" John ventured further; his curiosity genuine. The room seemed to hold its breath, the very air anticipating the reply.

"Busy with government affairs," Thomas responded, his hazel eyes averting slightly, a practiced discretion there. "Still not quite himself since... well, since your mother."

John nodded, the unspoken words hanging between them like the heavy drapes that muted the city's clamour outside the tall windows. It was a silence filled with understanding, an acknowledgment of shared grief that needed no articulation.

"Kip is coming," John suddenly announced, a spark igniting within him at his mention of his cousin's name. "Prince Christian. In a matter of days." His voice held a tremor of excitement, barely perceptible, yet enough to send ripples through the quietude of the chamber.

"Indeed, my lord?" Thomas said, arching an eyebrow ever so slightly. "The house will be honoured by his presence." His words were simple, but his gaze lingered just a moment too long, discerning the undercurrents of John's enthusiasm.

"Having you here," John began, his heart tripping over the sentiment he wished to convey, "it means more than you can know, Tom." He moved closer, his slight frame dwarfed by the expanse of the room, yet his presence seemed to fill it entirely. "We've grown up together, haven't we? Since those summers at Langley…"

Langley Hall, the family's country estate, stood proudly amidst the Norfolk countryside, its limestone facade gleaming under the sun's golden rays. The grand Corinthian portico welcomed visitors with timeless elegance, while the 40-ft high coffered hall whispered echoes of past grandeur. Oak parquet floors bore witness to generations of footsteps, and the air carried scents of beeswax, tapestries telling stories of old, and the comforting embrace of wood smoke from crackling fires.

Set against a backdrop of 2,000 acres of parkland, woodlands and farmland, Langley Hall exuded an aura of tranquillity and nobility that spoke to its storied history and secluded splendour.

"Indeed, my lord," Thomas echoed, allowing himself the faintest of smiles, one that crinkled the corners of his eyes and softened the formality of his stance. "It has been my honour, and it will continue to be."

The polished, perfumed room felt safer than Eton's busy grounds. In this setting of old wealth and inherent elegance, John could envision a world where he didn't need to bury his desires so deeply.

"Thank you, Tom," John said, his voice hushed as though the walls themselves might overhear. "For everything."

Thomas merely inclined his head, the gesture speaking volumes of their shared history, the quiet bond formed over years of silent understanding. A heavy silence descended; the potential energy of change was tangible as day yielded to twilight, the future remaining unseen.

The late afternoon sun slanted through the tall windows of John's new bedroom, casting long shadows across the polished parquet floor and illuminating fine motes of dust that danced in the air.

The room was a stark departure from his spartan chambers at school, with its heavy draperies and the stately bed that seemed too grand for just one occupant. He stood by the fireplace, where the embers of a fire crackled softly, adding a gentle warmth to the room.

"Tom," John began, turning towards his valet with a contemplative gaze, "actually the matches were splendid," abandoning his aristocratic reserve for a moment, "though I would have traded all the cheers for a quiet afternoon in Norfolk." His voice held a wistful note as he spoke of their shared past, and the many hours as boys they practiced cricket on the lawns of Langley Hall, a time unburdened by the weight of his title.

A FORBIDDEN LOVE

John nodded, a faint smile tugging at his lips. "I'm eager for Kip's arrival. It's been too long since we've roamed the fields of Norfolk together," he said, his blue eyes brightening at the mention of Prince Christian. "And I am grateful for you, Tom. Your companionship...it is a comfort amidst these stone walls."

Thomas and John shared a meaningful gaze, their understanding going beyond words. "It is my pleasure to serve you, Jonny," Thomas said, using his friend's childhood nickname with ease. "And I trust you won't accidentally give the prince another scar this year?"

John chuckled at the memory of the boating accident that had left his cousin with a small scar above his eye. "I guess I'll never live that down," he replied.

"Probably not, my lord," Thomas agreed with a smile. A slight pause, "now, is there anything else your lordship needs?"

John paused; "bathroom?" he inquired. He gestured to the two doors on either side of him.

Tom walked over to one of the doors and opened it. The guest room's adjacent door leads to Prince Christian's quarters. He then opened the opposite door, revealing the bathroom.

"Oh yes, I remember now. Aunt Victoria had it installed for one of her long stays while Kip and I were still stuck sharing a tin bath in the nursery." John's mind was filled with happy memories.

"Shall I draw you a bath, my lord?"

"Yes, please. I need to wash off all the soot from my skin and hair."

"Of course, my lord," Tom said as he started towards the bathroom. "It should take about ten minutes to fill up. And I'll return to dress you for dinner around 6:30 pm. Is that alright with your lordship?"

"Absolutely, Thomas. Thank you." With that, John's valet disappeared into the adjacent room and the sounds of running water filled the bedroom.

John's heart ached as he heard the bathroom door close, signalling Thomas' departure. He fell onto the bed with a heavy sigh, taking in his luxurious and strange new surroundings. The watercolour painting of Langley Hall above the fireplace immediately caught his eye, painfully reminding him of his mother's absence. He stood up and moved closer to the painting, and could not help but run his fingers over her signature: *'Isabella.'*

"Mama, why did you have to leave us?" John whispered, tears forming in his eyes. His gaze drifted to a group of boys playing cricket in the painting, a bittersweet reminder of happier times with Tom and Kip. However, he quickly realised that those days were gone and would never return, overshadowing the memories.

A hot bath was a rare luxury for John, something he had missed during his days at boarding school with twelve boys sharing one room with six baths and fighting for first dibs on the lukewarm water. Even when Kip was still there, they had to work together to ensure they both got decent baths. But now, John was alone and small compared to the other boys his age, only getting leftover baths before the younger ones.

Feeling relaxed and refreshed, John dried himself off and put on the dressing gown provided by his valet. It suddenly hit him that he did not even know what clothes he had or where they were located.

A FORBIDDEN LOVE

"I have a valet now," he muttered to himself with a mix of excitement and melancholy before pulling on the chord to call for Thomas.

As Thomas entered, John could not help but feel overwhelmed by all the changes happening in his life. "Where are my clothes? And what clothes do I even have now?" he asked playfully, shrugging his shoulders in amused confusion.

"My apologies, my lord. I neglected to show you earlier, fearing that it may slip your mind that you now have a valet in all the excitement of the day," Thomas said with a small bow.

He gestured to the nearest wardrobe and opened its doors, revealing a new wardrobe provided by John's father. "Your lordship's allowance was quite generous, and I made sure the tailors left room for growth since your Easter measurements. There is also an allowance for future adjustments." John blushed at the mention of his father's wealth.

"Do you think I have grown since Easter?" he asked, feeling self-conscious. Thomas gave him a once-over before giving his verdict.

"Yes, my lord, I believe so. You've certainly gotten taller," he said, holding up a white dinner shirt against John's shoulders and chest. "But perhaps you just need to fill out a little more sideways."

The comment stung, reminding John of his slight stature compared to the other boys his age, and he could not help but feel a pang of jealousy as he looked up at his tall, handsome servant, Thomas.

He had always been the smallest one among them, and it seemed even more apparent now as they prepared for dinner. "It's not fair!" he exclaimed, unable to hide his frustration.

"Please do not be upset," Thomas replied calmly, trying to reassure him. "You are still growing, and besides, I am four years older than you and with a very tall father."

John nodded reluctantly, understanding the logic behind his servant's words. But as Thomas helped him put on the shirt that was intentionally sized with room for growth, John could not help but resent his cousin Kip who had recently written about his own sudden growth spurt. "I can hardly keep up with all these giants in my life now," he joked bitterly.

But deep down, John secretly enjoyed the attention Thomas gave him during their first dinner-dressing ritual. He soaked up every compliment and adjustment from his servant's skilled hands. And as they stood before the mirror, John felt a sense of sadness wash over him when the process was over.

"I miss the simpler days in the nursery," he sighed, side-tracking himself from this train of thought, as Thomas expertly tied his silk tie.

"Indeed, my lord. But you look very handsome in this formal attire," Thomas said proudly.

John smiled gratefully at his servant's words and silently thanked him for making him feel special amidst all the changes happening around them.

"Is papa home yet?" John asked, turning to catch Thomas' reflection in the mirror.

"Yes, my lord, an hour or so since. He will be in the Blue Room shortly," Thomas informed him, his voice carrying the subtle blend of formality and familiarity that had come to define their relationship.

A FORBIDDEN LOVE

With a nod of acknowledgment, John took a deep breath, steeling himself for the evening ahead. The prospect of seeing his father stirred a complex mix of emotions within him—pride, trepidation, and an indefinable longing for approval. As he moved towards the door, each step was a silent echo in the chamber of his heart, a reminder of the roles they both must play in the intricate dance of aristocracy.

The hush of the Blue Drawing Room was a living entity, wrapping around John as he sat ensconced in the embrace of a winged leather armchair. The air was rich with the scent of beeswax and old wood, the silence only deepened by the soft creaks of the ancient floorboards. He could feel the weight of history in these walls, the generations of Langleys that had preceded him, their eyes following from oil-painted canvases.

His own heart seemed to beat in time with the distant ticking of the grandfather clock, each second stretching into eternity as he awaited his father's presence. Then, the cadence of measured steps approached—a herald to the moment he both longed for and dreaded—and John leapt to his feet, his pulse quickening.

The door swung open and the earl entered, the light from the gas lamps gilding his prematurely white hair. His eyes, those mirrors of familial legacy, landed on his son, and his stern visage softened into a beam of unabashed pride. "I say old boy, what a sight this is for an old man!" he exclaimed, striding forward with the authority of his station and taking John's hand in a firm clasp. The warmth and strength in his father's grip sought to bridge the distance of months spent apart. "Welcome home son," he whispered, and though quiet, the words resonated like a clarion call.

"Thank you, papa," John replied, his voice steady despite the fluttering within.

With a nod, the earl released John's hand and crossed the room to pour himself a drink from a crystal decanter, the amber liquid catching the light as it swirled into the glass. He settled opposite John, the elder man's countenance now etched with the lines of duty and expectation.

They spoke then of trivialities—the mundane and familiar tales of school term, cricket matches, and the comfort of John's new quarters—each word a steppingstone across the chasm of their shared reserve. And yet, beneath the surface of casual inquiry, there flowed an undercurrent of unspoken emotions, a yearning for connection beyond the bounds of propriety.

"And work, papa?" John ventured, threading the needle of curiosity.

A heavy sigh deflated the earl's stature, almost imperceptible save for the tightening at the corners of his eyes. "The Balkans," he murmured, skirting the edge of exasperation as he offered a succinct summary laced with the gravity of international
tension, which had not eased despite his work on the Treaty of London.

John absorbed the information, the gears of his mind whirring with the implications, the world outside their bubble of aristocracy encroaching with silent, inexorable force.

"But enough of that," the earl concluded with a finality that severed the thread of darker discourse. The door reopened; a servant's voice sliced through the air, as if summoned by their thoughts.

"Dinner is ready to be served, my lord."

A FORBIDDEN LOVE

A nod from the earl lightened the room's shadowy corners. "Let us go through and see what Mrs Elliot has for us tonight," he said, a note of levity returning to his voice as they rose in unison.

As they moved toward the dining room, the echo of their footsteps was a testament to their lineage, a rhythm set long before either of them had drawn breath—a dance of heritage and expectation choreographed by the silent witnesses lining the hallways of their storied home.

The dining room stretched before them, a grand tableau of polished mahogany and gleaming silver. Candles flickered in ornate holders, casting dancing shadows across the damask tablecloth.

John took his place to his father's right, at the long table which could have accommodated eight diners, acutely aware of the empty chair where his mother once sat. The absence felt like a physical presence, a void that neither he nor his father seemed able to breach. A quick glance towards his mother's portrait above the marble mantel piece, helped to fill part of that void.

As the first course was served, a delicate consommé that steamed in fine bone china bowls, John found his thoughts drifting to Kip's imminent arrival. The prospect of his cousin's company brought a warmth to his chest that even the richest soup could not match.

"I trust you're looking forward to Christian's visit," his father remarked, his keen eyes catching the subtle shift in John's demeanour.

"Very much so, Papa," John replied, careful to display nothing more than cousinly enthusiasm.

"As am I," his father nodded, a rare smile softening his features. "The boy brings a certain... vitality to the house."

John felt a flush creep up his neck at his father's words, grateful for the dim candlelight that concealed his reaction. He took a sip of water, using the moment to compose himself.

"Have you any plans for his stay in the country?" the earl inquired; his tone casual but his gaze sharp.

John set down his glass carefully. "I thought we might go riding, perhaps take a turn about the grounds, and then indulge his maritime interests and take the boat out and about."

"Capital ideas," his father agreed. "Though do be mindful of propriety, John. Society keeps a close watch, especially on people like us, so don't forget to reintroduce yourself in the village. Afterall, one day it will be your village and your villagers. And be sure to lead the village on Sundays."

A chill ran through John at the subtle warning in his father's words. Did he suspect? The earl continued, "and it will do you both well to reconnect before..." He trailed off, leaving the unspoken future hanging between them like a gossamer thread.

John felt a tightness in his chest at the implication. Before what? Before they were both thrust into the roles society demanded of them? Before the carefree days of youth slipped away entirely? He focused on the delicate china before him, tracing the intricate blue pattern with his eyes as he gathered his thoughts. Did he detect a flicker of something—was it understanding? Sympathy? — passing across his father's face.

A FORBIDDEN LOVE

John's father emptied the last drops from his crystal glass and pushed himself to stand, a contented smile gracing his lips. "My dear boy, please forgive me," he addressed his son with tiredness in his voice, "but I think it is time for me to retire." John stood up immediately, concern etched on his face.

"Are you feeling quite well, papa?" he asked, noting the lack of traditional nightcaps in the drawing room.

"Tomorrow, I face a mountain of cables at the Foreign Office, and I must make an early start and have breakfast there," he reassured his son, placing a comforting hand on his shoulder. "I will do my best to be back by six pm so we can catch up some more and make some plans."

He gave his son's shoulder a squeeze before nodding towards the door. "Goodnight, son."

"Goodnight, papa. It is wonderful to be home and I do understand your duties at the Office," John replied with a warm smile. He placed his hand over his father's, "and tomorrow, I will use the day to arrange and try on all my new clothes to make the most of your investment in me."

Father and son exchanged nods of respect before Bolton moved forward to open the door for the earl. "I will inform Bates that you have retired for the evening, my lord," the butler stated dutifully.

"Thank you, Bolton. Goodnight." With that, the earl exited the room, leaving behind a sense of warmth and familial love. However, John reflected for a moment on his father's words, and he could not escape the concern he felt about how much work he was doing. After all he was twenty years older than his mother and now entering his mid-sixties.

As if sensing the young lord's worry, Bolton stepped closer and spoke in a hushed tone. "Don't fret too much about your father, my lord. He is a strong man."

"I know, Bolton. Thank you," John replied, feeling reassured.

"Now, my lord, would you like a drink in the drawing room? The evening papers are still there," offered the butler.

"Yes, I think I will," John said, as he was escorted to the drawing room. There, Bolton poured him a generous glass of brandy.

"Thank you, Bolton. You remembered my preference," John remarked with fond nostalgia. He could not help but remember the first time he had indulged in this spirit with his cousin as they once snuck drinks into the nursery. A slight flush rose to his cheeks at the memory.

"We were all young and foolish once, my lord," Bolton said with just a hint of disapproval, recalling the same incident.

"Even you, Bolton?" John asked with a wide grin.

"Yes, even me, my lord," Bolton admitted with a small smile on his lips. He handed John the glass and asked, "will there be anything else?"

"No, not tonight thank you. I will finish this drink and then retire for the night," John replied confidently. Bolton raised an eyebrow and fixed his gaze on John. "Oh, and I'll send for Thomas when I'm ready to go upstairs."

"Very well, my lord. I bid you goodnight," Bolton said with a nod before silently exiting the room.

A FORBIDDEN LOVE

Pleased with himself, John whispered under his breath, "I think I passed that test." He looked around the grand room and remembered that he was alone. Perhaps it would be best to get some rest and clear his mind he thought. He stood up and reached for the cord, taking a big sip of his drink before doing so.

Soon after, the heavy door swung open.

"Did you need something, my lord?" It was one of the older footmen.

"Yes, James," he said, finishing his drink in two large gulps. The brandy warmed him as it went down, and he let out a small gasp. John set the empty glass on the mantlepiece. "Could you inform Thomas that I'll be going up now?"

"Of course, my lord." The footman opened the door and stepped aside for John to pass.

"Goodnight, James."

John strode purposefully through the entrance hall, swinging himself around the newel post at the bottom of the stairs - something he had always done despite the constant disapproval from adults. He landed on the fourth stair and quickly turned left, continuing his playful ascent up the first flight.

However, by the time he reached the second floor, he had lost momentum and moved slowly. Instinctively, he headed towards the narrower staircase that led to the nursery floor and attics before realising his mistake and entering his new bedroom.

John stumbled onto his bed, a little tipsy from the brandy he had just downed. As he lay there with his eyes closed, he could feel the bed shifting beneath him.

"Ooops," he muttered with a giggle. A few minutes passed in a haze of drunken thoughts and amusement before he heard the door open. John rolled over, struggling to lift his head. "Ah, Thomas, ready to read me a bedtime story like Nanny used to do?" John asked with a smile as he took in the sight of his valet.

"If you wish, my lord," Thomas replied with a broad smile, "but perhaps getting you into bed first would be more suitable?"

With that, Thomas stepped towards the bed and took John's hands, helping him sit up. The tie needed to come off first, but every time Thomas released one hand, John slumped backwards or sideways.

Resigned to John's antics, Thomas sat on the bed next to him and clasped him in place with one arm while using his other hand to remove the delicate silk tie. He then unbuttoned John's waistcoat and dress shirt.

Progress was slow, but eventually Thomas removed all of John's upper garments - much to the younger man's amusement. He let him flop backwards onto the bed, arms out-stretched, revealing tufts of armpit hair and a bony ribcage and chest.

"Yes," John said to himself with a chuckle, "plenty of room for growth." Thomas neatly folded and stored away the clothes, as he contemplated his next move.

He selected a nightshirt from a drawer and shook it out before noticing the name label sewn into its collar: *Langley, Ld Jn*.

Carefully putting it on over John's head and threading each arm through the sleeves, Thomas lifted him back up and pulled it down over his torso. Once John was settled back down in bed, Thomas easily took off his shoes, socks, and garters. With the waistband loosened, Thomas slid John's trousers off from his ankle.

Lord John's valet thought for a moment and changed his approach then pulled the cord to summon James. While he waited for him to arrive, he neatly piled up the clothes. The footman appeared and entered silently, quickly taking in the scene.

"The brandy?" he offered.

"Yes, the brandy," Tom whispered. "But perhaps some coffee now?"

"Very wise, Mr. Cooper," James replied with a wink.

While they waited for the coffee, Tom carefully brushed out any creases in John's suit and removed any lint from it. Satisfied with his work, he placed the suit back into the wardrobe and neatly folded the shirt and put away the shoes. He would send the socks to the laundry in the morning along with the shirt.

A quiet knock at the door signalled James' return with a tray. Tom made space on one of the bedside tables and allowed the footman to set down the tray before dismissing him for the night. With John now awake, Tom moved him up in bed so he could sit up, but every touch seemed to make John squirm ticklishly.

"Shush, shush Jonny, let's get you sitting up."

"Do I have to?" John complained groggily. "Mmmm, I smell coffee," he mumbled with half-opened eyes. "I do love coffee."

"I know," Tom replied. "Sit up and you can have some." John needed no further convincing. Ever since his mother introduced him to coffee during a trip to France and Italy years ago, he preferred it over traditional English tea.

Tom made a small cup of creamy sweet coffee and handed it to John while holding onto his hand as he sipped it slowly at first, but then gulped it down.

"Perfect, Tom," John said after taking his first sip.

"I'll make you another one," Tom said as he took the empty cup from John's hands. As John sat up on the bed, he noticed his old nightshirt.

"Looks like I'm back in school uniform already," he joked, pulling at the shirt.

"There are some new silk pyjamas in the wardrobe, my lord. Would you like to try them sometime?" Thomas attempted to divert the young lord's attention from his troubles and noticed that it seemed to work.

"That would be lovely, Thomas. I never could have worn such things at school, but perhaps at Cambridge this autumn?" The coffee was kicking in and John looked forward to starting university.

"Yes, my lord. How are you feeling now?"

"Much better, thank you. I apologise if I made a fool of myself or embarrassed you," John blushed slightly as he realised his behaviour may have been a bit indulgent. Thomas began to stand up, but John reached for his arm and guided him back down to sit on the bed.

"My lord?"

A FORBIDDEN LOVE

"I am still learning all of this, and I will be relying on you to guide me through any bumps in the road," he spoke quietly with great thought. "But I would never want to compromise your position with the other servants, and especially Bolton," he said sincerely.

"I will not let that happen, please do not worry about such things. And…" he looked into John's eyes, "whatever happens between us in the privacy of your rooms will stay between us. I promise you that as a friend and as your valet."

John looked down, feeling unworthy of such a pledge. "And besides, it was Mr. Bolton who recommended me to your father."

"Really?" John's face lit up with surprise.

"The earl initially wanted to hire an experienced valet for you, but someone who did not know you personally. Mr. Bolton gently suggested that someone more familiar with your ways would be better suited, therefore I was selected. And under Mr. Reeve's tutelage, I received six months of training at Langley," there was pride in Thomas' voice.

"I had no idea. I just assumed Papa chose you because we were childhood friends," John smiled. "So Mr. Bolton convinced Papa to change his mind?!"

"Yes, my lord. Mr Bolton is really quite fond of you, despite his stern exterior. All summer we have had to sit in silence as he read the cricket reports from your school matches, so I would say he is also proud of you. But you must never let him know that, because he would consider that improper or inappropriate in his world."

"Of course not, Thomas," John took a deep breath and continued, "if you don't mind, when we are alone in my room, could we maybe be a little less formal?" John held his breath, "in my eyes, you have always been my friend before my valet. And I think I would miss that friendship."

"As you wish, my lord," Thomas teased. John frowned at his response, feeling disappointed. But he could not keep a straight face as Thomas reached forward and tickled his ribs, causing an involuntary giggle. "You're still ticklish then Jonny," he laughed.

"Oh, you trickster! For a moment I thought you were serious," they both laughed heartily, the tension from earlier now gone.

"Perhaps, you could help me in one small matter?" asked Tom.

"Of course, anything," Jonny replied.

"I will promise to honour our friendship in private of course, but could you perhaps call me *Mr Cooper* to the other servants? That I haven't reminded you sooner is entirely my fault. I should have mentioned it at the station, but I was so pleased to see you looking so well, that it slipped my mind completely," Thomas felt sorry that he had had to mention such a thing.

John blushed and said, "Oh my gosh, I am so sorry Tom, I forgot in the excitement. I will try my best… Cooper," he grinned.

"Thank you, Jonny," he returned the smile with a nod. "Well then," Thomas stood up and straightened his uniform. Sleep now, young man. "Goodnight, Jonny. Sleep well."

"Goodnight, Tom. And thank you." John was soon sleeping soundly.

A FORBIDDEN LOVE

Thomas awakened John the next morning by flinging open the curtains and letting the bright morning sunshine flood in. John, feeling slightly groggy from the previous night's drinking, rubbed his eyes dramatically against the light.

"Good morning, my lord," Thomas greeted with a mischievous grin. "How are you feeling?"

"Good morning, Thomas," John replied, forcing a smile through squinted eyes. "I'm feeling alright."

"That good, eh, Jonny?" Thomas attempted, but ultimately failed, to hide an *'I told you so'* expression. He added, pausing dramatically: "It is convenient therefore, that I have requested tray service for your breakfast—a one-time exception."

John sat up in bed and watched Thomas move around the room, arranging his clothes for the morning. "That looks nice," he commented upon seeing the suit being laid out for him.

"It's the latest fashion, apparently," Thomas noted, examining the lightly tweeded grey jacket. "Single-breasted, with a shorter cut than usual and made from a nice, cool, thin material," he said, picking up the trousers. "And these have slight pleats at the top for extra comfort," Thomas added, looking pleased.

"The waistcoat and shirt?" John inquired with genuine interest.

"The waistcoat," Thomas said, returning to one of the wardrobes. "I thought this one would be suitable for daywear," he replied, holding out a silk-fronted single-breasted waistcoat in a simple grey to match the suit. Reaching for the shelf of neatly folded shirts, he added, "and finally, a plain white shirt for the new rounded collars."

"Papa must have spent a fortune on me!"

"His lordship wanted to ensure you have plenty of clothes for the summer, and for your time at Cambridge in the fall," Thomas explained, just as a soft knock announced the footman's arrival with John's breakfast tray.

After dismissing the servants, Jonny leisurely enjoyed his breakfast, savouring the quietness before dressing and making his way to the morning room. The sunlight filtered through the large floor-to-ceiling windows, illuminating the morning newspapers arranged on what used to be his mother's writing desk. He poured himself a cup of coffee from the waiting tray, settled into a wingback chair by the fireplace, and opened *'The Times'*. Yet, his concentration wavered, interrupted by the thought of his cousin's impending visit in a few days. Each blink brought forth the image of Christian's striking face, his jet-black hair, and those piercing blue eyes.

Over the past year, especially since their last meeting at Christmas, Jonny's feelings for Christian had deepened, becoming more intense and perplexing. He felt trapped in a whirlwind of emotions that seemed beyond his control.

Shame and disgust mingled with the fear of potentially bringing scandal to the family, yet he could not dismiss these feelings no matter how hard he tried. He felt torn between the comfort of having a few days to prepare for Christian's arrival and the dread of confronting his emotions.

Above all, he was resolute in not jeopardising his friendship with Christian or revealing the truth of his feelings, but the struggle within him was growing harder to ignore.

A FORBIDDEN LOVE

John was shaken from his thoughts by a knock at the door and the appearance of a footman. "Sorry to disturb you my lord, but a message has just arrived for you from the earl," he said, offering a small silver tray. John recognised his father's handwriting and took the folded note.

"That will be all for now, Robert," he told the footman before opening the note. He skimmed its contents rapidly, then re-read it slowly and deliberately to reassure himself amidst a rising panic.

He learned from the note that his cousin was expected in just over an hour, and this forced him to take several deep breaths to steady himself. Inside, relief, anticipation, joy, and a tinge of shame clashed within him as he recognised that his reaction to Kip's arrival differed from his previous reaction—indeed, from the expected reaction.

Determined, he vowed yet again that these new emotions must never show. A quiet knock at the door heralded Mr. Bolton's entrance. "Excuse me, my lord," Bolton said.

"Yes, Bolton, I assume you have also received a note from my father with the news," John replied, more as a statement than a question.

"Indeed, my lord. We understand his highness is arriving on the boat train at around one o'clock, and I have arranged for the carriage to meet him at the station." Bolton paused, awaiting John's nod of acknowledgment and approval.

"Of course," John responded, fully aware that Bolton was expecting further instructions. "And could you postpone lunch until two o'clock," he continued in a tone that brooked no argument.

"Very good, my lord," Bolton said with a gentle smile. "Also, Mrs. Elliot mentioned she could prepare some of the prince's favourite cold treats as a welcome, if you so choose."

"Yes, Bolton, that is an excellent idea. Please thank Mrs. Elliot for her thoughtfulness," John decided after a moment's reflection. "And let's have lunch here." Bolton nodded his approval, understanding—presumably—that the two young men would enjoy some privacy for their reunion.

John wrestled with his thoughts, uncertain whether to remain where he was, or to appear more at ease by returning to his room. Eventually, he ordered more coffee and tried to focus on the newspapers. Finding it impossible to concentrate, he began pacing the room, then moved to stand by the tall windows, watching the passing world in an attempt to calm himself. Time, for once, crawled; even the clock's ticking seemed to slow. A knock, followed by a footman, broke the heavy silence.

"My lord, the prince's carriage has just pulled up outside," the footman announced. John sprang to his feet.

"Thank you, Robert," he said, smoothing down his jacket and checking his buttons. Taking a deep breath, he stepped into the hallway. Standing in the centre of the mosaic-tiled floor, he watched through the open doors as the tall, lithe figure of his cousin elegantly emerged from the carriage. Bolton met him and led him up the steps, where at the door a footman accepted his cousin's hat and coat.

John took in the sight before him and his heart skipped a beat as he marvelled at his cousin's beauty—taller and more athletic than he had been at Christmas, yet still with the same piercing blue eyes and raven-black hair. John advanced toward his cousin and extended his hand.

"Welcome back, your highness," he said with a respectful nod. Kip gripped his hand, the coolness of his grip standing out against the warm, slightly damp, and nervous grip of his cousin.

"Thank you, my lord," Kip replied with a sharp nod in the Germanic manner. "My English home feels most welcoming." Christian gently squeezed John's shoulder with his free hand. "Good to see you, Jonny." John responded by reaching for his cousin's arm just above the elbow and patting it warmly.

"And you too, Kip. Now come in for some lunch," he said, guiding Kip to the morning room. "Mrs. Elliot has prepared something nice for you!"

Waiters brought trays of food and coffee, and placed them on various small side tables. Finally, alone, the boys looked deeply at each other as if set in some kind of spell that drew their eyes together.

"It is so good to be back Jonny," Kip took a bite of a cold meat sandwich and overtly savoured the taste to deflect away from his words. "I have missed Mrs Elliot's cooking too much." Christian, too, was struggling with his feelings and worked very hard to not give away too much. As for John, he was confused and uncertain, yet determined to never compromise his friendship. "Are we up on the nursery floor again?"

"Oh no, not this time," responded John, "that's no place for two young gentlemen now." He paused. "I even have a valet now," he said proudly.

"Quite the young English lord then. So, who is the lucky fellow that gets to dress you?" there was a glint of mischief in his voice which Kip immediately regretted, "not some crusty old ex-footman I hope." Jonny chuckled.

"No, not crusty at all! It's Thomas."

"Really, our Thomas?" Christian was incredulous, thinking Thomas was too young for such a responsible position.

"Yes, apparently Papa arranged it all with Bolton months ago and sent him to Reeves to be trained. It was quite the surprise for me when I got home."

"I am sure it was," agreed Christian. "I look forward to seeing him very soon then!" Christian lifted his head away from John's gaze and looked around the familiar room. "Do you remember the hours our mothers spent in here going through their correspondence and writing invitations for tea?"

"And how they banished us back up to the nursery if we were too noisy!" Both boys shared so many fond memories of their childhoods either here in Langley House, or in Norfolk at Langley Hall. But equally, both also shared the saddest of experiences together when their mothers died onboard the Titanic.

Ever since that dreadful day, each had found solace and comfort from their shared memories of their mothers, and they were never reluctant to mention them. They each hoped this bond, forged in tragic circumstances, would never break.

Easy and relaxed conversation followed, punctuated mostly with their shared recollections of the long summers spent at Langley Hall. Eventually, Christian felt the exertions of the previous day and yawned widely, "oh sorry Jonny, it's been long journey!"

A FORBIDDEN LOVE

"Of course, Kip, you must be exhausted," John said, though his tone wavered between genuine concern and a hint of reluctance as he stood to pull the cord. A few minutes later, a footman arrived.

"Ah, Robert, the prince and I are going up to our rooms now. Would you ask Mr Cooper to come up?" His voice carried the weight of protocol, yet there was a lingering trace of uncertainty.

"Certainly, my lord," the footman replied, and as he lingered by the door, the two young men ascended the stairs.

"Mr Cooper?" asked Kip as they moved together, "we have to call Thomas *Mr Cooper*?" Kip shook his head half in incredulity and half in humour, not quite knowing which was correct. John paused at the top of the main bedroom floor.

"Here we are, Kip," he said, motioning toward the room adjoining his own. He stepped over and opened the door to guide Christian inside.

Kip's eyes widened at the sight of the spacious room—a mix of wonder and trepidation mingling in his gaze. John continued, moving to the side door, and opening it with a hesitant flourish. "And here is my room, and through there," he pointed uncertainly to a door on the opposite wall, "is the bathroom we can share. If that is alright for you?"

"Of course it is," Kip replied, though his voice held a quiet note of doubt, as he glanced around John's room before moving to open the bathroom door. "All of this is for us?" He asked, his words resonating with both admiration and a trace of incredulity.

John chuckled softly, the sound tinged with a mix of nostalgia and the unsettling realisation that Kip's surprise mirrored his own reaction just the day before.

"Yes, how splendidly grown up we are now!" he remarked, a tentative laugh shared between them. Just then, a quiet knock disrupted their mirth, announcing Thomas.

"My lord, your highness, how can I help?" Thomas said, his tone meticulously formal yet betraying a subdued smile as he struggled to contain his amusement. Kip exchanged a conflicted glance with Jonny, perplexed by this unexpected formality from a childhood friend now grown. Yet, as his eyes flitted back to Thomas, the subtle smile slowly revealed its warmth, softening his lingering reservations.

"Oh, Thomas, you nearly had me there!" Kip exclaimed, stepping forward with a warmth that belied his inner turmoil. He shook the valet's hand. The enthusiasm in his grip removed his hesitation. "It is good to see you, old friend."

"Thank you, Kip. We have both been eagerly awaiting your arrival," Thomas replied, scanning the open doors with a keen eye. "I assume Jonny has given you the guided tour?" His gaze fell on Kip's room—bare of trunks or luggage—and the question that lingered in the air. "You are wondering where your luggage is?" Christian shrugged, an ambiguous smile playing on his face confirming Thomas' suspicions. "I have taken the liberty of unpacking for you, and the small chest with your personal things is on the table by your bed."

"Thank you, Tom; that was very kind, especially since I am traveling alone," Kip said, his gratitude mingling with a hesitant frustration at his own inability to fully rely on others.

A FORBIDDEN LOVE

"If you need any help with anything during your stay, your uncle has put me at your disposal," Thomas offered, his pride and pleasure edged with a hint of solemn duty.

Kip smiled wistfully as he reached over to slap Thomas gently on the arm. "Thank you, Tom, but ever since the Academy I've grown used to looking after myself." His words hung in the air, a collision of independence and the pain of relinquishing old comforts. "But it is comforting to know that I can rely on you should I need anything."

In that moment, their reunion felt bittersweet, a mix of heartfelt welcome and the tension of changes too swift to settle. As they all allowed themselves to look forward to the summer ahead, a lingering cloud of unspoken conflicts remained.

The earl would not be home for dinner, and John arranged for a simple supper to be brought up for him and Kip later. Once Thomas had departed, Kip removed his jacket with a pained smile, then tossed himself onto his bed as if to escape the unsettling cocktail of nostalgia, warmth, and a dawning awareness of the responsibilities that now lay ahead.

"This is the biggest bed I have ever had to myself," Kip said, spreading his arms and legs wide, yet there was an underlying tension in his voice.

"You should try to get some sleep before supper," advised Jonny, his words tinged with concern. Kip patted the bed next to himself, caught between wanting company and needing solitude.

"Yes, Jonny, I will do it soon, but come sit and chat for a while first," he smiled, though it seemed forced, "just like you used to do for me at school." Kip, in particular, had struggled with sleepless nights, only finding rest when Jonny was nearby.

"Of course," Jonny agreed, sitting down and leaning back against the headboard, though he felt a knot of worry tightening in his chest. "Is everything alright, Kip?" He studied his cousin's athletic form, marvelling at his outward strength but sensing an inner turmoil.

"Oh yes, thank you, Jonny..." Kip hesitated, his tiredness muddling his emotions. "Maybe, as nanny used to say, I'm just a little '*over-tired*'," he admitted, though the words did not quite capture the storm within.

"Yes, perhaps you are. Now close your eyes," Jonny instructed, though a part of him questioned if rest was truly what Kip needed.

Kip complied, and Jonny gently placed a hand on his cousin's forehead, lightly stroking his eyebrow with his thumb, a gesture as much for his own reassurance as Kip's. As Kip drifted into sleep, Jonny carefully moved off the bed, his heart heavy with unspoken worries. He paused at the door, casting one last lingering look back, unsure if he was leaving Kip or his own uncertainties behind.

John settled at his desk, spending some quiet time refining his latest sketches. Immersed in his art, he found both an escape from his worries and a resurgence of the happy memories of hours spent with his mother learning the craft. He would lean back in his chair after each small adjustment to his pencil drawing to appraise his work, all the while recalling his mother's gentle advice: '*Learn when to stop, Jonny—it's often the imperfections that make your work more personal.*'

A FORBIDDEN LOVE

A couple of hours later, feeling confident that he had struck a perfect balance between his need to improve the drawings and his mother's advice, John noticed that even though the evening sun still shone brightly outside, it was nearly eight o'clock. Quietly, he opened the door to Kip's room, only to be greeted by the sight of Kip sitting up in bed with a book in hand. "Oh, you're awake," he observed and stepped inside.

"Yes," Kip said warmly, "I peeked earlier and saw you deeply focused on your sketches, so I decided not to interrupt."

John quickly reassured him, "I wouldn't have minded at all." Then, with genuine concern, he asked, "have you managed to sleep at all?"

Kip set his book aside and replied, "yes, for about an hour or so. I think I'll take a bath and maybe have something to eat if that's alright with you?"

"Perfect," John replied. "I'll call the kitchen to have supper sent to my room around nine, and then I'll run you a bath. Besides, we both need an early night if we have an early start tomorrow." John detected the unspoken question on Kip's face, "it's the Eton-Harrow match at Lord's tomorrow."

"You're playing this time?" he asked, recalling John's previous disappointments.

"Yes!" John admitted, unable to hide his excitement. "I'm sorry I have to drag you along, though…" John knew Kip was no great fan of the sport despite the many hours they had played together as boys with Thomas.

"Absolute nonsense, cousin!" Kip countered, leaning forward to pat John's thigh gently. "I know how much this means to you, and therefore it means a great deal to me too." In that tender moment, their mutual affection and understanding filled the space between them, as if a new spark had ignited—or perhaps it was simply a heartfelt acknowledgement of what they both already knew.

For a few long seconds, they remained wrapped in that feeling, until John, fearing it might overwhelm him, broke the spell. He leapt from the bed and said, "I'll go let the kitchen know and get your bath running while you start getting ready."

Internally, Kip exhaled in relief that the moment had passed and his deeper feelings stayed hidden, though his nod betrayed a hint of his true emotions.

After taking baths, changing clothes, and having supper, the two boys settled into their nightwear and robes, sitting in the armchairs by the fireplace. Each held a crystal tumbler filled with brandy, sipping the warm drink in silence. They appeared thoughtful as they pondered quietly.

Kip eventually broke the silence, saying, "This must be difficult for you."

John nodded in acknowledgment, prompting Kip to continue, "I mean, all of this," gesturing around. "Becoming the young lord, with all the new responsibilities and rules that come with it."

"Yes," John replied, feeling relieved the question had not been more probing. "But you could say I've been preparing for this my whole life, and at least I have Thomas to guide me."

"That might be true, Jonny, but that doesn't mean it will be easy," John thought about how well Kip understood him and silently agreed with a nod.

"Besides, Kip, you'll have to handle the same thing one day," John sighed.

A FORBIDDEN LOVE

"Maybe, but being at the academy keeps me away from that cold castle and all those duties and expectations," Kip said with a forced smile and wished to end the conversation as it was moving towards aspects of his life that saddened him. "Now, my dear cousin," Kip finished his drink and stood up slowly, "it's time for me to get some proper sleep."

"Of course," John said, raising his glass. "Goodnight, Kip. Thomas will wake us in the morning."

"Goodnight, Jonny."

A FORBIDDEN LOVE

CHAPTER TWO:
TENSIONS RISING

The boys were up and ready for breakfast in good time to take their carriage to the cricket ground. Once inside and moving, "forgive me, Kip," John said, a touch of remorse threading through his words. "I couldn't have missed this match, and I am sorry if it's not your cup of tea."

Kip tapped Jonny's thigh with his knuckle and smiled, the scar above his right eyebrow lifting slightly. "I wouldn't be anywhere else," he assured, his voice laced with an unspoken understanding that ran deeper than perhaps both boys realised. "And besides," he continued, "nowadays, I am strictly a cup of coffee man because of you and my aunt." He raised both of his eyebrows in an admission of the power Jonny held over him.

The hallowed turf of Lord's Cricket Ground lay resplendent under the late morning summer sun, its emerald expanse a stage for sporting theatre. Amidst the thrum of excitement and the murmur of expectant spectators, Lord John Langley stepped onto the field with an air of quiet confidence. His cricket whites clung to his slight frame crisply, the fabric whispering against his skin as he moved. Christian, tall and composed, watched from the pavilion's shade.

Eton were to bat first and John strode out to open the innings. As he readied himself at the crease, there was a palpable anticipation in every sinew of his body—an eagerness to prove his mettle before his cousin's watchful gaze. Despite not being an avid follower of cricket, Kip held a secret pride in John's skills.

With the crack of leather on willow, John danced an elegant ballet upon the pitch, his movements blending athleticism and grace in equal measure. The crowd's applause rolled like distant thunder, but the clamour faded into irrelevance as Christian's eyes followed each fluid stride, each poised swing of John's bat. Every cheer was a testament to their shared past, every run a silent victory in the language only they understood. Just short of fifty, they dismissed him, and as he walked toward the pavilion, he heard polite applause and slightly more raucous applause from Kip.

After a pleasant lunch, it was Harrow's turn to bat, and John took to the field. He wasn't renowned for his bowling, but his captain gambled and gave him the ball—they needed wickets. The moment John's arm unfurled to deliver a ball that would shatter the wicket, time seemed to suspend. Kip leaned forward, his heart quickening as the batsman faltered, the stumps breaking in a triumphant cascade.

A shared look, heavy with unvoiced emotions, bridged the distance between pavilion and pitch. John's blue eyes sparkled, seeking Kip's approval in the sea of faces.

"He's my cousin, you know!" Kip declared to a stranger beside him, the words carrying a weighty pride that felt like a clandestine caress across the crowd's din.

The day wore on, the sky a vault of endless blue, and with each over, the tension in the match synchronised with that between the two young men. It crackled like static beneath the surface of polite society. In every stolen glance, each subtle nod, their connection deepened, underscored by the slow burn of something forbidden yet undeniable. They were players in a game far more intricate than the one unfolding on the field—a dance of glances and gestures fraught with the peril of discovery.

As the match drew to a close, the lengthening shadows cast a warm amber light over Lord's Cricket Ground. Both teams felt they were on the edge of something significant, a point from which there was no return. Harrow needed just six runs to win, while Eton required one wicket.

A firm hit sent the ball toward John, who made a spectacular catch to secure the winning wicket. In that moment, the crowd's roar seemed to fade, and John's triumphant smile softened as he exchanged a secretive glance with his cousin on the pavilion steps.

John enjoyed his newfound fame among his teammates as they enthusiastically celebrated their victory. Meanwhile, Kip chatted with a few boys he remembered from his Eton days, but his attention was mostly on watching his cousin relish his moment in the spotlight.

He felt a profound, albeit undeserved, pride in his cousin. In quieter moments, Kip realised his feelings for his cousin were changing. He recalled the many times in Germany when he had daydreamed about John, and now, in this moment, his heart swelled in his cousin's presence.

The evening descended upon Mayfair as they arrived back at Langley House. They were a little late, and it was a bit of a scramble to ready themselves on time for dinner. John was taking a bath, but Kip soon interrupted him by knocking and entering
the bathroom.

"What?" exclaimed John, hurriedly covering himself with his hands as he jerked upright in his bath - somewhat embarrassed by his vulnerability.

"Sorry, I just wanted to ask you to save the water for me!" He laughed loudly.

"What's so funny now?"

"I am just remembering that it wasn't so long ago that we were sharing baths," Kip raised his eyebrows to emphasise his mock surprise at John's sudden shyness.

"Fine, fine, you just surprised me," John smiled at his cousin. "Give me five minutes and it is all yours." Kip skipped back to his room, leaving the bathroom door open. Less than five minutes later, Kip appeared in the door again, wearing only a small towel around his waist.

"Well?" Kip asked. For the first time, John noticed his cousin's defined torso, a fine trail of hairs popping above the towel to his belly button, and an ample covering of hair on his shins. "Let me get a towel for you."

He reached over John and pulled a towel from the shelf behind the bath. John could not help but notice the definition in Kip's body as he stretched, nor the thick patch of matted armpit hair - and for a moment there was an intoxicating natural body odour that could have suffocated him.

John could feel he was losing physical control as he felt his own arousal looming. Kip, perhaps sensing his cousin's unease, acted the perfect gentleman and opened the towel out in front of him and turned away slightly to allow John to stand and then wrap himself in the outstretched bath sheet.

"Thank you, Kip," John said with a sense of relief that his potential embarrassment was now concealed.

A FORBIDDEN LOVE

"Now scoot Jonny," Kip dropped his towel and stepped into the bath, "it's my turn!" John headed to the door and turned to Kip.

"...and," he saw Kip's now naked body in full frontal perspective. He paused, and possibly audibly gulped, at the sight before him, "... and don't take too long," he croaked. Kip smiled in acknowledgement and sunk slowly down into the water.

An hour or so later, the dining room of Langley House became a stage for decorum and veiled sentiments. The silverware gleamed under the flickering candlelight, casting elongated shadows across the white tablecloth as a silent ballet of footmen glided between the guests.

At the head of the table sat the earl, his stern countenance softened by the wine's warmth and the day's success. Lord John, still flushed from the exertions of the match, exchanged furtive glances with Prince Christian across the laden table.

Each smile they shared was like a secret handshake, an unspoken affirmation of their mutual admiration. As they recounted the day's highlights, their voices danced around each other, never quite touching but always harmonising in the recounting of John's athletic prowess.

Christian found himself seated across from John at the formal dining table, his uncle presiding at the head. The click of silver on fine china punctuated the conversation as John recounted the day's match.

"And then, just as I thought the ball was past me, I managed to snag it!" John's eyes sparkled as he mimed the diving catch.

Christian chuckled, captivated by John's animated retelling. "It was a sight to behold," he added. "I've never seen anything like it."

The earl's eyebrows rose slightly. "I must say, Christian, I'm surprised to hear such enthusiasm from you about cricket. As I recall, you were never much of an enthusiast."

Christian felt heat creep up his neck. "Well, I..." he began, flustered.

John came to his rescue. "Kip's always been supportive of my cricket, father. Even if he prefers sailing himself."

Christian shot John a grateful look. "It's true," he mumbled. "I always enjoy watching John play."

The admission hung in the air, weighted with unspoken meaning. Under the table, Christian's knee brushed against John's, a fleeting touch that sent a jolt through him. When he dared to meet John's eyes again, he found them filled with a warmth that made his breath catch.

The older man cleared his throat. "Well, it's good to see family supporting one another. Now, shall we move on to dessert?"

As the footman approached with a tray of delicate pastries, Christian discovered a different kind of hunger consuming him, one he feared but also hoped would never be fulfilled.

Dinner concluded with the earl excusing himself again earlier than was customary, citing the need for rest before the strenuous days ahead. The boys, now left to their own devices, made their way to John's room.

A modest request for a tray from the servants ensured privacy and a supply of libations to fuel the night's confidences. John's room was now a little more of a sanctuary than it had been before, held an air of seclusion, heightened now by the dim glow of the hearth. They settled onto the settee, closer than space requuired, their sides brushing with the semblance of casualness.

The fire crackled and popped, its light casting dancing shadows that seemed to sway with the rhythm of their lowered voices. Kip casually removed his tie, throwing it on the chair opposite, before unfastening and removing the stiff collar of his shirt. As usual, John struggled with his tie and Kip reached forward. "Let me Jonny," and Kip quickly unburdened John of his tie, similarly tossing it aside. "Better?"

"Yes, thank you Kip," he then released the tension in his collar. "That's better. Today was...remarkable," John continued, his tone a mix of reflection and wonder, the words floating in the air like mist.

"Indeed, it was," Christian concurred, his gaze lingering on John's profile, studying the contours illuminated by firelight. "But not solely because of cricket." John's mind whirled contemplating what Kip could mean by that - was it the reunion with his old school friends, the conversation at dinner with his father, or, and this was the most alluring, or was it frightening, the moments in the bathroom? Initially, at least, Kip gave no further clues as to his meaning.

The conversation meandered through topics both inconsequential and profound, each exchange thick with the unvoiced knowledge of the world beyond the room's protective walls. And yet, within this hallowed space, guarded by silence and secrecy, they allowed themselves to drift ever so slightly into the realm of what could be, rather than what should be.

As the embers slowly faded, and the hour grew late, their discourse threaded through laughter and earnest whispers, a tapestry weaving together the uncharted trajectory of their hearts. In the quietude of the young lord's chamber, they discovered a solace that defied the tumultuous times looming ahead, a fragile peace in the eye of an impending storm. An almost tacit agreement between themselves that something was different now.

The low hum of conversation and the occasional clink of glass against the mahogany side table filled the room as John shifted slightly, his leg brushing against Christian's. The touch was brief, ostensibly accidental, but it sent a current through them both that seemed to buzz in the quiet space between their bodies. They each drew a breath, neither willing to acknowledge the moment yet unable to dismiss it.

"Remarkable match today," murmured Christian, making an easy diversion, his voice a soft baritone that resonated with John's own thrumming nerves.

"Indeed," John replied, his lips curving into a smile that did not quite reach his eyes. "Though I fear my performance paled compared to the thrill of your company."

Their gazes locked, heavy with unspoken thoughts, and for a fleeting instant, the world beyond the flickering flames of the fireplace ceased to exist. A log shifted, sending sparks spiralling upwards, tearing their attention away from the precipice they each felt they now teetered upon.

"Tomorrow's excursion should prove enlightening," Kip said, attempting nonchalance as he glanced away. "The marvels of science await us."

"Ah, yes," John concurred, the corners of his mouth twitching into an earnest grin. "But forgive me if I find myself more drawn to the stillness of the natural history museum for a spot of sketching."

"Of course," Christian agreed, his voice light, but his eyes dark with something akin to yearning.

A FORBIDDEN LOVE

They lingered a while longer, the dying fire casting a warm glow over their features. Eventually, the inevitable pull of time tugged at their sleeves, prompting reluctant goodbyes. As they parted, the ghost of their proximity haunted the cool air of Kip's room through the adjoining door.

The next morning dawned bright and clear, the streets of London already bustling as John and Christian made their way to the South Kensington museums. The Natural History Museum loomed before them, its terracotta facade both intricate and imposing.

"Shall we start here?" John suggested, gripping his sketchbook tightly. Christian nodded, following him up the steps. Inside, the soaring arches and elaborate stonework immediately caught John's artist's eye. He settled onto a bench, flipping open his sketchbook with practiced ease. His pencil flew across the paper, capturing the sweeping lines of the architecture.

Yet, as he worked, John found his gaze continually drawn to Christian. His cousin wandered the exhibits, examining fossilised remains and taxidermied creatures. The sunlight streaming through the tall windows caught in Christian's raven hair, creating a halo effect that made John's breath catch.

Surreptitiously, John began to incorporate Christian's figure into his sketches. The firm line of his jaw, the elegant curve of his neck, the way his hands moved as he gestured at an interesting display. John lost himself in the act of creation, barely aware of the passing of time.

"What are you working on so intently?" Christian's voice startled John from his reverie. He snapped the sketchbook shut, his cheeks burning.

"Oh, nothing really," John mumbled. "Just some rough sketches of the building."

Christian's eyebrow quirked, a knowing look in his eyes. "I see," he whispered. "Well, shall we move on to the *Science Museum*? I'm eager to see their new aviation exhibit."

As they left the Natural History Museum, John could not shake the feeling that something fundamental had shifted between them. The air seemed charged with possibility, and every accidental brush of their hands sent sparks dancing along his skin. What lay ahead, he wondered, both thrilled and terrified by the prospect.

They settled on a bench as John continued to sketch, but Christian moved away, examining the exhibits. But it was not the intricate machinery or new technology that captured his attention. Instead, his eyes kept darting to Christian's lithe form, tracing the elegant line of his jaw, the curve of his shoulders.

"Jonny," Christian called out, causing John to slam his sketchbook shut. "Come look at this marvellous contraption!"

John approached cautiously, clutching the book to his chest. "What is it?"

Christian's eyes sparkled with excitement. "Some sort of new engine, I believe. Fascinating, isn't it?" His gaze dropped to the sketchbook. "May I see what you've drawn?"

John's heart raced. "Oh, it's nothing really. Just rough sketches."

Christian reached for the book, but John instinctively pulled it away. A look of hurt flashed across Christian's face, quickly replaced by curiosity.

"Come now, Jonny," Christian teased, his voice low. "What secrets are you hiding in there?"

A FORBIDDEN LOVE

John swallowed hard, the air between them suddenly thick with tension. "No secrets," he lied, his voice barely above a whisper. "Just... private thoughts."

The hushed ambiance of the *South Kensington Science Museum's* cavernous halls enveloped Lord John Langley and Prince Christian as they retreated into a secluded alcove, away from the prying eyes of the afternoon crowd. The cool, tranquil air set the stage for their hushed dialogue, accompanied by the distant hum of voices.

"Show me what you've drawn," Christian's voice was low, yet the request carried the weight of a command.

"Later," John murmured, pulling the book closer to his chest, an almost imperceptible tremor running through his slender fingers. "It's not ready to be seen." The words lingered between them like a whispered secret, laden with unspoken significance.

Christian withdrew his hand, the corner of his mouth curling up in a knowing smile that belied the twinge of disappointment at being denied a glimpse into John's inner world. He nodded, accepting the boundary set by his cousin, his gaze lingering on the leather-bound enigma that John guarded.

He quickly changed the subject in order to hide his initial disappointment of not getting to see the contents of the sketchbook, "What do you dream of?" John's eyes widened for a second, shocked at such directness from his cousin almost inducing a self-inflicted panic. Kip noticed the subtle signs of turmoil in this cousin's eyes, and perhaps realising that there was something else between them, quickly added, "I mean your career after you leave Eton and Cambridge."

John's fingers traced the edge of his sketchbook, relieved, his eyes fixed on a distant point. "I'm not sure," he admitted. "Father expects me to follow him into politics or the civil service, but..."

"But?" Christian prompted gently.

John turned to face his cousin, their eyes meeting. "But I dream of studying art in Paris. Of creating something beautiful and lasting." He paused, a wry smile tugging at his lips. "Terribly impractical, I know."

This was the kind of dream confession Kip felt he could deal with and, his relief now showed too, but still he felt gratitude for being trusted with this information.

Christian's hand found John's knee, squeezing it lightly. "Not impractical. Brave." The touch sent a jolt through John's body, and he struggled to maintain his composure.

"What about you, Kip? Still set on the navy?"

A shadow passed over Christian's face. "It's expected of me. The family legacy and all that." He sighed, removing his hand and then running it through his raven hair. "Sometimes I wonder too if there is not more to life than following in our fathers' footsteps."

John nodded, understanding all too well. "We're meant to be the next generation of leaders, aren't we? But what if we want something different?"

The air between them grew thick with unspoken and forbidden possibilities. John's heart raced, aware of every point where their bodies almost touched.

"So, Kip," John began, his voice barely above a whisper. "What do you really dream of? Beyond the sea and your father's expectations?"

"Yes, there are many times when I wish to set my own course... to find a harbour where I can drop anchor and truly be myself."

A FORBIDDEN LOVE

Their shared admission lingered in the air; a delicate connection forged from their deepest desires. In this serene corner of the museum, surrounded by the whispers of history, they found comfort in each other's presence - two souls united in navigating the treacherous waters of societal expectations.

"Maybe," Christian added softly, his hand grazing against John's with deliberate intention, "we can both find a way to carve our own paths, even if it means braving through storms?"

"Maybe," John repeated, allowing the warmth of Christian's touch to seep into his skin, an unspoken promise that hung in the charged atmosphere of the museum.

The intensity of their conversation left both boys feeling exposed and burdened with newfound longings. It was as if they had silently formed an unbreakable bond, based on a mutual understanding of the pressures they faced. They spent the rest of the afternoon lost in thought, contemplating this newfound support between them.

As the earl could not attend their scheduled dinner that evening, Thomas had arranged for them to spend the evening at a West End music hall, followed by dinner at a nearby restaurant. He dressed Lord John as per usual, but also took a moment to admire Prince Christian's attire.

"You look quite the elegant young prince, if I may say so," Thomas beamed with pride.

"Oh, you may certainly say so, Thomas. Anytime and as often as you'd like," replied Christian with a smirk.

"Now, my lord, I have your tickets downstairs and have booked a carriage to take you to *The Savoy* for dinner. It should arrive in about forty-five minutes. Would you care for a drink in the Blue Drawing Room while you wait?" John and Christian exchanged glances and both agreed that John's room was more comfortable.

"No thank you, Thomas. We'll have a drink in my room and be ready to leave by eight o'clock," said John, slipping into the authoritative tone of his father.

"Very well, my lord," acknowledged the servant, recognising his young master's decisiveness. "If there is nothing else, I will await you in the hall at the designated time."

"Thank you, Thomas. That will be all for now," John dismissed his valet with a nod. As the door closed behind him, John let out a sigh of relief.

"Quite the young lord," commented Christian playfully. "I better get you a drink before you send me to the Tower." He poked his cousin in the ribs as he made his way to the drinks tray.

The evening draped itself in shadows across John's chamber, the flickering flames of the fireplace casting an intimate dance of light and darkness on the mahogany walls. Christian lounged on the plush settee, a glass of port balanced precariously on his knee, his gaze lingering on the sketchbook that John held just out of reach. The air, heavy with the cloying scent of cedarwood and a subtle undertone of lavender from the linen, seemed charged with a magnetic tension.

"Come now, Jonny, don't be such a bore," Christian teased, his voice low and smooth, echoing off the silk damask-clad walls. "You've been guarding that book as if it were the crown jewels."

A FORBIDDEN LOVE

John, sitting adjacent yet miles apart in this moment of playful confrontation, hesitated. His fingers tightened around the leather-bound sketchbook, the one confidant to his clandestine thoughts and secret yearnings. His heart thrummed a nervous rhythm against his ribs; the thought of exposing its contents left him feeling exposed, vulnerable.

"It's nothing, really. Just idle scribbles, Kip," he protested, his voice betraying the quiver of uncertainty that rippled through him.

But Christian, with the determination of one well-versed in naval strategies, leaned forward, his athletic grace clear even in this simple action. He snatched the book with a dexterity born of years spent on rowing teams, dodging John's half-hearted attempts to reclaim it.

"Idle scribbles do not cause such fervent protection," he said, a mischievous twinkle lighting up his blue eyes, the scar above his brow a testament to their shared past.

"Please, Kip, I…" John began, but the words died in his throat as Christian flipped open the cover, his fingers tracing the edges of the paper with an almost reverent touch.

Christian's breath caught. There, amidst quick sketches of pastoral landscapes and architectural studies, was a portrait of him, captured with an intimacy that transcended mere artistic observation. The likeness was undeniable—every line and shadow meticulously rendered to reveal more than just his physical form, but the essence of his spirit, the depth of his soul.

For a suspended heartbeat, they were both ensnared in the silent tableau; two young men on the precipice of discovery, the kindling of emotions too complex to name. Christian looked up, his expression a mélange of awe and something far more dangerous. "John...this is...I had no idea you..."

"Thought of you?" John finished for him, the words falling between them like drops of rain in the night's stillness. "I couldn't help myself. You're always there, in the back of my mind, somehow finding your way onto the page."

Their eyes met and locked, a myriad of unspoken confessions swirling in the depths of their gazes. The room seemed to shrink around them, the air thick with the heat of the fire and the palpable intensity of their connection.

Outside, the world of Edwardian propriety and societal expectations loomed, but here, in the seclusion of John's bedroom, they hovered on the edge of a revelation that could either bind them together or tear them apart.

"John..." Christian's voice was a whisper, barely audible over the crackling of the logs. But he did not need to finish. The portrait had said everything that needed to be said, and a long pause followed. "I think we should move downstairs for the carriage."

Amid the raucous cacophony of laughter and clinking glasses, Lord John Langley and Prince Christian found themselves in a world apart from their recent confessions. The West End music hall thrummed with life, its smoke-filled air lending a hazy, almost ethereal quality to the surroundings. Gaslights flickered, casting dancing shadows over the spirited crowd that packed the space, their bodies moving to the ragtime melodies that vibrated through the floorboards.

A FORBIDDEN LOVE

Seated at a small table, tucked away in a dimly lit corner of the hall, necessity pressed the two young men close, the heat of their thighs touching through the fabric of their well-tailored trousers. John's heart pounded a rhythm that drowned out even the boisterous tunes of the band on stage, each beat an echo of the intensity between them.

Christian, ever the embodiment of poise, leaned in closer to John under the pretence of better hearing his words over the din. But the intent behind the movement was unmistakable, his breath warm against John's ear as he spoke. "I can scarcely hear myself think."

"Perhaps that is for the best," John replied, his voice laced with a mixture of jest and earnestness that mirrored the ambiguity of their situation.

In the close confines of their secluded spot, John caught the scent of Christian's cologne—a subtle hint of bergamot and sandalwood that mingled intoxicatingly with the pervasive odours of tobacco and spilled beer. The fragrance was as familiar as it was disarming, evoking memories of stolen moments and unguarded glances.

Their eyes met occasionally, a silent language developing between them, each look laden with the weight of unvoiced desires. As if drawn by an invisible force, John would find his hand brushing against Christian's under the table, their fingers grazing in a touch that seemed accidental but lingered just long enough to suggest intention.

The act of watching the performers became secondary to the charged connection that pulsed between them. The vibrant flashes of colour from the stage costumes, the laughter and applause of the audience—it all faded into the background, overshadowed by the silent drama unfolding in their private corner.

John could feel the warmth of Christian's leg against his own, each point of contact sending a jolt of awareness through him. There was a tremor in his hands, imperceptible to the casual observer, as he struggled to maintain a facade of composure.

Christian, meanwhile, exuded a calm that belied the fire that John knew burned within him—a fire mirrored in his own heart. As the music swelled, reaching a crescendo that seemed to shake the very walls of the music hall, so too did the tension between them build—an exquisite pressure that promised both danger and delight.

For one night, they allowed themselves to be nothing more than two young men enraptured by the heady thrill of proximity, their shared secret a delicate dance of longing and restraint amidst the smoky revelry of Edwardian London.

The echoes of laughter and clinking glasses from the music hall trailed behind Lord John Langley and Prince Christian as they stumbled into the cool night air, the haze of cigarette smoke clinging to their clothes like ghosts of the revelry left behind. The London streets, bathed in the dim glow of gas lamps, hummed with the usual nocturnal symphony, but to them, the city felt hushed, as if it were holding its breath.

"Archduke who?" Kip slurred, squinting at the bold black letters splashed across the late edition newsstands. His voice carried a playful lilt, tinged with the slight buzz of spirits they had imbibed.

A FORBIDDEN LOVE

"Someone important, I suppose," John replied, the words rolling lazily off his tongue. He offered a dismissive wave, his thoughts ensnared by the warmth that still lingered from Kip's touch, the memory of their knees pressed together through the evening.

"Too far removed from us to matter tonight," Kip added, an impish grin tugging at the corners of his mouth.

They shared a look, one laden with unspoken emotions simmering just beneath the surface, the frivolity of their banter unable to mask the intensity of the connection pulsating between them.

As they ambled back to the townhouse in Mayfair, the impending storm of war felt distant, less immediate than the personal tempest brewing in their hearts. They moved through the streets like spectres, wrapped in the comfortable silence that comes from knowing another soul as deeply as your own.

Upon entering the lavish drawing room at Langley House, the mood shifted. The earl was a still figure amidst a storm of tension, his gaze sharp upon the senior civil servant who stood rigid before him. Their conversation ceased abruptly; the atmosphere was heavy with implications that neither John nor Kip could fully grasp.

"Boys," the older man called, a flicker of concern crossing his usually impassive features. "Please, sit."

They complied, sinking into the plush chairs, the undercurrents of urgency palpable. With a curt nod, the earl dismissed his civil servant, who exited with a haste that betrayed his composure.

"Europe is on the brink," the earl began, his voice low and grave. "I must travel abroad to aid the diplomatic efforts following this... assassination."

"Norfolk?" Kip murmured, exchanging a glance with John. There was excitement in the prospect of retreat, a shared anticipation for days spent away from the prying eyes of society, where they could explore the uncharted waters of their relationship.

"Yes, tomorrow," John's father confirmed, his blue eyes steeling over. "You'll be safer and better looked after there with me away."

A shiver of foreboding rippled through the room, the scent of old parchment and lavender suddenly oppressive. The dim light cast shadows that danced upon the walls like omens, whispering of changes to come—of a world on the precipice of transformation.

John met Kip's gaze, the silent communication between them now laced with a new tension, a shared understanding that their time together was a precious commodity, threatened by forces beyond their control.

As they rose from their seats, their hands brushed briefly, a fleeting contact that spoke volumes.

"Goodnight, Father," John said, his voice steady despite the tumult within.

"Goodnight, Uncle," echoed Kip, his tone equally composed.

As they retreated to the sanctuary of John's room, the house settled around them—a grand stage awaiting the unfolding drama of adolescent love amid the spectre of looming war.

A FORBIDDEN LOVE

Viscount Langley and Prince Christian c 1908

A FORBIDDEN LOVE

CHAPTER THREE:
ESCAPE TO NORFOLK

Lord John pushed open the heavy oak door to his bedroom, the familiar scent of cedarwood and lavender enveloping him as he entered. The room, usually a sanctuary, felt different tonight—charged with an electric undercurrent of unease. Christian followed close behind, his presence both comforting and disquieting.

"Nightcap?" John offered, his voice barely above a whisper. He moved towards the crystal decanter on the sideboard, desperate for something to occupy his trembling hands.

Christian nodded, sinking into a nearby armchair. "Please. I think we both need it after... that news."

As John poured the amber liquid into two cut-glass tumblers, he noticed the row of packed trunks and cases lining the far wall. The sight sent a shiver down his spine, a tangible reminder of the impending change looming over them.

"I hadn't realised how many there were," Christian murmured, following John's gaze.

John handed him a glass, their fingers brushing momentarily. "Neither had I," he admitted, settling into the chair opposite. "It's as if the reality of it all has suddenly... materialised."

The weight of unspoken words hung heavy between them. John took a sip of his drink, relishing the burn as it slid down his throat. In the flickering lamplight, he studied Christian's profile—the powerful jaw, the scar above his right eyebrow, the troubled furrow of his brow.

"Do you think..." Christian began, then faltered. He swirled the liquid in his glass, eyes downcast. "Do you think things will ever be the same?"

John's heart clenched. He wanted to reach out, to offer comfort, but something held him back.

Instead, he said softly, "I don't know. But whatever happens, we'll face it together. Won't we?"

Christian looked up then, his blue eyes meeting John's with an intensity that made his breath catch.

"Always," he promised, his voice thick with emotion.

As they sat in contemplative silence, John could not shake the feeling that they were standing on the precipice of something monumental. The packed bags seemed to loom larger, a stark reminder of the uncertain future that awaited them beyond the safety of these walls.

The ticking of the mantle clock echoed in the hushed room, each second amplifying the tension that simmered between them. John's fingers traced the intricate pattern on his glass, his mind swirling with conflicting emotions. Shame and desire battled within him, threatening to overflow.

Across the room, Christian shifted in his chair, the leather creaking softly. John glanced up, catching a flicker of something—longing? regret? — in his friend's eyes before Christian quickly looked away.

"I suppose," Christian murmured, his voice barely above a whisper, "we should try to get some sleep."

A FORBIDDEN LOVE

John nodded, unable to trust his voice. The weight of their unspoken feelings pressed down on him, making it difficult to breathe. He wanted to say something, anything, to bridge the chasm that had opened between them, but the words stuck in his throat.

Instead, he stood abruptly, the sudden movement causing Christian to start. "I should ring for Thomas," John announced, his voice sounding unnaturally loud in the quiet room.

As he moved towards the bell pull, John felt the atmosphere shift. A silent understanding passed between them—whatever had almost transpired earlier would remain unexplored, at least for now.

Christian rose as well, setting his barely touched drink aside. "Yes, of course," he agreed, a hint of resignation in his tone. "It's late, and tomorrow will be... eventful."

John's hand hesitated on the bellpull. He turned, meeting Christian's gaze one last time. The air crackled with unspoken words and unfulfilled desires. For a moment, John allowed himself to imagine closing the distance between them. Consequences be damned. But the moment passed. With a deep breath, John tugged the bellpull, signalling the end of their evening together.

Christian moved towards the adjoining door, his steps slow and hesitant. As he reached for the handle, he paused, turning back to face John. The moonlight streaming through the window cast half his face in shadow, accentuating the conflict etched across his features.

"Jonny, I..." Christian began, his voice thick with emotion. He swallowed hard, struggling to find the right words.
"What I mean to say is..."

"Wait," John interrupted, his heart racing. He took a step forward, then stopped, caught between the urge to close the distance between them and the fear of what might happen if he did. "Christian, I think I understand. But perhaps we shouldn't..."

The sound of approaching footsteps in the hallway silenced them both. Christian's hand fell away from the door handle, and John retreated a step, the moment of vulnerability evaporating like mist in the morning sun.

A soft knock preceded Thomas' entrance. The valet's keen eyes took in the scene before him—John's flushed face, Christian's rigid posture, the palpable tension in the air—and a flicker of concern crossed his features.

"You rang, my lord?" Thomas asked, his voice gentle and unassuming.

John cleared his throat, grateful for the distraction. "Yes, Thomas. I'm ready to retire for the evening."

As Thomas moved to assist him, John caught a last glimpse of Christian slipping through the adjoining door. The soft click of the latch echoed in his ears, a stark finality to the evening's unresolved emotions.

Thomas began his usual bedtime routine, but John could feel the valet's observant gaze upon him. As he helped John remove his jacket, Thomas spoke softly, "If you'll pardon me for saying so, Jonny, you seem troubled this evening. Is everything alright?"

John hesitated, his fingers fumbling with his cufflinks. The weight of unspoken words pressed against his chest, threatening to suffocate him. He looked up, meeting Thomas' concerned gaze in the mirror.

A FORBIDDEN LOVE

"I'm... I'm not sure, Thomas," he admitted, his voice barely above a whisper. Thomas paused in his task, his hands stilling on John's shoulders. In a moment of rare intimacy, he stepped closer, his reflection joining John's in the ornate mirror.

"Sometimes, Jonny, the burdens we carry are too heavy for one person alone," Thomas said softly, his Norfolk lilt more pronounced in the room's quiet. John felt a lump forming in his throat, the kindness in Thomas' voice threatening to unravel his carefully maintained composure. Without warning, Thomas broke protocol, turning John gently and pulling him into a supportive embrace.

The unexpected gesture of comfort broke something inside John. He sagged against Thomas, allowing himself a moment of vulnerability he had never dared show before. The scent of soap and laundered linen enveloped him, reminding him of simpler times, of childhood comforts long forgotten.

"It's alright, Jonny," Thomas murmured, his hand patting John's back awkwardly but sincerely. "Whatever troubles you, you're not alone."

John's mind raced, a whirlwind of conflicting emotions. Gratitude for Thomas' unwavering loyalty warred with shame at his own weakness. The warmth of the embrace both soothed and unsettled him, a stark reminder of the touch he truly craved but dared not seek.

After a long moment, John pulled away, straightening his posture and clearing his throat. "Thank you, Thomas," he said, his voice steadier now. "I... I appreciate your kindness. I'm sure I'll be quite alright in the morning."

Thomas nodded, a small smile playing at the corners of his mouth. "Of course. A good night's rest often puts things in perspective."

As Thomas resumed his duties, John felt a wave of relief wash over him. The valet's quiet presence was a balm to his troubled soul, a safe harbour in the storm of his emotions. Here, at least, he could find a moment of peace, free from the suffocating expectations of his station and the tumultuous desires of his heart.

The following morning, they departed in two carriages - one for the young cousins and another for their baggage and Thomas - heading to catch a train to Norwich. Sitting alone in a luxurious first-class compartment, they chatted aimlessly and reminisced about their childhood spent at the grand estate. For now, they put aside the troubles and shock from the previous night.

John reached into one pocket of his new jacket and pulled out a small dark blue box. He placed it on the table between them, adorned with gold edging and the crest of a prestigious London jeweller. "I have something for you, Kip," he said with a smile. "It was meant to be a birthday present, but I couldn't get it in time. I just picked it up last week, so I decided to wait until you were here."

Kip looked surprised and slightly puzzled. "I wasn't expecting anything," he said as he picked up the box and ran his fingers over its velvet surface. "You already gave me that biography of Lord Nelson for my birthday."

"That was my second choice," John chuckled. "This," he tapped the box gently, "is what I really wanted you to have. So go ahead, open it before I take it back." He teased as Kip's hand tightened around the box.

"Alright, alright," Kip laughed as he snatched the box away playfully. He brought it close to his face, peering at it suspiciously. "It's not going to explode or something, is it?"

A FORBIDDEN LOVE

John could not help but smirk at the thought. "No, of course not! Although that might have been entertaining," he joked as Kip unlocked the catch on the box and slowly opened it.

His eyes widened and his mouth hung open in surprise as he saw what was inside - a pair of square gold cufflinks with the Langley coat of arms hand-painted and enamelled on each one. The inside of the top lid held a small brass panel engraved with *'For Kip, from Jonny. April 1914'*.

"I thought these might remind you of where you'll always have family and a home," John explained, but Kip had already realised their significance.

"Oh, my goodness, I never expected this," Kip's words came out in a stutter. "Jonny, thank you. They're absolutely beautiful," he said, holding them in his palm, "and they will be treasured forever. Just like the giver will be."

John leaned over and gently placed his hand on top of Kip's, which was holding the cufflinks. "I truly hope so," he whispered before removing his hand. "Now, move over and let me put them on for you." John maneuvered around the table and almost sat on Kip's lap as he squeezed into his seat next to him. Kip willingly presented each wrist to John so he could replace the old cufflinks with the new ones. Kip held out his arms in front of himself and admired his gift.

"Jonny, they're stunning. Absolutely perfect," he said, turning to face John. "Just like you." In a swift motion, he gave Jonny a quick kiss on the forehead before playfully pushing him back towards his own seat. Despite their noticeable blushing and shy smiles, the two boys were content and happy in this moment of genuine affection.

The limestone facade of Langley Hall rose before them, its grandeur casting long shadows across the manicured lawns. John's breath caught in his throat, a mixture of awe and trepidation coursing through him as the carriage pulled to a stop. Beside him, Christian's eyes widened, his usual composure momentarily forgotten.

"Good Lord," Christian whispered, his voice barely audible. "It's even more magnificent than I remembered."

John nodded, unable to form words as they stepped out onto the gravel drive. The air was crisp with the scent of freshly cut grass and blooming roses, a stark contrast to the stuffy confines of their journey.

A line of staff stood at attention, their starched uniforms a testament to the estate's unwavering adherence to tradition. Mr. Reeves, the butler, stepped forward with a slight bow. "Welcome home, Lord John. Your Highness," he intoned, his voice carrying the weight of centuries of protocol. "I trust your journey was a pleasant one?"

John found his voice and thanked Reeves. He noticed the tension in Christian's shoulders and wondered why. The aged butler informed them they had prepared adjoining chambers with a view of the terrace for their stay, before guiding them towards the library where they saw a table filled with their favourite treats from their childhood.

"Look Christian, Mrs. Heath has made all our favourites!" John exclaimed, reminiscing about all the goodies they had eaten during their younger days in the nursery. Reeves hovered nearby with a footman, awaiting further instructions.

"We should sit down, Kip," John suggested. They both sat down, and attentive servants served them tea. John realised he was now the host and master of the house, with Reeves looking to him for direction.

"As there will only be the two of us, I don't think we need a formal dinner every night. Perhaps we could have hot trays brought to the music room instead?" John looked up at Reeves for approval before continuing. "However, if my father arrives, we will have to change our plans." Reeves gave a slight nod of agreement.

"Will your highness be requiring a valet?" asked Reeves, turning to Christian.

"No thank you, Reeves," Christian replied confidently. "Since attending the naval academy, I have learned to largely fend for myself." He glanced at John and added, "But if I do find myself in need of assistance, I will ask my cousin's valet."

"Very good, your highness," nodded Reeves before addressing John. "And are there any other instructions for your stay, My Lord?"

"I think breakfast at nine am in the breakfast room will be sufficient, and perhaps a picnic basket for lunch if we are out for the day." John thought before adding, "I'll inform Mr Cooper each evening beforehand."

"Understood, my lord," said Reeves before turning to leave. "And if there is anything else you require, please do not hesitate to ask."

"Thank you, Reeves," John dismissed him before adding, "Oh, and please extend our thanks to Mrs. Heath for the delicious treats."

"Certainly, my lord," nodded Reeves as he left the room with a flick of his finger to summon the footman.

As soon as they were alone, both boys burst into quiet giggles. "Did I pass again, Kip?" asked John.

"With flying colours, my lord!" Kip replied enthusiastically. "And no formal dinners? Thank goodness!"

John chuckled and explained, "I just remembered that's what Mama used to do when Papa was away. She preferred the more relaxed and informal atmosphere if it was just the four of us." This had included Kip's mother as well.

"Very true! There are far too many starched collars in London for my taste," agreed Kip, thinking briefly of his late mother.

John raised his teacup in a toast. "To no starch and happy days ahead!" They clinked their cups together.

"To us and fun," added Kip with a grin. The boys heartily helped themselves to the cakes and tarts before them.

After a few minutes, Kip surveyed the room, taking in his surroundings as if for the very first time. "This was always my favourite room," he said, hesitating before continuing.

"Because it's where we spent most of our time with our mothers?" John offered, and Kip nodded. "Well, here or out on the terrace," he added, pointing to the french doors. "Especially when we were getting too rowdy."

"Or getting bored with their game of *'find a book with a whatever in the title'*," Christian chimed in with a smile.

A FORBIDDEN LOVE

"Oh yes, the hours we spent searching every nook and cranny on those library ladders while they whispered away," John chuckled at the memory of their competitive and often fruitless searches. "But I did always wonder what they had to talk about for so long each day..." Jonny trailed off, lost in his own memories.

"You didn't know?" asked Kip, his tone serious once again.

John tilted his head in confusion. "No, I always thought it was just womanly things, like fashion or party planning."

"You really didn't know? I always assumed you did and that's why we never talked about it," a look of realisation dawned on Kip's face as he quickly concluded that he had been wrong about his cousin's apparent indifference over the past few years.

"Please Kip," John leaned forward, "tell me now?"

"Of course," Kip patted the cushion next to him, motioning for John to sit beside him. "But let's make sure there are no servants around." John obliged and turned sideways to face Kip.

"Don't worry, we're completely alone," their eyes met as Kip continued. "It turns out that my mother discovered my father had been having an affair with another woman, since before I was born..." his voice trailed off and his usual cheerful demeanour faded. John's expression shifted to one of shock and sympathy.

"Oh Kip, that must have been terrible for you," he placed a gentle hand on Kip's arm, "and your mother. I'm so sorry," he squeezed his cousin's arm in support. Kip looked down, a faint smile tugging at his lips from the kind gesture.

"And I must apologise to you, Jonny."

"Me? Why would you apologise to me?" John now placed a hand on Kip's shoulder.

"Please forgive me, Jonny," Kip's voice was quiet and trembling with emotion. "But when you didn't mention it to me during our last term at Eton after I found out, I had assumed Aunt Victoria would have told you about it and therefore that such infidelities didn't matter to you. And that hurt me. I'm sorry for ever thinking that way about you." Tears welled up in Kip's eyes, not for the memory of his father's betrayal, but for the wrong assumptions he had made about his cousin.

"That's right, I remember now, how unhappy you were during most of our last term," John placed a hand on each of Kip's shoulders and drew him closer, looking deeply into his eyes. "But I promise, I only thought it was because you were leaving...nothing else. I did not mention it, because well, I was a coward, as the thought of you leaving made me sad too." The boys nodded at each other before pulling apart slightly. "Feeling better now, Kip?"

"Yes, thank you," John smiled triumphantly at Kip's words. "What's that look for?"

"For us, and for no more secrets or unspoken feelings between us. Promise me?"

"Yes, Jonny. I promise," Kip said solemnly. "And you must promise me the same."

John placed a hand over his heart. "I promise my German prince. Now let's finish these cakes, before Thomas thinks we have gotten ourselves lost," John chewed a mouthful of the rich fruitcake before adding," and we can talk some more about this later. When you are ready to." It was not posed as a question, but a simple statement of what would happen soon.

As they ascended the grand staircase, John's mind raced. Adjoining chambers – adult quarters. The significance struck him. This was not the nursery floor above of their childhood visits; they were being treated as young men now.

Christian leaned in close as they walked, his breath warm against John's ear. "Adjoining rooms? How very... adult," he murmured, a hint of mischief in his tone.

John felt heat rise to his cheeks, his pulse quickening. "Behave yourself," he hissed back, though he could not quite suppress the thrill that ran through him at the implication. They paused at the top of the grand staircase, taking in their surroundings. To the right were his parents' rooms, occupying the front corner of the central block and extending through several connecting rooms above the main entrance.

These rooms included a study for his father, a drawing room for his mother, and two bedrooms. On the opposite front corner was Princess Victoria's suite, previously known as the *Dowager Wing* with its own set of stairs rising from opposite the Music Room.

They turned left and gazed down the main corridor that stretched the full length of the main block - a quarter of it serving as a gallery above the great hall. There were eight doors on the right-hand side, none of which they had ever entered in their lives.

"I wonder which ones are ours?" John said, turning to Kip, who shrugged in response. Just then, Thomas appeared at the far end of the corridor, making his way over from the servants' hall in the left-hand wing of the hall via the Dowager's staircase. He walked purposefully towards them.

"My lord, your highness, are you lost?" he asked with a smile, almost teasing.

"Not exactly lost, but unsure of where to go," replied John. Thomas stopped at the fourth door along from where they stood.

"My lord," he opened the door and gestured inside.

"*The Garden Suite*?" John whispered in amazement, turning to Kip, "Mother spent a fortune refurbishing these rooms for some Duke or Duchess."

"It was actually for the Duke and Duchess of Norfolk," explained Thomas, "for their first visit in 1910, if I recall correctly." He led them into the first room. "This will be your room, my lord. And if you will follow me," he gestured and opened a connecting door. "This is your shared day room or drawing room." He stepped towards the french windows and opened them, "and this is the terrace balcony overlooking the gardens."

Giving the boys a moment to take in the breathtaking view outside, Thomas walked over to the door opposite the one they had entered and opened it. "This," he announced while gesturing for them to enter, "is his highness' room."

The room was just as lavishly decorated and furnished as John's room but with warmer colours. "And finally, if you'll follow me," Thomas continued as he opened a door on the same wall, "we have the bathroom." He flipped a switch, illuminating the space with electric lights. "These were the first electric lights in the county for a country house," Thomas boasted proudly.

A FORBIDDEN LOVE

"Mother was so proud of that!" Jonny exclaimed with a laugh. He took in the sight of the sparkling white French-style tiles with a border of *forget-me-not* flowers, all accented by polished brass plumbing fixtures.

Thomas then moved towards the only closed door left and opened it. "And now we're back where we started," he stated as they all re-entered John's spacious bedroom. Pointing to the large four-poster bed, he added, "I've already laid out appropriate clothing for the rest of the afternoon, should you wish to change. Is that to your liking, our lordship?"

"Yes, Thomas, thank you," replied the young lord. Thomas turned to Christian and asked respectfully, "Is there anything I can assist you with your highness?"

"No thank you Thomas," replied the prince.

John thanked Thomas and sent him on his way, saying they would call if they needed anything else. As soon as the door closed behind Thomas, both boys inspected their new rooms. The staff's efficiency pleasantly surprised them.

Their clothes now filled the closets, wardrobes, and drawers. John noticed Thomas had also set out two photograph frames on the writing bureau near the window. In one frame was a picture of him with his parents when he was a small child, and in the other was a more recent photo of him and Kip posing together with cricket bats under a tree at the front of the Hall.

A wistful smile crossed John's face as he looked at his mother in the first picture, but it quickly turned into a happy one when he saw Kip in the second photo. Turning to the bed and dresser, he examined the outfit that Thomas had kindly laid out for him. It was all new to him - a fashionable ensemble comprising breeches, a double-breasted waistcoat in a light brown herringbone pattern, and a soft white shirt with a low collar.

On the dresser were a pair of cufflinks, a matching cloth cap, and a bright red bow tie. "Well done, Thomas," he murmured to himself, pleased with what he saw. He called for Kip through the open doors. "Come see my latest new outfit!"

Kip entered the room and was beckoned over to inspect the clothes on the bed. "Very stylish for a handsome young gentleman," he complimented, causing John to blush.

"Do you have something similar?" John asked anxiously, not wanting his cousin to feel out of place.

"Of course, don't forget that these fashions often start in Europe before making their way to London," Kip replied playfully, always looking for friendly competition. "Why, what do you have planned for this afternoon?"

John turned to Christian with excitement in his eyes. "How about a ride? I've already told the stables to expect us, and the weather is perfect."

Christian's face paled slightly at the suggestion; regretting having opened that door of possibilities with his question. "A ride? John, you know I'm not comfortable with horses."

"Nonsense," John insisted, already heading towards the door. "It'll be splendid. You can ride *Midnight* – she's as gentle as a lamb." Still uncertain, but not wanting to disappoint his cousin, Kip reluctantly agreed with a nod and a resigned sigh.

"Very well, if it will make you happy Jonny," Kip conceded, unable to resist John's infectious smile.

A FORBIDDEN LOVE

"Off you go then!" John ushered his cousin back towards his own room. "Let's get dressed!" he said excitedly. Kip left reluctantly, but not before John thanked him, to which Kip casually waved his hand; dismissing the need for gratitude.

Kip was the first to emerge from his room, dressed in similarly modern style clothing and a thick linen outfit in dark blue. His perfectly tied bow tie matched his stockings, and he held a Panama hat in his hand. He cleared his throat loudly to get John's attention, who was still struggling with his own bow tie. As John turned around slowly, Kip placed his hat on his head at a jaunty angle. "So, what do you think? Will I pass muster?"

John took a long look at his cousin, admiring how handsome he looked. His heart raced a little at the sight. "I would say so...very much so," he said, feeling the blood rush to his cheeks again. He struggled to find more words, all of which were stuck on repeat in his mind – *'beautiful Kip'* - and kept them to himself, too afraid to reveal his true feelings.

"Let me fix that knot for you," he whispered, taking John's hands away from the bow tie. His touch was gentle yet electric.

After a few seconds of adjustment, Kip stepped back proudly. "There you go, perfect," he declared. They held each other's gaze for a few lingering moments before breaking into wide smiles.

Finally, finding his voice again, John quipped, "quite the dandies we are, aren't we?" They chuckled softly together. "Let's see what the horses think about our outfits at the stables."

As they made their way to the stables behind the east wing, John could not help but revel in the familiar sights and scents. The earthy aroma of hay and leather, the soft nickering of horses – it all felt like coming home. He swung himself easily into the saddle, his body moving with practiced grace.

Christian, on the other hand, approached his mount with visible trepidation. John watched, a mixture of amusement and fondness bubbling up within him, as his cousin awkwardly clambered onto *Midnight's* back.

"There you go," John encouraged, urging his own horse forward. "Just relax and let her do the work."

As they set off at a gentle trot, John could not help but steal glances at Christian. The prince's usual poise was gone, replaced by a charming vulnerability that made John's heart ache with an unnamed longing. The afternoon sun caught in Christian's dark hair, highlighting the furrow of concentration between his brows.

"You're doing splendidly," John called out, tamping down the urge to reach out and steady his cousin. "Just keep your back straight and your heels down."

Christian shot him a look that was equal parts gratitude and exasperation. "Easy for you to say," he grumbled, his knuckles white on the reins. "You were practically born in the saddle."

As they rode side by side, John found himself acutely aware of the space between them – so close, yet impossibly far. The rhythm of the horses' hooves seemed to echo the beating of his heart, a constant reminder of all that remained unspoken between them. John could not resist a playful smirk.

A FORBIDDEN LOVE

"Come now, Kip. You command ships with ease, yet a simple mare defeats you?" He chuckled softly; the sound carried away by the gentle breeze. "Perhaps we should find you a rocking horse upstairs in the nursery instead?"

Christian's blue eyes flashed with mock indignation. "I'll have you know, Jonny, that the sea is a far more predictable mistress than this... this four-legged menace." He shifted uncomfortably in the saddle, wincing slightly. "At least on a ship, the deck doesn't actively try to unseat me." Their laughter mingled in the air, a moment of lightness amidst the weight of unspoken tensions.

As they approached the village, John felt a familiar tightening in his chest. The transition from boyhood to manhood carried with it new responsibilities, new expectations, and the sound of hoofbeats on cobblestones filled the air. John inhaled deeply, savouring the scents of freshly baked bread and blooming gardens.

He noticed the subtle shift in the villagers' demeanour as they passed – the respectful nods, the murmured "Good day, young Lord Langley."

A surge of overwhelming emotions washed over John, a potent mix of pride, responsibility, and insecurity. His grip on the reins tightened as he rode alongside Christian, trying to maintain a composed facade.

"They seem quite taken with you," Christian observed in a low, contemplative voice.

John's jaw clenched slightly. "They're good, hardworking people," he replied through gritted teeth, struggling to keep his tone neutral. "I can only hope I live up to their expectations."

As they continued their ride, John was acutely aware of Christian's gaze on him – searching, curious, and perhaps even longing. He could not help but wonder what his friend saw when he looked at him – the young lord, the dutiful son, or something else entirely? Their eyes met briefly, and a jolt of electricity shot through John's body. He glanced away, focusing on the path ahead. The silence between them grew heavy with unspoken words and lingering looks.

Clearing his throat, Christian spoke again. "I've always been envious of how comfortable you are here," he said in a hushed tone laced with both admiration and desire. John's heart raced at the implications of his friend's words. Dare he hope for something more?

"It's home," he replied softly, meeting Christian's gaze once more. "And now that you're here...maybe it could be your home too one day?" His voice trembled with vulnerability as he expressed his deepest desires. Christian hesitated, averting his cousin's intense gaze to gather his thoughts. Did he dare reveal his true feelings? After a moment, he looked back at John with a mixture of sadness and longing in his eyes.

"Yes," he said quietly, "living at Langley with you would be far better than my cold and lonely life in my father's castle in Germany."

A spark of hope ignited in John's heart, but Christian's next words brought him crashing down. "But the cost would be too high," he continued, his voice tinged with fear. "As your current heir, it would mean something terrible had happened to you, my dear cousin. I couldn't bear that thought."

A glimmer of relief mingled with disappointment in John's eyes as he realised the depth of Christian's feelings for him. He could only hope that one day they could find a way to be together without such dire consequences.

A FORBIDDEN LOVE

As they continued through the village, they settled for a moment by *the Langley Arms*. News of John's visit had been passed on to its occupants, and more greetings followed. Each *'my lord'* felt like another weight settling onto John's shoulders, a constant reminder of the mantle he was destined to inherit. He could not help but wonder if Christian noticed the change, if he understood the subtle shift in John's world.

As they rode on, their easy conversation faded into an uneasy silence. John could not help sneaking glances at Christian, but he quickly looked away when their eyes met. The tension between them was palpable, especially after their earlier conversation and mutual promise, and charged with unspoken words and unfinished thoughts.

Christian cleared his throat. "John, I..." he started, then trailed off as his voice faltered. John's heart raced in anticipation. He turned to face Christian fully, their horses drawing closer.

"Yes?" he prompted, barely above a whisper. For a moment, it felt like time stood still. John's entire world narrowed down to Christian's piercing blue eyes, filled with uncertainty and something deeper that made his breath catch in his throat. He leaned in slightly, drawn by an invisible force. But before Christian could speak, the sound of approaching hoofbeats shattered the moment. John jerked back, his face flushed with embarrassment and a hint of frustration.

Thomas rode up beside them, his posture relaxed but his gaze sharp. "A beautiful day for a ride, isn't it my lord? Your highness?" he said casually, yet with knowing eyes.

John nodded, struggling to find his voice. "Indeed, Thomas. And I assume my father had no influence over your decision to join us?"

"Your father simply asked that I keep an eye on you," Thomas replied smoothly, pausing before adding with a sly smile, "...during your adventures." Christian caught on quicker than John did.

"Jonny, I think he means this," he pointed to the scar above his eye.

"Of course," John said indignantly, provoking laughter from his companions. But soon enough, he joined in their merriment. Thomas let the moment linger before speaking again.

"If I may suggest, my lord, we should start heading back to the Hall. There is much to be done before dinner."

"Haha, our timekeeper and bodyguard!" John said, urging his horse into a canter.

As they continued their ride, John could not shake off the feeling of Thomas' watchful presence. His valet seemed to catch every fleeting look, every moment of hesitation between him and Christian. And yet, his expression remained neutral, his demeanour respectful and unobtrusive. John wondered what Thomas thought of their bond, if he sensed the underlying emotions that threatened to consume them. The thought both thrilled and terrified him, adding another layer to the already complex web of feelings he had for Christian.

As they trotted towards Langley Hall, John could not help but feel both relieved that he had finally expressed his secret hope to Christian, and yet regretful because of how others might judge this. The day's adventure had initially lifted his spirits, but he felt the weight of the many added unspoken words.

But approaching the magnificent limestone facade, the familiar tension, which constantly seemed to lurk beneath, returned.

A FORBIDDEN LOVE

"Let's race to the stables!" Christian suddenly called out with a mischievous twinkle in his eye. Thomas looked a bit concerned. John's heart leapt at the challenge.

"You're on!" he exclaimed, urging his horse forward. They thundered down the last stretch, hooves pounding against the ground, wind blowing through their hair. For those exhilarating moments, all thoughts of propriety and hidden desires disappeared. John laughed freely and without worry, as he inched ahead of Christian.

They arrived at the stables in a cloud of dust and excited shouts, dismounting with flushed cheeks and gleaming eyes. As John's feet touched the ground, he found himself standing face to face with Christian, their breaths mingling in the small space between them.

"Well ridden, your highness," John murmured, keenly aware of their closeness. Christian's gaze flickered to John's lips before meeting his eyes.

"You too, my lord," he replied in a deep voice. The air crackled with unspoken possibilities. John's fingers itched to reach out and bridge the gap between them. But like spun sugar, the moment passed too quickly as Thomas approached to take their horses. Christian followed suit, his movements less fluid, a grimace of discomfort flickering across his face as he stretched his sore muscles. "I fear I shall be feeling this ride for days," he groaned, a rueful smile playing at the corners of his mouth.

"A small price to pay for such a glorious afternoon," John replied, his tone light, yet his eyes held a depth of emotion that belied his casual words. As they ascended the steps to the grand entrance, their shoulders brushed a fleeting contact that sent a shiver down John's spine. A young footman swung the great oak doors open, revealing the soaring expanse of the great hall, the intricate plasterwork of the ceiling glinting in the afternoon light.

John turned to Christian, a sudden weariness settling over him. The day's adventures had been a respite, a chance to forget the looming spectre of war and duty, but now, within the walls of the hall, reality came crashing back. "Shall we go straight up?" John asked, motioning towards the staircase with a neutral tone.

Christian hesitated, his eyes searching John's face for any sign of uncertainty. For a moment, John thought he might speak and address the unspoken truths that hung between them. But the moment passed and Christian simply nodded, a small, wistful smile forming on his lips. "Lead the way," he murmured softly, his voice almost lost in the hall's vastness.

"Thank you, Robert," John said to the footman. "Please let Mr Cooper know we have gone upstairs." The footman nodded respectfully.

As they made their way up, their footsteps echoing on the polished floors, John felt the weight of the future pressing down on him. The stolen moments of the day had been a gift, a glimpse of what could be, but deep in his heart, he knew it was a dream that could never come true. But for now, he held onto the memory of the sun on his face, the wind in his hair, and Christian's warmth by his side. It was a slight comfort, a glimmer of hope in the darkness ahead, but it gave him strength to face whatever was to come. Both boys entered John's room and sat down on his bed to take off their boots.

Kip let out a slight groan. "Are you sore?" John asked.

"Just a little," Kip replied. "But nothing a hot bath and a drink or two won't fix." His reassurance eased Jonny's concerns and lightened the mood.

46

"I'm glad," John said sincerely. "Because I do feel a bit guilty for making you ride."

"Nonsense," Kip chuckled. "It was my idea to gallop, remember?"

"Are you sure?" John asked. Kip rubbed the inside of his thighs and groaned loudly in mock agony. John laughed and then pushed his cousin back onto the bed before standing up.

"Let me ring for Thomas then and see what arrangements are being made for dinner," John suggested. A few minutes later, Thomas arrived.

"Dinner at eight?" John asked.

"Yes, Jonny," responded Thomas. "Unless you would like it a little later?"

John thought for a moment before saying, "actually, let's make it nine o'clock so we don't feel rushed. Kip perhaps needs a longer bath than normal." He easily slipped back into his role as master with a confident tone.

"Very well. I will inform the kitchen," Thomas nodded before adding, "I have also prepared a drinks tray in your drawing room, and an ice bucket with some of the local ginger beers you seemed to have enjoyed previously."

"Aha, Thomas, you know us too well," Kip chimed in cheerfully.

After a moment of consideration, Thomas replied, "yes Kip. I think I probably do." There was no malice or threat in his statement, just a simple observation. He smiled broadly at both boys and said, "is there anything else I can assist you with?"

John briefly glanced at his cousin and noticed the slight blush on his cheeks that mirrored the warmth he felt himself. "No, thank you," he said confidently. "I shall ring when I am ready to dress," recalling his failed attempt at the bow tie earlier. Thomas nodded respectfully at Lord John and Prince Christian before letting himself out of the room.

"Well, if you can walk of course, shall we go through for a drink before taking our baths?" John was playfully mocking his cousin. Kip strode into the drawing room with a wide-legged gait, pretending to be in pain with every movement.

John paid no attention to his cousin's antics and instead opened two bottles of ginger beer from *The Langley Arms* in the village. "Already recovered, I see?" John teased as Kip's limp disappeared and he eagerly grabbed one of the chilled bottles.

"Of course," Kip replied with a wink, clinking their bottles together for a toast. They both took long sips, relishing the refreshing drink. The french doors were open, letting in a cooling breeze. They sat in silence, enjoying the view of the gardens below as the sun set. Without a word, John got up and retrieved two more bottles before making another toast.

"To friendship," he whispered.

"Always," Kip echoed. As they sat in contented quietness, fatigue from the day's activities setting in. Eventually, John stood up and declared that he would run a bath for Kip.

"I can do it myself," Kip protested weakly, straightening up in his armchair.

"Don't be ridiculous, just relax," John insisted as he made his way to the bathroom. Kip settled back into his chair, taking a sip of beer, and closing his eyes with a smile on his face.

A FORBIDDEN LOVE

At that moment, he was completely content with his cousin and their friendship. He could not think of anywhere else he would rather be at that moment. All he could hear was the soothing sounds of running water and the birds in the garden, allowing John to return and sit back down unnoticed.

John sat for a good five minutes, simply taking in the sight of his cousin. He realised this was the first time he had seen Kip with no visible worries since his arrival. Then, slowly but surely, his thoughts turned more troubling as he also realised that he had never found his cousin so handsome and, for a moment, even attractive.

John fought to push those thoughts away, feeling ashamed at the direction they were heading. He remembered his promise to be open with Kip and felt genuine guilt for keeping secrets. He furrowed his brow and reminded himself that this was how it had to be. Some things were better kept hidden. Just then, he noticed Kip beginning to stir.

"Hey Kip," John said softly, causing his cousin's eyes to snap open, slightly startled. "It's time for your bath."

"Yes, yes, of course," Kip replied, meeting John's gaze. "Thank you for reminding me." He sat up but paused, gesturing towards the half-empty bottle of beer in his hand. "But...I'm taking this with me!" With new-found energy, he jumped out of the chair and headed to his room to undress.

John settled back into his seat, trying to relax by gazing out at the gardens through the open doors. He searched for familiar details in the distance to distract himself from his thoughts.

The sound of water splashing from the bathroom gradually faded into the background as he focused on the peaceful sounds of nature outside. Time seemed to slow for those minutes of solitude.

"Jonny! Jonny!" Kip's call from the bathroom shattered the peace. Instinctively he turned around, a little concerned, then realisation dawned on his face and he smiled.

"I know what you want," he said, too quiet to be heard. He got up, walked to the drinks trolley, and opened another bottle. The bathroom door was wide open, so he knocked gently before entering. Kip turned to watch Jonny enter. He was red-faced because of the hot bath, but he grinned and then laughed when he noticed the two beers in John's hands.

"Ha, seems like there is someone else who knows me too well," referring to Thomas' earlier comment.

"That's what friends are for Kip," he placed the beer carefully into his outstretched hand and turned to leave, not wanting to show any inappropriate interest in his cousin's athletic form.

"No wait Jonny, please?" Kip sat up in the bath and leaned over its edge to face Jonny. "Could we chat for moment or two?"

John hesitated, unsure if he could fulfil the request. Kip was sitting naked in the bath, and John was afraid his gaze would betray his shameful interest in his cousin. He quickly produced a plan to protect himself and said, "yes, of course, Kip." He grabbed a chair from the corner of the bathroom and placed it slightly behind Kip before picking up a folded towel and placing it over his lap to hide any potential embarrassment.

A FORBIDDEN LOVE

"I don't know about you, Jonny," Kip began as he relaxed back into the bath, "but I always do my best thinking in here - whether it's making sense of the day or planning for the next." John nodded in agreement.

"What's on your mind, Kip?" he asked. Kip turned to face him quickly, catching John's gaze.

"First of all, I want to thank you for everything today," he paused and held John's eyes with his own, "especially your gift and the sentiments behind it." Kip's smile was genuine and warm. "And also, for letting me feel so... happy for the first time in a long while."

"Thank you, Kip. Hearing that means a lot to me," another wave of guilt washed over John as he thought about how he could not be completely honest in return. "And what have you been planning in this bath?" Kip lifted himself again against the edge of the bath, giving Jonny a clear view of his toned and smooth chest. "Well?"

"I was thinking, hoping, that maybe we could take the *Isabella* out for a small voyage?" This question provoked surprised laughter from John. "What's so funny now?"

"It's already arranged for tomorrow. It was supposed to be a surprise. Thomas rode down to the boatyard before meeting us this afternoon..." John explained.

"Well, it's still a surprise to me, so thank you, Jonny," Kip raised his bottle and took a large gulp in salute of his friend.

"Now," John flicked open his pocket watch, "you have ten more minutes, and then it's my turn!" He stood up, clutching the towel against himself, and headed for the door.

"My towel!" called Kip after him. Jonny only stopped once he was safely hidden in the doorway before tossing the folded towel back to Kip, who caught it with a smirk. Finally, John felt relaxed enough to undress and prepare for his own bath, eventually hearing Kip announce it was ready for him.

Feeling refreshed, John and Christian made their way to dinner on time. The conversation was simple and centred around reminiscing about their previous adventures at Langley. After a quick drink, they were ready to retire relatively early. John called Thomas upstairs.

"Thomas, we're ready to retire now. It's been a long day," John yawned to emphasise his point. Christian said goodnight and went to his own room.

Thomas followed John into his room and helped him out of his dinner clothes. While at the wardrobe, he brought out a pair of new pyjamas. "These will be nice and cool for these warm summer nights."

"Thank you, Thomas," John slipped on the top and fastened it up. "One more thing, Thomas," the valet tilted his head in anticipation. "I think we would like breakfast in the drawing room up here instead of downstairs."

"Very good. It will be brought up at nine o'clock," Thomas replied as he watched John put on the bottoms. "Will there be anything else, Jonny?"

"No, thank you, Tom," John replied with another yawn.

"Did you have a nice day overall?"

"It was perfect, Tom. Perfect," John smiled as he settled into bed.

"Good to hear, Jonny. Goodnight."

A FORBIDDEN LOVE

A FORBIDDEN LOVE

CHAPTER FOUR:
A SAILING ADVENTURE

The following morning arrived with a flawless sky of azure-blue. As the heat haze began to appear in the distance, Thomas pulled back the heavy curtains in John's room at precisely eight-thirty. Feeling the rising temperature, he opened the windows wide to let in some cool breeze. Turning to his master who was rubbing his eyes and waking up, Thomas greeted him, "good morning, Jonny. What a beautiful day it is."

Jonny grunted slightly but managed to smile, "thank you Tom." Thomas nodded his head in acknowledgment.

"They will bring breakfast up at nine," he paused before asking, "Shall I wake the prince?" He motioned towards the adjoining door. John eagerly nodded, ready to start the day. Sitting up in bed and throwing off the heavy quilt, he stretched his arms out and let out a final yawn.

Enjoying a few quiet moments of reflection, he gazed out at the blue sky before muttering to himself, 'truly a beautiful day'. With that, he swung his legs over the bed and noticed the slippers and dressing gown laid out by Thomas on the rug and bed respectively, and smiled before putting them on.

Jonny's grin quickly faded when he noticed his morning arousal. Memories of lectures from the housemaster at Eton about the dangers of self-abuse and giving in to carnal urges flooded his mind. "Not today," he pleaded with himself as he made some adjustments and tightened his dressing gown belt around his waist.

He walked into the shared drawing room and out onto the small balcony overlooking the terrace below, confident that his embarrassment was hidden, if not yet relieved. After a few minutes, he heard Kip stirring and heading to the bathroom. "Finally," he muttered with a smile.

Five or ten minutes passed. Jonny admired the beautiful view before him when Kip quietly approached and expertly poked him in the ribs, causing just the right amount of surprise.

"Good morning, cousin!" Kip exclaimed. Jonny jumped, jolted out of his peaceful thoughts.

"Bloody Hell Kip," Jonny rarely used profanity and clutched at his heart. Initially, Kip burst into laughter, but stopped when he noticed his cousin's genuine shock.

"I'm sorry Jonny," he placed both hands on Jonny's shoulders, "I'm just excited for today," he explained. Jonny's face softened into a smile.

"It's fine, you just startled me while I was deep in thought," he reassured Kip with a warm look in his eyes. "Anyway," he continued, "breakfast will be up soon and I need to use the bathroom." He excused himself.

He returned just as two footmen arrived with the breakfast trays. He noticed coffee instead of tea, scrambled eggs, toast, some sliced meats as preferred by Christian and, that most modern of beverages, orange juice. They pulled a small table from the wall and set it for two, then, after dismissing the footmen, the two friends ate.

"John, imagine the wind as our silent companion, the sails billowing with whispered secrets of the water," Prince Christian mused finally, his eyes alight with a passion that only the prospect of the open water could ignite. John noticed how, for the first time during this visit, his cousin became truly alive, the passion obvious in both his words and his eyes.

He had always admired Christian's sailing prowess from afar, but the way he spoke of the water and sailing, almost as a lover, was new to him. John could not help but smile at his cousin's passion.

"I have never heard the poet in you before Kip," John was almost teasing.

Whilst his young master and his cousin took their breakfast, Thomas Cooper, ever the attentive valet, was meticulously packing a picnic lunch prepared by Mrs Heath. His hands wrapped sandwiches in waxed paper, fingers deftly tying twine around bundles of fresh fruit.

The aroma of baked bread and cured meats filled the kitchen. Thomas selected a spot of rich Stilton, a nod to Christian's favoured palate, and a flask of sweet elderflower cordial, a bottle of fruity red wine and half a dozen bottles of ginger ale (packed in a modern *'ice box'*). These were then laid out on the rear of a two-horse rig, ready for young adventurers to inspect.

"Is there anything more I can get for you, my lords?" Thomas inquired, his hazel eyes glancing up from the hamper now brimming with victuals and refreshments.

"Only your good company and keen eye, Thomas," Christian said, clapping the valet on the shoulder with a familiarity bred from years of shared confidences.

"Indeed, we're much obliged to you, Thomas," John added, his voice soft but sincere.

As the trio completed their preparations, laughter and light jests punctuated the morning air. With each compass, chart, and piece of safety equipment checked and stowed, their camaraderie tightened like the knots that would soon secure the sails.

"Let us make haste to the boatyard; *'Isabella'* awaits her crew," Christian declared, his tone infused with the promise of adventure.

Thomas took the reins whilst the cousins sat in the rear with the hampers. Simple conversation, the kind reserved for those who shared an unspoken understanding, marked the journey to.

As they travelled the mile or so to the boatyard, John felt the weight of the world lifting from his shoulders, buoyed by the anticipation of the day ahead and the comforting presence of his companions.

The morning mist clung to the boatyard like a shroud, tendrils of vapour curling around the moored vessels as if reluctant to release them to the day. Standing proudly among its hardworking peers was *'Isabella'* — a sleek, single-masted, gaff-rigged yacht. Gleaming white paint coated the flat-bottomed hull, perfect for sailing the shallow Broads, contrasting with the dark teak of the cockpit and forward cabin.

Her name, elegantly inscribed in gilded lettering upon her stern, was a homage to John's late mother, and each glance at those graceful curves brought a bittersweet ache to his heart.

A FORBIDDEN LOVE

The Estate's Boatman and his young assistant warmly welcomed the group. He removed his cap and gave a nod, "good morning, my lord, your highness," he said in a thick Norfolk accent as he gestured towards the cart, "and Mr. Cooper," acknowledging Thomas.

"Good morning, Boaty!" The cousins responded, realising that they had only ever known the Boatman by their childhood nickname for him.

"I hear from Mr. Cooper here that your highness has joined the navy and will skipper today."

Kip blushed slightly, "I promise to take good care of her."

"I have no doubt you will. You were always an attentive student, she will be safe with you," replied the Boatman.

Christian led the way up the gangplank with confidence and determination. "She's more than just a yacht, Jonny," he said over his shoulder in a low, reverent tone. "She's a link to our past and all the adventures we had, and those yet to come."

John followed suit, running his hand along *'Isabella's'* smooth wooden rail and feeling the history pulsing through it. The scent of recently applied deck oil enveloped him as he stepped into the cockpit; for a moment, he could almost hear his mother's laughter echoing in the air.

The excitement was palpable as they prepared to set sail and loaded provisions into the cabin. As Christian re-familiarised himself with every rope and sail line, the weight of their family lineage seemed to lift, replaced by the promise of freedom that only the open water could offer.

With everything ready to go, Jonny informed Thomas that they would return around six pm, giving them seven hours on the water. Kip hoisted the mainsail and caught a slight breeze. "Cast off Boaty!" He called out, "and Jonny, take in the forward line first."

"Your highness, remember in these light winds, everything will happen slowly. Keep an eye on the reeds on the windward side for any gusts," advised the Boatman using his vast experience. He untied the bow mooring and tossed it onto the deck before gesturing to his assistant to release the stern. As the yacht inched along the quayside, he used a long boat hook to give it a firm push towards the centre of the river. There, it caught the natural flow of the water and more wind, and Kip adjusted the rudder to stay on course.

"Very nicely done," mumbled the Boatman to himself before turning to Thomas. "The prince is a skilled sailor, and with these winds, they won't get far before it changes direction mid-afternoon." Thomas raised an eyebrow in question.

"What does that mean?" he asked.

"It means, Mr. Cooper," he smiled, "that the afternoon wind will bring them back home without fail."

"That's reassuring," nodded Thomas with understanding and relief.

"Watch closely now," Christian instructed, his eyes alight with the thrill of his element. He moved about with an effortless grace, pointing out the cunningham, the mainsheet, explaining the purpose of each with an infectious enthusiasm. "Sailing is about harnessing the wind, not fighting it — feel her direction, work with her. Although there is not much wind today."

A FORBIDDEN LOVE

John nodded, taking in every detail, observing how Christian's hands manoeuvred the tiller, making minute adjustments that spoke of an intimate knowledge of the craft. There was an artistry to Christian's command — a dance between man and nature — and John felt a surge of admiration for the deft way his cousin bent the elements to his will.

They glided slowly eastwards along the River Chet through its narrow waterways, where the reflection of overhanging foliage dappled the surface of the water with moving shadows. The reeds rippled in the yacht's wake. Christian's voice was a steady beacon amidst the whispers of the wind, guiding John through the language of the sea. Each term, each technique, was a shared secret, drawing them closer in a world of their own making.

"Starboard tack now, we're coming about," Christian announced, his tone laced with excitement. As he orchestrated the manoeuvre, John marvelled at the precision, the careful timing required to pivot gracefully within the confines of the channel.

"Seamanship isn't just skill, it's instinct," Christian confided, a smile touching the corner of his lips as he caught John's gaze. "Like recognising the subtle shift in the breeze or the change in someone's expression."

The words hung between them, charged with an unspoken meaning, and for a heartbeat, the world beyond the slight sway of *Isabella* ceased to exist.

Only the rhythm of the waves against the bow, the creak of the rigging, and the silent language of their glances filled the space — a symphony of silent acknowledgments and unvoiced desires. As the yacht glided gracefully through the water, the sun piercing the remnants of dawn's mist, there was a sense of unity — not just between the two young men, but with the elements themselves.

The morning's expedition had transformed into something far greater than a mere display of nautical prowess; it had become a voyage into the depths of camaraderie and burgeoning affection, navigated by the steady hands of Prince Christian and the eager heart of Lord John Langley.

The *'Isabella'* glided silently upon the gentle ripples of the interconnected waterways, a graceful swan amidst the verdant tapestry of the Norfolk Broads. The soft whisper of reeds brushing against the hull was like a secret conversation between old friends.

Thatched cottages with their quaint gardens, windmills and a ruined abbey dotted the shoreline, little pockets of the evidence of civilization that seemed to exist in harmonious accord with the wildness surrounding them. John took in the scenery with wide eyes, each bend in the river unveiling another picturesque village or expanse of lush marshland.

From the bow of the yacht, he could see dragonflies darting above the water's surface, their iridescent wings catching the sunlight in fleeting moments of brilliance. The air carried the scent of damp earth and budding flowers, a fresh, invigorating perfume that filled his lungs with each breath.

"Look there," Christian pointed towards a heron standing stoically at the water's edge, its grey plumage blending seamlessly with the reeds. "Nature's sentinel," he mused, his voice a low murmur barely audible over the lapping waves.

John followed Christian's gaze, absorbing the stillness of the scene. There was a beauty here that transcended words, a peace that settled into the bones. For a time, they sailed in companionable silence, the world beyond the

A FORBIDDEN LOVE

Broads forgotten, as if the looming spectre of conflict between their nations had no place among these tranquil waters.

Suddenly, the serenity shattered. A shout pierced the calm, jarring, and urgent. Christian's head snapped towards the sound, his blue eyes narrowing as they spotted the source—a wayward dinghy, its inexperienced occupants struggling with the tiller, veering dangerously close.

"Hard alee!" Christian commanded, his hands flying to the mainsheet with practiced ease. The *'Isabella'* heeled sharply, the wind filling her sails as she responded to her master's touch, carving a path clear of the impending disaster.

John's heart thudded in his chest, a rush of adrenaline flooding his system as he clung to the rail. He watched, wide-eyed, as Christian navigated the crisis with the same effortless grace he had shown earlier, but now with a fierce determination that set his jaw and furrowed his brow. Christian averted the near collision; the dinghy passed harmlessly by, its occupants shouting apologies over their relief.

"Good God, Kip," John breathed out, his voice trembling slightly with the remnants of fear. "That was...remarkable."

A smile brightened Christian's features, erasing the intense look he had just moments ago. "Being prepared is essential when on the water," he stated confidently, a hint of pride in his voice. "The unexpected is all part of the adventure."

As the yacht glided through the calm waters, John could not help but admire his cousin. His skilful handling of the boat and quick thinking were not only impressive but also comforting in a world full of uncertainty. As they continued on their journey, their bond deepened with each passing moment, strengthened by their shared interests and unspoken trust that had formed from previous close calls in life. John watched as Christian expertly navigated the yacht while he retrieved his satchel and sketchbook.

Sitting comfortably on the cabin roof, John sketched Christian below him in the cockpit. He could not help but notice the intense look of concentration on Christian's face as he took in everything around them. And when the wind caught Christian's loose-fitting shirt, revealing his chiselled chest and stomach, John felt a powerful desire to capture this moment and preserve it forever on paper.

After a few uninterrupted hours, the *'Isabella'*, her white sails a stark contrast against the verdant expanse of the Norfolk Broads, glided toward a sheltered inlet. Here, the water was still as glass, reflecting the azure sky and the dancing reeds along the bank. Christian deftly maneuverer the yacht to a gentle stop, securing her with a practiced hand.

"Here we are," he announced with quiet satisfaction, his blue eyes scanning the secluded cove they had chosen for their respite. "A perfect spot, wouldn't you say?"

John could only nod, the serenity of the place seeping into him, easing the residual tension from their earlier brush with danger. They disembarked onto the soft earth, shoes sinking ever so slightly into the damp ground. The sweet scent of wildflowers and the gentle rustle of leaves in the soft breeze filled the air.

Thomas, though not present, had prepared a picnic basket with thoughtful precision, its contents now spread upon a checkered blanket. There were sandwiches wrapped in parchment, fresh fruit that glistened like jewels, and a bottle of wine, its dark green glass cool to the touch. Christian and John settled onto the

A FORBIDDEN LOVE

blanket, the distance between them negligible, an arm's length that felt both entirely proper and charged with something more.

They ate in silence at first, the only sounds the calls of distant birds and the occasional soft splash of fish breaking the surface of the water. As the meal progressed, the conversation flowed more freely. It started with shared memories, laughter over incidents long past, but soon, the talk turned to more serious matters—the thundercloud of war gathering on the horizon.

"I can't help but worry about what lies ahead," Christian admitted, his voice barely above a whisper, as if speaking louder might summon the very fate he feared. "We stand on the brink of something dreadful, and I fear for us—all of us."

John felt a shiver run through him despite the warmth of the sun overhead. "Yes, it's all anyone talks about these days," he responded, his gaze drifting across the water. "The uncertainty is unbearable at times."

"Would you fight, John? If it came to that?" Christian's question hung heavy between them.

John looked into Christian's eyes, seeing there the same conflict that churned within his own heart. "I suppose I must," he whispered, the weight of duty settling on his shoulders. "It's expected of us, isn't it? To defend our country, our family's honour..."

Christian's voice, tinged with bitterness, asked, "Even if it means fighting those we care for on the other side?" His scar, a pale line, seemed to speak of old wounds and new fears. John reached for a grape, rolling it between his fingers as he contemplated the enormity of the question.

"I pray it never comes to that," John murmured, and in that moment, they shared a look that conveyed more than words ever could—a mutual understanding of the precariousness of their position, caught between loyalty and love.

Christian nodded, absentmindedly playing with the blades of grass next to him. "Let's not focus on such bleak thoughts," he suggested, though his expression betrayed his words. "We have today, and today is good."

"Today is good," John repeated, allowing himself a small smile filled with hope. They continued to converse as the day progressed, their voices growing quieter and their words more intimate.

Kip lay back in the grass, turning towards Jonny with his head propped up on his hand. "Do you truly want to be an artist?" he asked softly. Jonny mirrored Kip's position and replied with enthusiasm.

"More than anything else!" Kip's eyes shone with sincerity at his cousin's declaration.

"Do you think your father would allow it?" John considered the question.

"I believe Mama could have persuaded him... but now I highly doubt it," a hint of sadness crossed his face. Kip furrowed his brow thoughtfully.

"Your father loved Aunt Victoria very much, didn't he?" the gears turning in his mind were almost audible.

"Of course he did," answered John, slightly confused by the question.

"Well," Kip said triumphantly, "then remind your father of that when you mention your desire to attend art school and how you know your mother would have supported you." Kip raised an eyebrow as a finishing touch. John narrowed his eyes as he contemplated Kip's suggestion.

A FORBIDDEN LOVE

"Yes," he finally responded, "that could work, but..." Jonny gathered his thoughts before continuing, "I wouldn't want my father to think I manipulated him in such a crude manner."

"Maybe, but doesn't it also show him just how much this means to you?" Kip countered. "And if you show your papa how much this matters to you, like you've shown me, then how could he possibly say *'no?'*" Kip grinned widely, "especially to that face!"

Kip reached out and lovingly brushed Jonny's cheek. "I could never say *'no'* to you..." he quickly withdrew his hand, adding in a softer tone, "about anything."

The words hung heavily in the air as Kip wondered if he had revealed too much about his true feelings. "Are you suggesting I use my charm and good looks as weapons?" Jonny chuckled at his own words.

"Exactly! How else would you ever convince me to go for a ride?" both boys laughed heartily before settling into a comfortable silence with their thoughts. Jonny sat up and locked eyes with Kip.

"And what about your dream of sailing, Kip? Would your father approve?" Jonny asked quietly, but Kip's response was a loud, mocking laugh that startled his cousin. "Kip?" concern laced his voice at the unexpected response.

"I'm sorry, Jonny. Talking about my father tends to bring out the worst in me sometimes," Kip apologised sincerely. They sat in silence for a while as Kip gathered his thoughts, unsure if he should reveal everything. Jonny could see the internal struggle written on his cousin's face.

"Please, Kip?" he prodded gently. Christian removed his hand from supporting his head and laid back to look up at the clouds above as he gathered his thoughts.

"Even though castle walls are thick," Kip began mysteriously, "voices still carry through them." He took a deep breath before continuing. "My parents' arguments and fights filled my childhood within those castle walls for as long as I can remember." But whenever we had guests, they put on a facade of happiness."

Jonny looked at Kip with surprise and regret in his eyes. "I never knew, Kip," he offered an apology.

Kip sighed heavily, saying, "The aristocratic way dictates that nobody should ever know."

"That is until your dear mama somehow learned the truth, and offered her help." John was genuinely touched by the affection Kip held for his mother.

"How did she manage to help?"

"I can only assume that she saw my mother wasn't happy and eventually figured out why," Kip closed his eyes before continuing, "my father's affair, of course." There was a hint of pain in Kip's voice as he spoke.

"He began the affair before he had even met my mother. Apparently, my grandfather disapproved of her and thought she was an *'unsuitable'* wife for a prince. But he continued seeing her even after marrying. And when Mama passed away, I confronted him about it. He said that was simply the way things were."

"That's when you left Eton and went to the naval academy?" Johnny asked, putting the pieces together.

A FORBIDDEN LOVE

"Yes," Kip confirmed with a nod. "My father blamed your mother for being a bad influence on my mother and encouraging her to move back to England. He said she got what she deserved by leaving him for *New York* with your mother."

"Your father actually said that?" John asked incredulously.

"Yes, those were his exact words," Kip replied bitterly.

Johnny felt anger boiling inside him at the thought of Kip's father treating his own family and Kip's mother so poorly.

"Bloody hell, Kip. I had no idea," he said honestly.

"That's why I have never talked about my father fondly," Kip explained. "You see now why I am so pessimistic about ever being able to achieve my dream of sailing. My father would never allow it, and he thinks I am *'too English'* already."

There was a sense of resignation in Kip's voice as he spoke about his dreams being crushed by his father's control. "But please don't let my sad and unhappy story ruin our time together," he said, trying to put on a brave face.

Jonny's eyes squinted in deep thought for a moment, all the while his eyes firmly fixed on his cousin's forlorn demeanour as he stared into the clouds. His heart was bursting with an emotion he struggled to recognise. All he knew for certain was that Kip needed his help and that it was his duty to do that. Jonny picked up a small bread crust and tossed it onto Kip's chest to get his attention. Kip turned onto his side to face Jonny again.

"Kip, the only thing I know for certain about this whole mess is what my mama would have done," stated Jonny with a new certainty in his voice.

"And pray tell then dear cousin," Kip replied earnestly.

"Mama would have helped you, as I promise now to do in her absence," offered Jonny.

"But how Jonny?" Kip's genuine curiosity immediately hooked him into his cousin's plan.

"Mere details Kip!" Jonny teased and then chuckled. "But, give me until the end of the day and I promise I will have a plan." Kip nodded in acceptance that he trusted Jonny enough to know that indeed some plan would evolve in Jonny's mind over the rest of the day.

The picnic ended not with a resolution to their fears, but with a deepening bond forged in the fires of looming uncertainty. As the shadows lengthened upon the water, they packed away the remnants of their repast, each movement deliberate, an attempt to savour the tranquillity of the moment before facing the world again. The air was thick with the scent of damp earth and lingering wildflowers, the peacefulness of their secluded spot reluctant to release them from its embrace.

As he stowed the last basket away, "it was quite the feast," said Christian in a low and warm voice.

"Thomas deserves all the credit," John replied, glancing up to catch Christian's gaze. A smile flickered across his cousin's face, but it was the unspoken gratitude in his eyes that sent an inexplicable shiver down John's spine.

Together, they returned to the *'Isabella'*, their hands occasionally brushing while they passed the coiled ropes and secured the sails. Each touch was like a spark, igniting something delicate and dangerous between them. John felt the heat rise to his cheeks, hoping the cooling breeze off the water would disguise his body's betrayal.

A FORBIDDEN LOVE

Christian stepped aboard first, offering his hand to John. It wasn't necessary—the gap was small, and John was surefooted enough to manage—but the gesture was intimate, compelling. Their fingers lingered together for a fraction longer than needed, and when John stumbled slightly, Christian's grip tightened, steadying him with an ease that spoke of deep familiarity.

"Careful there, Jonny," Christian chided gently, though his eyes danced with mirth. "We can't have you taking a swim before we've even left the mooring."

"Thank you, Kip," John managed, finding his footing on the deck. "I'll endeavour to keep my clumsiness at bay."

Christian showed no sign of releasing John's hand until he was certain of his balance. Only then did he let go, turning his attention to the rigging with a sailor's expertise. He instructed John on the finer points of setting the mainsail, his voice carrying over the gentle lapping of water against the hull. With each term and technique, John's admiration for Christian's skill grew, alongside an awareness of the fluid grace with which he moved.

As *Isabella* caught the wind, the yacht began its journey back towards the village. The closeness of the cockpit allowed for shared secrets and silent confessions. As Christian navigated the yacht with a steady hand, John studied the lines of concentration that formed on his cousin's brow. The scar above Christian's eye—a testament to past adventures and youthful folly—seemed now to be a mark of distinction.

With the sun dipping lower, it gilded the waterways with a soft, golden light. With an open stretch of Broads ahead, Kip beckoned Jonny to sit with him by the tiller and allowed him his first turn to steer the yacht.

The boat sliced through the stillness as if it were part of the landscape itself. Villages nestled amidst the marshlands passed by, picturesque and serene, as if plucked from a painter's dream. Soon the turning back onto the *River Chet* appeared in the distance, and recognising it, Jonny instinctively ceded the tiller to Kip. "No, no Jonny, you have the helm," Kip ordered. "I'll take the rigging, just listen for my orders."

"Port bow, watch for the skiff," Christian's voice cut through the silence, sharp but calm.

John's heart lurched as he spotted another boat emerging suddenly from around a bend. But Christian's watchfulness and clear instructions averted what could have been a graceless collision, and relief washed over John in a warm tide, glad to have pleased his cousin. The trust he placed in Christian's abilities only deepened, the tension between them shifting into something akin to awe.

"Nicely done," Kip murmured, his words were full of pride and carried away on the breeze.

Their journey continued, marked by quiet conversation, and shared laughter that rang out across the waters. As they sailed onward, the setting sun cast long shadows, and the world seemed to hold its breath.

The intimacy of their shared tasks wove around them a cocoon of camaraderie, within which lingered glances and *'accidental'* touches became the language of their unspoken bond.

A FORBIDDEN LOVE

As the estate boathouse and jetty came into view, the return to Langley Hall loomed ahead, yet the desire to stretch these stolen moments into eternity was palpable. They both knew this day would soon become a memory, a point of light in the encroaching dusk of uncertain futures. But for now, as the *'Isabella'* glided homeward with John and Christian side by side, the connection between them pulsed like a living thing—a secret promise made beneath the vast expanse of the changing sky.

The yacht's hull gently kissed the wooden frame of the jetty expertly steered by Kip, a soft thud heralding their arrival at the arranged rendezvous point. Thomas stood there, his figure a stable silhouette against the waning light. He reached out to secure the rope eagerly thrown by John.

"Timely as ever, Tom," Christian remarked with an amiable smile, but there was a slight tremor in his voice that betrayed the day's exertions and deep conversations.

"Always, your highness," Thomas replied, his hazel eyes flickering briefly over the young men. In the dusky glow of twilight, he noted the rosy hue on John's cheeks and the bright spark in Christian's eyes—telltale signs of more than just the crisp air.

His lips quirked up in a knowing half-smile, though it vanished as quickly as it appeared, his discretion impeccable as always. Thomas stepped back, allowing them space to disembark while observing their interactions with the quiet wisdom of one who has seen hearts speak without words. The two young friends moved with an ease born of shared secrets, their laughter mingling with the lap of water against the dock.

"Thank you, Cooper, for meeting us," John said, his voice laced with a subtle reluctance to conclude the day's adventures. "It's been... quite the journey."

"Of course, my lord. I trust everything was to your satisfaction?" Thomas inquired, though he already knew the answer. The bond between the boys was palpable, woven through the very air like a delicate thread of silver.

"Beyond satisfactory," Christian interjected, his gaze lingering on John, who nodded in silent agreement. Their shared experience on the *'Isabella'* had drawn them closer, each moment etching itself into memory with the permanence of ink on parchment.

As they bid farewell to the yacht, stepping onto the solid ground of the estate's private mooring, there lingered a momentary hesitation—a collective breath held before the plunge back into reality. The finality of disembarking weighed on them with the gravity of an ending, yet within that weight was the buoyancy of something new and uncharted.

"We need to get loaded up and head back," Thomas stated, breaking the spell that seemed to hold the boys at the water's edge.

"Let's," John agreed, casting one last look over his shoulder at the Isabella, empty picnic basket in hand. It was more than a boat; it was a vessel that had carried them away from the constraints of their worlds, if only for a fleeting span of hours.

With the cart loaded, they made their way back. As the grand limestone façade of Langley Hall loomed ahead, its windows reflected the last few hours of daylight.

A FORBIDDEN LOVE

Inside there already awaited the warm glow of the golden sunlight and the comforting scents of beeswax and old tapestries, but it could not rival the freedom of the open water or the intimacy of shared confidences under an endless sky.

"Quite the day, wasn't it?" John murmured, his mind replaying every smile, every touch, every word exchanged.

"Indeed," Christian responded, his voice low and infused with an emotion he dared not name. "One for the journal, I'd say."

They entered the hall, the grandeur of the Palladian mansion enveloping them once more. The door closed behind them with a resonant click, sealing away the echo of sails and the whisper of the river. But within the walls of Langley Hall, the sense of fulfilment from their sailing expedition remained—an invisible but indelible mark on the tapestry of their lives.

Thomas watched them go, his observant eyes missing nothing. He understood the language of subtlety, and he carried the knowledge of their deepening bond with the same care he gave to every task. With a last glance at the horizon where the *Isabella* now rested, he turned and followed his charges into the gathering calm of evening.

In his chamber, John stood before the mirror, his fingers working at the buttons of his sweat-stiffened shirt with an unfamiliar clumsiness. During a quick bath, he washed away the smells of the day from his skin and hair. His blond hair, once tousled by the wind, now lay damp against his forehead. He changed into a well-tailored suit; the fabric hugging his slight frame with an almost consoling embrace. He hesitated at the cravat, fingers brushing the silk as if each fold held a secret he wished to unravel.

Christian, meanwhile, emerged from his quick bath with the grace of a man stepping out from a tempest's eye. His black hair slicked back, he donned his attire, the edges of his jacket aligning with the precision of a naval uniform. The scar above his brow was barely visible now, yet it drew John's gaze whenever they met.

The music room welcomed them with open arms, the flames of candles dancing on the walls, casting shadows that played out scenes of unspoken desires. A meal had been laid out—simple fare that did nothing to distract from the complexities simmering between them. They sat opposite each other, the piano silent for now, though the air thrummed with the unsaid melodies of their hearts.

"Your mother would have loved to see you sail today," Christian said softly, breaking the silence as he passed a dish of
roasted lamb to John. The reference to the late Countess drew a bittersweet smile from her son, who nodded in quiet acknowledgment.

"Her *Isabella* carried us well," John replied, the yacht's name spoken like a tender caress. "As did your expertise."

Their conversation flowed with the ease of a river finding its course, yet beneath the surface swirled currents of what could be. Every glance held a touch longer than necessary, every laugh a note too fond. The clink of cutlery and glasses punctuated the spaces between words, a staccato accompaniment to their dance around the truth.

As the evening wore on, the light outside faded completely, leaving only the warm glow within. But the darkness beyond the windows seemed less daunting, less impenetrable, with the memory of their day still fresh, an anchor in the uncertainty that lay ahead.

They rose together and headed upstairs to their shared drawing room. Their steps through the great hall echoed, the sound a reminder of the vastness of Langley Hall and the smallness of two souls within it. Yet even as they retreated, the bond that had grown between them stretched taut, unbroken by distance or decorum. John stood hesitantly between his bedroom and the drawing room.

"I'm going to change into something more comfortable before we have a well-deserved drink," he explained, beginning to remove his cravat and unfasten his stiff shirt collar.

Kip nodded in agreement and disappeared into his own room. John carefully laid his clothes on the bed, taking some time to decide what to wear next. He settled on his pyjama bottoms and dressing gown, unsure if he could find the energy to change again later. Before heading to the drawing room, he pulled the cord to summon Thomas.

He walked towards the french windows, their heavy drapes pulled back to reveal a sliver of moon rising on the horizon. Resting his forehead against the cool glass, he watched as mist drifted over the expansive lawns of the estate. The darkness outside reflected the turmoil within him; both holding secrets hidden in shadows. With no sign of Kip yet, John opened two bottles of ginger beer in preparation. Just then, Thomas appeared.

"You called for me, my lord?"

"Oh yes, thank you Tom. I thought I would save you a trip later by getting ready for bed now," John explained. "If Kip is half as tired as I am, one or two drinks should have us asleep within the hour," he chuckled. "Especially since Kip did most of the work on the yacht."

"Of course, Jonny, you both looked rather tired... but happy, as you returned to the Hall," Thomas smiled warmly.

"Thank you, Tom, and yes we are both very happy," John felt at ease.

"If there's nothing else Jonny, I'll tidy away your clothes from today and wake you at eight-thirty for breakfast at nine o'clock?" John nodded.

"If I need anything else, I'll ring for you. But for now, I'll say goodnight," a tired but genuine smile on John's face.

"Very well, my lord," feigning formality. Thomas turned towards the bedroom door. "Goodnight Jonny," he playfully winked. "And please wish Kip a good night from me as well."

As John wondered what Kip was up to, he strode to his cousin's door and entered his room. "Come on Kip, the beer is getting warm," he noticed Kip pulling a loose shirt over his head and flashed a smile at him.

"Oh, I think I may be a little overdressed," Kip remarked, noticing John's casual attire. "Well then, I won't need this," he removed the shirt and tossed it onto his bed. Although John desperately tried to look away, his cousin's bare torso captivated him as he struggled with his shirt. He knew Kip had caught him staring, their eyes meeting for a long moment. But there was no hint of disapproval or disgust in Kip's expression; if anything, John thought (or hoped?) it was approval.

A FORBIDDEN LOVE

John walked to the bathroom door where Kip's dressing gown hung. "Here, just wear this instead," he said, throwing it over.

"Yes, perfect. Thank you, Jonny," Kip slipped his arms into the sleeves and turned slightly away, feeling a bit exposed by his lack of clothing. He quickly removed his trousers and underwear before securing the robe around his waist. Turning back to face John, he asked, "so what did I hear about a beer?"

"Let's sit down," John motioned towards the door and their drinks, waiting for them. They settled into armchairs that offered a view of the gardens outside. Kip eagerly took a sip of his beer before settling in for a long drink.

"That hit the spot, Jonny," he relaxed into the comfortable chair, using its back to support his tired head and shoulders.

"Well, you did most of the work. You deserve it," John sympathised.

"Not all of it, you helped too," he chuckled, "I'll turn you into a sailor yet!"

Christian's laughter echoed in John's ears, warm and rich, just as it had throughout their eventful day. It stirred something deep within John, a yearning that he could not quite explain. He recalled the confident way Christian handled the ship's tiller, his eyes shining with excitement over mastering the unpredictable winds. John could not deny his admiration for Christian's skill, but it was the patient way he explained nautical terms and the quiet pride in his voice that had captured John's heart.

As he gazed out the window, a shiver ran down John's spine not from the cold, but from recalling their near-disaster earlier that day. The memory of Christian's quick reflexes steering them away from potential disaster filled him with gratitude and another emotion he could not name.

After their laughter died down, John caught his reflection in the window: his blue eyes seemed deeper, shadowed by the intensity of the day, and a flush still lingered on his cheeks from their exciting adventure. He took a deep breath, trying to calm his racing heart – a futile effort when every beat seemed to chant Christian's name. Steeling himself for what was to come next, John turned to face Christian again.

"Christian," he said seriously, using his cousin's full name to grab his attention, "do you want to hear my plan to help you?" Kip sat up straighter in his chair, leaning forward intently towards John.

"Of course I do. If you really think you can help me," Kip replied quietly. John stood up and walked over to the drinks trolley to pour them each a large brandy, feeling Kip's eyes following his every move. When he turned around and handed Kip his drink, John met his gaze without hesitation. He took a moment to compose himself before speaking.

"Well Kip, here's how I see it," he fixed his gaze on Christian's eyes, "when we both turn twenty-one, we can do whatever we want with our lives – with or without our fathers' approval or support."

Kip furrowed his eyebrows as he considered John's words. "You see, when we turn twenty-one, we'll both have access to our trust funds from Grandpapa. And I'll also receive a substantial inheritance from my dear mama." Understanding dawned on Kip's face.

"Yes, I have a small inheritance from my mother as well, but it won't be nearly as much as yours," Christian interjected.

"Do you remember Harrison from school?" Christian nodded. "Well after you left, I was in the same dorm as him. We were both on the house cricket team, so we used to chat quite a bit.

Nothing too serious, but he mentioned that his family had a small villa in the south of France and..." John paused for dramatic effect, "a magnificent yacht that they often rented out to wealthy Americans when they weren't using it." He let that sink in for a moment before continuing, "so I think between our trust funds...well, we could afford to buy a small villa and yacht together. I could pursue my passion for painting while you teach rich Americans how to sail or take them on excursions."

"You would really do that for me? Use your trust funds to help me?" Kip hesitates for a moment, "and you came up with this plan in just a few hours?" Both boys share a broad smile.

"Of course I would do it for you, even right now if I could - especially now that I understand how difficult things are with your father. But," Jonny pauses, considering the weight of his next words, as he realised they would reveal his long-held feelings. He takes a deep breath, "to be honest, I didn't come up with this plan today. I've been thinking about it ever since we lost our mothers. I missed you so very much when you went back to Germany that making this plan was the only thing that kept me going sometimes." A look of concern or maybe relief crosses Kip's face.

"My leaving Eton made you that unhappy, Jonny?" John nods slowly. "Well, you weren't alone in that, I promise," he chuckles before adding, "I used to dream every night of escaping from the Academy, sneaking onto a freighter, and showing up at some English port to find you. Then I could secretly take refuge somewhere here - hidden from everyone except each other and Tom."

The confession of their feelings shocked neither boy; instead, they find solace in them. There is still an underlying sense of shame or confusion about what these feelings mean, but their primary response is one of relief, as they no longer feel alone in whatever it is between them.

"I think I may prefer your plan though, Jonny," Kip finally says. Jonny gives him a quizzical look while taking a sip of his drink. "I'm not sure how long I could have lasted living in the hayloft, eating scraps of smuggled food... and never getting a proper bath!" They laugh nervously as they realise the implications of their plan. Kip raises his glass to toast with Jonny, "my cousin's plan!"

"To our plan," Jonny corrects with a smile.

CHAPTER FIVE:
UNSPOKEN FEELINGS

Wednesday July 29th, 1914

John and Christian had fallen into a comfortable routine, alternating between leisurely rides around the estate and adventurous boating trips. But even in this idyllic setting, their conflicting desires surfaced.

Sundays were a particularly difficult day for John, as he struggled with the expectations of his noble upbringing and his own yearning for a simpler life. He was expected to lead a procession of the household staff to the church in the village. Despite the warmth of the villagers, and the fond memories of being baptised by the local vicar, John could not shake off the inner turmoil caused by his hopes playing against everyone else's expectations.

Outside of this idyllic setting, the tensions in Europe grew, as if mirroring those the young lord was experiencing himself. In response to the assassination Austria had mobilised its army ready to fight Serbia, and had received a guarantee from Germany to support them if Russia responded. Jonny and Kip were aware, through the daily newspapers brought up from London, that the delicate balance of alliances could lead to a serious war between the Great Powers.

The current international situation was the main topic of conversation at a recent tea party with the Parish Councillors and Church Wardens. The dark shadows of a war only reinforced John's feelings, of being torn between his sense of noblesse oblige, duty and his growing desire for a life without obligation.

Meanwhile, John and Kip's private conversations on their boating trips and rides allowed them to be more open and vulnerable with each other; but they still found themselves dancing around their intense physical attraction, fearful of the consequences and societal judgement.

The lessons drilled into them at school about the dangers of same-sex relationships weighed heavily on their minds, adding to the already tumultuous conflict within themselves. How could something feeling so right also be considered so sinful? As they continued to navigate their feelings for each other, John and Christian knew that they would have to tread carefully in order to protect both their hearts and their reputations.

On this day, the sailboat again glided alongside the boathouse, its white sails billowing against the amber sky. Their latest trip out had been to the ruins of *St Olave's Priory*, a site that John had been keen to sketch. As was their routine, Thomas was waiting for them with a cart to return them to the Hall.

"Good day my lord, your highness?" Thomas asked.

"Of course it was Thomas!" Jonny responded, forgetting the required formality, and almost skipped to the cart as he clutched his sketching satchel and an empty picnic basket.

Once they had arrived back at the Hall, two footmen appeared to take away the empty baskets and the boys jumped down onto the gravel, "Cooper, as we are a little early today, I think we will take coffee and a slice or two of Mrs Heath's fruit cake upstairs in our drawing room."

A FORBIDDEN LOVE

"Very well my lord, I will send a footman up shortly, and return myself to lay out your evening wear for dinner," Thomas smiled inwardly as he realised Jonny had said *'our'* drawing room.

"Thank you, Cooper," said John as they stepped into the house and raced up the main staircase. They passed through John's room, and he casually tossed his satchel onto his bed.

"Do you mind showing me your work from today later?" asked Kip, genuine interest clear in his tone.

"Of course—we have no secrets between us now," replied Jonny, his voice edged with pride. Was he proud of his art or of their bond? "But first, I need to tidy up the main piece before you see it. I'll do that while you're in the bath."

"Shall we go through then?" Kip guided Jonny to the shared drawing room, which had quickly become their favourite place of sanctuary. As they entered, a wave of heat and humidity greeted them. "We should open these doors," said Kip, hurrying over to the french doors and flinging them wide open.

"It's been quite humid and sultry today," observed John, peering out the window at a distant grey haze. "Maybe there'll be a storm later on? What does my skipper think?" he teased with a smile.

Kip also gazed out at the haze and looming clouds. "I wouldn't dare take a boat out in weather like this," he declared in a mock-serious tone. "I'd batten down the hatches and strap myself to the mast!"

The boys laughed, though their merriment lessened when Robert, the footman, arrived with coffee and cake. "Thank you, Robert, but we can manage from here," said John dismissively. "Shall I pour?" As they took their first sips of steaming coffee, beads of sweat began forming on their brows. Kip released a deep sigh, apologising to Jonny before removing his shirt and settling back down.

"That's better," he remarked.

"Yes, indeed," thought John, as his face lit up at Kip's actions. Though neither spoke it aloud, their eyes and expressions revealed their mutual attraction.

Kip felt a mix of satisfaction at having made Jonny react, and inner conflict mixed with shame for enjoying it as much as he did. Despite the underlying tension, both of them had silently vowed not to act on these forbidden desires. In that moment, simply knowing the depth of the other's feelings was enough to bring comfort, even if any hope for more was deliberately kept at bay. This unspoken truce sufficed, as for now, it eased their feelings of guilt and shame.

"Well," said Jonny with a playful look at his cousin, "when in Rome, right?" He stood up, removed his shirt too, and then sat back down a little self-consciously. It was clear he did not possess the same confidence in his physique that Kip did.

"Look at us," laughed Kip. "We look like two farm labourers in the middle of harvest!" As always, Kip's humour eased the awkwardness of the situation. In truth, both young men were comfortable with their mutual physical attraction, yet equally determined and too ashamed to ever act on it, whether through words or actions.

Easy conversation resumed as they recounted their day together, every stolen glance at one another's bodies a tacit acknowledgment of their predicament rather than a moment of discomfort. Eventually, Jonny directed his cousin to his bath, mindful of his promise to finish his sketches.

A FORBIDDEN LOVE

John undressed, loosely wrapped his dressing gown around himself, and settled on his bed with his sketchbook. After contemplating his work for a few minutes, he smiled and began making adjustments, once again losing himself in his art. Finally, he was happy with his work and carefully closed his sketchbook before moving into the bathroom to rouse Kip. As he entered, all he could see of his cousin were his feet over the end of the bath and his head leaning over the other.

Clearly, he had nodded off. Jonny smiled at the peaceful scene and, for a moment, considered waking him with a startle as a prank. Instead, though, he tiptoed to the bath and placed his hand on Kip's shoulder to wake him, "Kip, it's time now." Slowly, his cousin raised his head and turned to face Jonny, and his eyes opened.

"Ah, Jonny," he smiled warmly. "I must have dozed off for a moment."

"Yes, just a moment I am sure," Jonny chuckled. "Lucky you didn't drown!"

"Imagine my obituary headline, *'Sailor Prince drowns in bath'*," Kip sat up and laughed raucously as Jonny shook his head in resignation at the comment. Kip composed himself for a moment and made his most mischievous face before adding, "well you could always have got in and rescued me." He playfully slapped the water in front of himself.

"Come on Sailor Prince, we need to be getting on to be ready for dinner." Jonny moved to grab one towel on the rack and passed it to Kip. He quickly stood and wrapped himself in the proffered bath sheet, and left John to take his own bath.

With Thomas' compliance, because of the continuing heat and humidity, both young men eschewed wearing dinner jackets, and wore light cotton waistcoats with their shirts and bowtie. As they arrived in the Music Room, their table was, as always, immaculately set out ready for the food's arrival. A large set of french doors that led to one end of the terrace were wide open, letting in a slight but cooling breeze. With their usual efficiency, two footmen appeared with trays at exactly eight pm. After this, they hovered to provide drinks and move away finished plates.

As they savoured the meal, their conversation flowed easily, touching on everything from literature to politics. John found himself captivated by Christian's wit and charm, hanging on every word. The presence of the servants, and propriety, kept any controversial thoughts from ever being spoken.

Once the last plates were cleared away and servants dismissed, Christian leaned back in his chair, a thoughtful expression crossing his face. "You know, Jonny, I was thinking about that magnificent grand piano in the corner. It's been a long time since I've heard you play."

John felt a flutter of nervousness in his stomach.

"Oh, I'm terribly out of practice," he demurred, fidgeting with his napkin. "I wouldn't want to subject you to my rusty skills."

Christian's eyes softened. "Nonsense. Your talent is natural, cousin. I'm sure it would be a delight to hear you play again."

John hesitated, torn between his desire to please Christian and his fear of revealing too much through his music. He had always found it easier to express his deepest emotions through the keys than through words.

"Please?" Christian pressed gently. "For me?"

A FORBIDDEN LOVE

Unable to resist the earnest look in Christian's eyes, John nodded, rising from his chair. "Very well, but don't say I didn't warn you."

The polished wood of the grand piano gleamed in the soft lamplight, beckoning him forward. John settled onto the piano bench, his fingers hovering over the keys as he took a steadying breath. He was acutely aware of Christian's gaze upon him, filled with encouragement and something deeper that John dared not name. Meanwhile, Christian had poured them a large brandy each and settled next to his cousin on the bench.

They lapsed into a comfortable silence, shoulders still touching, as they sat side by side. John's fingers absently traced the keys, not quite playing, just feeling the smooth ivory beneath his fingertips, working through his mind to find a piece to play.

Decision made; John began to play. The first notes of Debussy's *'Clair de Lune'* filled the air, the melody drifting through the open french doors and into the summer night. The music seemed to weave a spell around them, the rest of the world falling away, until there was nothing but the two of them, the piano, and the shimmering notes that hung in the atmosphere around them.

Their unspoken truth hung between them, as tangible as the notes lingering in the air. John felt a sudden urge to lean in, to close the scant distance separating them and press his lips to Christian's. But the weight of propriety and the fear of rejection held him back, rooting him in place.

Christian leaned in closer, his breath warm against John's cheek. "I've always loved watching you play," he murmured, taking a sip of his drink, his voice barely audible over the music. "The way you lose yourself in it, like nothing else matters."

John's fingers faltered for a moment, his heart stuttering at the intimacy of Christian's words. He could feel the heat of his body, the press of his shoulder, the scent of his cologne mingling with the beeswax and old wood of the music room.

Christian's lips curved into a playful smile, breaking the tension that hung between them. "You know, Jonny," he said, his voice light but tinged with a deeper emotion, "when we have our villa in France, I'll make sure to buy you a grand piano. Something worthy of your talent."

John felt a rush of warmth flood his chest. The casual mention of their shared dream, spoken aloud in this intimate moment, made it feel more real than ever. He chuckled softly, grateful for Christian's ability to diffuse the intensity of the moment.

"Oh? And where exactly will you put this grand piano, Kip?" John asked, falling easily into their familiar banter. "I thought the villa was going to be filled with your sailing trophies."

Christian's eyes sparkled with mischief. "We'll make room. Perhaps we'll have a music room with a view of the Mediterranean? You can play while I watch the sunset."

The image settled in John's mind, vivid and alluring. He could almost feel the warm breeze from the open windows, hear the distant crash of waves. In that imagined future, there was no threat of war, no societal expectations - just the two of them, free to be who they truly were.

"I'd like that," John murmured, allowing himself to lean slightly into Christian's shoulder.

A FORBIDDEN LOVE

The grandfather clock in the hallway chimed softly, reminding them of the world beyond this room. Yet neither made a move to leave. The notes of Debussy seemed to linger in the air, a gossamer thread connecting this moment to their dreamed future. Forcing himself to focus back to the music, John let the familiar notes of Satie's *'Gymnopédie No. 1'* flow next from his fingers.

The piece had always held a melancholy beauty for him, a sense of longing that seemed to echo the ache in his own heart. As the last notes faded away, John noticed the silence that settled over the room. He could feel Christian's gaze on him, could hear the soft rhythm of his breathing. Slowly, feeling as if he were moving through water, John turned to face him.

Beside him, Christian's eyes had drifted shut, his expression one of pure rapture. The music had washed over him, carrying away the doubts and uncertainties that had plagued him for so long. In this moment, there was no war looming on the horizon, no expectations to be met, no roles to be played. There was only the music, and the man beside him, and the love that burned between them like a beacon in the darkness.

Christian's eyes were open now, dark, and fathomless in the flickering candlelight. They searched John's face, as if seeking answers to questions he dared not ask aloud. John could see the vulnerability there, the raw, unbridled emotion that Christian so rarely allowed himself to show. It was a sight that took his breath away, a glimpse into the depths of a soul that he had come to know as intimately as his own.

In that moment, the world seemed to fall away, leaving only the two of them suspended in a moment of perfect understanding. The silence stretched between them, heavy with the weight of all that remained unspoken, all that they yearned to say but could not find the words to express.

And yet, in that silence, John found a strange sort of peace, a sense of belonging that he had never known before. For also in that moment, he knew that whatever lay ahead, whatever trials and tribulations they might face, he would face them with Christian by his side.

They were bound together by a love that transcended the boundaries of class and country, a love that would endure through the darkest of nights and the brightest of days. And though the road ahead might be fraught with danger and uncertainty, John knew he would walk it gladly, so long as he had Christian's hand to hold, and his heart to guide him home.

"I've never heard it played quite like that before," Christian said softly, his eyes fluttering open to meet John's gaze. "It's as if you've captured something... ineffable."

John's fingers trembled slightly on the keys. "I suppose I was thinking of... of us," he admitted, his voice barely above a whisper. Christian shifted on the piano stool, his thigh pressing more firmly against John's.

"Us?" he echoed, a note of hope in his voice.

John's heart pounded. He turned slightly, acutely aware of their proximity. "Our friendship, our plan, I mean. How it's changed, grown deeper over the years." They sat again in silence for a moment, the air between them thick with unspoken words. John's mind raced, torn between the urge to lean closer and the fear of crossing a line that could not be uncrossed.

Christian cleared his throat. "Play something else?" he asked, his voice husky. "Something... passionate."

A FORBIDDEN LOVE

John nodded, his fingers finding the keys once more. As he began to play Chopin's *'Nocturne in E-flat major'*, he felt Christian's gaze upon him, intense and searching. The music swelled, mirroring the tumult of emotions in John's chest.

As he reached a particularly moving passage, he felt Christian's hand brush against his own, ostensibly to turn the page of the sheet music. The touch, brief as it was, sent a jolt of electricity through John's body. Their eyes met, and for a moment, the rest of the world fell away again.

The haunting melody drifted through the air, filling the music room with its ethereal beauty. As John's fingers danced across the ivory and ebony keys, a shadow fell across the threshold. Thomas had paused in the doorway as he was returning to the servants' hall. He had been upstairs to lay out Jonny's night wear, having been told he would not be needed at bedtime.

The valet's eyes widened slightly as he took in the scene before him. Lord John and Prince Christian sat side by side on the piano stool, their bodies angled towards each other, shoulders touching. As the music swelled, Christian leaned in closer, his eyes half-closed in rapture.

Thomas observed the young men with a mixture of fondness and concern. He noted the way John's slender frame seemed to relax under Christian's gaze, his usual rigidity melting away. Christian's hand rested dangerously close to John's thigh, fingers twitching as if longing to close the gap.

"They're like two halves of a whole," Thomas thought, a bittersweet ache in his chest.

He knew all too well the dangers that lurked beyond these walls for two young men like them. As if sensing his presence, John's eyes flickered towards the door. Thomas quickly stepped back, melting into the shadows of the hallway. He lingered for a moment, listening to the final, plaintive notes of the piece. "I shouldn't intrude," Thomas murmured to himself, his voice barely a whisper.

With practiced stealth, he retreated down the corridor, leaving John and Christian to their private moment. As he walked away, Thomas' mind whirled with conflicting emotions. He felt a deep, brotherly affection for both young men, having watched them grow from boys into the fine gentlemen they were becoming.

And yet, he could not shake the fear that gripped his heart. "May God watch over them," Thomas prayed silently, his steps echoing softly in the empty hallway.

He knew their path would not be an easy one, but he vowed to do what he could to protect them, even if it meant turning a blind eye to moments like these. He felt a pang of sympathy for the young men, caught between the demands of duty and the yearnings of their hearts.

Thomas knew all too well the weight of societal expectations, the constant pressure to conform to a rigid set of norms and values. And yet, in moments like these, when the world fell away and all that remained was the music and the connection between two souls, he could not help but feel a glimmer of hope.

As the music swelled to a crescendo, Christian's hand moved to rest lightly on John's back. It was a gesture so intimate, so full of unspoken longing. John's voice, soft and hesitant, barely carried over the music. "Christian, I..."

"Shh," Christian murmured, his fingers tracing small circles on John's back. "Just play. Please."

A FORBIDDEN LOVE

And though there was still so much left unsaid, so many feelings that remained unspoken, John knew they had time. Time to explore this new and fragile thing between them, to nurture it and watch it grow.

Time to dream of a future that they could call their own, a life that they could build together, brick by brick. For now, it was enough to be simply here, in this moment, with the one person who understood him better than anyone else in the world. As the night stretched on, John let himself sink into the warmth of Christian's presence, the steady rhythm of his breathing a soothing balm to his troubled soul.

John's exertions and his intense emotions caused his forehead to bead with sweat. "Let's sit for a while," and he led Christian to a pair of armchairs. Jonny sat and finished his drink, holding it up to Kip, "would you mind?" Kip took the glass and refilled it after he emptied his own, and then sat down on an armchair next to Jonny.

"Thank you, Jonny," Kip said, leaning towards his cousin and raising his glass. "The music and your playing were beautiful." He clinked his glass against John's.

"Thank you, Kip," John replied, feeling his cheeks warm with a blush. "It was my pleasure." They held each other's gaze for what felt like an eternity, sharing a moment of mutual contentment.

Suddenly, a bright flash lit up the dark sky outside, briefly illuminating the terrace and gardens. Moments later, they heard the rumble of thunder approaching and passing overhead. Both boys stood up together and moved towards the open french doors, looking out at the horizon.

A few minutes later, the sky flashed again, and the thunder followed more swiftly, indicating the storm was drawing nearer. Realising this, they turned to each other.

"Shall we?" Kip asked, pointing upwards. Jonny nodded eagerly and stepped back inside to pull the cord to summon a footman.

"You go up, Kip. I'll follow once the footman arrives," Jonny said, mindful of his duties. The footman arrived after a few minutes, allowing Jonny time to finish his drink and grab two bottles of ginger beer from the drinks trolley. "Please inform Mr. Cooper that the prince and I have gone up now and that I won't be needing him again tonight."

"Very well, my lord," the footman replied. With that, Jonny skipped past the footman and dashed towards the grand staircase.

A FORBIDDEN LOVE

'Kip on Isabella' July 1914

A FORBIDDEN LOVE

CHAPTER SIX:
THE STORM'S EMBRACE

Jonny burst through the door of his bedroom, his heart racing with anticipation. The sight that greeted him sent a jolt through his body - Kip was already there, lounging on the edge of his four-poster bed. His jacket, waistcoat, and tie lay discarded on a nearby chair, leaving him in just his crisp white shirt and trousers.

"There you are!" Kip exclaimed, jumping up with a mischievous grin. "I was beginning to think you'd lost your nerve." Jonny felt a flush creep up his neck as he took in Kip's dishevelled appearance.

"Never," he replied, trying to keep his voice steady. Kip laughed, the sound sending a shiver down Jonny's spine.

"Well, hurry up then. We don't want to miss the best part of the storm." As Jonny fumbled with the buttons of his own jacket, Kip's eyes sparkled with nostalgia.

"Remember when we were boys? How we used to dare each other to stay out in the rain the longest?" then he laughed loudly, "and sneak past nanny's room to get to the roof!"

"How could I forget?" Jonny chuckled, his fingers trembling slightly as he removed his tie. "You always won."

"Only because you let me," Kip teased, moving closer. The scent of his cologne, mixed with the earthy smell of impending rain wafting through the open window, made Jonny's head spin. Jonny's mind raced as Kip helped him with his waistcoat. Was this how it had always been between them? This electric tension, masked by years of friendship? Or was it just his own desperate longing colouring his perceptions?

"There," Kip said softly, his hands lingering on Jonny's shoulders. "Now you're ready for an adventure."

Jonny swallowed hard, acutely aware of Kip's proximity. "Lead the way then," he said, his voice barely above a whisper.

As they moved towards the door, another low rumble of thunder echoed in the distance. Jonny's heart thudded in response, not just from the thrill of the approaching storm, but from the storm of emotions Kip's presence always stirred within him. Kip's hand closed around the cool glass of the ginger beer bottle, condensation beading on its surface.

"Come on," he whispered conspiratorially, a mischievous glint in his eye. "Before Nanny catches us."

Jonny's heart raced as they slipped out of his bedroom, their footsteps muffled by the plush carpet. The familiar corridors of Langley House seemed different in the dim light, charged with an air of secrecy and adventure. Their laughter echoed softly as they climbed the Dowager's stairs and ran along the top corridor, a melody of shared memories and unspoken desires. Jonny's fingers brushed against Kip's as they climbed the narrow stairs to the roof, sending a jolt of electricity through his body.

As they emerged onto the rooftop, the air was thick with anticipation. Jonny inhaled, tasting the metallic tang of the approaching storm on his tongue. They made their way to the stone balustrade, their shoulders touching as they leaned against it.

A FORBIDDEN LOVE

"There," Kip breathed, pointing to a distant flash. "Did you see it?" Jonny nodded; his eyes fixed on the horizon. But he found his gaze drawn irresistibly to Kip's profile, illuminated for a moment by another streak of lightning. He wondered if Kip could hear the thundering of his heart, louder even than the storm that approached.

"It's beautiful," Jonny murmured, unsure if he meant the lightning or the boy beside him. Kip turned to him, eyes shining with excitement.

"Just like old times, eh?" he breathed, his voice barely able to be heard over the growing wind. Jonny swallowed hard, acutely aware of how close they were standing.

"Just like old times," he echoed, wishing desperately that it could be something more.

The first fat droplets of rain splattered onto the stone balustrade, warm and heavy with summer's promise. Jonny tilted his face skyward, closing his eyes as the rain fell in earnest. The sensation was exhilarating, each drop a gentle caress against his skin.

"So, who is going to stay the longest?" Kip's voice was playful, tinged with nostalgia.

Jonny opened his eyes, turning to find Kip getting similarly drenched, his raven hair plastered to his forehead. Their laughter mingled with the patter of rain, a harmonious counterpoint to the growing rumble of thunder. Jonny was acutely aware of how Kip's shirt clung to his athletic frame, outlining every contour. He felt suddenly self-conscious of his own slight build, wondering if Kip noticed the way the fabric adhered to his skin. A brilliant flash of lightning illuminated the sky, followed almost immediately by a deafening crack of thunder. Jonny instinctively stepped closer to Kip, their arms brushing.

"Getting scared, Johnny?" Kip teased, but there was a gentleness in his eyes that belied his words. Jonny shook his head, droplets flying from his darkened blond hair.

"Never," he said, mustering a bravado he did not quite feel. "You?"

Kip's gaze locked with his, intense and unreadable. "Not a chance."

The air between them crackled with an energy that had nothing to do with the storm. Jonny's heart raced, torn between the thrill of the tempest and the magnetic pull of Kip's presence.

He wondered how long they could stay out here, suspended in this moment of shared defiance against nature and society's expectations. Another flash, another boom, closer still. Neither boy moved, each silently daring the other to be the first to retreat, to break the spell that held them captive on the rain-lashed roof. A blinding flash of lightning split the sky, followed instantaneously by a deafening crack of thunder.

The acrid scent of ozone filled the air as a nearby oak tree burst, only two hundred yards away, into flames, its ancient branches illuminated in a terrifying spectacle.

"Bloody hell!" Kip exclaimed, grabbing Jonny's arm. "We need to get inside, now!"

Jonny's heart leapt into his throat, adrenaline surging through his veins. Without a word, they sprinted towards the roof access door, feet slipping on the rain-slicked lead. The storm's fury seemed to chase them, the wind whipping at their sodden clothes.

A FORBIDDEN LOVE

As they stumbled into the safety of the house, Jonny's legs trembled beneath him. He leaned against the wall, panting heavily, acutely aware of Kip's proximity.

"That was... exhilarating," Jonny managed between breaths, a nervous laugh escaping his lips.

Kip's eyes sparkled with a mix of fear and excitement. "Thought we were goners for a moment there. Come on, let's get dried off before we catch our death." They made their way to Jonny's bedroom, leaving a trail of wet footprints on the polished wooden floors. Once inside, Kip immediately began rummaging through the linen closet in their shared bathroom.

"Here," he said, tossing a thick towel to Jonny. "Get out of those wet things before you freeze." Jonny caught the towel, his fingers brushing against Kip's. He turned away quickly, focusing on the fireplace to hide the flush creeping up his neck.

"I'll, uh, get the fire going," Jonny mumbled, fumbling with the matches. His hands shook slightly as he struck one, the small flame dancing in the room's darkness. As the fire slowly came to life, its warmth chased away the chill that had settled into Jonny's bones.

He could hear Kip moving behind him, the soft rustle of fabric as his friend dried himself off. Jonny's mind raced. How many times had they changed in front of each other without a second thought? Why did it suddenly feel so... different?

Jonny turned, towel clutched to his chest, to find Kip standing closer than he expected. The firelight danced across Kip's damp skin, highlighting the curve of his collarbone and the hollow of his throat. Jonny swallowed hard; his mouth suddenly dry.

"Here, you missed a spot," Kip said softly, reaching out to brush a droplet of water from Jonny's cheek. His touch lingered, warm, and gentle, sending a shiver down Jonny's spine that had nothing to do with the cold.

"Thanks," Jonny whispered, his voice barely audible over the crackling fire. He cleared his throat, trying to regain his composure. "We should, um, finish drying off."

They moved closer to the fire; the heat seeping into their bodies as they towelled themselves dry. Jonny could not help but steal glances at Kip, noticing how his wet shirt clung to his lean frame, how his dark hair curled slightly at the nape of his neck.

"Remember when we used to do this as boys?" Kip asked, breaking the charged silence. "After getting caught in the rain during one of our adventures?"

Jonny laughed softly, grateful for the distraction. "How could I forget? We'd come back looking like drowned rats, and nanny would scold us something fierce."

"But she always had towels waiting for us and a hot drink," these were indeed happy memories for both.

As they reminisced, their hands occasionally brushed against each other, each touch sending sparks of awareness through Jonny. He lingered longer than necessary, savouring the casual intimacy of the moment. Once dry, they settled on the rug by the fire, nursing the last of their ginger beer.

A FORBIDDEN LOVE

The storm continued to rage outside, but in here, time seemed to stand still. Jonny stared into the flames, lost in thought. He could feel Kip's presence beside him, solid and comforting, yet thrumming with an undercurrent of tension that he could not quite name. Kip moved briefly to the drawing room, and he returned with two large brandies
. "This will warm you up," he whispered as he passed one to Jonny. Before he sat back down, he pulled his damp shirt off over his head and placed the towel around his shoulders. He reached towards Jonny and took hold of his shirt to pull it off too. Jonny offered no resistance, concentrating instead of keeping hold of his drink. Wrapped again in his towel too, both boys settled, the flames of the fire gently illuminating their faces.

"Penny for your thoughts?" Kip finally murmured, his voice low and husky.

Jonny turned to look at him, struck by the intensity in Kip's blue eyes. "I was just thinking..." he began, then hesitated, unsure how to put his swirling emotions into words, "... about how many things can change and yet remain the same."

"*Plus ça change, plus c'est la même chose*," offered Kip.

In this moment, it seemed that both boys had accepted that something had changed between them, despite their uncertainty about its exact meaning or nature, whilst it also seemed that they could still play their childhood games. These inherently contradictory thoughts played on the minds of both as they silently finished their drinks.

The fire crackled, casting flickering shadows across Kip's face as he rose, extending a hand to Jonny. "Come on, you look exhausted. Let's get you to bed."

Jonny took Kip's hand, feeling a rush of warmth at the contact. He allowed himself to be guided to the massive four-poster bed, its mahogany frame gleaming in the firelight. Kip's touch was gentle as he eased Jonny onto the plush mattress.

"You don't have to tuck me in," Jonny protested weakly, even as he sank into the softness of the down pillows. "I'm not a child anymore."

Kip chuckled, his fingers lingering as he pulled the heavy green silk damask covers up to Jonny's chin. "No, you're certainly not," he murmured, his gaze roaming over Jonny's face. "But I will take care of you all the same."

The tenderness in Kip's voice made Jonny's heart clench. He watched as Kip moved away, shivering slightly in his still-damp clothes.

"You're cold," Jonny observed, concern colouring his tone. "Why don't you..." he hesitated, then pushed on, "why don't you join me? For warmth."

Kip froze, his back to Jonny. The silence stretched, punctuated only by the patter of rain against the windows and the low rumble of distant thunder.

"Are you sure?" Kip asked finally, his voice barely above a whisper.

Jonny's pulse quickened. "Yes, we always used to," he breathed, lifting the covers in invitation.

After a moment's hesitation, Kip slipped into the bed beside him. The mattress dipped, and Jonny was acutely aware of his proximity, and the heat radiating from his body.

"This feels... warmer," Kip murmured, his breath warm against Jonny's ear. Jonny nodded, unable to form words. This moment shifted their relationship; however, he remained uncertain how.

A FORBIDDEN LOVE

All he knew was that having Kip beside him felt right, felt like coming home. Kip lay motionless, his heart thundering in his chest. The soft glow of the fire cast dancing shadows across the room, mirroring the tumultuous emotions swirling within him. He could feel the warmth of Jonny's body mere inches away, tantalising and forbidden.

"Jonny?" Kip whispered, his voice barely audible above the patter of rain against the windowpanes.

"Mm?" Jonny mumbled, already half-asleep.

Kip swallowed hard, wrestling with the words caught in his throat. "I... I'm glad we're friends."

Jonny shifted slightly, his arm brushing against Kip's. "Me too," he murmured drowsily.

The innocent touch sent a jolt through Kip's body. He clenched his fists, fighting the urge to reach out and pull Jonny closer. The scent of rain and wood smoke lingered in the air, mingling with the familiar notes of Jonny's cologne. Kip closed his eyes, allowing himself to be enveloped by the comforting sensations.

"We can't stay like this forever, can we?" Kip whispered, more to himself than to Jonny. But Jonny's steady breathing told him his friend had already drifted off to sleep. Kip lingered, enjoying intimacy's fleeting nature. Eventually, with a quiet sigh, he carefully extricated himself from the bed. As he stood, Kip gazed down at Jonny's peaceful form.

"One day," he murmured, "one of us will have to be brave enough to say it out loud." He reached out, his fingers hovering just above Jonny's tousled hair, before withdrawing. "But not tonight. Tonight, this is enough."

With one last lingering look, Kip padded silently towards the door, leaving Jonny to his dreams. Kip's hand trembled as he grasped the brass doorknob, its cool surface a stark contrast to the warmth he'd just left behind. He paused, turning back to cast one last glance at Jonny's sleeping form. The flickering firelight cast dancing shadows across his friend's face, softening the handsome features that Kip knew so well.

"Sweet dreams, Jonny," Kip whispered, his voice inaudible above the muffled rumble of thunder outside.

As he eased the door open, a gust of cool air rushed in, carrying with it the scent of rain-soaked earth. Kip slipped into the darkened drawing room; his bare feet silent on the polished oak floor. The storm still raged beyond the windows, flashes of lightning briefly illuminating the ornate wallpaper and family portraits. Kip leaned against the closed door, his heart pounding. The tempest outside seemed to mirror the tumult of emotions within him – desire and fear, hope and despair, all swirling together in a dizzying maelstrom.

"What am I doing?" he murmured, running a hand through his damp hair. "This can't... we can't..."

Another peal of thunder shook the house, as if in response to his unspoken doubts. Kip straightened, squaring his shoulders as he made his way towards his own room. Each step felt heavy, laden with the weight of unspoken truths and forbidden longings.

As he reached for the handle of his bedroom door, a floorboard creaked behind him. Kip froze, his pulse quickening. Had Jonny awakened? Would he call out, ask Kip to return? But the moment passed in silence, broken only by the steady drumming of rain against the windows.

A FORBIDDEN LOVE

Kip exhaled slowly, a mixture of relief and disappointment washing over him. "Goodnight, Jonny," he whispered once more, before slipping into his room and leaving the storm – both outside and within – behind closed doors.

A FORBIDDEN LOVE

CHAPTER SEVEN:
A WORLD TURNED UPSIDE DOWN

3rd August 1914

The late afternoon sun cast a golden sheen upon the limestone facade of Langley Hall, its grandeur undisturbed by the faintest whisper of conflict. Yet as Thomas Cooper, his hands steady despite the tremor in his heart, clutched the telegram delivered moments ago, the tranquillity of the Norfolk estate seemed to shudder beneath the weight of impending war.

With the urgency of a storm gathering on the horizon, Thomas mounted his horse and galloped across the parkland. His keen eyes scanned the verdant expanse for Lord John and Prince Christian, the young men blissfully unaware amidst their ride that the world was tilting on its axis. Upon finding them, he reined in his steed with a practiced ease that belied his anxious haste. The boys slowed their mounts, concern etched in their youthful features as they regarded Thomas' uncharacteristic intrusion.

"Forgive me, my lords," Thomas began, voice betraying none of the turmoil within as he extended the missive. "A telegram from London."

Lord John's slender fingers, which had often graced cricket bats and reins with equal finesse, trembled ever so slightly as he took the paper. His striking blue eyes, mirrors to a soul that danced on the edge of forbidden desires, widened in disbelief as he read aloud the stark words that heralded a new epoch.

"Germany has declared war on France," he murmured, the syllables falling like stones into the stillness of the countryside. Beside him, Prince Christian's raven locks stirred in the breeze, his athletic form rigid with tension as he absorbed the gravity of the message.

"Papa has summoned us back to London," John continued, his voice a resonant echo in the vastness surrounding them, "because Britain might be dragged into it."

The scent of wildflowers and freshly turned earth hung heavy in the air, a poignant reminder of the carefree summer days that were now slipping through their fingers like grains of sand. The boys shared a glance that spoke volumes—of adventure and camaraderie, of a bond forged in the innocence of youth, now threatened by the drums of war.

"Kip," John whispered, the name an invocation, a plea. His cousin's piercing blue gaze met his, and in that silent communion, they understood their lives were about to fracture along the fault lines of a world divided. The gentle rustle of leaves seemed to mourn the end of their halcyon days, while the distant bleating of sheep carried a sombre note that mirrored the boys' sudden plunge into adulthood.

The rolling fields of Langley Park, once a playground of endless possibilities, now lay under the shadow of an uncertain future. "Let us return to the hall," he continued at last, his tone carrying the weight of his noble lineage and the unspoken dread of what lay ahead. They turned their horses back, the languid pace a stark contrast to their racing thoughts.

Thomas followed, casting a protective gaze over the two figures riding ahead. He knew the fabric of their lives was unravelling, thread by thread, each moment drawing them closer to a parting that might be their last. The waning

A FORBIDDEN LOVE

light painted the scene in hues of bronze and amber, as if nature itself wished to preserve the memory of the day before war stole its innocence.

Lord John's valet hurried inside and moved through the hallways of Langley Hall with a silent urgency, his presence a steady undercurrent in the flurry of activity that had commandeered the once tranquil hall. Footmen hustled past, arms laden with empty leather trunks and satchels, their faces etched with solemn determination. The air was thick with the tang of beeswax and old tapestries; each polish of furniture, each fold of fabric seemed to whisper a poignant adieu.

In Jonny's chamber, Thomas handled the young lord's garments with reverence; he smoothed and folded each shirt intimately, revealing years of unspoken knowledge. He packed the mahogany wardrobe trunk methodically, placing a copy of Shakespeare's sonnets—a treasured gift from Kip—on top, a silent acknowledgment of a friendship deeper than words could express.

The atmosphere in the house was hushed, as if the very walls braced themselves against the coming change. Whispers floated down the oak-panelled corridors, catching in the coffered ceilings, and drifted out into the manicured gardens where roses bloomed in oblivious splendour.

Outside, Kip and Jonny walked side by side from the stables, their footsteps in harmony over the gravel and then stone steps of the grand portico. Each step was a measured tread through shared history, the rustle of leaves a reminder of whispered confidences and laughter now tempered by the gravity of the times.

"Remember when we built that fort?" Kip nodded toward a copse of beech trees behind the servants' wing, a smile touching his lips but failing to reach his eyes. "We were invincible kings of our own realm."

Jonny's laugh, soft and restrained, carried a note of nostalgia. "And you fell from the ramparts chasing away imaginary invaders."

"Feels like we're walking through a dream," Kip murmured as they emerged into the entrance hall.

"More like waking from one," Jonny replied, his eyes drifting back over the idyllic countryside beyond the door.

A footman greeted them in the entrance hall and then led them into the library, where a light afternoon tea awaited. They sat rigidly on a small settee by the unlit fireplace, each picking hesitantly at the neatly arranged sandwiches and cakes. Their gazes remained fixed on the dimming light outside, where Kip's raven hair appeared even darker as shadows crept in.

Breaking the heavy silence first, Jonny said, "I suppose Papa is worried that Britain might join the war now?"

Kip turned toward his cousin, his emotions swirling inside him. "And we will become cousins at war," he replied. That blunt remark, and the turmoil it stirred, stood in stark contrast to the gentle intimacy of just the previous night when he had carefully tucked a blanket around Jonny as he slept.

A soft knock at the door announced Reeves' entrance. "Excuse me, my lord, your highness," he said respectfully, nodding to both. "In light of the earl's telegram, I thought it best to inform you of the preparations for your return to London."

"Of course, Reeves, please continue," Jonny responded, swiftly embracing his new role as an adult.

A FORBIDDEN LOVE

"Mr. Cooper is supervising the footmen as they pack your belongings, and they should finish shortly," Reeves explained. Both Jonny and Kip nodded in acknowledgment. "We will serve dinner at eight o'clock in the music room."

"And what about the arrangements for tomorrow?" Jonny inquired next.

"Breakfast has been scheduled for eight o'clock, and to ensure you can catch a train arriving in London just after noon, carriages will depart at nine," Reeves concluded. "Is everything to your lordship's satisfaction?"

"Yes, quite satisfactory, Reeves," Jonny replied with a nod. "Thank you, that will be all for now." The elderly butler bowed slightly before taking his leave.

Finally, Kip spoke in a tone mixed with admiration and vulnerability. "I don't know how you do it, Jonny." Jonny raised his eyebrows in puzzled surprise, not quite grasping his cousin's meaning. "I mean, how you slip back into *Lord John*' whenever necessary, remaining so calm... so strong..." Kip's words trailed off, then he patted his chest. "Inside, I feel panic, fear — my heart races like it might burst while my thoughts become a chaotic, cotton-wool mess." Gently, Jonny reached out and placed a comforting hand on Kip's thigh.

"Sometimes..." Jonny began, his voice faltering as he searched for the right words. "I truly don't know myself. But what I am absolutely certain of," he paused and gave Kip's leg a gentle squeeze to underscore his next words, "is that whatever strength I do have comes solely from your presence." The meaning of his words settled between them, and Kip moved his hand to rest over Jonny's.

"Really?" Kip whispered, his eyes moistening with the threat of tears.

"Yes, and always." In that moment, each young man drew strength from the other, and the shock of their recall to London faded slightly.

"Alright," Jonny said, holding Kip's hand as he stood up and pulling him along, "let's go upstairs and get ready for dinner," his voice cutting through the tension like a calming tune.

"Of course," Kip replied, letting go of Jonny's hand as slowly as he could.

As they returned to the Garden Suite through Jonny's door, they encountered Thomas, who was closing the lid of a trunk. "My lord, your highness," he said, releasing the lid. "I've taken the liberty of laying out tonight's attire for both of you, and tomorrow's clothes are still in your wardrobes," he said, looking to Christian for approval. "Does that meet your highness' approval?"

"Of course, Thomas," Kip agreed, "that's perfectly fine. Thank you for your thoughtfulness."

Thomas nodded, "the footmen will be back shortly to take away the rest of your luggage, leaving one trunk each for tonight and the morning."

"Thank you, Thomas," Jonny acknowledged.

"We've set dinner for eight o'clock tonight," Thomas smiled, checking his pocket watch, "which gives you plenty of time to prepare."

"Excellent. If I need anything else, I'll let you know, but Kip has become quite good at tying my ties now," Jonny said, glancing at his cousin, and for the first time since they received the news, they both shared a warm smile.

"Very good, my lord, your highness," Thomas nodded and left.

"Well," Kip said, his smile lingering, "if ever there was a time for a drink, I think it's now."

A FORBIDDEN LOVE

"Lead on, Macduff," Jonny replied, and they both went to their drawing room. Jonny sat down first as Kip poured two generous brandies. He handed Jonny his drink, sat on the edge of his armchair, and raised his glass.

"I'm not sure what we should toast to," Kip mused, and then, "how about the future, or rather our future?"

"Yes," Jonny replied, "to our future and whatever it may bring."

The sound of clinking glasses filled the air. The two young men settled into their chairs, each retreating into their own thoughts. They reflected on their shared summer and marvelled at the growth of their friendship, yet they couldn't shake the fear of what might come next and the associated shame and rejection. Could they endure in a world that did not understand them? Almost as if their minds were in sync, they realised that perhaps a separation was necessary to prevent them from crossing a line they could never return from. However, the idea of their parting and the reasons behind it sent a shiver down their spines.

They moved to the dining room; a table for two had been set. Candlelight flickered, casting a golden glow on the fine china and silverware, but doing little to illuminate the growing chasm between them. They took their seats, each acutely aware of the other's presence, yet unwilling to breach the delicate barrier that propriety demanded.

Jonny reached for the bread, his hand trembling imperceptibly, before passing it to Kip. Their fingers brushed, a fleeting touch that electrified the air between them. Kip's gaze lingered on Jonny's face, tracing the lines of uncertainty etched there.

The meal progressed in near silence, broken only by the clink of cutlery against porcelain. They ate mechanically, the sumptuous fare a stark contrast to the austerity of their conversation. Each bite was an effort, a reminder of the feasts they had shared in times of careless joy, now overshadowed by the spectre of war. Their eyes met, conveying what words could not. In those depths, they saw the reflection of their own fears, the realisation that dreams might remain just that—inaccessible and distant in the wake of coming battles.

As dinner concluded, they rose from the table with the reluctant grace of courtiers at the end of a masquerade. The candle flames quivered, casting elongated shadows that danced mockingly on the walls.

In their shared silence, the boys understood: this was the twilight of their innocence, the prelude to a night that promised no gentle dawn. They moved wordlessly, their familiar ritual needing no direction. Thomas poured out two glasses of aged brandy with practiced hands before retreating, leaving them in their private world.

The crystal decanters on the sideboard caught the last light, casting prismatic patterns that flickered like distant stars against the rich blue wallpaper. Jonny settled into an armchair; his slender form wrapped in the embrace of velvet cushions.

He watched Kip pace by the tall french windows, his raven black hair absorbing the room's dimming glow.

The silence between them was deep, a well of shared memories and unspoken thoughts. "Beautiful, isn't it?" Kip murmured finally, gesturing towards the darkening panorama outside. "Feels as if we could just step out and time would stand still for us."

A FORBIDDEN LOVE

"Would that we could," Jonny replied, his voice a mere whisper, betraying a yearning that mirrored Kip's own. He took a sip of the brandy, the warmth spreading through him, a fleeting comfort against the chill of inevitability.

Kip joined him, sinking into the companion chair. They sat there, side by side, each lost in the labyrinth of their musings. The mantel clock's pendulum marked the passage of moments too precious, too few.

"Last night," he began, his confession halting, "when I helped you to bed, something shifted inside me." The admission hung between them, heavier than the humid night pressing against the windowpanes.

Jonny's breath caught, his heart thrumming a frantic cadence. The truth of their affection was a treacherous current they both navigated, charting courses meant to avoid the rocks of society's scorn. Yet here, in the sanctity of their drawing room, honesty found its voice.

"Kip," he said, the name a talisman against the fear gripping his chest, "our friendship—it's the compass that guides me. Always."

The brandy warmed their lips but could not thaw the frost of a future, and the uncertainty of a farewell looming with dawn's first light. In the room's quiet, they made an unspoken pact—to hold fast to the bond that defined them, to bury deeper the longings that dared not speak their names.

When they retired, the house slumbered around them, and their steps were soft upon the creaking oak. Each man carried the weight of his heart, encased in armour wrought from years of convention and expectation.

In the solitude of their respective chambers, they surrendered to sleep's elusive embrace, their final night at Langley Hall a requiem for innocence lost, for a love never to be declared. And as the darkness enfolded them, the bittersweet taste of brandy lingered on their tongues—a memory to be cherished, a sorrow to be borne.

4th August 1914

The planned early start ran as efficiently as it should, and a brightening day shone upon the Norfolk countryside as the train's whistle pierced the silence. John and Christian stood on the platform of the station, an air of solemnity shrouding them like the thick fog that clung to the ground. The sombre beat of their hearts seemed to echo the rhythmic chugging of the steam engine as it came to a halt, its arrival an ominous harbinger of the war that loomed at midnight.

With quiet efficiency, they boarded the first-class compartment, the leather seats offering cold comfort as they settled into the space meant for travellers, but now transformed into a vessel carrying them toward an uncertain future.

The train lurched forward, the landscape outside blurring into a tapestry of green fields and sleepy hamlets, soon to be lost to them, perhaps forever. In the intimacy of their shared confines, John's slight form brushed against Christian's athletic one, a fleeting touch that sparked a silent storm within.

Yet, between them stretched an emotional chasm, wide and unbridgeable, filled with whispered confessions from the night before and the haunting spectre of unspoken desires. As villages slipped by, replaced by the encroaching cityscape, they sat side by side, close enough to sense each other's warmth yet distant in their shared resolve to honour the friendship that was their guiding star.

A FORBIDDEN LOVE

Meanwhile, Thomas travelled in the third-class carriage, his observant eyes taking in the surrounding faces—faces marked by apprehension and the dawning realisation that the world they knew was shifting beneath their feet. He leaned back against the hard wooden bench, a stark contrast to the comfort afforded to his young lords, yet his concern lay not with his own discomfort but with theirs.

As the train rattled along, Thomas allowed himself a moment of reflection, pondering the role he would play in this rapidly changing tableau. His loyalty to John and Christian was as unwavering as the tracks beneath them, and he felt the weight of responsibility settle upon his shoulders.

He understood the challenges that awaited them all—the tug-of-war between duty and desire, the battlefields both literal and figurative that they would have to navigate.

His hazel eyes, usually warm and reassuring, held a glint of steely determination as he thought of the boys. They were no longer just the carefree lads who had roamed the estate, laughing and dreaming under the vast Norfolk skies. They were now pawns in a game played by nations, and Thomas vowed silently to shield them as best he could from the worst of the storm that was about to break.

The train sped on, carrying its passengers away from the innocence of yesterday and toward the heart of an empire on the brink of war. Inside, the two young men sat ensconced in their polished wood-panelled sanctuary, each lost in thought, their knees occasionally touching in a quiet affirmation of their bond. Outside, Thomas watched as the pastoral serenity gave way to the soot and clamour of London, a city ignorant of the last hours of peace it was to enjoy.

The carriage rattled over the cobblestones, its wheels echoing in the wide streets of Mayfair. As it turned onto the elegant thoroughfare where Langley House stood sentinel, John could not help but notice how the pale façade of his family's townhouse seemed to mirror his own taut expression. He exchanged a glance with Christian, whose stoic mien belied a tempestuous undercurrent that rippled beneath the surface. A flurry of activity enveloped the boys upon entering the grand vestibule, and someone directed them to the earl's study.

There, Christian's father, the German Naval Attaché, towered in the midst of this controlled chaos, his commanding voice slicing through the din as he orchestrated the departure arrangements with Bolton. His presence was like a barometer of tension, the lines on his face etched deeper by the gravity of war's approach.

"Christian," he called, beckoning his son with an authoritative flick of the wrist. "Your things must be ready to be collected by eleven o'clock tomorrow morning."

John watched as Christian nodded, his raven black hair catching the light from the crystal chandelier overhead, casting angular shadows across his handsome features. Their eyes met briefly, the unspoken acknowledgment of their shared predicament hanging heavily between them. The underlying tension between Kip and his father was now apparent to him.

John's father was busy at his desk reviewing and signing various documents, and finally looked up to greet the boys, "I am sorry to have recalled you both early, but events seem to have overcome us, and Prince Frederick and Christian must now return to Germany immediately."

A FORBIDDEN LOVE

He handed Frederick the papers that he had just signed, "these should suffice to grant you both passage from Tilbury tomorrow." The elder prince nodded sharply in acknowledgement as he took the papers.

The earl then explained for the benefit of the boys that the British government had just issued an ultimatum to Germany that morning at 11.00am. Essentially, if Germany did not withdraw from Belgium within twelve hours, Britain would declare war.

"Now, with business and arrangements concluded, let us go through for some lunch before Prince Frederick has to get back to the embassy."

Lunch was a hurried affair, with cold cuts and cheese laid out on the long mahogany table usually reserved for more sumptuous feasts. They ate mostly in silence, the clinking of silverware punctuating the air, heavy with the ticking of the grandfather clock—a relentless reminder of time slipping away.

"Kip," Jonny said softly, "tomorrow, Tilbury." His voice was steady, but his blue eyes held a stormy sea of emotion.

"Midday," Kip replied, the word feeling like a stone in his mouth. There was a finality to it that made his heart clench.

With no respite for their fathers at either the embassy or the Foreign Office because of the ultimatum, they decided that with the house empty, to dine in the West End. John gave Thomas instructions to make a reservation somewhere he recommended. A last evening together before the world they knew would change irrevocably.

As they departed from Langley House a few hours later, the departing sun casting long shadows through the windows, stretching across the intricate plasterwork like silent sentinels bidding them farewell. The West End awaited them with its gilded theatre marquees and throngs of people blissfully unaware of the precipice upon which they all teetered.

In the dimming light, the boys walked side by side, their footsteps falling in sync. The proximity comforted and cursed them, soothing their souls while reminding them of what they could never say aloud.

They would have dinner at a discreet establishment known for its intimate alcoves and the low hum of conversation—a place where secrets could be shared beneath the veil of propriety. It promised a veneer of normalcy even as the world outside braced for the unknown.

A FORBIDDEN LOVE

A FORBIDDEN LOVE

CHAPTER EIGHT:
ONE LAST NIGHT

They arrived at a small restaurant tucked away on a quieter side street. The warm glow of gaslight spilled from its windows, promising respite from the frenetic energy outside. As they entered, the din of the streets faded, replaced by the gentle clink of cutlery and a murmur of hushed conversations.

The *maître d'* led them to a secluded table in a dimly lit corner. John sank into his chair, grateful for the relative privacy. Christian sat across from him, his blue eyes searching John's face with an intensity that made John's breath catch.

"Well," Christian began, unfolding his napkin with practiced grace, "shall we peruse the wine list? I believe a good Bordeaux might be just the thing to lift our spirits."

John attempted a smile, though it felt strained. "An excellent suggestion. Though I fear it may take more than wine to accomplish that particular feat."

Christian's laugh was low and rueful. "Perhaps you're right, dear cousin. Perhaps you're right."

As they studied their menus, John found his gaze continually drawn to Christian's hands – strong and capable, yet capable of such gentleness. He remembered the feeling of those hands on his shoulder earlier that day, a gesture of comfort that had nearly undone him.

The silence between them grew, charged with all they longed to say but dared not voice. John's mind raced, grasping for some neutral topic of conversation, anything to break the tension that stretched between them like a taut wire. But as he met Christian's eyes over the flickering candlelight, John knew no words could adequately express the tumult of emotions roiling within him.

So, he remained silent, allowing the unspoken to fill the space between them, a bittersweet acknowledgment of all that might have been.

The waiter approached their table, his footsteps barely audible on the plush carpet. John straightened, grateful for the interruption.

"Are the gentlemen ready to order?" the waiter inquired softly. Christian's eyes flicked to John, a silent question. John nodded, almost imperceptibly.

"Yes, I believe we are," Christian replied, his voice steady. "I'll have the veal." As Christian placed his order, John found himself studying the curve of his cousin's jaw, the way the candlelight caught the planes of his face. He startled when the waiter turned to him expectantly.

"Oh, um, yes. The salmon, please," John managed, a flush creeping up his neck.

The waiter departed, leaving them once again in a cocoon of silence. John reached for his water glass, desperate for something to occupy his hands. As he did so, his fingers brushed against Christian's, sending a jolt through him. He jerked back, nearly upsetting the glass. Christian's hand darted out, steadying it. "Careful there," he murmured, his touch lingering a fraction too long.

John swallowed hard. "Thank you," he whispered, unable to meet Christian's gaze.

The restaurant hummed around them, a gentle cacophony of clinking cutlery and muted conversations. Yet to John, it felt as though they were utterly alone, suspended in a moment outside of time.

A FORBIDDEN LOVE

"Jonny," Christian started, speaking in a low and urgent voice. "I..." But whatever he had been about to say was lost as the waiter reappeared, bearing a bottle of wine.

John exhaled shakily, torn between relief and disappointment. As the ruby liquid splashed into their glasses, John found himself wondering what Christian had been about to say. The weight of unspoken words hung heavy between them, a tangible presence at their table.

When the waiter returned with their meals, John startled, drawn from his reverie by the man's expectant gaze. The waiter departed, and John's hand twitched atop the starched linen tablecloth, aching to reach across the table, to brush his fingers against Christian's, to offer some semblance of comfort, of connection.

But he remained still, paralysed by the weight of propriety, of the expectations that bound them. Instead, he watched as Christian sipped his wine, the bob of his throat as he swallowed, the way his lips glistened in the muted light. Each subtle movement was a reminder of their intimacy, of the stolen moments they had shared, the whispered confessions and fervent touches.

Now, in the restaurant's hush, those memories felt distant, like fragments of a fading dream. John's chest constricted, a dull, persistent ache that seemed to swell with each passing moment. He longed to shatter the silence, to give voice to the tempest raging within him, but the words remained stubbornly lodged in his throat, choked back by the fear of what they might unleash.

Christian leaned forward slightly, his elbows resting on the table, his hands clasped loosely together. The movement drew John's gaze, and he found himself staring at the faint scar above Christian's eyebrow, the one he had gotten as a boy during some reckless adventure. It was a detail he had known for years, yet it felt suddenly unfamiliar, as if he were seeing it for the first time.

"You're thinking too much," Christian said softly, his voice low enough that it would not carry beyond their table. "I can always tell."

John swallowed hard, his fingers tightening around the stem of his water glass. "Perhaps I have a lot to think about."

Christian's expression shifted. A flicker of something—regret? longing? —passing across his face before he masked it with a practiced ease. He leaned back in his chair, his posture casual, but his eyes never left John's. "You don't have to carry it all alone, you know."

The words hung in the air, heavy with meaning, and John felt a sudden, desperate urge to say something—to confess everything, to lay bare the tangled mess of emotions he had been carrying for so long. But the words caught in his throat, trapped by fear and uncertainty, and instead he murmured, "It's not that simple."

Christian's jaw tightened, but he did not press. Instead, he reached for his wineglass, his fingers brushing against the stem with deliberate care. The silence stretched between them, thick and suffocating, until the arrival of their meals provided a momentary distraction.

The food was exquisite—rich, fragrant, beautifully presented—but John barely tasted it. He picked at his plate, the clink of his fork against the porcelain echoing in his ears. Around them, the restaurant hummed with the indistinct murmur of conversation and the occasional burst of laughter, a stark contrast to the quiet tension at their table.

A FORBIDDEN LOVE

Christian ate with measured precision, his movements graceful and controlled, but his gaze kept drifting to John, lingering for a heartbeat too long before shifting away. John could feel the weight of those glances, the unspoken questions they carried, and it made his chest ache with a kind of longing he could not name.

"You're not eating much," Christian observed after a while, his voice carefully neutral.

John set his fork down, his appetite non-existent. "I'm not very hungry."

Christian hesitated, then reached across the table, his hand hovering near John's for a moment before he pulled it back, as if thinking better of the gesture. "Jonny..."

The way he said his name—soft, almost pleading—sent a shiver down John's spine. He looked up, meeting Christian's gaze, and for a moment, the rest of the world faded away. There was something in Christian's eyes, something raw and vulnerable, that made John's breath catch in his throat. But then Christian looked away, his expression shuttering once more, and the moment passed, leaving John feeling adrift. He stared down at his plate, the rich aromas of the meal suddenly overwhelming, and wondered how something as simple as dinner could feel so fraught, so impossibly heavy.

Eventually, John risked another glance at Christian, only to find those piercing blue eyes already fixed upon him, swirling with a maelstrom of emotions. In that fleeting moment of connection, John saw his own fears, his own desperate longing, reflected back at him. That silent acknowledgment, a shared understanding of the upcoming trials and necessary sacrifices, was apparent.

"And," Christian whispered, emphasising the secretive nature of what he was about to say, "we'll always have our plan." A thin, nervous smile appeared on Jonny's lips.

"Yes, yes we do Kip," John replied, but beneath the trepidation and the aching sadness, there was something else, something warm and fierce and unshakable. It was a promise, unspoken but no less binding, a vow that transcended the boundaries of time and distance. In that instant, John knew, with sudden, unshakable certainty, that their bond would endure, no matter what the future held or how long they were parted.

The realisation settled over him like a mantle, a quiet, steadying strength that suffused his limbs and calmed the racing of his heart. He reached for his glass, his fingers trembling only slightly as he raised it in a silent toast. Across the table, Christian mirrored the gesture, his eyes never leaving John's, a wealth of understanding passing between them in that wordless exchange.

As they sipped their wine, the silence that enveloped them no longer felt oppressive, but rather intimate, a cocoon of shared emotion and unspoken promises. For now, in this fleeting moment of connection, they could forget the trials that awaited them, the long, lonely months of separation that stretched ahead.

At this time, they could simply be John and Christian, two hearts beating as one, bound by a love that would weather any storm. They chose to walk back to Langley House, and as they entered the streets of Mayfair, they noticed that earlier, the area had been lively, but now a quiet anticipation hung in the air, reflecting their own conflicted feelings.

As they got closer to the House, they began to be aware of the distant murmur of a large crowd coming from the direction of Buckingham Palace.

A FORBIDDEN LOVE

They paused momentarily as the strains of *'Rule Britannia'* drifted over the rooftops from the direction of the Victoria Memorial.

"Listen, Kip, I think Papa was right," John murmured. He referred to the earl's earlier mention of the ultimatum being given to Germany, which had a deadline of eleven pm. Kip checked his pocket watch and saw it was thirty minutes past eleven. "I think Britain and Germany are at war," he said gravely.

The boys continued their walk home, chilled by the turn of events. Gas lamps spilled golden light onto the pavement, their flickering glow giving the scene a surreal quality, quickly turning into a nightmare. With each step, the Mayfair townhouse loomed closer, its elegant facade a reminder of the inevitable separation ahead. As they walked, John's hand brushed against Christian's, the touch sending a shiver through him. He longed to intertwine their fingers and cling tightly, but propriety and the fear of being watched held him back.

Beside him, Christian's breathing was steady, his profile sharply outlined against the darkening sky. John couldn't resist glancing at him, trying to memorise every detail—the firm line of his jaw, the gentle curve of his lips, the way the lamplight flickered in his eyes. He wanted to capture this moment, to hold it as a memory against the lonely nights to come.

As they neared the townhouse, the realisation of the war's onset filled John with a sense of urgency, a desperate need to voice everything he had left unsaid. But the words were stuck in his throat, blocked by a wave of emotion that threatened to overwhelm him. How could he articulate the depth of his feelings, the consuming love that filled him? How could he make Christian understand he was as vital as the air John breathed, the heartbeat in his chest?

The wide oak door closed behind them with a gentle click, and the sudden quiet of the empty house wrapped around them like a blanket. In that silence, their breathing echoed loudly, and the sound of their clothes moving was a sharp whisper against the stillness. They lingered for a moment in the foyer, the unspoken words hanging heavily between them.

Suddenly, they heard the hall boy hurrying to the inner doors. "Sorry, my lord, your highness, I should have been here to let you in," he said nervously.

"Don't worry, Charlie," Kip assured the boy, "we won't mention it to Mr. Bolton." He gave the hall boy an exaggerated wink.

"Is the earl home?" John asked.

"No, my lord. He left a few hours ago for Downing Street," Charlie replied shyly, then gained enough confidence to continue. "His Lordship left a note for you." The hall boy retrieved a small silver tray from a side table, where a folded piece of paper had been awaiting John's return. John immediately recognised his father's handwriting as he opened and read it, then folded it twice and tucked it into his waistcoat pocket.

"Very well, Charlie, you can lock up now and go down," John paused before adding, "and please inform Mr. Cooper that I won't need him again tonight."

"Thank you, and good night, my lord," Charlie said with a deep nod towards John, then turned to Christian, "your highness," and nodded again.

The cousins moved towards the stairs, and once they reached the top, they stopped, standing close enough to touch, yet still separated by their own fears and doubts. Christian's eyes were dark in the dim light, his expression unreadable. For a long moment, they simply gazed at each other, trying to memorise the other's face as if to etch it into their souls.

A FORBIDDEN LOVE

"Here," John said, pulling out the note and handing it to Kip, "it is as we feared. Papa will not be home tonight." John beckoned his cousin towards his room with his eyes and as the bedroom door clicked shut behind them, the sound was sharp and final in the stillness.

The room was dimly lit by the warm glow of a single lamp, casting long shadows across the mahogany panelling and deep green silk damask. John moved to the sideboard, his movements slow and deliberate as he poured two generous measures of brandy into crystal tumblers. The amber liquid caught the light, glinting like molten gold as he handed one glass to Christian.

Kip accepted the drink, his fingers brushing against John's in a fleeting caress that sent a shiver down his spine. He watched as John lifted his own glass to his lips; the brandy disappearing in a single, desperate swallow. John's hand trembled slightly as he set the empty tumbler down, his eyes dark and haunted in the lamplight.

"Jonny," Christian murmured, his voice low and gentle. He stepped closer, one hand coming to rest on his shoulder, a steady, comforting presence. "Talk to me. Please."

John shook his head, a bitter laugh escaping his lips. "What is there to say? Tomorrow, you'll be gone, off to fight for Kaiser and country, while I remain here, trapped in this gilded cage." He reached for the decanter, pouring himself another measure of brandy with unsteady hands. Christian's grip on his shoulder tightened, his thumb rubbing soothing circles against the tense muscles.

"Jonny, you won't be trapped forever. The war can't last. And when it's over, we'll be together again, just like we planned."

John drained his glass, the brandy burning a fiery path down his throat. He could feel the alcohol taking effect, a warm, numbing buzz spreading through his limbs.

He swayed slightly on his feet, and Christian's arm slipped around his waist, holding him steady. "You're going to make yourself ill, don't forget we've already had wine," Christian said at last, his voice low but firm.

It was not a reproach, not exactly, but there was an edge to it that made John's shoulders tense. He turned, meeting Christian's gaze for the first time since they had entered the room, and found himself struck by the concern etched into his cousin's expression. It was rare for Christian to let his guard down like this, and it made something in John's chest tighten uncomfortably.

"I'm fine," John replied, his voice clipped. He reached for the decanter again, but Christian was there before he could

pour, his hand closing over John's wrist. His touch was warm, grounding, and for a moment, John could not breathe.

"You're not," Christian said quietly, his fingers tightening slightly. "And you know it."

John's jaw clenched, but he did not pull away. Instead, he stood there, frozen, acutely aware of the heat of Christian's hand against his skin, the way his pulse seemed to quicken beneath that touch. He wanted to say something, to argue, but the words stuck in his throat, tangled and useless. Christian's thumb brushed lightly over the inside of his wrist, a gesture so small and fleeting that John might have imagined it, but it soothed him.

"Just a small one then Kip," he reassured, pouring a finger of brandy into both boys' glasses.

Christian's arm tightened around John's waist as he struggled to support him. "Alright," Christian said softly, guiding John to the edge of the bed. He could sense his cousin's discomfort and his own presence was both a comfort and a torment. John closed his eyes, taking in the familiar scent of sea salt and cedar that clung to Christian's skin.

"Let me take off your jacket, Jonny," Christian whispered, his fingers brushing against John's collar. "May I?"

John nodded, unable to speak. He felt Christian gently remove his jacket from his shoulders, followed by the careful removal of his shoes. Every innocent touch sent sparks of longing through John's alcohol-clouded mind.

"All better now," his voice a low rumble that John could feel in his bones. "You should rest." John slowly opened his eyes and found himself face-to-face with Christian.

"Will you stay?" he asked impulsively, before realising what he was saying. "Just... for a little while?" Christian's expression softened, a mix of tenderness and something else, more intense.

"Of course," he whispered. "I'll stay as long as you need me." John began giggling uncontrollably as he fumbled with the studs on his shirt collar.

"Help me, Kip!" he pleaded. Kip gently pulled away John's hands and placed them on his own shoulders.

"Let me," Kip murmured. Slowly and deliberately, he unfastened each stud until the shirt was partially open. He knew he had to stop before things went too far and irreparably damaged their friendship. He remembered how close he had come to betraying them both the night of the storm. But he also could not deny the feeling of lust that had been building between them and that he could not easily dismiss.

As Jonny glanced down at Kip's slender fingers working on his shirt, he could not help but be mesmerised by the sight and sensation of Kip's fingers lightly brushing against his smooth chest. But he knew they needed to stop, as they had back at Langley House, worried about what would happen if they went too far and shocked each other with their true desires. They both felt like they were teetering on the edge of a dark abyss, pulled down by their deepest secrets and basest instincts.

As Kip finally opened Jonny's shirt completely, it would only take one more fleeting moment before they reached the point of no return. Kip's hands hovered briefly and dangerously by the waistband of his trousers, but then Kip noticed Jonny's neatly folded pyjamas at the foot of the bed, and the tug of regret snapped him back to reality.

Christian's hands smoothed over the vibrant silk of John's pyjamas, the fabric jarring and unexpected compared to his usual understated style. A smile played at Christian's lips as he pulled back, realising this was his chance to put an end to things before they went any further, and hopefully avoiding any feeling of rejection for Jonny.

Once again, he would use his charm and humour to deflect from his true feelings. His eyes sparkled mischievously as he held up the brightly patterned pyjamas in shades of crimson and gold.

A FORBIDDEN LOVE

"Goodness gracious, Jonny," Christian chuckled warmly. "Are you planning to signal for help with these? Or perhaps light a small fire?" With that comment, Jonny let out a silent sigh of relief as he realised Kip was trying to pull them both back from the brink.

John laughed and glanced down at his flamboyant pyjamas. "You can thank our mutual friend Tom for these," he explained with a tinge of regret that he wasn't brave enough to have made this choice for himself.

"Let's see how they look on!" Kip eagerly suggested, not wanting Jonny to feel rejected by his change of plans. They took off Jonny's dress shirt together and replaced it with the pyjama jacket. After buttoning it up, Kip threw the bottoms to Jonny and picked up the discarded shirt to hang it up. "Put these on while I take care of your shirt and trousers."

Kip turned away to give Jonny privacy as he changed into the pyjama pants, allowing him to avoid exposing himself or displaying any arousal. In that moment, Kip discreetly made some adjustments of his own to control his own desire and not make John uncomfortable.

Once John was back on the bed, Christian hesitated before sitting down next to him. He could see the conflict within his cousin, torn between longing to be close to John and fear of what might happen if he acted on those feelings.

"You do look quite dashing," Christian said with a wink, hoping to coax a smile out of John and ease the tension between them.

As their quiet laughter died down, John fell back onto the bed, exhaustion weighing heavily on his eyelids. Christian hesitated again, unsure if he should stay or leave. But eventually, he lowered himself onto the bed and sat gingerly next to John, aware of every inch separating them. The mattress sank under their combined weight and Christian could feel the warmth radiating from John's body. His heart raced as he struggled with conflicting desires - to close the distance or maintain a safe distance to avoid rejection.

"Are you alright?" John asked in a soft voice barely above a whisper.

Christian forced a smile, trying not to let his emotions show. "Of course, Jonny. Just thinking."

He carefully arranged himself on the bed to sit by John's waist, conscious of every movement. As he sat there next to John, he could not help but take in his cousin's scent - a mix of cologne and brandy. It was almost overwhelming, in a way that Christian was finding increasingly difficult to resist.

As John settled back against the pillows and closed his eyes, Christian watched him with a heavy heart. He wanted so badly to comfort him and tell him all the things he could not say out loud. But for now, all he could do was sit there beside him and silently offer his support.

"Just give me a moment," Kip said as he got up from the bed to collect the rest of John's clothes and put them away. This gave him another opportunity to question his feelings and actions towards Jonny. But eventually, he couldn't resist the urge, and need, to be close to him and reassure him before he left, especially in the light of the evening's news.

Quickly and quietly, Kip removed his own jacket, tie and collar and shoes before opening the top couple of buttons on the shirt. Slowly, hesitantly, he lowered himself back onto the bed next to John, who had turned away to face the other direction. Christian held still, afraid to make any sudden movements or breathe too loudly.

A FORBIDDEN LOVE

He did not want to ruin this delicate moment between them. As Kip initially laid on his back next to John, he could not help but wonder if John had turned away as an invitation for closeness or as a barrier to keep their relationship strictly platonic. His mind raced as he struggled with conflicting thoughts and emotions, determined not to break the resolve he had made the day before.

John lay perfectly still, his eyes closed, feigning sleep while his senses heightened with every subtle shift of Christian's body beside him. The warmth emanating from his cousin's proximity sent a tremor through him, one he desperately hoped Christian would not notice. He savoured the closeness, committing every sensation to memory – the soft whisper of Christian's breath, the faint scent of sea salt that clung to him even after months away from the naval academy.

In the room's silence, John's thoughts raced. What did this mean? Christian's presence in his bed, so close yet agonisingly distant, felt charged with unspoken meaning. Hope bloomed in his chest, fragile and dangerous. But fear coiled around it, threatening to suffocate the tender emotion before it could take root.

Shame burned through Kip, hot and sharp, as he imagined how it would feel to press his body against John's, to learn the shape and texture of his cousin's skin. It was a wanting he could never voice, a longing he had carried so deep and for so long he scarcely knew how to separate it from the fabric of his own soul. He had broken away once already after the storm, but his resolve was wavering.

"Jonny?" Christian's whisper cut through the stillness, barely audible. "Are you awake?"

John's heart leapt, but he kept his breathing steady, unsure whether to answer. Before he could decide, he felt Christian shift closer, hesitantly, as if drawn by an invisible thread. The mattress dipped further, and suddenly Christian's arm draped over him as he turned onto his side, pulling him into a tentative embrace.

Yet here, in the quiet stillness of John's room, with the soft sound of his cousin's breathing and the faint scent of brandy and cologne, Christian felt his carefully constructed walls finally begin to crumble irreversibly.

He wanted this, wanted it with an intensity that terrified him. But how could he risk the only genuine friendship he had ever known, the only person who saw past the titles and the expectations to the vulnerable, uncertain boy beneath? How could he bear to see disgust or rejection in those beloved blue eyes? And yet, how could he let this moment pass again, knowing it might be the last time they ever lay together like this, the last chance to show John the depth of his feelings, the truth of his heart?

Christian's breath caught in his throat, his pulse pounding in his ears as he slowly, tentatively, let his hand come to rest on John's stomach. The contact was electric, a jolt that seemed to light up every nerve ending in his body and it was quite deliberate, he realised, finally accepting to himself the truth of his feelings and desires.

Tomorrow, the world would intrude with all the horrors a war might unfurl, and its cruelties and compromises. But tonight, in the shelter of each other's arms, they could simply be two boys in love, holding fast to a perfect, shining moment, a memory to light in the darkest of days to come.

John did not dare to move or to speak, terrified of shattering this fragile, perfect moment. If he pretended to sleep, he reasoned, he could savour it just a little longer, this feeling of being held, cherished, loved.

A FORBIDDEN LOVE

Even if it was only a beautiful illusion and it would allow him to keep hidden his true desires. But then Christian's arm tightened around him, pulling him closer, and John's breath caught in his throat. The heat of Christian's body seeped into his own, igniting a flame that threatened to consume him. He could feel every point of contact between them, a searing brand that marked him as Christian's own.

The silence stretched taut, the only sound the thundering of John's heart in his ears. Surely Christian must hear it, must feel the tremble in his limbs, the hitch in his breathing? There was no hiding now, no pretence of indifference or mere cousinly affection. Time seemed to slow, each second stretching out into an eternity as they lay connected, their bodies fitting together like two halves of a whole, two spoons in a cutlery tray. The rhythm of their breathing synchronised, their heartbeats echoing each other in a private symphony. In this cocoon of shadows and silk, the world outside faded away, reduced to a distant echo.

John's mind drifted, thoughts fragmented and hazy, yet each one imbued with a profound sense of significance. The warmth of Christian's body against his, the gentle rise and fall of his chest, the soft puff of his breath against his neck - every sensation felt amplified, heightened, as if his very skin were alive with electricity.

Did this mean being truly seen and truly known? To have someone look into your soul and accept every dark corner, every secret shame? In Christian's embrace, John felt a sense of belonging, of rightness, that he had never known before. It was terrifying and exhilarating all at once, like standing on the edge of a cliff and finally, finally finding the courage to fly.

Slowly, hesitantly, John moved his hand to cover Christian's where it rested on his stomach. He felt Christian tense for a moment, then relax. John gave a gentle squeeze, a silent reassurance, a question, an answer – all wrapped up in one slight gesture.

For a long, suspended moment, neither of them moved, the air heavy with unspoken words. Then, with a soft, shuddering sigh, Christian twined his fingers with John's, squeezing gently, a silent affirmation, a promise. He pulled John closer, tucking the smaller boy's head under his chin, wrapping him in an embrace that felt like safety, like home.

John slowly and deliberately guided Kip's hand from the fabric of his pyjamas to the smoothness of the skin beneath. Both shared a new feeling. These were not butterflies in Jonny's stomach but soaring eagles, and for Kip, all his doubts evaporated into absolute resolve to claim his cousin's heart and desires.

They spoke no words, made no declarations, and for the first time, needed none. In the language of touch and breath and heartbeat, they said everything that mattered. I am here. I see you. I love you. And for now, in another fragile, perfect moment, that was enough.

In the room's quiet, the only sound was the soft, even breathing of the two boys, their chests rising and falling in gentle unison. The warm glow of the firelight painted their features in soft, muted shades, casting long shadows on the walls and lending an almost dreamlike quality to the scene.

John allowed himself to drift into a state of calm, relying on the steady beat of Christian's heart near his ear. It was a soothing sound, like a lullaby promising safety and serenity, pushing away any lingering fears and doubts. In Christian's embrace, everything outside seemed to vanish - the world with its

A FORBIDDEN LOVE

expectations and pressures, its strict rules, and harsh judgments - leaving only this intimate haven.

As John became aware of his own arousal, feeling Kip's hand just inches away on his stomach, he cautiously turned towards him. He gently guided Kip's hand to his hip and feared that he may have ruined the moment when he stirred. But to his relief, Kip simply rolled onto his back and whispered, "come here Jonny."

He offered his chest for John to rest his head on and moved his hand down to rest on John's thigh, pulling it over his own arousal. As realisation dawned upon John about what his leg was resting on, Kip pulled him closer so that their aroused bodies pressed together. "Mmmm, much better," Kip said quietly and contently.

John then reached to place his hand inside Kip's open shirt, feeling the firmness of his chest as he wrapped his arms tightly around him - as tightly as a drowning sailor would hold on to a life raft.

For Christian, being held like this by John was a revelation, bringing clarity amidst the chaos of his emotions. He had spent so long denying his feelings, burying them beneath layers of charm and wit and feigned indifference. But now, with John's warmth enveloping him, feeling the softness of his cousin's hair against him - Christian knew he could no longer pretend. This bond between them was real; it went beyond friendship or family or any label society may try to put on it.

Laying there intertwined, their breaths mingling, it felt as if the air itself had changed - charged with something new, fragile, and infinitely precious.

The future loomed ahead of them, a vast unknown canvas waiting for them to fill with their own colours. But in this moment, there were only the two of them, holding on to each other as sleep claimed them, their unspoken feelings lingering like a promise, a whispered secret shared between two hearts. The quietness of the room cocooned them, enveloping them in stillness and tranquillity, even as the outside world continued on, oblivious to the small miracle unfolding within these walls.

In the morning, there would be questions to answer, decisions to make, paths to choose. But for tonight, nestled in each other's arms, John and Christian could simply exist - their love blazing like a flame against the darkness, guiding them through whatever storms may come.

And so, they slept; two boys on the brink of manhood, their destinies intertwined in ways they couldn't even fathom. Their bodies played out a subtle dance and positions changed during their sleep without ever waking each other. The future may have been uncertain, but in these fleeting moments of perfection, they had one another - and that was more than enough. It was everything.

As the sun rose outside, Kip and Jonny occasionally stirred awake. Each checked to make sure that they were not still dreaming before drifting back to sleep. Kip was the first to fully awaken, disturbed by the noise of early deliveries outside. He noticed Jonny lying on his side, wrapped around him with his head resting on his chest. Kip tried to resist pulling his hand away from where it rested on Jonny's hip under his pyjamas, instead opting to gently caress the soft skin with his fingers. Slowly, Jonny responded by stroking Kip's bare chest, initially jolted by a moment of panic like Kip had experienced earlier.

A FORBIDDEN LOVE

Using his free hand, Kip placed his palm against Jonny's cheek as he looked down at him. "Good morning, Jonny," he whispered. A smile spread across Jonny's face as he took his hand off Kip's chest and placed it over the one on his cheek. Both boys had found the reassurance each needed.

"Morning, my prince," Jonny eventually replied after a long pause. There was a satisfied silence between them. "Thank you, Kip, for..." He was interrupted by Kip placing a finger softly over his lips.

"Shhh, no need for thanks," Kip said softly. "We both... well, we finally found each other." As these words were absorbed and accepted, their doubts faded away. Mixed emotions bubbled beneath the surface, but there was no regret. Jonny was usually more eloquent than Kip, able to find just the right words in any situation, but now speech failed him.

Still, he could not remain silent. "Kip, what about everything else? The shameful stuff?" he whispered.

Kip knew this question was coming and that he needed to answer it, but he was surprised that Jonny was the one that asked it. His heart raced as he considered how to respond. He defaulted to his usual approach, gently removing his hand from underneath Jonny's and taking hold of it. A reassuring squeeze eased his cousin's nerves as he then quickly moved it down to rest over his obvious arousal.

"You mean this stuff?" Kip said in a hushed voice, squeezing Jonny's hand around his covered erection. Jonny gasped, half in shock and half in unexpected pleasure. Kip was keenly aware that he kept his hand where it was and continued to gently hold him. Encouraged by this, Kip slid his own hand from Jonny's hip to hold on to his cousin's manhood. This time, Jonny's gasp expressed pure pleasure.

Kip's hand remained there briefly, then he gently removed it. "Little time remains," he noted, eyeing the clock. "Thomas will be up soon."

Jonny started, but Kip's soothing voice calmed him down. "No need to worry, Jonny," he smiled. "There's just one more thing I need to do... and then I think no more words will be needed."

With a mischievous grin, Kip leaned forward and placed one hand on each side of Jonny's face. He gazed deeply and longingly into his eyes before pulling their faces together. Their lips met gently at first, eyes closing, then the kiss deepened. Their lips parted as passion took over, and both felt overwhelmed with emotion, wondering how their hearts had not burst. They eventually pulled away, feeling exhausted yet content.

"Now," Kip said, leaning in to peck Jonny's forehead, "I should head back to my room." Jonny nodded slowly. "We wouldn't want Thomas catching us *in flagrante delicto*," he winked.

Despite Kip's usual light-hearted tone, there was truth to the potential scandal it could cause. Kip quickly gathered his clothes and shoes before moving to the connecting door. Jonny chuckled at his cousin's use of school Latin.

"Of course not. I'll come through after Thomas leaves." For now, he lay back on his bed, hands behind his head, reflecting on the past few hours. Although he should have felt tired, the realisation invigorated him that, for the first time, he and Kip were truly in sync, their feelings finally mutual. He felt a calming sense of peace as he contemplated the details of their plan, recognising that it was no longer just a fantasy but soon to be their reality.

A FORBIDDEN LOVE

Kip, in the next room, shared the same thoughts. Both boys smiled in their silent connection.

Within ten minutes, there was a gentle knock, and Thomas entered. Jonny sat up, "oh, you're already awake, my lord." Thomas closed the door and went to open the curtains.

"Good morning, Tom, yes, it was noisy outside," Jonny replied with feigned innocence. "Has the news gotten out?"

"Yes, good morning, Jonny," Thomas said, glancing out the window. The street buzzed with the news; the early papers already circulating, he sighed. "People are excited, and large crowds have gathered in support of the war."

"But it won't last long, will it, Thomas?" Jonny's happiness quickly faded.

"I hope not, Jonny," Thomas replied, lacking conviction, as he moved to the wardrobe. "A day suit?" Jonny nodded, pondering the tone of Thomas' voice. Jonny watched as his valet efficiently laid out his clothes and tidied up. "Will Kip need waking?"

"I've already heard him moving around, but thank you anyway, Tom," Jonny said seriously.

"Very well, my lord. Would you like assistance getting dressed?" Thomas asked, returning to a formal tone as the gravity of the situation weighed on him.

"No, thank you, Tom," Jonny replied, trying to lift the suddenly heavy mood. "But don't worry, Kip and I will be on time for breakfast!" He smiled.

"Of course, Jonny," Thomas said, attempting to lighten the atmosphere before nodding and leaving the room.

A FORBIDDEN LOVE

CHAPTER NINE:
CHRISTIAN'S DEPARTURE

Jonny slumped back down onto his pillow. The bed seemed too large now, too empty without Kip's presence. He reached for the pillow Kip had used the night before, hugging it close to his chest. It still smelled like him - a comforting blend of sandalwood and something uniquely Kip. Jonny closed his eyes, allowing himself to be lost in the memory of last night. They had lain together, limbs intertwined, speaking in hushed tones about their plans for the future. Kip had traced the contours of Jonny's face with gentle fingers, as if committing every detail to memory.

Jonny realised he could not allow himself to be overtaken by those emotions, so he leapt out of bed to break their spell. He quickly made his way to the bathroom, and once finished, he knocked loudly on Kip's door before stepping inside.

"Breakfast downstairs in fifteen minutes," he announced in as casual a tone as possible, only to notice several of Kip's trunks thrown open with their contents scattered across the bed. "Decided not to leave?" he teased, quickly aware of how cruel that comment might sound.

"I wish the decision were mine," Kip replied with a serious note of resignation, "but it seems someone packed all my clothes away last night, leaving me with nothing to wear today!" His smile soon returned. "Maybe I should travel like this?" he added, sweeping his hand over the towel wrapped around his waist before turning to face Jonny. Jonny's eyes widened at the sight of Kip's lean, smooth torso.

For the first time, his obvious attraction did not seem like a betrayal but rather an affirmation of his true feelings. Kip noted Jonny's look with quiet satisfaction, taking in the sight of his cousin standing in the doorway wearing nothing but a loose dressing gown. "*Touché*," he thought to himself then slowly looked Jonny up and down

. "But perhaps we shouldn't distract ourselves right now?" His smile was wicked, teasing, and sensual.

"No, Kip," Jonny laughed, pulling the belt on his dressing gown tighter around himself, "perhaps we shouldn't." He tried to convince himself that this was the right decision, but the disappointment on Kip's face told a different story.

Both understood it was not a rejection but merely a postponement; their time would come eventually. Breaking the silent gaze, Jonny added, "the bathroom is free, and don't worry about repacking—I'll ask Thomas to handle it while we have breakfast."

"Very well, my lord," Kip replied with a mock bow of deference.

Jonny got dressed while Kip used the bathroom, then sat at his desk to review his sketches. In a flash, Kip passed behind him, making his way back to his own room. "Ten minutes, Kip!" Jonny called after him. After a few minutes of deliberation, Jonny selected several sketches from that summer. Once satisfied with his choices, he carefully signed and dated each one before placing them in an old brown leather document wallet. Kip appeared at the connecting door with his arms opened wide, and Jonny turned toward him.

"Do I pass his lordship's high standards?" Kip joked, aware that his comment hinted at more than just a reference to his attire. It was clear that the days of dancing around their feelings were now behind them.

"Always, Kip," Jonny admitted in admiration, a gulp in his voice. "You could wear a potato sack and still exceed all my expectations."

Both boys savoured the new freedom that came with the honesty they had shared only a few hours earlier. Jonny slowly rose and walked over to Kip, holding out the sketches. "These are for you—some of my sketches from the summer to remind you of the adventures we've had."

Kip took the wallet and held it close to his chest before saying, "I'll look at them later, when I'm alone and missing you the most." He turned quickly to return to his room, placing the folder on an unopened trunk to hide the sadness that crossed his face.

Composing himself, he rejoined Jonny, urging, "Let's eat breakfast."

The newspapers lay on the breakfast table like harbingers of doom, their headlines stark against the crisp white linen. Jonny immediately saw the newspapers and his heart sank as he read the bold print: *WAR DECLARED*. Beside him, Kip reached for a paper, his fingers brushing Jonny's as he did so. The brief contact sent a shiver through Jonny, a momentary respite from the dread that had settled in his stomach.

"It says here that it'll be over by Christmas," Kip remarked, scanning the commentary. "French forces will prevail on land against Germany."

Jonny nodded, clinging to that glimmer of hope. "Perhaps it will be a quick affair, then. Demonstrate power, then return home for the holidays." But wars were never as simple as the papers made them out to be. Hearing the dining room door open, they saw Mr. Bolton enter, worry etched onto his typically stoic face.

"My lords," he said, bowing slightly. "I have the morning's arrangements for you." Jonny set down his coffee cup, giving the butler his full attention. He could feel Kip's gaze on him, but he kept his own eyes on Bolton, afraid that if he looked at Kip, he might break.

Bolton continued, his deep voice filling the room, "They will load his highness' luggage shortly. The carriage will be ready to depart within the hour."

Jonny nodded; his throat tight. An hour. He only had that much time left with Kip. "Thank you, Bolton. Could you ask Cooper to repack some of the prince's trunks first though?"

"Of course, my lord." Bolton bowed again, then turned to leave, the door closing softly behind him.

A heavy silence settled over the breakfast table, the weight of their shared future pressing down upon them. Jonny's gaze drifted to the window, the pale morning light filtering through the gauzy curtains, casting a soft glow upon Kip's face.

In that moment, he looked almost ethereal, a vision of beauty and strength that Jonny longed to hold on to forever. Jonny rose from the table. "Let's take our coffee in my room while Thomas finishes your packing." His voice was steady, but his eyes conveyed a deeper meaning, a need for these last moments of privacy.

A FORBIDDEN LOVE

Kip nodded, following suit. Their gazes locked, a silent understanding passing between them as they made their way out of the dining room and up the grand staircase. The plush carpet muffled their footsteps, the portraits of Jonny's ancestors lining the walls bearing witness to their ascent.

Once inside Jonny's bedchamber, Kip closed the door softly behind them. The warm glow of the morning sun bathed the room, dust motes dancing in the shafts of light streaming through the tall windows. The faint sounds of the servants' activities drifted through the walls, a reminder of the world beyond their sanctuary.

Jonny gestured towards the settee near the fireplace, and they settled close to one another, their thighs barely touching. The intimacy of their proximity was both comforting and electrifying, a bittersweet reminder of all they stood to lose.

"I've been thinking," Kip began, his voice low and urgent. "About what comes after the war." Jonny turned to face him, his heart racing.

"What do you mean?"

Kip took a deep breath, his eyes searching Jonny's face. "I'm going to leave the navy. When this is all over, I want to come back to England. To you."

Jonny's eyes widened, a flicker of hope igniting in his chest. "But your father... your family..."

"I don't care." Kip's voice was fierce, his jaw set with determination. "I'm willing to risk his disapproval, even estrangement, if it means I can be with you."

Jonny's breath caught in his throat, his vision blurring with sudden tears. He reached out, his fingers grazing Kip's cheek. "You would do that? For me?"

Kip leaned into his touch, his eyes soft and earnest. "For us, Jonny. For the life we could have together."

Jonny swallowed hard, his heart swelling with a love so profound it ached. He knew the risks; the sacrifices Kip was willing to make. And in that moment, he knew he would move heaven and earth to make their dream a reality.

"Then we'll find a way," he whispered, his forehead resting against Kip's. "No matter what it takes, we'll find a way to be together."

He squeezed Kip's hand, his voice low but resolute. "We'll make it work; I swear it. My allowance is more than enough for both of us, and I'm certain Father would support our plan."

Kip's eyebrow arched sceptically. "The earl? Are you sure?"

"He's more understanding now than you might think," Jonny murmured, remembering moments of unexpected kindness from his often-distant father. "And even if he isn't, we'll find a way."

The sound of footsteps in the hallway broke the spell as the servants moved the last of Kip's trunks downstairs, and they reluctantly pulled apart, Kip rising to his feet and moving towards the window. Jonny followed, standing beside him as they watched the servants loading Kip's luggage into the waiting carriage.

Their hands found each other, fingers intertwining as they stood side by side, drawing strength and comfort from each other's presence. The sunlight filtered through the lace curtains, casting a soft glow over their faces, and for a moment, the world outside ceased to exist.

A FORBIDDEN LOVE

It was just the two of them, their love a tangible force that seemed to fill the room, enveloping them in its warmth. And as they stood there, watching the preparations for Kip's departure, they knew that no matter what the future held, they would face it together. Jonny allowed himself to believe, just for a moment, that their love could conquer anything. Even the looming spectre of war and the chasms of societal expectation that threatened to tear them apart.

Jonny took a deep, steadying breath, his mind racing with possibilities.

"We'll need a plan," he said, his voice low and urgent. "A way to stay in touch, even when you're away."

Kip nodded; his brow furrowed in thought. "I'll write to you as often as I can obviously."

Jonny's heart clenched at the thought of any contact, a lifeline to sustain them through the long months apart. "I will ask Papa to find a way for me to write," he promised, his fingers tightening around Kip's. "No matter how long it takes, I'll be here, waiting for you to come home to me."

Kip's eyes shone with unshed tears, a smile trembling on his lips. "I'll hold onto that, every day, every moment we're apart. The thought of coming home to you, of building a life together, will keep me going, no matter what." They fell silent, letting the weight of their promises settle over them like a comforting blanket.

Outside, the distant sounds of the carriage being loaded drifted through the window, a stark reminder of the farewell that loomed ahead. Hand in hand, they looked through the window, gazing out at the bustling activity below. The polished carriage reflected the sun. It was a scene Jonny had witnessed countless times before, but never had it held such a poignancy, such a sense of finality.

As if sensing his thoughts, Kip's hand tightened around his, a silent reassurance, a promise of the future they had vowed to fight for.

And as they stood there, side by side, their bodies barely touching but their souls entwined, Jonny felt a flicker of hope, a glimmer of light amidst the gathering darkness. No matter what happens, they would face it together, their love a beacon to guide them through the storms ahead.

As the servants secured the last trunk, they stepped back, their task complete. Kip turned to face Jonny, his eyes glistening with unshed tears. Without a word, he pulled him into a fierce embrace, his arms wrapping around him as if he never wanted to let go. With a heavy sigh, Kip stepped away from the window, tugging Jonny with him. "We should go down," he said, his voice thick with emotion.

"I love you," Kip whispered, his breath warm against Jonny's ear. "No matter what happens, no matter where this war takes us, that will never change."

Jonny's heart swelled. The words he had longed to hear finally spoken aloud. "I love you too," he breathed, his own voice trembling with emotion. "Forever and always."

Their lips met in a passionate kiss, a seal of their unspoken vow. It was a kiss that spoke of love and longing, of hope and desperation, of a future that hung in the balance. Jonny poured every ounce of his heart into that kiss, every unspoken word, every secret desire. When at last they parted, Kip's hand rose to Jonny's cheek, his thumb brushing away the single tear that had escaped.

"No tears, Jonny," he murmured, his voice gentle but firm. "This is not goodbye, merely a brief parting. We will be together again, I swear it."

A FORBIDDEN LOVE

Jonny nodded, swallowing hard against the lump in his throat. He knew Kip was right, knew that they had to be strong, to face the challenges ahead with courage and determination. But oh, how he wished they could stay in this moment forever, safe in each other's arms.

With a deep breath, Kip stepped back, his hand falling from Jonny's cheek. "Come," he said, his voice steady despite the emotion that swirled in his eyes. "It's time."

He moved to the door, his hand resting on the handle for a moment before he turned it, the click of the latch sounding unnaturally loud in the room's stillness. And then he was stepping through, releasing Jonny's hand as he did so.

Jonny followed, his steps heavy as they made their way down the grand staircase, the portraits of their ancestors seeming to watch their descent with solemn eyes. The entrance hall stretched out before them, vast and echoing, the very air seeming to hold its breath in anticipation of the farewell to come.

The household staff stood assembled in the entrance hall, their faces sombre and respectful as Kip and Jonny descended the last steps. Bolton stepped forward, his bearing as impeccable as ever, a light woollen coat and hat in his hands.

"Your coat, your highness," he said, his voice resonating through the cavernous space.

Kip inclined his head in acknowledgment, allowing the butler to assist him into the garment, the fine fabric settling over his shoulders like a mantle of duty. Bolton held out the hat, his gloved hands steady as Kip took it from him. "On behalf of the household, your highness, I wish you a safe journey and a swift return."

Kip nodded, his lips curving into a smile that did not quite reach his eyes. "Thank you, Bolton. Your service, as always, has been exemplary." He turned to face the assembled staff, his gaze sweeping over their faces, taking in the mixture of respect, concern, and even a hint of fondness that he found there. His eyes met the young hall boy from the night before and he winked. These were the people who had made Langley House a home for him, who had served him with unwavering loyalty, and who now stood witness to his departure.

"I want to express my gratitude to each and every one of you," he said, his voice carrying through the hall. "I hope to return to Langley House soon, under happier circumstances."

A murmur of agreement rippled through the staff, heads bowing in deference. Kip's gaze lingered on them for a moment longer, committing their faces to memory, a touchstone of normalcy to carry with him into the uncertain future. With a final nod, he turned to Jonny, his eyes searching the other boy's face. Jonny met his gaze, his own eyes bright with unshed tears, his lips pressed together in a thin line. Kip's hand twitched at his side, aching to reach out, to offer one last touch of comfort, but he resisted the urge.

Instead, he inclined his head towards the door, a silent invitation. Jonny nodded, his shoulders squaring as he fell into step beside Kip. Together, they crossed the entrance hall, their footsteps echoing on the polished marble floor.

As they reached the threshold, Kip paused, his hand resting on the door handle. He glanced back over his shoulder, taking in the sight of the household staff standing at attention, a tableau of loyalty and respect.

A FORBIDDEN LOVE

His gaze shifted to Jonny, drinking in the sight of him, etching every detail into his memory. Then, with a deep breath, he passed through the open the door and stepped out into the watery sunlight of the London morning, Jonny following closely behind.

On the top step, Kip turned to face Jonny, his posture straightening as he stood to attention. With a fluid motion, he lifted his hat in a formal farewell; the brim casting a shadow across his face. Jonny mirrored his stance, his own back ramrod straight, his chin lifted in a show of resolve. Their eyes met, a wealth of unspoken emotions passing between them. Kip extended his hand, his fingers trembling almost imperceptibly. Jonny grasped it, his grip firm and steady, a lifeline in the tempest of their feelings.

"I will write," Kip whispered, his voice low and urgent. "As often as I can. And when this blasted war is over, I'll come back to you. I swear it."

Jonny nodded; his throat too tight to speak. He squeezed Kip's hand, hoping the gesture would convey all the things he could not say. "I'll be waiting," he managed at last, his words a hoarse rasp. "Always."

Kip's lips quirked in a sad smile, his eyes shining with unshed tears. He released Jonny's hand, his fingers trailing across the other boy's palm in a final, lingering caress. Then, with a deep breath, he bounded down the steps, his long legs carrying him swiftly to the waiting carriage. Jonny stood at attention, watching as Kip settled himself inside, his heart clenching at the sight of him.

As the carriage began to move, Kip leaned out of the window, his hand raised in a slow wave. Jonny lifted his own hand in response, his eyes locked on Kip's, refusing to look away even as the distance between them grew.

The carriage rolled down the street, the clatter of hooves on cobblestones echoing in the morning's stillness. Jonny watched until it disappeared from view, his vision blurring with tears he knew he had to hold back.

He stood there for a long moment, hand still raised in farewell, his heart aching with all he had left unsaid. The future stretched before him, vast and uncertain, but he clung to the memory of Kip's promise, a glimmer of hope in the gathering

darkness. With a shuddering breath, Jonny lowered his hand, his fingers curling into a fist at his side. He turned back to the house, his steps heavy with the burden of his emotions, but his head held high, determined to face whatever lay ahead with the same courage and resolve he had seen in Kip's eyes.

Jonny stepped into the entrance hall, the cool shadows a stark contrast to the bright morning light outside. The click of the door echoed in the stillness, and he paused, his hand resting on the polished wood as he composed himself. "Bolton?" he called, his voice steady despite the tremor in his heart.

The butler materialised from the shadows; his expression was carefully neutral. "Yes, my lord?"

"Please inform me when the earl returns," Jonny instructed, his tone even. "I shall be in my room."

"Very good, my lord." Mr. Bolton bowed, his eyes flickering briefly to Jonny's face, a flicker of concern in their depths.

Jonny nodded, then turned and ascended the grand staircase, his hand trailing along the smooth banister. Each step seemed to weigh him down, the emptiness of the house pressing in on him, suffocating in its silence. He reached his bedroom, its familiar scent enveloping him as he closed the door behind him.

A FORBIDDEN LOVE

For a moment, he leaned against the solid wood of the door, his eyes falling closed as the events of the morning washed over him. Kip's whispered words, his gentle touch, the promise of a future together - it all seemed like a dream now, a fragile hope that the harsh realities of war could shatter.

A sob rose in Jonny's throat, and he pressed his hand to his mouth, stifling the sound. He slid to the floor, his back against the door, and drew his knees to his chest, his shoulders shaking with the force of his emotions. Tears streamed down his cheeks, hot and bitter, as he finally allowed himself to feel the full weight of his grief.

The thought of Kip, alone and in danger, tore at his heart, and he ached with the longing to be with him, to protect him from the horrors that lay ahead. But he knew that was impossible. Their paths and duties were predetermined, so all he could do was pray for Kip's safety and hope for their reunion.

In the solitude of his room, Jonny wept, his tears a silent testament to the depth of his love and the strength of his resolve. He would endure this separation, this uncertainty, for the sake of the future they had dreamed of together. He would wait for Kip, ready to build their promised life together when the war ended and the world healed.

With a heavy heart, Jonny made his way to the bathroom, splashing cool water on his face to erase the evidence of his tears. He stared at his reflection in the mirror, hardly recognising the haunted eyes that gazed back at him. The weight of their secret, of the forbidden love they shared, seemed to press down on him, threatening to crush him beneath its burden. He turned away, unable to bear the sight of his own despair.

"I will come back to you," Kip had promised.

Jonny clung to those words now, using them as a talisman against the darkness that threatened to engulf him. He would be strong, for Kip's sake, for the sake of the love they shared. He would endure whatever trials lay ahead, secure knowing that someday, somehow, they would be together again.

Until then, he would carry on, his heart full of love and his mind fixed on the hope of tomorrow.

A FORBIDDEN LOVE

CHAPTER TEN:
LETTERS ACROSS ENEMY LINES

In the days following Christian's departure, John distracted himself with preparations for his move to Cambridge. Thomas gently urged him to visit various bookshops to get him out of the house and also encouraged him to return to his favourite museum with his sketchbook. Conversation was still somewhat subdued as John worked through his emotions. However, the news that his father would be home for dinner for the first time in several nights lifted his spirits the most.

Thomas fussed over John as he got him dressed for dinner, and John was now comfortable with this level of attention from his valet. As Thomas made the final adjustments to his tie, he stepped back to admire his handiwork. "You seem in a better mood today, Jonny?" he asked cautiously. Thomas' informal tone in private was comforting to John.

"Yes, I think I am, Tom. It will be nice to spend some time with my father tonight," he replied softly.

"Of course, you must have missed him these past few days," Thomas sympathised, drawing a smile from Jonny. "Now," he gently patted John on the shoulder, "let's get you down to the drawing room." He moved to the door and opened it.

In the serene stillness of the Blue Drawing Room, the fire crackled softly, casting flickering shadows on the richly decorated blue wallpaper. The heavy velvet curtains shut out the night, enveloping Lord John Langley in a world of flickering light and moving shadows. The familiar scent of lavender polish and the lingering presence of old parchment filled the air; the weight of the Langley family history was almost tangible. A footman knocked and entered, carrying a small silver tray with a letter on it.

"My lord, the earl asked me to give this to you when you came downstairs," John took the letter from the tray and instantly recognised Christian's handwriting. "Would you like me to pour you a drink, my lord, while you wait?"

"No... no thank you," Jonny replied, slightly flustered by the sight of his cousin's letter. "I will wait for the earl to come down."

"Very well, my lord," the footman gave a slight bow before departing and leaving John alone with his letter. He brought the envelope to his lips, feeling its texture and any familiar scent. His mind and heart raced, and though he wanted to tear it open, he paused. Instead, he picked up the paper knife left by the footman and carefully slit the top. Inside, he found a single folded sheet, which he gently extracted with trembling fingers. Taking a final deep breath, he unfolded it.

'*MV Yarmouth, August 4th, 1914,*' the letter began. '*My dearest Jonny, Father suggested I write a note to express my gratitude to you and the earl for hosting me this summer. I shall leave it onboard with some of his correspondence for delivery to your father's office. I trust this letter reaches you safe and well.*' Jonny could almost sense Kip's thoughtful pause before he continued, '*Above all, I want to thank you, my dear friend, for the adventures we shared over the summer and the strength I felt from our close bond.*

My only regret is leaving you so soon after we discovered the real depth of our friendship.' Jonny smiled, picturing Kip's teasing yet knowing wink as he acknowledged their shared secrets.

Kip went on, '*I find great comfort sitting here alone with my thoughts, trusting in your resolve and promise to rescue me after the war.*

A FORBIDDEN LOVE

Indeed, it is only the knowledge of this that will sustain me through the challenges ahead. My father has informed me I must return to the Academy immediately and take my officer's examination in the spring of next year.' Jonny let this news settle before reading the final lines, *'Dear cousin, I must end this brief note now. My hopes rest on our future plans, but for now, my sincerest wish is that we find a way to stay in touch. I understand this may not be possible during a war between our nations, but I will never give up hope. Until we meet again, I leave you with my fondest good wishes. Yours, as always, Kip.'*

John read Kip's note over several times before he heard his father step into the drawing room. Standing up, he greeted him with a formal nod, "Papa."

The earl's face lit up with a broad, albeit tired, smile that revealed his delight at seeing his son. He motioned for John to sit again and then signalled to Bolton to pour some drinks. With his drink in hand, the earl dismissed the butler.

"Well," his father began, "I see you've received Christian's letter." He nodded toward the note still clutched in John's hand. "Any news?"

"He wrote to ask me to pass on his thanks for hosting him this summer," John replied. The earl's smile widened at his nephew's kind gesture, though he soon noticed a familiar expression on his son's face.

"Is there something else on your mind, John?" he asked gently. "You have that look your mother used to have when she was about to ask me something that might trouble me." His smile was warm and reassuring, though. John took a sip from his drink before continuing. It was ironic—when he was a boy, his father often seemed impatient with him, as if urging him to simply *"to spit it out,"* but now their dynamic had changed.

"Well," John began, "Kip wondered..." he paused, realising he could not put everything on his cousin, "I wondered if there might be a way for us to keep writing to each other?"

"Mmmm," the earl mused, watching his son's face shift from polite curiosity to earnest supplication. "Oh, my dear boy, I could never resist that look from your mother either."

"Could you maybe find a way?" John urged.

"No promises, mind you, but I'll see what I can do," the earl replied, savouring the relief and happiness blossoming on John's face. A warm sense of satisfaction bloomed in his chest, a feeling he knew his beloved wife would have shared.

"Thank you, Papa!" John exclaimed. The conversation then shifted to John's preparations for his move to Cambridge, with his father offering sage advice on adapting to life there. "And will Thomas be coming with me?"

"Of course he will; you need not worry about that," his father said with a knowing chuckle, having already spoken to Thomas about it. "Just remember, never underestimate the value of a loyal manservant."

"Of course not, never," John replied, his relief clear. At that moment, a knock at the door announced dinner, and for the first time since Kip's departure, John felt completely at ease—grateful that his father would help keep them in touch and reassured that Thomas would be there to guide him in Cambridge. For the next hour, John entertained his father with lively accounts of their time in the countryside, and at last, the earl enjoyed the company of his son and heir.

A FORBIDDEN LOVE

After dinner, father and son returned to the drawing room and eased into comfortable chairs with a drink in hand. John sat on the edge of a silk-upholstered armchair, gently swirling his port in the glass while his eyes remained fixed on the deep ruby liquid. The comforting warmth of the alcohol echoed his mood as he savoured the attentive company his father had offered over the past few hours.

Across from him, the earl settled into his favourite wingback chair, watching John with a detached, measured interest. His fingers drummed a slow, steady beat on the armrest, the only sounds in the quiet room aside from the persistent ticking of the old grandfather clock standing in the corner.

Taking a deep breath, John finally allowed the words he had rehearsed all evening to escape. "Papa," he began softly, "thank you for your time tonight—I know you must be tired." For just a moment, the earl's drumming paused, the smallest hint that he had heard his son. Maintaining a steady gaze and an unreadable expression, he replied in a deep, rumbling voice reminiscent of distant thunder,

"My dear boy, I only wish I could have done it sooner. Is there anything else you'd like to discuss?" His tone remained kind and inviting.

John placed his glass on the side table, the crystal resonating against the polished wood, and leaned forward, resting his elbows on his knees while clasps of his hands held tight.

"Kip mentioned at Langley that his father had had an affair. I wasn't aware of it, and learning about it was quite a shock." He looked up, meeting his father's gaze with a mixture of curiosity and inner turmoil.

The earl's eyes narrowed slightly, a subtle twitch in his jaw betraying his reaction. He leaned back, allowing his fingers to resume their steady rhythm. "Secrets, John, are a currency in our world," he explained in a measured tone. "People trade, barter, and, yes, often whisper them behind closed doors."

John's heart pounded like a drum, each beat marking his anticipation and apprehension. It felt as though he were teetering on the edge of a precipice, with one misstep threatening to send him plunging into the unknown.

Yet there was also a thrill—a sense of exhilaration at finally delving into the subject that had haunted him all summer. "And mama chose to help Aunt Victoria?" he ventured. A soft chuckle escaped his father.

"Of course she did," the earl replied, a warm smile passing briefly over his features as he recalled the memory.

"So, you didn't disapprove of her *'interference'*?" John pressed, even though he already suspected the answer.

"As you should well know, Jonny, no one could ever hold a long-lasting disapproval for your mama. When she suggested a trip to *New York* with your aunt to help her escape an unhappy marriage and re-evaluate her future, I naturally supported the idea." His expression darkened as he recalled the tragic events of their voyage on the *RMS Titanic*. "In hindsight, maybe I shouldn't have."

The fire crackled and snapped, its sound ricocheting around the room like a sudden gunshot. Startled, John's nerves jangled, yet the earl remained unmoved—his steady gaze and sad expression unchanged. The interplay of light and darkness swirled along the wallpaper, with shifting shadows like demons locked in combat with angels. And in that eerie atmosphere, John waited; his breath caught and heart pounding, yearning for his father to reveal more about the secrets that had cast such a long, haunting shadow over his recent life.

A FORBIDDEN LOVE

In a sudden flash, memories of his aunt surged through John's mind—her laughter resonating through the halls of Langley Hall and her eyes shimmering with joy. Back then, he had been too young and absorbed in his own world to notice the quiet melancholy that must have lay behind her smile. The earl then set his glass down, the base clicking against the polished wood of the side table. Leaning back in his chair with his fingers steepled beneath his chin, he murmured, "if we must discuss secrets John, sometimes it is better to let them lie, not to probe too deeply into the past."

John's mouth grew dry and his tongue felt heavy as he reached for his own glass, relishing the coolness of the stem against the warmth of the room. The port was sweet and full-bodied, a burst of flavour that anchored him. "Only *'sometimes,'* Papa?" John almost whispered. His father shook his head slightly and smiled.

"So, like your mother," the elder remarked.

"I'll take that as a compliment," John replied with a smile.

"As it was meant to be, dear boy, as it was meant to be," the earl said, taking a long sip as if carefully choosing his next words. Leaning in slightly, John listened in eager anticipation.

"Let me tell you about the last conversation I had with your mother," the earl began, his tone now serious and measured. "I believe the time is right."

Intrigued, John hung onto every word. "We had just arrived in Southampton, and you stepped out of the carriage to supervise the unloading," his father recalled, a note of pride colouring his tone.

"I was about to follow you, but your mother gently took my elbow and asked me to sit back down for a moment, then she simply told me to be kind to you and not to repeat my father's mistakes." He let the words fade before adding, "She said it out of love—for the sake of both of us, I believe."

"You have never spoken much of my grandfather, Papa," John mused carefully over his words. "Was he unkind to you?" His father rose to take John's glass, refilling it before handing it back and settling into his armchair once more.

"This may take some time to explain," he said after a long sip. "Yes, your grandfather was unkind to me, though he genuinely believed he was doing what he thought was best for me when he arranged my first marriage, but it was for the family's prestige rather than my own happiness."

John recalled the sombre gravestone in the Langley churchyard for *'Countess Amelia'.* "It wasn't a happy union, but I fulfilled my duty and secured an heir," hence the inscription of *'Infant Lord Edward'* there too John realised. "Within weeks, I lost both wife and my successor. Then my father only took a month to find me another potential bride, even as I was mourning my son."

John was utterly spellbound; he had never known his father to be so candid. "What did you do, Papa?" John asked, knowing nothing of this chapter in his father's life. His father chuckled softly in response.

"I ran away!" John's eyes widened at this revelation. "Well, I joined the diplomatic service and got myself posted abroad, so not as romantic as it might seem. Work kept me away from my father's schemes and marriage plans, but he made it clear how disappointed he was in me," the pain of those years was evident on the earl's face, but then he suddenly brightened.

A FORBIDDEN LOVE

"Then, while on leave years later, I met your mother at a dinner. For the first time in my life," his cheeks flushed with embarrassment, "I fell in love." John let his father's confession settle for a moment.

"So did grandfather finally accept your choice?" John's father burst into laughter.

"Of course not! He forbade me from marrying what he called *'new money'*, insisting I should never marry beneath my station. To stop me, he not only cut off my allowance but also withdrew all support, arguing that our union would render us outcasts in society," he declared with a triumphant smile. "But we ignored his warnings, and within a year, he had passed on, leaving us free."

Leaning closer to his son, he added, "I suppose what your mother was trying to tell me is that I should trust you to make your own decisions too." Pausing for a few moments to let his words sink in, he softly patted his son's knee. "Just be careful not to be reckless with this new freedom, promise me, son?"

John considered his father's words with caution, wondering if there was an unspoken hint about his friendship with Kip, though he quickly dismissed the thought, realising his father had not seen anything inappropriate.

"I promise I'll do my very best, Papa," John replied, giving his father a reassuring look.

"I couldn't ask any more from you. I only wish your mother were here to guide and advise you," his father said with quiet resignation.

"Me too, Papa, me too," Jonny responded, sitting up straighter. "We're both doing the best we can, so thank you, Papa, for sharing all of this tonight," John concluded.

The earl's face remained composed and unreadable, though there was an unmistakable glint in his eyes that John could not quite decipher. He hoped it signified understanding, a silent acknowledgment of the emotions that were now stirring within him. But he was not sure, not yet. Slowly, John's father rose, pulled the cord to summon a footman, and bid Jonny goodnight.

John then sat quietly for several minutes as he finished his drink. The time since Christian's departure had left him feeling alone, and without Thomas' attentions, it might have been even worse. Yet the intimate, honest conversation he had just shared with his father filled him with hope that the coming months might be better than he feared.

He also reflected on how, in just a few short hours, his relationship with his father had deepened, and he found comfort in the thought that his father might be more sympathetic to his situation than he had ever imagined.

In the following weeks, John and his father settled into a companionable routine, sharing breakfast and dinner together on most days. Their conversations ranged from early setbacks in the land war to his father's disappointment over the failure to pursue a diplomatic solution.

Jonny sensed that his father was deliberately trying to truly understand him for the first time, openly seeking his opinions and never dismissing them. For the first time, he began to see the kind, considerate side of his father—the same side that had perhaps attracted his mother—a stark contrast to the publicly cold and calculating persona he usually displayed.

A FORBIDDEN LOVE

One night in mid-September, father and son were enjoying a post dinner drink again in the blue drawing room, when the earl reached into an inside pocket in his jacket and pulled out a small envelope. "Sorry son I had almost forgotten about this," he handed over the envelope. John's confused face showed that the writing wasn't Kip's; the letter was addressed to his father.

"Papa?" he asked quietly.

"I have finally found a solution for you John," the earl said suddenly, his voice cutting through the silence like a knife. "Inside are the details you need to be able to write to Christian." John looked up, his eyes meeting the earl's gaze. There was a spark there, a glint of triumph that sent a shiver down John's spine.

"How?" John said nervously as he tried to contain his obvious glee.

"The Portuguese Embassy in Lisbon," the earl continued, a small smile playing at the corners of his mouth. "I have a contact there who has agreed to act as an intermediary. Your letters to Christian will pass through his hands, direct to the German Embassy in Lisbon discreetly and securely."

John's breath hitched, a mix of relief and apprehension washing over him. Our Portuguese Embassy. A neutral ground in the battlefield of their forbidden correspondence. He could almost see the letters now, sealed with wax and whispered promises, traveling across borders and battle lines. He was about to ask who this contact was, but his father had already recognised the unspoken question on his son's lips.

"Don't worry Jonny, it is someone I can trust implicitly, somebody I once helped to get out of a tricky situation he had found himself in," the earl reassured his son.

"So, he sort of owes you?" asked Jonny. His father smiled wisely.

"Not really Jonny, you see real friendships are not as transactional as you might initially think," his son's eyes squinted slightly as he tried to understand the words. "We were brought together by circumstances, he was a young man out of his depth and he needed help, and he felt that I was the one that could, or rather would, help him."

"So, you were kind to him?" Jonny felt a surge of pride in his father and an enhanced understanding of the man he was.

"Yes, I suppose I was," he replied humbly. "I saw him at a meeting in the Foreign Office last week. He has just been appointed as our Ambassador in Lisbon. He asked about you, and I casually mentioned your situation. Then, this morning, his note appeared on my desk."

"So, he was just returning your kindness?" Jonny asked, and his father nodded in agreement. "I'm curious about how you met him, though," Jonny added, "without breaking any confidences, of course."

"It was in the '80s when I was *Charge d'Affairs* in *Tangiers*, and the note's author had just joined us as a junior agent," the earl explained, choosing his words carefully. "He was fresh out of university and a bit naive."

He paused, watching his son's reaction and anticipating his response to the rest of the story. "To put it simply, he found himself in a difficult situation, facing the threat of blackmail," John's eyes widened in surprise, "because a local boy tried to use a past encounter as leverage against him."

A FORBIDDEN LOVE

John blushed at the mention of *'with a local boy'* and tried to keep his composure. "Don't be so shocked, Jonny. In that region, such things are more common than you might think. He was still young and did not deserve to lose a promising career over one indiscretion."

John's mind raced, torn by this revelation: his father had shown understanding and support for his young colleague when society would have expected disapproval and condemnation. "What did you do to help?" he stammered.

The earl's face lit up with triumph. "I confronted the blackmailer and called his bluff."

"Is that all you did, Papa?" John sensed there might be more to the story.

"I may also have hinted at some severe consequences and the might of the British Empire coming down on him," he burst into hearty laughter, and his son quickly joined in. The earl raised his glass, the crystal catching the light like a captured star. "To discretion, John," he said, his voice a low rumble. "And to the bonds that transcend boundaries."

John raised his own glass, the port swirling like a dark sea. As he took a sip, the rich liquid warming his throat, he could not shake the feeling of standing on the edge of a precipice. The path ahead was shrouded in fog, the outcome uncertain. But for now, there was hope. Hope, and the promise of words whispered across the void.

A couple of weeks later, it was time for the earl and John's final dinner together before his departure for Cambridge. The dining room at Langley House was an elegant space, the walls adorned with ancestral portraits and the table set with gleaming silver and fine china. Yet beneath the veneer of normality, an undercurrent of tension ripples, the impending separation and the uncertainties of war casting a pall over the meal.

"Is everything ready for tomorrow then son?" asked the earl.

"Yes, thank you papa, I believe that Thomas has everything in hand," John smiled, "I really do not know what I would do without him now."

"Yes, he is a good man, like his father is, and his grandfather was too," the earl mused for a moment. "Did you know that the Coopers have been tenants at Home Farm since the reign of George III?" John shook his head. "Well, you cannot buy that kind of loyalty my boy. Try to remember that."

"Of course, papa."

Father and son continued an easy conversation for next couple of hours. The earl regaled John with some of his youthful adventures in Cambridge whilst gently warning him about the dangers of excess. Finally, as they finished their last drink in the drawing room, father asked son a serious question, perhaps one that had been playing on his mind for some time, "are you happy to be going to Cambridge," then he paused, "I mean following me to university?"

"Why would you ask me that?" John genuinely wondered having never expressed any doubts to his father.

"Well, it just seems to me sometimes that you are more like your mother than me, and perhaps you would prefer to study elsewhere or even study something artistic?" John's heart raced a little as he realised that his father really did seem to know him a lot better than he thought. "Be honest Jonny, please?" John took a deep breath.

A FORBIDDEN LOVE

"Papa, I have thought sometimes that maybe one day I might go to an art school," his father nodded slightly in acknowledgement of what he had already suspected, "but I will try my best at Cambridge first, and see how things develop if that is agreeable for you?" John realised, in that moment of candour between the two, that he should at least do that for his father. "I hope I haven't disappointed you."

"My dear boy, of course not. In fact, I think your plan to try it first and then see how things go is a very mature one. I could not be prouder," his usually deep voice was gentle and reassuring.

"Thank you, papa," the earl batted away the words with a flick of his wrist.

"Well, I shall retire now," he said as he moved to pull the chord, "I hope everything goes well tomorrow, and if I cannot get up to visit you then we shall see each other in Langley for Christmas," he turned towards the door, "good night son."

"Good night papa, and thank you."

October, 1914.

The lodgings in Cambridge were a stark contrast to the opulence of Langley House, but they held a certain charm that John found comforting. The rooms were small, the furniture worn, but the scent of beeswax and old books filled the air, a familiar smell that reminded him of home. Thomas moved about the room, unpacking John's belongings with a quiet efficiency, his presence a calming force amidst the storm of emotions within John.

Thomas looked up, catching John's gaze. A soft smile played at the corners of his mouth, a silent acknowledgment of their shared bond. "You'll be alright here," he said, his voice a gentle murmur. "It's a new beginning, a chance to find your own way." John nodded, a lump forming in his throat. He turned back to the window, the sunlight warming his face.

A new beginning, yes, but also a continuation of a journey started long ago, a journey filled with shadows and secrets, and the promise of love that transcended boundaries. And as he sat there, the world outside bustling with life, he knew that no matter what lay ahead, he would face it with courage, with hope, and with the unwavering support of those who understood the complexities of his heart.

The ancient stones of Cambridge seemed to whisper secrets as old as time itself, their cool indifference a stark contrast to the warmth John had left behind in London. The October wind whipped through the quadrangle, sending leaves skittering across the cobblestones like frightened mice.

John stood by his window, watching the scene unfold, his breath fogging the glass. The chill seeped into his bones, a physical manifestation of the loneliness that gripped him.

The first week passed in a blur of lectures and introductions, each day bleeding into the next with a monotonous regularity. The other students moved in packs, their laughter echoing through the hallowed halls, a stark reminder of John's solitude.

A FORBIDDEN LOVE

He found himself retreating further into his shell, his thoughts a tangled web of longing and despair, and his days at Cambridge unfolded like a series of watercolour paintings, each one bleeding into the next with a hazy, dream-like quality. John was adrift in a sea of unfamiliar faces, the grand stone buildings and manicured lawns feeling more like a gilded cage than the promised land of academic freedom.

One afternoon, as the rain lashed against the windowpanes, John found himself drawn to his writing desk. The mahogany surface was smooth beneath his fingers, a stark contrast to the tumultuous emotions roiling within him. He opened the top drawer, revealing a carefully hidden bundle of letters. The sight of Christian's familiar handwriting sent a shiver down his spine, a mixture of anticipation and dread.

'*My dearest Jonny,*' he read, his heart quickening, '*The world grows darker with each passing day, yet thoughts of you are my guiding star...*' John closed his eyes, Christian's voice echoing in his mind.

When he opened them again, the room seemed to pulse with an aching emptiness. "I miss you terribly," John whispered to the empty air, his voice thick with emotion. He reached for a sheet of paper, dipping his pen in ink.

As he wrote, pouring his heart onto the page, Thomas quietly entered the room. John looked up, a fleeting smile crossing his face. "Another letter for the Portuguese Embassy, Jonny?" Thomas asked, his tone neutral but his eyes knowing. John nodded, a faint blush colouring his cheeks.

"Yes, Thomas."

"I shall make you some coffee, and then leave you to write your reply," Thomas knew by now that John liked to read and write his letters in private.

Jonny smiled appreciatively and his gaze then drifted to the window, where autumn leaves danced on the breeze.

Finally, alone with his pen and paper and his thoughts, Jonny began:

'*My rooms, November 4th 1914, My Dearest Kip, Cambridge is a labyrinth of stone and shadow, a world away from the warmth of our summers. The days stretch out before me, an endless expanse of lectures and solitude. Yet, in the quiet of my chambers, I find solace in your words, a lifeline amidst the growing despair.*'

As the days turned had into weeks, the exchange of letters had become a ritual, a sacred communion between two souls adrift in a sea of uncertainty. Each missive was a testament to their evolving feelings, the emotional depth of their correspondence a stark contrast to the superficial interactions that filled John's days.

'*I dreamt of you last night,*' John continued, his words a whispered confession. '*Of the sun on your face, the wind in your hair. Of the laughter that danced in your eyes, a beacon of light in the darkness. I find myself searching for you in the crowds, your face a phantom that haunts my dreams. The war casts a long shadow, a spectre that threatens to engulf us all. Yet, in your letters, I find a sliver of hope, a promise of a future unmarred by conflict.*'

Their correspondence had become a sanctuary, a haven where they could express their deepest fears and most fervent hopes. The war raged on, a relentless beast that threatened to consume them all. Yet, in the quiet of his chambers, John found solace in the knowledge that somewhere, across the sea, Christian was thinking of him, his heart a beacon of love amidst the chaos.

A FORBIDDEN LOVE

As the first tendrils of winter crept into the air, John found himself drawn to the fireplace, the crackling flames a comforting presence in the gathering darkness. He held Christian's latest letter to his chest, the paper crinkling softly beneath his touch. The words were etched in his heart, a testament to their love, a promise of a future yet unwritten. He concluded his letter, *'Until we meet again, my dear cousin,'* his words a whispered vow. *'Until the storm passes, and the dawn breaks anew. Yours as ever and always, Kip.'*

The lamp flame flickered, casting eerie shadows on the faded tapestry that adorned John's wall. The room, sparsely furnished with heavy, ancient wooden pieces, bore the weight of history and the chill of the Cambridge night. John sat at his desk, his breath misting slightly in the cool air, his eyes fixed on the worn photograph of Christian tucked into the corner of his mirror. The silence was overwhelming, a stark contrast to the bustling days filled with lectures and the distant murmur of war news.

Thomas entered quietly; his footsteps muffled by the worn rug. "Your letter, Jonny," he said softly, "if it is to catch the last collection?"

His hazel eyes met John's briefly, a silent understanding passing between them. John reached for the envelope, and passed it to Thomas.

"Thank you, Thomas," John murmured, his voice barely above a whisper. He watched as Thomas nodded, and then took the envelope from Jonny's outstretched hand.

On December 5th, John and Thomas travelled straight to Langley Hall, where John planned to spend Christmas with his father. After a hectic first term he was looking forward to the peace and quiet that his ancestral home would offer. They arrived for the first time in a motorcar taxi, and the view as it turned from the tree-lined approach to face the hall was no less impressive than it had always been.

Christmas at Langley Hall in his mother's time had always been a joyous time, filled with grand dinners and parties. However, since her death the house was quieter. The earl hosted a lunch for the parish council and then all the tenants and their families were invited on Christmas Eve for a musical event and late tea in the ballroom in memory of the late Countess. Another tradition begun by her was that all the staff had Christmas Day to themselves except for serving an early dinner for John and his father.

The earl spent most of his time during the day in his study, reviewing and responding to the government papers he received by courier most days. Meanwhile, John and Thomas would take a ride around the estate and tenant farms. Thomas introduced him to many of the older tenants so that he could begin to learn about the workings of the estate. On quite a few occasions they stopped off on their way back to the Hall to have a drink in *The Langley Arms* and the days between Christmas and New Year passed by pleasantly.

Again, once John and Thomas were back in Cambridge the weeks passed quickly, and Kip's letters continued to arrive, each one a lifeline in a world consumed by war. John loses himself in Christian's words, in the vivid descriptions of life at sea and the whispered promises of a future together. John remained open in his mind about whether or not to stay at Cambridge as, with the war nowhere near a conclusion, there was no need to hurry his decision.

A FORBIDDEN LOVE

John reads and rereads Christian's replies again and again until the pages are worn and the ink smudged. In those precious pages, John finds a reflection of his own heart, a love that burns bright and true despite the distance that separates them.

With each exchange, the words grow bolder, the sentiments more impassioned. What began as tentative expressions of affection blossom into fervent declarations of devotion, the language of love flowing between them like a secret code. John writes of his love, of the way Christian's smile can light up a room, of the way his laughter can chase away even the darkest of clouds. He writes of the dreams they have shared, of the future they have imagined together, a future that seems so fragile now in the face of the gathering storm.

In April 1915, a letter arrives that shatters the fragile peace John has found. With shaking hands, he unfolds the paper, his eyes scanning the words with growing dread.

'My dearest Jonny,' the letter begins, *'I write to you with news that fills me with both pride and trepidation. They promoted me to lieutenant and assigned me to active duty on a warship. It is a great honour, but it means that I cannot write as often, if at all.'* John's heart clenches, an icy fear seeping into his bones. He knows what this mean, Kip will be at the forefront of the war, and in constant danger.

'I do not know what the future holds, my love,' Christian's letter continues, *'but I want you to know that you are always in my thoughts and in my heart. You give me the strength to face whatever lies ahead, and the hope of a life together when this war is over.'*

Now fear lingers for John, an icy hand gripping his heart. What if Christian never returns? What if John faces the rest of his life alone, haunted by the ghost of a love that never fully blossomed? He shakes his head, banishing the dark thoughts. He cannot afford to indulge in despair, not now. He has a duty to fulfil, a legacy to uphold.

John resolved to reply immediately as he was unsure if his last letter would get through in time. *'My dearest Kip,'* he began, his hand trembling slightly. *'Your letter has reached me, and with it, a blend of joy and despair that I cannot express. Joy, for the love that echoes across the miles, and despair, for the silence that now looms ahead.'* He paused, the nib hovering over the paper as he gathered his thoughts.

He now realised that he must do his duty too. *'I have made a decision, Kip. I am joining the Officer Training Corps. I cannot sit idly by while the world burns around us. I hope you understand, my dear friend. I hope that this war will not divide us further, that our love will remain a beacon in the darkness.'*

His heart ached as he wrote, the words flowing from his soul. The ticking of the clock on the mantelpiece seemed to echo the countdown to their inevitable separation.

He folded the letter carefully, sealing it with a drop of wax. The flame of the candle flickered as he pressed his signet ring into the warm wax, the Langley crest leaving its imprint. He stared at the sealed letter, a sense of finality washing over him. As he prepared to send Thomas to post to catch the last post, John imagined Christian aboard his warship, the salty spray of the sea on his face, the wind whipping through his raven hair. He pictured him reading his letter, his blue eyes scanning the words, a faint smile playing on his lips. The image was both comforting and heart-wrenching, a stark reminder of the distance between them.

A FORBIDDEN LOVE

And so, with a heavy heart and a steely resolve, John begins to prepare for the trials ahead. He will join the Officer Training Corps, just as he told Christian. He will fight for his country, for his family, for the chance to build a world where love like theirs can flourish without fear. As he stands there, watching the sun dip below the horizon, John feels a flicker of something that might almost be hope. The road ahead is long and uncertain, but he knows he will walk it with Christian by his side, even if only in spirit.

"Wait for me, my love," he whispers into the gathering dusk. "I will come back to you, no matter what it takes. This, I swear." And with that, John turns away from the window, ready to face whatever the future may bring. For in the end, he knows, their love is the only thing that truly matters.

A few hundred miles away, a single candle lit Christian's small study bedroom at the navy academy. Its light flickered across John's last letter almost animating his cursive script. He wondered if this would be his last letter and said a silent prayer hoping his letter arrives in time for a reply to get back to him before his active service started in ten days' time. As with everything to do with his cousin; he would have to wait and hope.

In this moment though, he took out the cufflinks Jonny had given him and moved them between his fingers. He found solace in their familiar touch and the sentiments that they represented.

A FORBIDDEN LOVE

CHAPTER ELEVEN:
THE BATTLE OF JUTLAND, 1916

It had been over a year since Jonny and Kip had last exchanged letters, and each of them clung to both their memories and their future plans. The simple certainty of their eventual reunion motivated them to press on, taking life one day at a time.

The previous autumn, John enrolled in his university's Officer Training Corps and ultimately by the end of January he was involved in the training new infantry battalions destined for front-line reinforcement. As was customary John had Thomas as his batman—a personal soldier-servant—and Thomas soon enlisted in the Regiment alongside him. In a Thetford training camp, they mastered the skills essential for trench warfare.

Meanwhile, following his graduation from the Academy, they assigned Kip to the *SMS Frankfurt*, a recently completed light cruiser. Trained as a gunnery officer, he was responsible for relaying firing solutions from the bridge to the ship's guns. Up to that point, his assignment had consisted of short training missions and target practice—a typical routine for most of the *German High Seas Fleet*, which was held in port by Britain's *Grand Fleet*.

31st May 1916

Great secrecy surrounded the plans that unfolded on the night of May 30th, as officers aboard the *SMS Frankfurt* received their briefing for the next day's operations. The plan was for the entire *High Seas Fleet* to sail into the North Sea to ambush the British *Grand Fleet*. The operation was expected to decisively shift the war in Germany's favour.

Christian's cruiser squadron was to cover the rear, positioned behind the main body of battleships, with orders to sink any critically damaged British vessels. As the sun rose, Kip, standing on the bridge, could not help but marvel at the sight of nearly a hundred combat ships setting out to confront the *Grand Fleet*. His father was in command of one of the forward battleships, the *SMS Pommern*. However, the attempt to surprise the British would ultimately fail, as the *Grand Fleet*, with over one hundred and fifty warships, repelled the German attack.

They steamed north during the morning hours; by afternoon, Christian's squadron had separated from the main fleet to begin a reconnaissance mission to find the Royal Navy's cruisers. In the distance, Kip could just make out the plume of smoke rising from distant battles.

Then, around four o'clock, they came under fire from superior British vessels but evaded the attack without harm. An hour later, they encountered a solitary British cruiser, and for the first time in actual battle, Kip ordered his gun crews to fire.

The vessel trembled as another volley roared from the forward turrets. Prince Christian clutched the railing, his gloves whitening his knuckles, while he surveyed the sea cloaked in smoke. Flames licked the skyline where British dreadnoughts clashed with German battlecruisers. It was not long before three British battlecruisers emerged to shield the beleaguered British cruiser.

A FORBIDDEN LOVE

SMS Frankfurt soon became the target of their assault. A jarring impact shook the ship as a shell detonated just shy of its hull. The pungent odour of cordite and burning metal saturated the salty air. Christian squinted against the acrid smoke, resolute as bursts of water erupted from the starboard bow, enemy shells consistently finding their mark.

Yet, in the solitude of his thoughts, terror gnawed at him. The overwhelming scale and intensity of the battle surpassed all he had ever imagined, even after years of preparation. With every fiery exchange, every booming broadside, death seemed to lurk just a heartbeat away—a roll of the dice with their lives on the line.

Unbidden, the image of John's face appeared in his mind—his warm eyes crinkling with laughter and his blond curls shimmering in the sunlight along the banks of the *River Cam*. This bittersweet memory struck him like a shard of shrapnel. Would he ever see his dear friend again, or would the cold depths of the North Sea claim him forever, another victim of this merciless war tearing them apart?

Then, in that very moment, the *Frankfurt* was struck. A searing flash, dazzling in its brilliance, yanked Christian from his reverie. The deck bucked underfoot as the shockwave of a nearby explosion slammed him against the bulkhead. A sharp, sudden pain slashed through his shoulder, robbing him of breath.

He glanced down through a veil of smoke and shock, watching crimson spread across the once-pristine white of his uniform—the fabric now torn and ragged. He knew, dimly, that shrapnel was the culprit; a stray fragment from a nearby hit just behind the bridge had found its target amid the chaos.

"Sir!" a strained, urgent voice called at his elbow. "You're wounded!"

Christian shook his head, battling the dizziness threatening to overtake him. He could not afford to weaken now, not with his men relying on him. "It's nothing," he rasped, his voice rough with pain and resolve. "Return to your post, sailor."

Forcing himself upright, he pressed his hand firmly against the wound. Despite the fresh blood seeping between his fingers where he held his chest wound, he set aside the pain and concentrated on the task ahead. The battle continued to rage around them, with enemy vessels reduced to mere silhouettes amid the smoke and spray. With little choice, the superior force compelled the *Frankfurt* to withdraw, returning to port the next morning.

Meanwhile, overnight, *SMS Pommern* encountered a formidable assembly of British ships and led its squadron into a direct confrontation. Damaged early in the exchange, it withdrew from the main force, but at around four in the morning, a British destroyer torpedoed it—one torpedo ignited a tremendous explosion that split the ship in two, causing it to sink with no survivors. Prince Frederick was lost.

John was at his regiment's training camp outside *Great Yarmouth* when the first reports of the battle began to emerge in the evening editions of the British press on 2nd June. However, it would not be until the next day that Jonny saw the first headlines about the battle. They talked about a *'great victory'* for the Royal Navy and the heavy losses on both sides. John read the reports in his field tent filled with dread.

"Please," he whispered, his fingers white-knuckled on the edge of his table. "Please, let him be safe."

A FORBIDDEN LOVE

Later that night and in the reassuring company of Thomas, John still felt numb. "Try not to worry too much Jonny, it is early days. We don't have too many details yet."

"Thank you, Thomas, I know what you are saying is true, but…" John's voice trailed off into silence.

"Here," Thomas handed him his hip flask filled with brandy, "have some of this and then try to get some sleep."

Sleep eluded him though, his mind haunted by visions of Christian amid the fury of battle. He saw the flash of those blue eyes, the curve of that beloved smile, and his heart ached with longing and fear.

"Come back to me," he murmured, his forehead pressed against the cool glass. "Come back to me, my love."

The night deepened around him, the distant stars obscured by clouds and smoke from the campfires. And still, John kept his vigil, his prayers, and his love a beacon in the darkness, guiding Christian home across the war-torn sea.

The next few days, John continued to scour the newspapers, every scrap of news was precious, every rumour a clue to Christian's fate. But as the days passed, and the reports grew grimmer, John felt his hope begin to falter. The toll of ships lost, of lives claimed by the pitiless sea, seemed to mock his prayers, and his desperate yearning for word of Christian's safety.

And so, he waited, torn between hope and despair, his heart a battlefield as fierce as any fought upon the seas. The hours stretched into days, the days into weeks, and still, he kept his watch, his love a flame that would not be extinguished, a light to guide Christian home.

A week after the battle, Thomas entered his tent with a letter. John's hands trembled as he opened it, the earl's familiar script dancing before his eyes. He scanned the words, his heart pounding, until he saw it: *'Christian is alive.'* A sob tore from his throat, and he sank into the chair, the paper fluttering to the floor. Relief crashed over him in waves, and he wept, his shoulders shaking with the force of his emotions. Thomas waited outside, knowing that Jonny need a few moments alone.

"My lord? Is everything alright?" Thomas eventually asked.

John nodded, a watery smile breaking across his face. "Christian is alive, Thomas. He's alive."

Thomas' eyes widened, and then he, too, was smiling, his relief palpable. "That's wonderful news, my lord. Truly wonderful."

John rose, clasping Thomas' shoulder. "It is, Thomas. It is." He drew a deep breath, his mind already racing ahead. "It seems that the Ambassador in Lisbon enquired directly with the German Embassy to find out for me." John was once again reminded of the nature of real friendship. "However, it seems that Prince Frederick was lost with his ship and Christian was wounded, but not seriously."

There was a long silence, and they simply stood for a moment, the silence between them rich with shared emotion. Then John straightened, his jaw set with determination.

"We'll make it through this war, Thomas. We'll make it through, and we'll find Christian again. I know we will."

A FORBIDDEN LOVE

Thomas' smile was gentle, his eyes shining with a faith that matched John's own. "I know we will, Jonny. I know we will." And with those words, they sealed a pact, forging a bond in the crucible of war and love. They would face the trials ahead together, united in their purpose, their hearts fixed on the hope of reunion, the promise of a future where they could all be free.

June 30th 1916

The antiseptic smell mixed with the sharp metallic odour of blood, creating a clashing aroma that lingered in the stale hospital air. Prince Christian lay still on the narrow bed, his bright eyes now clouded with pain and sorrow as they fixed on the cracked ceiling above.

Muffled voices echoed from afar through the thick stone walls, a constant reminder of the turmoil outside the quiet confines of his room. Memories of the battle—the burning agony as shrapnel tore through his flesh and the crushing grief of losing his father—haunted his drifting thoughts. He raised his hand, running his fingers along the uneven edge of the bandage wrapped around his brow, a stark symbol of his vulnerability. Though the physical pain had receded to a dull throb, the emotional wounds and deep scars in his heart promised a much longer recovery.

A nurse stepped in, her pristine white uniform a striking counterpoint to the subdued palette of greys and browns that enveloped his world. With a gentle touch, she examined his bandages while her soothing voice murmured, "You're healing well, your highness. The doctor says you should be able to leave soon.

Christian offered a slight nod and a reserved smile. "Thank you, nurse. I truly appreciate your help."

After she left, his eyes wandered to the small writing desk beside his bed, and a sudden longing surged within him. He yearned to write to John—to spill out his emotions, to share his sorrow and the tiny spark of hope that still flickered inside him—but he knew that was not possible at the moment. Instead, he reached for the drawer in the cabinet next to his bed and pulled out a bundle of old letters from Jonny.

With awkward care, hindered by the sling on his arm, he selected a random envelope and unfolded its contents. Tears fell, dampening the paper and smudging the ink. He did not try to brush them away, allowing them to bear witness to his grief.

Lying back on the bed, feeling a slight lightness in his heart for the first time in days, Christian closed his eyes, conjuring the image of John's face in his mind. In that instant, despite the enduring pain and loss, he believed he would persevere. For he knew that, ultimately, love triumphs. Still, the sorrow of his father's passing weighed upon him.

"Father..." he murmured, his voice breaking on the word. "I'm so sorry."

His eyes closed as he recalled the final time he had seen Prince Frederick, standing tall and proud on the bridge of his flagship. They had argued, as they were prone to do, about duty, honour, and the proper behaviour of a prince. Frederick had been so inflexible, so unwavering in his beliefs. And now, he was gone.

A FORBIDDEN LOVE

CHAPTER TWELVE:
INTO THE TRENCHES

September 1917

After the initial regimental training had finished at the end of 1916, John's unit was first assigned to a camp in Kent as it joined the reserves. His unit undertook further training before finally crossing the Channel in July and settling in the reserve camp twenty miles behind the front line. Here they would wait until they were called forward as required.

The earth trembled beneath John's feet as he stepped into the labyrinth of trenches, the cacophony of war assaulting his senses. The air was thick with the acrid stench of cordite and decay, making his stomach churn. Beside him, Thomas moved with practiced ease, his calm demeanour a stark contrast to John's wide-eyed disorientation. This was to be their first day in the reserve trenches which were a hundred yards behind the front line.

"Mind your head, sir," Thomas cautioned, guiding John to duck under a low-hanging beam. "The Fritz likes to aim for anything that sticks up too high, even this far away." This was a reconnaissance trip forward, to assess the trenches before calling the enlisted men forward the next day.

John nodded, swallowing hard against the lump in his throat. He had thought himself prepared for this, but the reality was far more overwhelming than he could have imagined. The constant barrage of artillery fire in the distance set his nerves on edge, each explosion sending tremors through his body.

As they navigated the narrow passages, John's thoughts drifted to the elegant corridors of Langley House. How different this world was from the one he had left behind. The duckboards beneath their feet creaked ominously, and John found himself longing for the solid oak floors of home.

"Watch your step here," Thomas warned, pointing to a section where the boards had rotted away. "And always keep your back to the wall when passing others. Less chance of knocking someone into the mud."

John followed Thomas' lead, pressing his back against the damp sandbags. The earthy smell mingled with sweat, decay and fear, creating an atmosphere thick with tension. As they moved, John could not help but notice the way Thomas' uniform clung to his lean frame, a reminder of the physical toll this life had taken on his once-impeccable valet.

For a moment, their eyes met, and John felt a surge of something he could not quite name. Gratitude, certainly, but also a warmth that seemed at odds with their grim surroundings. He quickly averted his gaze, cheeks flushing with a mixture of embarrassment and confusion.

As they continued their tour of the trench system, Thomas pointed out various features – the fire step, the dugouts, the latrine. John tried to absorb it all, but his mind kept wandering to the letters tucked safely in his breast pocket. Christian's words, a lifeline to a world that now seemed impossibly far away.

"And here's where we'll be sleeping," Thomas said, gesturing to a cramped dugout. "It's not Langley Hall, but it'll keep us dry... mostly." John ducked inside, the musty air closing in around him.

"It's certainly... cozy," he managed, trying to mask his dismay.

123

A FORBIDDEN LOVE

Thomas chuckled softly. "That's one word for it, sir. But don't worry, I'll make sure you're as comfortable as possible."

The next day the men moved forward, efficiently assigned to their positions by the non-commissioned officers. As night fell, the darkness seemed to amplify every sound. John lay on his narrow cot, acutely aware of Thomas' presence just a few feet away. The intimacy of their shared space was both comforting and unsettling, stirring feelings John had long tried to suppress.

"Thomas?" he murmured into the darkness.

"Yes, Jonny?" The two were momentarily alone; the other lieutenant assigned to the cramped bunker was currently out in the trenches, checking on the watch.

"Thank you... for everything."

A silence fell before Thomas responded, his voice heavy with emotion. "No need to thank me, Jonny," he said after a brief pause, "now get some sleep—we have a long day ahead."

As John drifted off, the cacophony of war receded into the background, replaced by the steady cadence of Thomas' breathing. Amidst the hell of mud and blood, they had discovered a small haven in each other's presence—a delicate bond forged in the crucible of war.

When dawn broke on another cold, damp day, John, and Thomas ventured into the trenches to check on the men. Over the past six months, John knew each of them by name, learned details of their backstories—even tracking who had written to whom as he reviewed their mail sent home. Despite the grim conditions, morale remained buoyant, thanks to the deep sense of camaraderie born from their shared ordeal.

Although they had seen the devastation as wounded men were brought in from the front lines, they themselves had yet to experience combat. Everyone soon understood that they would either go to the front line or, if the Germans attacked, immediately be called forward.

All, except for Thomas and John were recent conscripts, most hailing from Norfolk. They were farm labourers, apprentices, factory workers, fishermen, boatmen, and a few sons of the well-to-do. Few were older than John or Thomas, and naturally looked up to their lieutenant and corporal for leadership and, to their surprise, comfort.

Many of the younger conscripts had only left home when called up and missed their families, but a few kind words and some genuine empathy went a long way in easing those homesick feelings. They encouraged close friendships, often forming between unlikely pairs—like the banker's son and a farm labourer, or the fisherman and the vicar's son.

After his morning rounds, in the dim light of late morning, John sat hunched over a makeshift desk, reviewing the men's correspondence home. Once he was alone—except for the sleeping fellow officer—he took out several of Christian's letters. His fingers traced the elegant script, each word a soothing balm for his war-weary soul. Even though a persistent scent of cordite drifted in the air, mingling with the earthy dampness of the trench, John's mind wandered far away, immersed in the warmth of Christian's words. He had not heard from Kip in over a year, but at least he knew he had survived the *Battle of Jutland*.

A FORBIDDEN LOVE

'My dearest Jonny,' he read, savouring the familiar term of endearment. *'The sea here reminds me of our summers in Norfolk. Do you remember that day we sailed and you somehow managed to whack me in the head with a boat hook?'* A bittersweet smile curved John's lip. He could almost hear the thud of wood striking Kip's forehead, feel the shock as he saw blood trickle from the cut, and picture the astonished expressions on both his and Kip's mothers' faces. And then there was Kip's laughter following the mishap, his humour once again dispelling the gravity of the moment: *"Haha, now I'll look like a real pirate with a scar."*

John picked up his pen and began writing with an urgency fuelled by a mix of longing and fear for what the coming days might hold.

'Somewhere in France, October 30th, 1917. My dearest Kip, if you are reading this letter, it means I might not be returning home. At least, not alive. I am deeply sorry that we will not get to carry out our plan together. However, I have made arrangements so you can proceed on your own. Please promise me you will at least try to find the happiness you truly deserve. The only genuine joy I have ever known came from the promises I have made to you.

That last night at Langley House was the brightest moment of my life, and I have no regrets about its meaning or significance. Live your life knowing that I am watching over you, and that I will be there to welcome you when your time comes. For now, I will keep your letters close to my heart literally; they are my shield against the insanity here. With all my love now and always, Jonny.'

He sealed the letter in an envelope and tucked it into his pocket, planning to give it to Thomas that evening along with an explanation. Just before midnight, John and Thomas found themselves alone once more.

"Thomas, I have something I want you to keep safe for me… just in case" John said, his voice wavering as he reached into his pocket and produced an envelope addressed simply to "Kip." Thomas took the envelope with a slow, almost reluctant nod, his eyes mirroring a turmoil he tried hard to conceal.

"I understand, Jonny," he replied after a long pause, tucking the letter carefully into his inner pocket.

"Do you really, Thomas? I mean, do you truly understand how important Kip is to me?" John's question was heavy with the burden of a truth he had long dreaded admitting, yet felt compelled in these circumstances to confess now. His heart pounded not only with anxiety over the secret's magnitude but also with the fear of facing Thomas' possible disapproval.

"I know exactly how much Kip means to you," Thomas murmured, locking eyes with John. There was a moment of quiet intensity, as if he was battling his own conflicted feelings. "I think I've always known, but it's become especially clear over these past few years." His smile, though meant to reassure, wavered with uncertainty.

"But—" John hesitated, his voice catching on the cusp of his confession, "but how?" Each syllable dripped with the gnawing worry that their secret was precariously exposed, vulnerable to another's notice.

"Don't worry, Jonny, no one else knows or even suspects," Thomas assured him, his tone both comforting and cautious. "I've made sure of that, and I'll always protect your secret." As he stepped closer, placing a hand on John's shoulder, a complex mix of trust and inner conflict played across his features. "I promise."

A FORBIDDEN LOVE

"Thank you, Thomas. I was so afraid you'd be ashamed of me, of us... but I needed someone to know the truth at least," John confessed, a single tear slipping down his cheek as a bittersweet wash of relief mingled with lingering fear. "How can I ever thank you?"

"Just by being happy, Jonny—both of you," Thomas replied matter-of-factly, though his words carried the weight of the struggle that might entail.

"Maybe you could come with us as well?" John ventured. Freed, if only momentarily, from the isolating burden of secrecy, he went on to describe their post-war plan: relocating to the south of France to buy a small villa. He spoke of taking an art course while Kip planned to operate a boat for paying tourists, even mentioning Kip's promise to buy him a piano—each detail mingled with hope, yet underscored by a pervasive uncertainty.

"It sounds like you've given this plenty of thought," Thomas remarked quietly, touched by the spark of joy in John's eyes even as he sensed the underlying hesitation.

"And of course, none of it would feel right without you watching over us. You'd have your own separate rooms away from the villa so you could build your own life too," John concluded, his tone both triumphant and trembling with a vulnerability that reflected his current dependence on Thomas. The heartfelt sentiment moved Thomas deeply, melting some of his usual reserve as he squeezed John's shoulder—a gesture laden with both affection and his own conflicted emotions.

"That is the kindest thing anyone has ever said to me..." his voice trailed off, caught between gratitude and an unspoken, lingering sorrow that such steps would be necessary.

"Then it's a deal," John declared with a fervent nod, masking the tempest of conflicting thoughts storming beneath his composed exterior.

"But let's survive this bloody war first, eh Jonny?" Thomas shot back, his voice steady despite the inner chaos, the looming uncertainties of both present and future casting shadows over them both like a heavy shroud.

"Yes, you're absolutely right, but there's something else I need to say," John pressed on with urgency. "I'm reminded of a conversation with my father just before I went up to Cambridge. He said, *'real friendships are not transactional'.*"

Thomas raised an eyebrow, curiosity piqued, trying to decipher John's deeper meaning. "In other words," John continued with intensity, "I didn't make the offer to you for after the war to settle any debt I might feel I owe you. I made it because you are my friend, our friend, and I fiercely want you to have a chance at happiness and freedom too."

Thomas stepped forward with determination, gripping John's hand in a resolute handshake, "it is indeed a deal then, Jonny."

November 19th, 1917

John stood rigid, his back pressed against the mud-caked wall, trying to steady his nerves as he surveyed the grim faces of his fellow soldiers. The tension was palpable, a living thing that writhed and coiled around them all.

A FORBIDDEN LOVE

"It won't be long now," John spoke to his assembled platoon, his usual composure betrayed by a slight tremor in his voice. "The offensive begins at dawn, and we move forward at the same time as part of the second wave." He folded the orders he has just received and placed them inside his top pocket.

Thomas nodded, unable to find his voice immediately, "now men, try to get some shut eye. Dismissed!" The men slowly shuffled away to their billets in the dugouts along this secondary trench system.

"I never imagined it would be like this," John whispered, more to himself than to Thomas. "The waiting... it's almost worse than I imagine the fighting will be." His fingers unconsciously sought the pocket where Christian's letters lay, a habit that had become as natural as breathing. The touch of the worn paper grounded him, even as his mind raced with thoughts of what lay ahead.

Thomas' eyes met his, a flicker of understanding passing between them. "It's the not knowing. Makes a man's mind play tricks on him."

A rat scurried past their feet, and John suppressed a shudder. He thought of the grand halls of Langley, of music and laughter, of Christian's smile. How far away it all seemed now, in this hell of mud and blood.

"Do you think we'll make it, Thomas?" The words slipped out before John could stop them, revealing a vulnerability he usually kept hidden.

Thomas was silent for a moment, his gaze distant. "We'll do our duty, Jonny. That's all any of us can do."

As the first light of dawn began to creep across the sky, a low rumble filled the air. It grew steadily, building to a deafening roar that shook the very earth beneath their feet. The British artillery barrage had begun. John's heart pounded in his chest; each beat a counterpoint to the thunderous explosions. He gripped his holstered pistol, knuckles white with tension.

"It's time," John said consulting his pocket watch, his voice barely audible over the cacophony. "Move the men forward along the communication trench. We will await our next orders there."

"Yes sir!" Thomas saluted the young lieutenant and he moved along the trench to usher the men forward. For the next hour they waited in the forward trench for news of the first assault. Each man was pressed hard against the trench walls, their fear and apprehension clear on their faces. Eventually a messenger appeared, salutes John and hands him a note and all eyes are upon him as he opens it.

"Corporal Cooper," John summoned Thomas to his side as he took out a folded map. "Here!" He stabbed his gloved hand on the map, "the first wave has reached *Lateaux Wood*, just north of *Bonavis*. We are to help them dig-in against any counter-attack." John took out his field binoculars and jumped on the firing step. Just through the smoke and haze of battle, he spotted a slight wooded rise about a mile in the distance above the ruins of a small village. "Corporal!" he summoned Thomas to join him and took out his pistol and pointed, "that way!"

Thomas roused and readied the men and all eyes were soon on John. He raised his whistle to his lips in his other hand, waited for second as he looked at the faces in the trench below him. *This is it* he said to himself, then let out a long shrill signal on the whistle.

He heard the reassuring voice of Thomas next to him, "stay low and keep moving," he shouted, "and look out for the Hun in shell holes!" They exchanged one last look, volumes spoken in that silent moment.

A FORBIDDEN LOVE

Then, with a surge of adrenaline and fear, they climbed out of the trench and into the chaos of what had been *No Man's Land* a few hours before, they were joined by multiple other units all along the line. The world around them was transformed into a nightmarish landscape. Shells exploded in great gouts of earth and flame, the air thick with smoke and screams. John stumbled forward, his legs moving of their own accord.

"Stay close!" Thomas shouted, his familiar presence a lifeline in the madness. As they advanced, John's thoughts turned once more to Christian. Would he ever see him again? Would he ever have the chance to speak the words that had long remained unspoken between them? With each step into the unknown, John Langley carried not just the weight of his duty, but the burden of a love that dared not speak its name.

The apocalyptic scene before them was beyond anything John had ever imagined. Shell craters pockmarked the earth like gaping wounds, filled with murky water and unspeakable debris. Twisted strands of barbed wire crisscrossed the hellscape, snagging on uniforms and tearing flesh. Acrid smoke burned John's eyes and throat, obscuring his vision in waves of choking grey as he kept his eyes fixed on the distant woods.

They crested a slight rise and found themselves at the edge of *Lateaux Wood*. The trees were splintered and broken; leaves stripped away by shellfire. In the dim light filtering through the smoke, John caught glimpses of khaki uniforms moving among the devastation.

Suddenly, a German soldier appeared from behind a shattered trunk, bayonet glinting. John froze, his revolver feeling impossibly heavy in his hand. Thomas reacted instantly, tackling the man to the ground. They grappled in the mud, a tangle of limbs and desperation. John's training kicked in. He raised his pistol, trying to get a clear shot, but the two men were too closely entwined. His hands shook violently.

"Do it!" Thomas yelled, pinning the German's arms. "Shoot, Jonny!"

The use of his pet name jolted John into action. He moved forward and took aim before he pulled the trigger. The bullet penetrated the German's neck passing over Thomas' shoulder. The man's eyes widened in shock, then glazed over.

As the body went limp, John stumbled backward, overwhelmed by what he had done. He had taken a life. The realisation hit him like a physical blow. Thomas scrambled to his feet, breathing heavily. "You alright?" John nodded numbly, unable to form words. "No time to dwell on it," Thomas said, his voice gentler than his words. "We need to dig in. This position won't hold itself."

As they began to carve out rudimentary trenches in the captured ground, John's thoughts whirled. He had imagined this moment countless times, but the reality was far worse than anything he had envisioned. The coppery taste of fear lingered on his tongue, mingling with the acrid smoke.

"I never thought it would be like this," John murmured, more to himself than to Thomas.

Thomas paused in his digging, meeting John's eyes. "Nobody ever does, sir. But we're still here. That's what matters now." John nodded, forcing himself to focus on the task at hand. As he dug, he could not help but wonder what Christian would think of him now. Would he still recognise the boy he had known, or had the horrors of war irrevocably changed him?

A FORBIDDEN LOVE

The sounds of battle continued to rage around them, but for John, they seemed oddly distant. In this moment, all that existed was the earth beneath his hands, the ache in his muscles, and the comforting presence of Thomas at his side.

They worked in silence, carving a temporary sanctuary in the blood-soaked earth of *Lateaux Wood*. With each shovel full of dirt, John felt a piece of his old self slipping away, replaced by something harder, more brittle.

As night fell, he whispered a silent prayer - not for victory, but for the strength to face whatever horrors tomorrow might bring. As he worked, the events of the day replayed in his mind. The face of the man he had killed, the friends he had seen fall. He thought of Christian, so far away and hopefully safe. Would he ever understand what John had experienced here? Could anyone?

Over the next couple of days, their position was effectively the front line. However, the Germans were distracted by the gains the British had made to the north of them, but they were still under constant artillery fire with no possibility of any further advance.

Along the whole part of this front the British now concentrated on consolidating their recent gains and reserves were brought to the front to relieve John's, however the German's had assembled a large counter-attack force which it used to make swift gains to the north.

November 30th, 1917

The dawn of November 30th broke with an ominous stillness. John, his uniform caked with mud and worse, peered over the hastily constructed parapet. The air felt heavy, charged with an electric anticipation that set his nerves on edge. And then it seemed as if the very gates of Hell had been opened.

The Germans targeted their position with artillery fire as they assaulted the woods through the village below. A messenger soon appeared amidst the heaviest part of the battle so far. John read the note and screamed for Thomas.

"Get the men ready to move out!" he was barely audible above the thunder of battle, "we're to head east along the ridge and road towards *Villers!*" Thomas mustered his troops and organised them into a rolling withdrawal as they were joined by more units from the west and north.

They moved cautiously along the recently dug trench line, fighting as they moved to prevent the German advance from over-running them. A scream cut through the air, different from the others. John's eyes locked onto a figure he recognised writhing just outside of the trench – one of their own, caught in the crossfire. Without thinking, he vaulted over the trench.

"Jonny, no!" Thomas' shout faded behind him as John crawled through the mud, bullets whizzing overhead. He reached the wounded soldier, a boy even younger than himself.

"I've got you," John gasped, gripping the boy's uniform. "Hold on." As he dragged the soldier back towards their lines, time seemed to slow. Every inch felt like a mile, every second an eternity. He could hear Christian's voice in his head, urging him on, telling him to be brave. "Almost there," John panted, more to himself than the wounded soldier. The trench loomed ahead, salvation just yards away.

A FORBIDDEN LOVE

A bullet kicked up dirt inches from John's face. He gritted his teeth, summoning strength he did not know he possessed. With a final, desperate heave, he tumbled back into the trench, the wounded soldier beside him. Thomas was there in an instant, pulling them both to safety. "You bloody fool," he hissed, but his eyes shone with pride. "That was the bravest thing I've ever seen."

John lay there, gasping for breath, the full weight of what he had done crashing over him. He had faced death and emerged victorious, if only for a moment. As the battle raged on around them, John closed his eyes, Christian's face vivid in his mind. For the first time since arriving at the front, he felt truly alive. However, once the adrenalin dissipated, he felt a searing pain erupt in his thigh, ripping a strangled cry from his throat. He looked down to see his uniform darkening with blood, the fabric torn where a bullet had found its mark.

"Thomas," he gasped, his vision swimming. "I think I've been hit."

Thomas' face paled as he assessed the wound. "We need to get you out of here, now."

As they stumbled towards their objective, the world around John became a blur of sound and fury. The earth shook beneath their feet, and he could taste copper on his tongue – blood or fear, he could not tell. "Stay with me, Jonny," Thomas urged, his voice tight with worry. "Just a little further." John's thoughts drifted to Christian, to the letters tucked safely in his breast pocket. Would he ever see him again? Would he ever have the chance to tell him...

Within a couple of hundred yards that seemed more like miles, their retreat came under the protective fire of the British positions to the east, but the threat from German artillery still remained. A deafening explosion rocked the air, and John felt a sharp, stinging sensation across his face and arms. Thomas cursed, pulling him closer.

"Shrapnel," Thomas muttered. "We're almost there, Jonny. Hold on." A deafening explosion rocked the earth, showering them with dirt and shrapnel. John felt a sharp sting across his cheek, and heard Thomas' muffled cry of pain as he took a hit to his shoulder. The world tilted sideways as they tumbled into the trench, a tangle of limbs and fear.

A makeshift dressing station materialised out of the smoky haze, a scene of controlled chaos. Men lay moaning on stretchers, while harried medics rushed between them. The air was thick with the heavy scent of blood and the acrid smell of antiseptic. Medics applied rudimentary bandages to both men's wounds and sent them to a field hospital behind the British lines.

As they stumbled through the winding trenches, John's thoughts drifted. He imagined Christian's face, worried and beautiful, reading his last letter. Would he ever see those eyes again? The pain and chaos faded, replaced by a strange, detached calm.

"Stay with me, Jonny," Thomas urged, his arm tight around John's waist. "We're almost there."

The field hospital, by its very size, was a vision from hell. Blood-soaked men lay moaning on makeshift cots, while harried medics rushed between them. The air was thick with the stench of antiseptic and death. Outside were laid hundreds of casualties, slowly being tended to by medics and nurses.

John's legs gave way, and he collapsed against Thomas. As darkness crept in at the edges of his vision, he heard Thomas' frantic voice: "Help! I need help here!"

A FORBIDDEN LOVE

The last thing John saw before consciousness slipped away was Thomas' face, streaked with dirt and blood, his hazel eyes wide with fear. John wanted to reach out, to tell him it would be alright, but the darkness claimed him before he could form the words.

December 8th, 1917

The antiseptic scent of the hospital room in Kent mingled with the fragrance of fresh-cut flowers, creating an odd juxtaposition that made John's head swim. Sunlight streamed through the tall windows, casting long shadows across the polished floor. He blinked, his eyes adjusting to the brightness after days of fitful sleep.

Thomas sat by the bed, his familiar presence a balm to John's frayed nerves. "How are you feeling, Jonny?" he asked, his voice soft with concern. John attempted a wan smile before surveying his raised and heavily plastered leg, relieved that it was still there. He pointed weakly at his bandaged leg. "Luckily, the bullet ricocheted off your thigh bone and missed a major artery."

"I think I know where it came out," he grimaced as he tried to sit up. Thomas chuckled, the sound warming John's chest. "Your humour's returned. That's a good sign." As John shifted in the bed, a sharp pain lanced through his side also. He winced, memories of the shelling flooding back.

"Shrapnel from when we were taking you to the dressing station." Thomas opened his hospital jacket to reveal his heavily bandaged shoulder, "I got a souvenir too."

"The men... did they... did Saunders?" John was asking about the young farmer who he had pulled back into the trench.

"Saunders is doing well, a couple of beds along from me in the ward upstairs, as for the others...," Thomas soothed, placing a gentle hand on John's arm. "Don't trouble yourself with that now. You need to rest." John closed his eyes, fighting back tears.

"I keep seeing their faces, Thomas. The men we lost. Was it worth it? All this... sacrifice?"

Thomas was quiet for a long moment. When he spoke, his voice was heavy with emotion. "I don't know if I can answer that, Jonny. But I do know that what you did out there... it was brave. Heroic, even."

John scoffed, opening his weary eyes to meet Thomas' gaze. "Heroic? No, Thomas, the real heroes are those that never made it back."

A FORBIDDEN LOVE

Lieutenant Lord John Langley, June 1917

A FORBIDDEN LOVE

CHAPTER THIRTEEN
BONDS OF WAR

May 1918

John, after four months of recovery and recuperation, returned to service; however, movement restrictions led to his reassignment from the front to a staff position. Along with this move, and in recognition of the way he had led his men, he also received a field commission to the rank of captain.

The envelope trembled in Lord John Langley's hand, its heavy cream paper bearing the official *War Office* seal. Sunlight filtered through the tall windows of his temporary quarters in *Montreuil-sur-Mer*, northern France, casting long shadows across the sparse furnishings—a military cot, a writing desk, and a single chair where Thomas sat, watching him with quiet concern. The army reassigned Captain Langley to a staff posting at its General Headquarters.

"Distinguished Service Order," John murmured, the words tasting foreign on his tongue.

Thomas rose from his chair, moving with the practiced efficiency that had characterised their relationship for years. "Congratulations are in order. Your father will be very proud." His voice carried that familiar Norfolk lilt, softened by years in service to the Langley family.

"Would he? I wonder if even he would find meaning in all this... this senseless waste. He worked tirelessly for peace in 1914." He gestured vaguely toward the window, beyond which lay the devastated French countryside.

"The men respect you," Thomas said. "They'll be pleased to see recognition for your actions at *Lateaux Wood*."

John closed his eyes; the mere mention of the battle conjuring images he had spent months trying to forget. The mud, the screams, the stomach-churning stench of death.

"I did nothing heroic, Thomas. I simply survived while others didn't."

"You led your men through hell, Jonny. That counts for something."

The room felt suddenly stifling. John loosened his tie, fighting the constriction in his throat. "This promotion... it takes me further from the front lines but closer to the machinery of death. Staff officer. Reading casualty reports while sipping tea in some requisitioned château."

Thomas' warm hazel eyes met his, steady and grounding. "Perhaps you might do more good there, than in the trenches?"

"Or perhaps I'll simply be another cog in the wheel, sending men to their deaths with the stroke of a pen." Energy seemed to sap out of him as he recalled the horrors he had been part of. "God, Thomas. When I think of those boys— barely men—in the mud in the woods..."

"You needn't think of it now, Jonny."

"But I must," John whispered. "Someone must remember them." He walked to the window, gazing out at the apple orchard beyond. The apple blossoms in stark contrast to his thoughts. Thomas appeared at his side, silent but present, his reflection in the glass a comforting shadow. How many times had Thomas stood thus, bearing witness to John's private moments of doubt and despair?

A FORBIDDEN LOVE

"I dreamt of Christian last night," John admitted, his voice barely audible. The confession hung between them, dangerous yet necessary. "I was playing on the piano for him in the music room at Langley Hall. Just as I did that summer before... before everything."

Thomas remained still, his silence neither judgmental nor encouraging, but he was reminded of how he had observed the two of them that night and he simply accepted their situation.

"I wonder where he is now," John continued. "If he misses my playing for him?"

"Music endures, Jonny, even in the darkest times," Thomas continued to try and reassure, "and besides, the German Navy has not ventured out of port since *Jutland*, so we must assume he is at least safe."

John offered a brittle smile. "It's been over two years since we were able to write to each other, but I suppose you are right - he is safe in port at least."

A discreet knock interrupted their moment. Thomas moved swiftly to the door, receiving a stack of papers from a young private who snapped a smart salute before departing.

"Your reports Captain," Thomas said, placing them on the desk. John's shoulders stiffened as he returned to the desk. The topmost page listed casualties from a recent offensive—names reduced to ink on paper, lives condensed to regiment numbers and dates of death.

"Two hundred and forty-three men," he read aloud. "In a single day. For what? A cricket pitch's length of mud that will be lost again by week's end." Bitterness seeped into his voice. "And here I sit, promoted for my service, while they lie in unmarked graves."

Thomas poured a measure of whisky from the decanter on the side table, placing it within John's reach. "You honour them by remembering. By questioning."

"Questions won't bring them back," John said, taking a grateful sip of the amber liquid. It burned pleasantly, momentarily distracting from the hollow ache in his chest. "Nothing will bring any of them back. I used to believe in glory, Thomas. In honour and duty and all those grand ideals my father espoused." John's voice cracked slightly. "Now I only believe in survival. In finding moments of humanity amid the barbarity."

Thomas stood at attention, his posture straight but his eyes gentle. "Then perhaps your new position offers opportunity for that, sir. To infuse humanity into decisions that might otherwise lack it."

John considered this, running his finger along the edge of the casualty report. "You always did see light where I see only shadow."

"Someone must, Jonny," Thomas replied, the ghost of a smile lifting the corner of his mouth.

Tomorrow, he would report his summary to headquarters, and continue to wade through the paperwork of war. But tonight, in this quiet room with Thomas' steadfast presence beside him, he allowed himself to feel both the honour and the burden of survival.

As darkness fell outside, John returned to the window, watching as stars appeared one by one above the scarred French landscape. Somewhere beneath those same stars, Christian might be looking upward too—separated by war, by nationality, by the vast, unbridgeable distance of opposing sides.

A FORBIDDEN LOVE

John pressed his forehead against the cool glass and closed his eyes, allowing himself one moment of weakness before tomorrow's facade of strength must begin.

The morning briefing room buzzed with the low murmur of officers comparing notes, the sharp scent of coffee mingling with tobacco and wool uniforms still damp from the morning mist. John stood by the wall map, his newly acquired captain's uniform still felt stiff and somehow fraudulent against his skin. He traced the red pins marking Allied positions, each one representing hundreds of men waiting in trenches, in foxholes, in hastily constructed shelters—waiting for orders that might send them to their deaths.

"Quite the collection of brass in here today," came a voice to his right, the accent unmistakably American, with vowels stretched wide like the streets of New York.

John turned to find himself facing a lieutenant about his own age, perhaps a year or two older. The man's blond hair, nearly the same shade as John's own, was cropped close beneath his cap, and his blue eyes held a directness that was simultaneously disarming and refreshing.

"Gentlemen," Colonel Hadley's voice boomed, silencing the murmurs. "I'd like to introduce Lieutenant Piotr Kowalski, our new liaison from the *American Expeditionary Forces.*"

"Lieutenant Piotr Kowalski," the man said, extending his hand. "Though everyone calls me Pete."

"Captain Lord John Langley," John replied, taking the offered hand. Pete's grip was firm, his palm calloused in a way that suggested familiarity with manual labour rather than just weapons training. "Though the *'lord'* part is merely a courtesy, I'm afraid."

Pete's eyebrows rose. "A real English aristocrat? Wait until I tell my mother back in *Brooklyn*. She'll never believe her son is hobnobbing with nobility."

Despite himself, John felt a smile tugging at his lips. "I assure you, Lieutenant, there's nothing particularly noble about reading casualty reports and coordinating artillery placements."

"Fair enough, but still—" Pete gestured vaguely at John, "—you've got that whole... I don't know... dignified thing going on."

Before John could respond, Colonel Hadley called the room to attention. As the officers arranged themselves around the large oak table, John found himself beside Pete, their shoulders nearly touching in the crowded space. The American smelled of bay rum aftershave and something else—perhaps the faint trace of cigarettes not quite British in their composition. John found himself oddly fascinated by the newcomer's easy smile, so at odds with the grim faces surrounding them.

As the briefing progressed, he could not help but notice how Pete's questions were incisive, revealing a keen intelligence beneath his affable exterior. The briefing concluded with typical military efficiency—updates on German positions, artillery batteries, supply lines. John took careful notes, his handwriting precise even as his mind wandered to the reality behind each statistic and strategic point.

When Hadley mentioned a particularly heavy bombardment near *Arras*, John's pen faltered, memories of mud and blood and screams momentarily overwhelming his carefully constructed composure.

"You okay there, Captain?" Pete whispered, his voice low enough that only John could hear.

John blinked, forcing himself back to the present. "Perfectly fine, thank you," he murmured, though his knuckles had gone white around his fountain pen.

Pete said nothing more, but when the briefing concluded, he lingered as other officers filed out and made his way towards Jonny, "Captain Langley, you wouldn't know where this Yankee could find a decent coffee in this place would you?"

John hesitated, his ingrained reserve warring with an inexplicable desire for company. "I might," he found himself saying. "Though I warn you, our definition of *'decent'* may differ from yours." John found himself smiling again, the expression feeling foreign on features that had grown accustomed to careful neutrality. "I believe I can help with that. My batman managed to procure some actual coffee beans last week—a minor miracle in these parts."

"Your what now?"

"My batman—ah, my personal servant. Corporal Cooper."

Pete's eyes widened. "You brought your butler to war? That might be the most British thing I've ever heard."

"He's not exactly…" John began, then hesitated, realising that trying to explain the nuanced relationship he had with Thomas was futile for an American so refreshingly direct. "Anyway, the coffee offer still stands if you're interested."

"Show me the way, Captain Langley," Pete said with a wide smile. "I haven't had a decent cup since *Paris*."

As they made their way to the improvised officers' mess, John felt a surprising calm wash over him. Pete's presence seemed to momentarily dispel the constant, lingering gloom of war. They settled at a small table near one of the room's large windows. Nearby, Thomas was stationed against the wall with several other officers' aides, and he quickly approached Jonny.

"Ah, Corporal Cooper, I assume," Pete declared, leaping to his feet and extending a hand toward Thomas. "My coffee saviour, I believe." Thomas raised an eyebrow at the young American's casualness and glanced toward Jonny, seeking a cue.

"This is Lieutenant Kowalski, an American Liaison Officer who has just joined GHQ," Jonny said with his customary formality, then added, "and I've promised him some of your excellent coffee."

"Very well, sir. I'll bring a large pot," Thomas replied with a nod as he headed into the service area.

"I'm guessing, Captain," Pete said, nodding toward the medal ribbon above John's breast pocket, "that you've seen some action in this war." There was something in Pete's tone—free from judgment and stripped of the usual bravado—that compelled John to answer genuinely.

"*Lateaux Wood.*"

"The German counter-attack last year," John confirmed. "I read about it. By all accounts, you were lucky to get out of there."

"Not everyone was lucky. I lost a lot of good men that day," John's face turned sombre once more, though he was surprised by Pete's knowledgeable response.

Pete emitted a low whistle. "No wonder you earned that fancy medal. Sounds like it was pure hell."

A FORBIDDEN LOVE

"An accurate assessment," John replied, surprised by his own candour. "And you, Lieutenant? Have you faced the front lines?"

"Two months near *Cantigny*, until they decided my Polish might be useful for intelligence work," Pete responded with a shrug. "Not the grand adventure I had imagined when I enlisted, but I can't complain."

John studied the American, noting the slight tension around his eyes hidden beneath his relaxed demeanour. "I suppose few things in this war have turned out exactly as anyone expected." At that moment, Thomas returned with the coffee and left them to their conversation. Pete grinned as he took his first sip of the steaming brew.

"Now that's good!"

"I'm sure that Thom... I mean Corporal Cooper, will be reassured to hear that," John said, accepting the compliment.

"So, Captain, what's the story behind you and Corporal Cooper?" Pete asked. Normally, John would have found such a question impertinent, but he felt completely at ease with Pete. Grateful for a chance to discuss something beyond the war, he replied:

"We've known each other our whole lives. When we were boys, we used to play together at my family's country home with my cousin. In fact, his father managed the farm on the estate for my father," John explained, pausing to calculate mentally, "and our families have been associated for nearly two hundred years."

"Wow!" exclaimed Pete, "that's longer than my country has existed!" Jonny chuckled at the remark.

"And then, when I was seventeen, my father hired him as my valet when I went off to university, and, well," John said with a warm smile, "we've stuck together ever since."

"So, he's your friend too?" Pete teased; Jonny playfully placed a finger on his lips as he whispered.

"Yes, but you mustn't let anyone else know. It's not exactly proper or the way we do things," John confided, feeling a wave of relief at finally sharing this secret with someone other than Christian. Remarkably, he had only spent two hours with this man, yet here he was, divulging his private truth.

"Understood," Pete replied with a conspiratorial wink. "Is it more of a lord and peasant issue, or is it the divide between an officer and his enlisted men?" John was taken aback by the young American's keen insight.

"Somewhat of both," John admitted with an honest chuckle. "It would be far more problematic for Thomas than for me, which I both understand and respect. So," he added, fingers steepled contemplatively, "we behave properly in public."

A smile lit his face as he recalled a conversation they had had three years earlier at Langley House. "Sometimes he has to remind me not to be too informal around others."

"Your little secret is safe with me, Captain, but..." Pete said coyly, his smile taking on a mischievous quality, "such restrictions do not exist in the American army."

This final remark puzzled John—was it simply an observation about the cultural and social contrasts between them, or, he quickly dismissed the thought, a subtle hint of interest in Thomas?

137

A FORBIDDEN LOVE

When the topic turned to his American roots, Pete spoke of his Brooklyn upbringing, reminiscing about his childhood spent on the streets of *Brooklyn* and his family's business nestled deep within *New York City's* Polish community. His words mingled pride with nostalgia.

"It must have been quite an adjustment," John mused, "transitioning from such a vibrant community to... well, this." He gestured vaguely at their current surroundings.

Pete's gaze clouded momentarily. "It was. Yet in some respects, it felt like an escape." He paused to choose his words carefully. "There were certain expectations, you know? The burden of tradition, family responsibilities..."

John felt a surge of understanding. "I understand that all too well," he said softly, thinking of his own fate and the unspoken pressures that came with his position. Their eyes met, and in that brief moment, John sensed a deeper connection—an unspoken understanding between them. He fleetingly thought of Christian, of secret moments and concealed desires, and wondered if Pete harboured similar hidden truths.

As they eventually parted ways, John found himself eagerly anticipating their next meeting—a feeling that was both thrilling and unsettling. Despite the war's lingering horrors, the spark of an unexpected friendship had begun to bloom in this unlikely setting.

The post-briefing coffee with Lieutenant Kowalski soon became a daily ritual for John, during which he noticed Pete's growing curiosity about Thomas' life. Their conversations were light and easy, yet each day, Pete's interest in his old friend seemed to deepen. John reassured himself that it was merely a reflection of their shared social standing.

Then one day, he observed Pete reaching for the coffee pot simultaneously with Thomas, and neither moved away as hastily as they normally would. It reminded John of the accidental touches he once enjoyed with Kip.

"Pete," John began, immediately regretting his choice of words but pressing on, "if you ever wish to meet Thomas socially, I would have no objections."

Pete's eyes widened in surprise. "But you mentioned that it isn't customary for officers to fraternise with enlisted men."

"At least not in the British army," John countered with a knowing smile. "But apparently that isn't the case in yours. As you once pointed out to me." He triumphantly noted the blush creeping up on Pete's cheeks. "Well, I must be off now, so I'll let you finish your coffee." As he walked away, he leaned in and murmured something into Thomas' ear.

Moments later, Thomas, standing by the table, addressed him: "Lieutenant, Captain Langley mentioned you had a question for me."

"Oh," Pete was momentarily taken aback, his usual self-assurance slipping away. "Oh, oh, yes, I have."

"And he mentioned that whatever it was, the Captain was happy with it," Thomas spoke softly, unsure of what John had agreed to.

Pete inhaled deeply, "do you know the village square?"

"Of course, sir," Thomas replied, a puzzled expression on his face.

"Then meet me at eight o'clock at *'Bar Rochelle'*?" Pete suggested anxiously.

"That's the bar frequented by the Americans."

A FORBIDDEN LOVE

"Exactly, Corporal," Pete confirmed, hoping they understood what he implied. Thomas pondered the words for a moment before realising the significance of the venue—a bar shared by both American officers and enlisted men, unlike the British bars, which separated officers from enlisted personnel.

"Erm, alright then, thank you, Lieutenant," Thomas nodded, clearing the table while lost in thought. An hour later Thomas found John at his desk in his quarters.

"Ah, corporal Connor, I was wondering where you were," John said with the cheekiest grin he could muster, "did you manage to speak to Lieutenant Kowalski?"

"Don't you *'corporal Connor'* me Jonny!" Thomas tried to maintain a serious countenance, but failed as his face broke into a grin.

"How did you know?" In truth, he had already accepted John's intervention, but he then worried he had made his feelings too obvious.

"Probably the same way you worked things out with Kip and I, and don't worry no one else will have noticed," he tried to reassure his friend, "and it took me a week, despite having known you all of my life. I did the right thing, didn't I?"

"It was a surprise I won't deny it and it made me examine my own feelings. But yes, I think it was a good thing you did."

"The lieutenant, I mean Pete, has said nothing to me specifically, so I don't want to make any assumptions, but I know that I spend more time talking about you when I am with him than anything else," John continued. "I may be completely wrong about there being any great significance to his interest in you when all he might want is a friend."

"And there was only one way I could find out?" Thomas acknowledged.

"Exactly. So, what did he say?"

"He asked me to join him in the American bar in the village for a drink tonight. Apparently, officers and enlisted men mix freely there."

"Good, then you won't feel out of place or awkward. And let's face it, he is a rather affable and likeable chap."

"Charming too," added Thomas.

"Oh yes, that he is!" Jonny himself blushed a little with this confession - and he had wanted to add *'handsome'* but chose not to, "now, go and enjoy yourself Thomas, you deserve it, go make a new friend."

Over the next several weeks, John increasingly found himself in Lieutenant Kowalski's company. What began as simple morning coffee sessions gradually turned into working lunches, occasional dinners, and long walks through the ruined village that served as their headquarters whenever duty permitted.

Pete's inexhaustible energy and straightforward manner provided a striking contrast to John's reserved nature, and he spoke more freely with the American than with anyone except Thomas.

Yet he always respected Thomas' privacy, never prying into the bond between him and Pete. All he knew for certain was that Thomas now carried himself with a lightness he hadn't seen since before the war.

"Really, you've never had a hot dog?" Pete asked one evening as they sat in John's quarters with a bottle of cognac between them—another of Thomas' remarkable acquisitions. John swirled the amber liquid in his glass and replied,

"I'm afraid Eton and Mayfair didn't exactly cater to *New York's* culinary traditions."

A FORBIDDEN LOVE

Pete chuckled, a rich, unguarded sound that John seldom heard these days. "When this is all over, I'm taking you and Thomas to *'Nathan's'*. They say they have the best hot dogs in the world."

"I shall hold you to that," John responded, comforted by the fantasy of a future beyond endless reports and telegrams laden with death. Thomas popped in to see if the officers were well-settled. "You've come at the perfect time, Thomas."

"Sir?" Thomas said.

"Close the door, Thomas," John ordered as he poured him a drink and gestured for him to sit at the end of the bed. There was something compelling in his command that left no room for argument. "And relax—a few minutes with us won't unravel England's social fabric or compromise the army's command structure."

"If you say so, Jonny, especially since this is an excellent brandy, well worth sharing," Thomas replied with a broad smile.

"By the way, Pete mentioned these *'hotdogs'* and promised he'd take us both to sample the best of them in *New York*," John said, happily noting how Thomas seemed to relax, his eyes lingering on Pete.

"I'd recommend at least trying one, as I did the other night at the American bar in the village. It was nothing like anything I've ever tasted before," Thomas added.

"I'm not sure that's the highest endorsement I've heard, Thomas," Pete quipped, and the three men broke into a comfortable, quiet laughter.

After finishing his drink, Pete stood up. "It's getting late, so I should head back to my quarters."

"Of course, Pete. Thank you for your company tonight, as always," John said warmly, rising to shake his hand. Then he turned to Thomas and said, "Corporal, would you kindly escort the lieutenant to his accommodation block? It's rather dark out there, after all," accompanied by a playful wink.

"Of course, sir. I'd be happy to," Thomas replied, saluting his captain. "Thank you, Jonny."

As the door closed, John's thoughts immediately drifted to Christian—raven-haired Christian with his serious eyes and stunning smile—somewhere across no-man's land in a German naval uniform.

The memory brought both warmth and a hollow ache to his chest as he watched his new friend depart with his oldest one. The ease with which Thomas and Pete interacted stirred bittersweet memories of his times with Kip.

The two men proceeded slowly and cautiously through the darkness across the courtyard, Pete's movements slightly
unsteady from alcohol. "That was really kind of Jonny to invite you to join us," he remarked.

"Yes, it was, even if it isn't exactly allowed," Thomas replied earnestly, teasing the Polish officer.

"Lighten up, Thomas!" Pete said, then noticed the broad smile on the Englishman's face. "I swear, I'll never quite grasp your British sense of humour."

A FORBIDDEN LOVE

After escorting Pete to his quarters, Thomas returned to Jonny's room. he knocked and entered. "I have safely returned Lieutenant Kowalski to his billet," he said, looking down at John who sat alone in his quarters, staring unseeing at reports that should have commanded his full attention. "Will there be anything else you require tonight?"

John looked up, desperate not to be alone with his thoughts. "Stay a moment, would you?"

If Thomas was surprised, he concealed it. He nodded and took a seat when John gestured to the chair opposite.

"Is something troubling you, Jonny?"

John closed his eyes briefly. "Everything, I think." When he opened them again, Thomas was watching him with the same steady gaze that had been a constant in John's life since childhood. Something about that unwavering loyalty broke the dam inside him. "I'm not sure I know who I am anymore, Thomas," John said, his voice barely above a whisper. "This war, this uniform, these responsibilities—they've changed me. And now there's Lieutenant Kowalski..."

"We are only friends Jonny," Thomas observed neutrally.

"Yes, I know, but even if you were more than that," John twisted his signet ring nervously, "it wouldn't matter to me of course. He's a kind man with a good heart." Thomas waited patiently as John struggled for words.

"But all I can still think about is Christian," John continued, the admission painful. "His face, his voice. As if I were betraying him somehow by spending time with Pete, which is absurd considering we haven't seen each other in years, may never see each other again."

"The heart doesn't always follow reason, Jonny."

John laughed bitterly. "Isn't that the truth." He stood, pacing to the window where the rain was streaking the glass. "Sometimes I dream he's dead, Thomas. I dream that a telegram will arrive announcing that Prince Christian was killed in action, and I'll never have the chance to... His voice broke.

"To what?" Thomas asked softly.

"To tell him that nothing has changed for me," John whispered, pressing his forehead against the cool glass. "That despite everything—the war, our families, these years apart—I still..." He could not finish.

Thomas was silent for a long moment before speaking. "If I may, Jonny, perhaps what you are feeling now isn't a betrayal of your feelings for Kip, but... a reminder that your heart is still capable of connection. After all you've seen and been through."

John turned, surprised by the insight. "I hadn't thought of it that way."

"Life continues, even in war. Perhaps especially in war." Thomas stood, straightening his jacket. "And if I might be so bold, I believe Kip would understand that better than most."

John felt a tear slide down his cheek, quickly wiping it away. "Thank you, Thomas. I don't know what I'd do without you."

"Fortunately," Thomas replied with the ghost of a smile, "that's not something you need to consider. I'll be here as long as you need me." With those words Thomas formulated a plan in his mind of how he might help Jonny recall some happier times with Kip.

A FORBIDDEN LOVE

After Thomas left, John returned to the window, watching raindrops trace lonely paths down the glass. Christian's face rose unbidden in his mind—not as he would last seen him, stiff and formal in his naval uniform, but years before, laughing as they raced their horses across the meadows of Langley Hall, young and carefree and oblivious to the future that awaited them.

The following evening, Jonny and Pete sat together in the officers' mess, a room buzzing with conversation that masked the surrounding war. Wisps of cigarette smoke layered beneath the low ceiling, diffusing the yellow lamplight into a soft, dreamy haze. Each man cradled a glass of champagne while Thomas, who had somehow come by the champagne bottle, attended to them. Jonny preferred not to know too much about the origins of Thomas' latest finds.

Leaning over the table to top off their glasses, Thomas casually whispered something into Pete's ear. Straightening up, he announced, "Captain Langley, I believe the Lieutenant has something to ask you."

Jonny arched an eyebrow. "I'm not sure I understand, Corporal."

"Your batman mentioned you play the piano," Pete explained, nodding toward the upright sitting in the corner—a graceful yet timeworn instrument likely taken from a French family's parlour. "And not just play. According to him, you're brilliant."

A blush warmed Jonny's cheeks. "Thomas exaggerates, and he knows I haven't played in years."

Pete's blue eyes twinkled with mischief as he embraced Thomas' little scheme. "Apparently, you could have been a concert pianist if you hadn't been born with a title."

Jonny made a silent vow to remind Thomas later about discussing personal matters. "My father would have disowned me at the mere suggestion," he joked at the thought.

The piano sat in the corner like an unspoken challenge, its brass candlesticks catching the light. Ever since his arrival, Jonny had avoided it, well aware of how music could dredge up buried emotions.

"Come on, Johnny," Pete urged, using the nickname reserved for their private moments. "The men here deserve something better than gramophone records and bawdy tunes."

"I'm not sure—"

"Just a single piece. For morale," Pete insisted, leaning closer so only Jonny could hear. "For me and Thomas."

Finally, he acquiesced with a quiet clink as he set down his glass. "One piece."

As Jonny walked over to the piano, the room's chatter dwindled to silence. The familiar weight of expectation settled on his shoulders—distinct from the burdens of command yet strangely intertwined. He lowered himself onto the bench and let his fingers hover with uncertainty over the keys, reacquainting themselves with their smooth, yellowed surface.

A fleeting thought crossed his mind about what Christian would say if he could see him now. He hesitated, pondering what to play. One might expect a martial, stirring piece—something like *'Rule, Britannia!'* or *'Men of Harlech.'* Yet his fingers seemed to have a different idea.

A FORBIDDEN LOVE

Instead, he settled on an old favourite, Debussy's *'Clair de Lune'*. The soft, opening notes filled the suddenly hushed room, resonating with memories of hours lost to practice and the pure joy of surrendering to the music.

The melody evoked visions of moonlight shimmering over water—a world of peace and transcendent beauty far removed from his own. At first, his notes came out hesitant, tentative. But as Jonny's fingers found their familiar rhythm, muscle memory took over.

He closed his eyes and allowed the bittersweet melody—a tune of longing and loss—to flow through him. His thoughts drifted: of Christian, of moonlit nights and brief, stolen glances; of Kip's warm laughter and the spark of understanding in his eyes; and of Thomas' steadfast presence, a lone rock amid tumultuous emotions. The music rose, carrying with it everything Jonny had left unsaid.

All conversation in the mess was abandoned except for the haunting strains of the piano. In the dim light by the door, Thomas watched on, his heart heavy for his young master. For a fleeting moment, he saw a glimpse of the free-spirited boy Jonny once was, before duty and expectations weighed him down.

The pace quickened as his fingers flew over the keys, channelling a swell of emotion into the music. Each note expressed a sentence he could not speak aloud, every crescendo a hidden confession. His playing became a bridge, spanning vast divides—across the Channel, past enemy lines, and over the years that had kept him apart from Christian.

In that moment, the room around him seemed to vanish. He was no longer Captain Lord John Langley, decorated and burdened by duty, but simply John—a seventeen-year-old once again, playing in the familiar music room at Langley Hall for Christian, their knees barely apart on the bench as golden summer light filled the space.

When the last notes dwindled into silence, John lingered motionless, his hands hesitating above the keys as if unwilling to break the enchantment. The stillness was complete: no coughs, no shifting in seats, no clinking of glasses. Slowly, he blinked, drawing himself back from that dreamlike state to the smoke-filled officers' mess and the looming war just beyond its walls.

Then someone exhaled audibly. "Good God, Langley, bravo!" a colonel called out from the back of the room.

Across the room, Pete observed him with a look that mixed wonder with a deeper, almost personal sentiment. "I didn't know," he remarked.

John felt suddenly vulnerable, as if he had confessed much more than his skill on the piano. He rose, giving a hesitant nod in response to the scattered applause that had emerged.

"Encore!" someone shouted.

"I'm afraid that's all for tonight, gentlemen," John responded, his voice steadier than he felt. "We have an early briefing tomorrow."

As he made his way to the door, accepting the compliments with nods, he caught sight of Thomas standing in the shadow near the entrance. The batman's face wore a quiet pride and recognition. Thomas, who had known him since childhood—who had packed his first cricket bat for Eton and helped him dress for his inaugural London Season—looked at him as if seeing an old friend long absent.

A FORBIDDEN LOVE

Their eyes met for a moment. Thomas offered a barely noticeable nod, silently acknowledging that for a few precious minutes, the John of before the war—the one who had raced horses with Christian through Norfolk fields and dreamt of beauty rather than death—had returned.

John slipped into the cool night, now able to breathe without restraint. The lingering strains of his music echoed in his mind, a brief escape from the impending war that would resume at dawn. As he walked across the courtyard toward his quarters, he failed to notice Pete and Thomas following until, after he shut his door, he found them waiting outside.

"The lieutenant mentioned that you and he might share a nightcap," Thomas mumbled.

"Yes," John replied slowly blinking. "Of course." He beckoned them inside. Each officer settled into a seat while Thomas poured them generous measures of brandy before excusing himself.

"That performance was incredible, John. It genuinely seemed to carry you away from all this," Pete remarked, nodding toward the scattered reminders of war in John's room.

"Thank you," John murmured. "Playing brought back memories of better times." Leaning closer to Pete, he asked, "what did Thomas say to you in the mess hall, exactly?"

Pete chuckled. "He only mentioned that I should ask you to play again, saying you're exceptionally gifted, and maybe the distraction would do you some good."

"Dear Thomas, he really understands me," John chuckled. Then he paused, weighing his next words. "What has Thomas told you about my cousin Christian?"

"You mean the boy you and Thomas used to spend time within the country?" Pete replied almost to himself. John nodded. "Not much—just that it's been a while since you've seen him. I suppose he's enlisted too then?"

"Not exactly." John ran a hand through his hair, struggling to find words that would not reveal too much about what he and Christian once shared. "He was... is... on my father's side of the family. My aunt married a German prince, which meant Christian ended up in the German navy."

"That must really complicate things," Pete observed, his tone free of judgment as he got straight to the heart of the matter.

John exhaled; aware he had been holding his breath. "You could say that."

"And you miss him," Pete stated plainly, not posing it as a question.

"I don't even know what I feel anymore," John admitted, staring into his nearly empty glass. "But in the end, we were more than friends." His words hung in the air as Pete considered them, while John worried that this confession could lead to his disgrace and dismissal from the army.

"So," Pete said calmly, "you were in love?" John silently agreed, too hesitant to meet his eyes. "Hey John, look at me." Slowly, John lifted his watery eyes to meet the American's gaze. "I assume Thomas is aware, so your secret is safe with both of us." A wave of relief washed over John, and he smiled.

A FORBIDDEN LOVE

"Thank you, Pete," John said, sitting up and regaining his composure. "That truly means a lot to me." At last, John had shared the one truth that defined him with someone other than Thomas. "And for what it's worth, I do know how I feel—I love Christian, even though it's been years, and we now find ourselves on opposite sides of a war."

"I'll drink to that, my lord!" Pete declared, clinking his glass against John's, sealing yet another bond of secrecy.

A few nights later, Thomas and Pete sat together at a table in the American bar, enjoying each other's company in a way that was, at least for Thomas, unfamiliar. "I had a good chat with Jonny the other night," Pete began, pausing as he realised, he was not breaking any confidences before continuing, "he told me all about Christian and how hard things are for him right now."

"Thank you, Pete. It is good that he doesn't have just me to confide in."

"Don't mention it, old boy," Pete replied, attempting an English upper-class accent as he reached across the table to tap Thomas' hand.

"So, what about you? What will you do once we finally stick it to the Kaiser and head home?" Pete asked, his tone stirred by memories of Jonny's plans.

The simple question, rarely posed, took Thomas by surprise. "I haven't really thought about it," he fibbed. "I plan to stay on with Jonny. It's what's expected of me, I suppose."

Pete snorted lightly. "Expected, huh? I know all about that. My folks expected me to take over my father's butcher shop, marry a nice Polish girl from the neighbourhood, have a dozen kids." He took a long swallow from his cognac. "Sometimes I wonder if I enlisted just to escape all those expectations."

Thomas examined Pete's face in the lamplight, noticing the tension in his jaw and the slight furrow of his brows. "And what would you choose if expectations weren't holding you back?" Pete turned to face him, a flash of vulnerability crossing his features.

"I'd travel. I'd see the world beyond *Brooklyn* and the battlefields. Maybe even settle somewhere where no one knows my name or what I'm meant to be." He gave a self-deprecating smile. "Sounds a bit foolish, doesn't it?"

"Not at all," Thomas replied softly. "I think it sounds incredibly brave."

Their eyes locked, and for a moment, Thomas felt as if he were looking into a mirror—not of his appearance, but of something deeper, more essential. The moment stretched, heavy with unspoken understanding, until Pete cleared his throat and looked away.

Nearly spent, the lamp oil cast long, shifting shadows over the small table where John and Pete sat. Outside, rain tapped against the windows, a soothing backdrop to the occasional distant rumble of artillery. Emboldened suddenly, Thomas asked, "So there isn't anyone special waiting for you back home?"

Pete leaned back in his chair, his American accent softening as he replied quietly. "No, there's no one special back there. Just here." His blue eyes met Thomas' with an intensity that stole his breath. "Do you understand what I'm saying, Corporal?"

The air between them seemed to thicken. Thomas swallowed hard as memories of the bond shared by Jonny and Christian in that summer of 1914 unexpectedly surfaced in his mind. "I believe I do, Lieutenant." The ensuing silence felt interminable, though it lasted only a few seconds.

A FORBIDDEN LOVE

October 1918

Under the October sky, the dark, still waters of *Wilhelmshaven* offered no reflection of stars or moon. Christian stood on his ship's deck, his hands gripping the cold metal railing as he stared into the endless black. Over two years had passed since his father's funeral, yet instead of grief, a deep emptiness lived within him.

"*Herr Leutnant,*" a soft voice called from behind. "You should come below. It's getting colder."

Turning, Christian saw Müller, his orderly—a thin young man whose already gaunt cheeks had grown even more hollow in recent months. "Just a moment longer," Christian replied, his gaze returning to the harbour. "The air up here feels... cleaner." Cleaner than the stale, oppressive atmosphere below decks, where men huddled in murmuring clusters that fell silent at the approach of officers.

"We're like ghosts," he murmured to himself as he peered into the darkness. "A ghost fleet manned by ghost men." Indeed, the *High Seas Fleet* had become just that—majestic warships moored in the harbour, their crews wasting away under the tightening British blockade. The British blockade prevented even the battered and repeatedly repaired *Frankfurt* from ever engaging in battle again.

"Permission to speak freely, sir?" Müller asked.

"Of course, Müller."

Müller's voice dropped to a barely audible whisper. "There was another incident on the *König* today. Three men refused to work, claiming they couldn't endure the rations we're providing."

Christian nodded, unsurprised. "And then?"

"They've been confined. But there are others like them." Müller glanced around, ensuring they were truly alone. "The men have gotten word that the *Admiralstab* has cancelled the final offensive."

"Is that confirmed then?" Christian asked, though he already suspected it was true.

Rumours had circulated for days—the high command scrapped their grand plan for one last glorious sortie against the British, not due to enemy action, but to the genuine fear that the crews would refuse to sail towards what they saw as certain death.

"As good as confirmed," Müller sighed, his breath forming a small cloud in the chill. "Your father would have…"

"My father would have followed orders," Christian interrupted sharply before softening. "Forgive me. It's been a difficult week."

"You did right by him in the end. He knew that," Müller replied.

After Müller left, Christian leaned against the railing again, allowing memories to surface. He recalled his father standing stiffly at Langley House, his face a mask of duty; he remembered the cold distance between them after discovering his father's secret affairs, and the pride that had kept them from bridging that gap, even as death neared.

"I should have tried harder," he murmured.

A FORBIDDEN LOVE

Inevitably, his thoughts turned to Jonny. Was he still in France? Was he still alive? The letters had stopped two years ago—impossible to send or receive across the divide of war. All that remained was a memory: Jonny at the piano in Langley Hall, sunlight streaming through tall windows as his slender fingers danced across ivory keys.

He closed his eyes, imagining those same hands now—perhaps poised over military dispatches, or wrapped around the grip of a revolver. Four years of war had transformed them both from boys into men who scarcely recognised themselves.

A distant commotion caught Christian's attention—voices raised from the forecastle, then quickly subdued. Another dispute over rations, perhaps, or something worse. The revolutionary murmurs were growing bolder each day.

"*Herr Leutnant*," Müller returned, his face more anxious than before. "There's trouble—the stokers are refusing to light the boilers for tomorrow's exercise."

Christian straightened, adjusting his uniform jacket with its frayed cuffs. "Tell the *Oberleutnant* I'll report immediately."

As he trailed Müller below decks, Christian felt the burden of his naval heritage settling over him as he reported the incident to his superior. Now, the duty to steer its unremarkable conclusion rested squarely on his shoulders.

Back in his cabin, he halted before a small, timeworn mirror. The reflection staring back was no longer that of the carefree youth who had set sail with gleaming hopes in 1914. Although his eyes kept their vivid blue intensity, they were now shadowed by memories of loss and hardship.

Lying atop his desk was a faded photograph, its edges softened by frequent handling—a snapshot of him and Jonny, both around twelve, holding cricket bats and beaming with the effortless confidence of childhood before the war. Christian briefly ran his fingers over it, engaging in the nightly ritual. "Truly a world apart," he murmured, not only referring to the physical distance but also the chasm that had grown between their lives, their nations, and their futures. Yet, in his heart, that delicate bond still flickered—a quiet flame he shielded from the swelling storms of revolution and defeat.

Meanwhile, the Allies, now bolstered by American forces, had mounted a fresh counter-offensive to reclaim the territory lost during the *'German Spring Offensive'*. Historians would later call this assault the *Hundred Days Offensive*, the final major campaign before Germany's forces collapsed. Amid these developments, Pete received orders to rejoin his unit at the front.

The October mist enshrouded the officers' quarters in Northern France, transforming the morning into a featureless, grey expanse. John stood by the window, observing Pete methodically stuffing his few possessions into a worn leather kit bag. The American's actions were deliberate and precise, a stark contrast to his usual exuberance.

"I guess this is what we all signed up for," Pete remarked, infusing his words with an attempt at cheerfulness. "You can't be a real hero sitting behind a desk at headquarters forever."

John traced patterns on the condensation-coated windowpane. "The reality of the front isn't like they describe it."

"I know." Pete hesitated, holding a neatly folded shirt between his hands. "Your experiences... they've taught me more than any manual ever could."

A FORBIDDEN LOVE

At that moment, Thomas entered to collect Pete's luggage, prompting John to turn as the floorboards creaked beneath his steps. In the dim light, Pete appeared diminished, his Nordic features more pronounced than usual. "Corporal, would you please escort the Lieutenant to his car?" John requested, giving them a moment of privacy.

Pete crossed the room with quiet footsteps muffled by the worn carpet. He paused just short of John, close enough to smell his bay rum shaving soap to be sensed. "I've never been good at goodbyes," Pete admitted. "My mother always says that's my worst trait."

Despite the heaviness in his chest, John felt a smile tug at his lips. "One of many I suspect."

"You wound me, Lord Langley." Pete clutched his heart in a dramatic gesture before regaining his composure.

Extending his hand in a formal, last gesture, Pete paused as John grasped it, feeling the rough calluses that matched his own. For a prolonged moment, they stood connected—a handshake that surpassed the constraints of convention.

"Keep your head down, old boy," John said, turning away to leave Pete in the company of Thomas.

"Well, as I've already said, I'm not very good at goodbyes," Pete confided to Thomas. "But don't let this place turn you into a ghost—you're far too alive for that."

"Just stay safe, Pete, that's all I ask," Thomas replied, stepping forward for a handshake before being pulled into a warm bear hug that brought their cheeks together.

"Now, Corporal, where's that car?" Pete regained his composure and marched out of the room. Thomas followed with the last bag, loading it into the awaiting vehicle. As Pete took his seat and closed the door, Thomas snapped to attention and delivered a crisp salute.

Later that evening, back in John's quarters, Thomas was serving coffee. As John took a sip, the familiar taste briefly transported him away from the mud and chaos of France. "Do you ever wonder if we'll recognise England when we return? Or if England will recognise us?"

Thomas moved to stir the fading embers in the fireplace. "I think, Jonny, that England will be waiting for us, just as we left her. Maybe a bit more worn out, like all of us."

"And what about those we left behind?" John's voice dropped to a near whisper. "What about those on the other side?"

Thomas straightened up, brushing his hands on his trousers. "I believe true connections endure even the harshest winters. Like the old oak at Langley that survived the great storm of '98."

John smiled faintly at the memory. "Kip and I used to climb that tree as boys. Father always said it had stood for five hundred years and would stand for five hundred more."

A comforting silence settled between them, interrupted only by the occasional crackling of the fire. "If—when—this war ends," John said, "I don't know what the world will look like. But I know I must find Kip."

A FORBIDDEN LOVE

"Then find him you shall, Jonny. And if you need help with that, just ask." The simple offer almost broke John's carefully maintained composure. He swallowed hard against the sudden tightness in his throat. "We've been through worse than this, haven't we, Thomas?"

"Yes, indeed we have, sir. The winter at *Messines*, for example."

"God, yes." John laughed softly. "I still can't feel my toes properly."

Thomas smiled, his eyes crinkling at the corners. "Whatever comes, we'll face it together. As we always have." John nodded, feeling the weight on his shoulders lighten a bit from being shared.

"As we always will."

A FORBIDDEN LOVE

A FORBIDDEN LOVE

CHAPTER FOURTEEN
ARMISTICE AND AFTERMATH

10.58 am November 11th, 1918.

Inside *Montreuil-sur-Mer's* General Headquarters, the atmosphere was as quiet and still as a tomb—a stark departure from the constant clamour that had accompanied the war. In the distance, the low rumble of artillery fire still resonated. Lord John Langley, slight in build yet burdened by the weight of his ancestry, stood outside with his valet Thomas, both surrounded by an eerie silence that seemed to steal the very breath from their lungs. Earlier that morning at five am, all sides had signed the Armistice—a document promising an end to the bloodshed—which was set to take effect precisely at 11am.

Outside the GHQ, John, flanked by Thomas and countless other officers and men, listened as the chimes of a grand clock echoed from the open windows of the Officers' Mess—marking the eleventh hour on the eleventh day of the eleventh month—while the distant rumbling ceased. John's blue eyes, usually alight with introspection, now mirrored the profound stillness surrounding him.

The relentless sounds of artillery and the agonised cries of dying men had long driven his nightmares, making this sudden quiet seem both strange and welcome. Despite his uniform being meticulously pressed, it did little to straighten the weary slump of his shoulders.

Thomas, ever the steadfast presence, remained close. His strong, well-practiced bearing and immaculate uniform exuded calm, although his Norfolk lilt was oddly muted. He understood his role not only by social order but also through the deep, unspoken bond he shared with the young lord at his side.

As whispers of celebration began to ripple through the group and seep from the adjacent rooms, a torrent of conflicting emotions surged within John.

While the streets rejoiced, his heart was a tempest of fear and longing, haunted by the image of Christian still in uniform, facing an uncertain fate overseas. He envisioned Christian's tall, graceful form aboard a ship, his raven hair tousled by the sea breeze, and the scar above his right eyebrow a lingering reminder of shared childhood adventures now overshadowed by the grim reality of duty.

"It's over," John murmured, the sound of his own voice feeling almost foreign. "The war... it's finally over."

Thomas nodded, his stoic expression softening. "Indeed, Captain. The world will never be the same."

John turned to his loyal valet, searching for words to capture the whirlwind of relief, disbelief, and underlying unease swirling within him. "I need to find out what will happen to the German fleet and then locate Christian."

"We will find him," Thomas replied with a certainty that required no further explanation.

That brief pause on Armistice Day soon gave way to the arduous tasks of assessing casualty figures and coordinating the return of over a million men to their homes. John felt a wave of relief wash over him, knowing Kip was out of harm's way. In just a couple of days, it became clear that the *German High Seas* fleet had to disarm in port and sail to *Scapa Flow* to be interned until final negotiations determined its fate.

A FORBIDDEN LOVE

Recognising that Kip was likely destined for Scotland, John immediately requested a transfer to *Dover*, where he would join a unit charged with evaluating the needs of repatriated soldiers. At the very least, this meant bringing him back to England—even if only to take part in the hectic work of managing the wounded and the missing.

The homeward journey via *Zeebrugge* and *Harwich* felt like a surreal odyssey, as the once-familiar landscape now bore the scars of war. As the train rattled through the countryside, John watched the passing scenes—a patchwork of jubilant villages and overwhelmed hospitals dotting the route.

In one town, the streets buzzed with laughing children and dancing couples, their faces glowing with the relief that followed peace. Bright, colourful flags fluttered from every window, while the air was rich with the aromas of freshly baked bread and roasting meats.

Yet, just a few miles further along the track, the scene shifted dramatically. The train passed a vast field hospital, its endless rows of white tents stark against the sky. The sharp scent of antiseptic and the metallic tang of blood filled the air, intermingling with the distant groans of the wounded.

John closed his eyes, his heart tightening at the dissonance. How could such a division exist in the world, suspended between extremes of joy and suffering? He felt torn apart, his emotions swirling in a confusing mixture of relief, anxiety, and deep loss. Next to him, Thomas stirred and broke the heavy silence.

"Are you alright, Captain?" he asked.

John shook his head, his voice a whisper. "I don't know, Thomas. I feel... lost. The war is over, but for me, it's as if it's only just begun."

He turned to face his loyal companion, his eyes haunted by memories of horrors—the mud-choked trenches, the screams of the dying, and the relentless pounding of guns—that replayed like an endless nightmare.

Now, with Christian still entangled in a web of duty and politics, John felt adrift in a sea of uncertainty. Would he ever see his cherished cousin again? Could they ever revive the deep, unspoken bond that had always simmered between them?

He tucked a telegram from his father into his breast pocket; the telegram advised him to write to Kip's ship once it reached *Scapa Flow*, but warned that all correspondence would be opened and censored. Billeted at a large seafront hotel in *Dover* with Thomas, John wasted no time once alone in his room—he immediately took up his pen to write to Kip:

Dover, 25th November 1918.
My dearest Kip,
It is with great relief that I can finally write to you again after so many years of separation. Thomas and I are doing well now, despite having suffered some injuries last year, and I hope you have been equally fortunate. I was deeply saddened to learn about your father. I know that even though things had been difficult between you in recent years, you must miss him terribly. I understand that you can still reply despite the censorship imposed on fleet correspondence, and it would be best if you write to my Mayfair address as I might be moved at any moment.

My sincerest hope is that this letter finds you safe and well. Ultimately, my greatest wish is that we might return to how things were on that last day we spent together all those years ago.

A FORBIDDEN LOVE

Forever yours, Jonny.'

Wilhelmshaven, 25th November 1918

The air reeked of salt and insurrection as Christian wound through the tight corridors of his vessel, the rhythm of boots striking the metal floor punctuating the rising shouts from afar. The *German High Seas Fleet* was in the midst of rebellion, its rigid structure beginning to crack like fragile ice. Red banners billowed across the decks against a sombre sky—a sky that had borne witness to the collapse of empires and the surge of anarchy.

Christian's heart pounded in step with the chaos, his blue eyes mirroring the turmoil swirling around him. With deliberate elegance, he advanced, each step a careful interplay between the man he was supposed to be and the one he longed to become. Sailors brushed past him with determined expressions, their faces etched with resolve as they fought to overthrow the officers who had guided them through the relentless storms of war.

Though he was an officer himself, and one who shared a bond with those he led, Christian felt an intense pull from opposing loyalties. His father's voice echoed in his mind like a steady drumbeat, urging him to remain steadfast—an embodiment of duty and honour. Yet, the part of him that craved the taste of freedom and the warmth of John's gaze murmured thoughts of defiance.

When he witnessed his respected captain being dragged from his quarters by the very men he had once led into battle, Christian's determination faltered. The captain's eyes—brimming with betrayal and resignation—met his, mirroring the fate that might soon be his. That silent meeting hung heavy over him, like a guillotine waiting to sever his bond with everything he had known.

The ship groaned beneath his feet, a massive steel beast wounded by its own crew, as it began its slow, inevitable journey north toward *Scapa Flow*. Standing on the deck amidst the triumphant cries of the mutineers, with the chilly sea breeze tousling his black hair, Christian's hand drifted to the scar above his right eyebrow—a memento of simpler days, a testament to innocence lost in the unyielding gears of war.

Leaving the German Navy meant forsaking the life destined for him since birth. It would be a rejection of his father's legacy and the burdensome expectations that weighed upon him like an anchor deep in the ship's hold.

Yet remaining would choke him under the uniform's ill-fitting embrace, in a world that no longer made sense. As the coastline blurred into a distant haze, isolation wrapped around Christian like a heavy shroud.
He found himself adrift, caught between the currents of duty and the instinct to survive—not only navigating the waters toward Scotland but also the murky depths of his own loyalties.

Every nautical mile taking him further from his homeland also nudged him towards an uncertain destiny, one that might let him follow the true north of his heart. With the lingering scent of revolution and red banners fluttering like the wings of a daring *Icarus*, Prince Christian stood determined. Despite the looming dangers and the internal strife that dulled his natural charisma and tempered his sharp wit, he remained resolute.

A FORBIDDEN LOVE

For now, he was a prince without a realm, a sailor without direction, embarking on the most dangerous voyage of all: the quest to discover who he could become when stripped of both title and country. It took more than a day before the grey waters of *Scapa Flow* lapped against the hull of the German warship with a sombre rhythm, each wave softly echoing the taste of defeat. On deck, Christian stood with his raven-black hair whipped by the biting November wind as the ship sailed into internment. Mist draped the *Orkney Islands*, their vague shapes like ghostly sentinels guarding the passage into captivity.

Here, amid the stark beauty of the northern isles, he first encountered a letter from John—a coded note that had navigated the perilous currents of wartime censorship. With trembling hands, Christian opened the already unsealed envelope, his heart quickening at the sight of John's familiar handwriting.

Though wrapped in seemingly ordinary language, the words carried a subtle undercurrent of longing and concern. Each sentence was like a lifeline thrown across a vast ocean of sorrow, reigniting a spark that the war threatened to snuff out. In the solitude of his cabin, Christian composed his replies with careful, guarded language, crafting messages that would slip past watchful censors while still conveying his deep affection.

'*Jonny*,' he wrote, using his own term of endearment, '*the northern skies are vast and empty, missing the stars that once witnessed our whispered confessions, and I too yearn for the fond memories of our last summer together. I even miss the horse-riding!*'

Their exchange evolved into a delicate dance of cloaked sentiments and silent promises, each letter standing as testament to the enduring strength of their bond. Yet, confined within this temporary limbo, Christian wrestled with a decision that could forever reshape his destiny.

Returning to Germany meant confronting a nation in chaos, a family shattered by betrayal, and a future burdened by duty. But to remain in England—John's England—was to boldly choose exile over honour, to forsake his lineage for the sake of love.

It was a decision as audacious as it was fraught with danger. The day eventually arrived when Christian's determination crystallised like frost on a windowpane. As he watched his fellow officers prepare for repatriation, their faces etched with the quiet resignation of soldiers accustomed to their fates, he understood he could not follow them. English soil rooted his heart, bound by invisible ties to a man whose love was both his most treasured secret and his truest truth.

"Are you certain of this, your highness?" one of his few loyal subordinates asked, a note of apprehension in his voice.

"More certain than I've ever been," Christian replied, his gaze fixed on the horizon where sea met sky—a junction of endless possibilities. "Former aristocrats, stripped of their estates, possess nothing within the fatherland. The only family I have now is in England."

News of his choice spread swiftly among the German sailors, chilling them like the first frost of winter. Whispered accusations of '*traitor*' and '*deserter*' clung to him like barnacles, yet he bore the isolation with the stoic resilience of a sailor venturing into uncharted waters.

As dusk settled over *Scapa Flow*, casting the ships in a spectral light, Christian felt the full weight of his decision upon his shoulders. Still, beneath that burden, a fragile sprout of hope emerged, stretching through the darkness toward the promise of a new dawn.

A FORBIDDEN LOVE

February 1919

  Bringing Christian back to Langley turned out to be far from straightforward. The authorities displayed reservations about releasing the former enemy combatant to Scotland instead of returning him to Germany. Meanwhile, John and Thomas had permanently returned to London after John took on a new role at *Victoria Station*, where he coordinated with the city's medical authorities to sort out the victims of a sweeping influenza epidemic in Europe.
  In the Mayfair townhouse, the atmosphere in the library was electric with anticipation as John paced back and forth, his steps softened by the thick Turkoman carpet. The quiet haven transformed; urgency now filled the room. Scattered across the mahogany desk like autumn leaves, telegrams held the key to unlocking Christian's freedom.
  John's blue eyes, clear and steadfast, now mirrored a turbulent inner storm as he examined the latest encoded message. He had become skilled at unravelling the bureaucratic shorthand that masked the true content of diplomatic communications. Although his father's contacts in the Foreign Office were proving to be a significant asset, he still faced a complex and trapping web of negotiations.
  Standing at the window of his father's study, Lord John Langley watched the busy street below. The frenzied activity had transformed the once serene Mayfair townhouse into a centre of intrigue. Diplomats, politicians, and military officials moved in and out, their conversations reverberating through the marble hallways as they debated the future of a post-war world.
  Yet, John's focus was not on the political manoeuvring around him; his mind was entirely preoccupied with one goal: securing Christian's release from the German Navy and ensuring his safe arrival in England. He had thrown himself into this mission with unwavering determination, tapping into every connection and resource available.
  "John, my dear boy," his father's voice interrupted his thoughts, "I have news from the Admiralty. They're open to negotiating Christian's release, but it won't be straightforward. Some still regard him as a traitor—a German prince who abandoned his country."
  John turned to face his father, his blue eyes burning with resolve. "I don't care what they think, Father. Christian isn't a traitor. He's a man of honour and courage who's followed his heart and conscience. I won't rest until he's safe and free."
  The earl sighed, the lines on his aged face deepening with concern.
  "I understand, John. But you must be cautious. The world is watching, and there are those who would use this situation against us and our family. We need to proceed carefully, wielding all our influence and diplomacy to navigate these perilous waters."
  John nodded, his jaw firm with determination. "I understand, Father. But I won't let Christian down. I'll do whatever it takes to bring him home."
  Pausing by the gleaming fireplace, John let his fingers trace the pulsing veins of the marble, finding a strange comfort in their intricate pattern—reflect his own tangled emotions. The conflict between his burning desire to expedite Christian's release and the daunting obstacles raised by warring governments coiled

A FORBIDDEN LOVE

tightly in his chest.

"John," his father called once more, his voice cutting through the silence like a tuned instrument, "we must be patient. Diplomacy is a delicate dance."

"I've grown weary of dancing, Father," John replied a little too impatiently, his tone tinged with steely resolve. With Christian's fate hanging in the balance, he knew there was no time to spare.

Taking a deep breath, John returned to the desk, his slender fingers methodically rifling through the documents with a renewed sense of purpose. Every letter he wrote was a deliberate arrangement of words designed to influence, soften resistance, and convince. He understood the might of language and employed it with the precision and grace of a master swordsman.

Late at night, when the last guests had departed and the house settled into an eerie calm, John sought refuge once again in the library's quiet. Surrounded by the soft murmur of ink on paper and echoes of previous conversations, he allowed himself to dream—envisioning a world where he and Christian could live unburdened by the relentless grip of war, facing only the battles of the heart.

In that tranquil solitude, hope glimmered like a candle flame—persistent and radiant—casting light upon the uncertain darkness that lay ahead. Thomas Cooper worked with steady precision amid the turmoil simmering within the Mayfair townhouse. He carefully sorted through piles of correspondence, arranging them into neat stacks on Lord John's grand mahogany desk.

The gentle rustle of paper provided a stark counterpoint to the unspoken urgency that filled the air like the threat of an imminent storm. His position had evolved from a mere valet into that of an essential ally in the mission to safely deliver Prince Christian down to England.

Together, they had seen the return of the troops, with John often accompanying Thomas to *Victoria Railway Station*, where exhausted and ailing soldiers disembarked. While Thomas offered compassionate assistance and reassuring words, John leveraged his influence and title to navigate bureaucratic obstacles, easing the soldiers' transitions back to civilian life or their placement in hospitals. Working side by side, Thomas' confidence in their cause deepened, and his regard for John evolved into something resembling brotherhood.

The days were long, frequently stretching into nights where sleep became a scarce luxury. They laboured in what had become an operations centre set in the library, where telegrams fluttered in like leaves caught in a ceaseless wind. The rich carpets and heavy velvet drapes absorbed the fervour of their hushed conversations, even as John marshalled every resource available to him.

Though the chill of the February evening seeped in through the tall sash windows, the warmth of their determination burned brighter than any fire. High stakes, personal truths, and national loyalties merged into an intricate tapestry with every passing hour, as the new post-war reality shifted the ground beneath their feet—yet they remained unwavering.

As night fell over London, draping the city in its mysterious embrace, the house in Mayfair stood out as an island of light amid a sea of uncertainty. Within its walls, two men forged a bond over their shared mission—a beacon of resolve in the ever-changing landscape of peace.

Outside, the late winter air carried a crisp promise of renewal, while within the precious confines of the historic townhouse, doubt lingered like an unseen spectre. Battle's scars deeply embedded themselves in the fabric of their lives,

A FORBIDDEN LOVE

indelibly marking their shared past. Although the Armistice had silenced the guns, the echoes of war's disruption still threatened to pull them apart.

In the quiet of that moment, John pondered the precarious path ahead. His heart clung to hope—a delicate vessel amid the storm of change raging beyond these walls. It was a hope not solely for peace, but for the liberty to love without barriers—to one day stand beside Christian, united not by the ties of birth that once divided them, but as men bound in spirit.

Christian's hardships paralleled John's, underscoring the deep bond between them. Far to the north, amid the icy waters of *Scapa Flow*, Christian faced his own trial—mutiny, internment, and the complete upheaval of his world. Still, hidden behind censored words and subtle hints, his letters revealed an unwavering devotion, a commitment that soared above the chaos of revolution.

As the firelight faded into encroaching darkness, John began to envision a future free from the shadows of war. He pictured Christian, not a dutiful prince, but Kip: the boy he treasured, the man who won his heart. He imagined them strolling through Langley Village, passing quaint thatched roofs and the lingering scent of woodsmoke, liberated from society's critical gaze. Across the landscape drifted their laughter; a more harmonious melody than he could play.

Closing his eyes, John inhaled as the aromas of cedarwood and lavender mingled with the imagined touch of sea salt on Christian's skin. He pictured their reunion as a timeless moment when the burdens of their choices would vanish like morning mist over Norfolk's fields at dawn.

Softly, John whispered "hope" to the empty room—a prayer, a promise. As he sealed Christian's letter with a kiss, he felt certain that their love, tested by the flames of war and the chill of separation, would endure. It was a love that transcended borders, flourishing in the fertile soil of a transformed world—a love embodying pure rebirth.

They gradually overcame one obstacle after another, and hope grew. By the end of February, the earl dispatched Thomas to the tailors to secure civilian clothes for Christian, while they all awaited a signed warrant from the Foreign Office; the earl had already drafted the necessary letter of guarantee to accompany it.

Exhaustion had become commonplace for both John and Thomas, yet one night Thomas noticed John looked a little feverish and urged him to retire early for rest. The next morning, Thomas struggled to rouse his master from a deep sleep, and it was evident that he was unwell. The family doctor was called, and he confirmed John was likely suffering from the so-called *'Spanish Flu.'* Though youthful and strong, the patient would require constant care.

A FORBIDDEN LOVE

A FORBIDDEN LOVE

CHAPTER FIFTEEN
REUNITED

Early March 1919

Christian received his travel permit and warrant on March 1st, and Thomas immediately sent a case of his clothing to Scotland. Finally, he would be home with Jonny within a couple of days.

They employed a nurse to supervise John's care, but Thomas took it upon himself to be ever-present. "Jonny," Thomas murmured, his voice tight with concern. He wrung out a cloth in the basin on the bedside table and laid it across John's burning forehead. "Please, you must keep fighting, Kip will be here soon."

John's eyelids fluttered but remained closed, his chapped lips parting slightly as he let out a weak moan. Thomas's hands shook as he checked John's pulse, counting the rapid beats against his fingers. Too fast. Much too fast.

Wetting the cloth again, Thomas moved it gently over the flushed planes of John's face, trying to cool the raging fever that held his master in its merciless grip. He adjusted the blankets, tucking them snugly around John's shivering frame despite the heat radiating from his skin.

In his mind, Thomas recited a silent, desperate prayer, pleading with God not to take the young man he had grown to care for so deeply. He could not lose him, not like this. Not when there was still so much left unsaid between them. Brushing back a lock of damp blond hair from John's forehead, Thomas let his fingers linger, wishing he could somehow absorb the sickness into himself. He would gladly bear it all if it meant sparing John this suffering. A coughing fit seized John's frail body, snapping Thomas from his reverie.

Thomas slid an arm beneath John's shoulders, lifting him gently as he pressed a glass of water to his cracked lips. "Drink, Jonny," he coaxed softly. "Please, you need to keep your strength up."

John sipped weakly, water dribbling down his chin before Thomas eased him back against the pillows. His breathing was even more laboured now, each inhale a painful rattle that made Thomas' chest constrict with fear. "Rest now," Thomas whispered, his vision blurring with unshed tears. "I'm here. I won't leave you."

He clasped John's limp hand between his own, willing his own strength into the fragile body before him. If love alone could heal, he knew John would be whole and well again in an instant. His only option was to faithfully tend to him and hope for it to be sufficient.

In the study, the earl paced before the fireplace, his footsteps heavy with worry. He crumpled the telegram in his fist; it was already creased and smudged from repeated reading, as though the words might change if he just stared at them long enough.

'PRINCE CHRISTIAN STOP RELEASE CONFIRMED STOP ARRIVING LONDON LATER TODAY STOP'

He should have felt relief. After weeks of dispatches and diplomatic wrangling, pulling strings with contacts in the Admiralty and calling in favours owed, he had finally secured Christian's return from *Scapa Flow*. The boy would be back on English soil within a day. But even that victory tasted bitter on his tongue,

A FORBIDDEN LOVE

overshadowed by the plague that had descended upon Langley House. With each passing hour, John seemed to slip further away, the *Spanish Flu* exacting its terrible toll despite all efforts to stop it.

The earl's hands shook as he tossed the telegram onto his desk, scattering the diplomatic papers and Admiralty correspondence that littered its surface. He had moved heaven and earth to bring Christian home, driven by the need to fulfil what might very well be his dying son's last wish. Now, he could only pray that John would live long enough to see his beloved cousin again. To speak the words that had remained unspoken for far too long. To find some measure of peace in Christian's arms before the end.

Sinking into his chair, the earl buried his face in his hands, shoulders shaking with silent sobs. All the power and privilege of his position seemed meaningless in the face of this unseen enemy that cared nothing for wealth or title. He would have traded it all - every acre, every shilling - to keep his son safe. But in the end, he was as helpless as any common man, left to watch and wait and plead for a mercy that might never come.

John's bedroom door burst open with a bang, startling Thomas from his vigil at John's bedside. He leaped to his feet, heart pounding, only to see Christian standing in the doorway, chest heaving and eyes wild with desperation.

"Jonny," Christian breathed, the single word carrying a wealth of emotion as he crossed the room in three long strides. He sank to his knees beside the bed, reaching out with trembling hands to cradle John's face. "I'm here, my love. I'm here."

John's eyelids fluttered open, his glazed eyes struggling to focus on the face hovering above him. "Kip?" he rasped, his voice scarcely more than a whisper. "Is it really you?"

"Yes, it's me," Christian assured him, tears streaming down his cheeks as he pressed a fervent kiss to John's forehead. "I came as soon as I could. I'm so sorry it took me so long."

John managed a faint smile, his hand twitching against the sheets as he tried to reach for Christian. "You're here now," he murmured. "That's all that matters."

Christian clasped John's hand in both of his own, bringing it to his lips and holding it there as if he could anchor John to life by sheer force of will. "I won't leave you again," he vowed. "I promise, Jonny. I'll be right here, no matter what."

For a moment, it seemed as though Christian's presence had wrought a miracle. Colour bloomed on John's pallid cheeks, and his breathing eased, losing some of its laboured quality. He gazed up at Christian with eyes that shone with love and longing, a hint of his old self surfacing through the haze of fever.

They lapsed into silence, their eyes speaking volumes even as their voices fell still. In that moment, the world outside the bedroom ceased to exist, the horrors of war and the spectre of death fading into insignificance. There was only this: two hearts, two souls, bound together by a love that defied all boundaries and conventions.

A love that had endured separation and hardship and now faced its greatest test in the crucible of John's sickbed.

A FORBIDDEN LOVE

"When I'm well again," John began slowly, his tone wistful and dreamy, "we'll go back to the Broads, just you and I. We will sail until sunset..." His words trailed off as a fit of coughing seized him, his frail body convulsing with the force of it.

Christian held him close, murmuring soothing nonsense as he rubbed John's back, his own heart clenching with fear and helplessness. When the coughing subsided, John sagged against the pillows, his face grey with exhaustion. Despite that, he clung to Christian's hand, his grip weak but insistent. "Promise me," he whispered, his voice thin and reedy. "Promise me, you'll remember our adventures. Remember us. No matter what happens, Kip. Promise me."

Christian swallowed hard, fighting back the sobs that threatened to overtake him. "I promise, Jonny," he said fiercely. "I will never, ever forget. You will always be with me, always."

Jonny smiled then, a beautiful, heartbreaking smile that said everything he lacked the strength to put into words. His eyes drifted shut, his breathing growing shallow and uneven.

Even so, Christian held on, pouring all his love and desperate hope into the fragile hand clasped within his own. Praying, pleading, bargaining with a God he scarcely believed in anymore, all for one more day, one more hour, one more precious moment with the man who meant everything to him.

As the night wore on, Christian kept his vigil at John's bedside, his eyes never leaving the pale, still face of his beloved. The room was hushed, the only sounds the crackling of the fire in the grate and John's laboured breathing.

Christian's own breath seemed to catch in his throat with every ragged inhale, his heart stuttering and skipping in his chest. He reached out a trembling hand to brush a stray lock of hair from John's forehead, his fingers lingering on the fevered skin. John looked so small, so fragile, his body seemed to sink into the plush mattress and pillows. Christian ached to gather him up, to hold him close and never let go, but he feared even the gentlest touch might shatter the tenuous thread holding John to this world.

"Stay with me, Jonny," he whispered, his voice cracking. "Please, my love. Fight. Fight for us." But even as the words left his lips, Christian noticed a change in John's breathing. It grew shallower, more rapid, and there was a bluish tint to his lips and fingertips that sent a bolt of pure terror through Christian's heart. "Thomas!" he cried out, his voice raw with panic. "Thomas, come quickly!"

He leapt to his feet, nearly toppling the chair in his haste. His hands fluttered uselessly over John's still form, wanting to help, to heal, to do something, anything. But he was helpless, powerless in the face of this invisible enemy that sought to steal away the very heart of him.

Thomas burst into the room, his eyes wide and alarmed. "Kip? What is it?"

"It's Jonny," Christian choked out. "He's... he's turning blue. His breathing... It's not right. Please, Thomas. Fetch the doctor. Hurry!"

Thomas took one look at John and blanched, his face going ashen. "Right away," he said, and dashed from the room. Christian sank back into the chair, gathering John's limp hand in both of his own. Tears streamed down his face unchecked as he pressed fervent kisses to each knuckle, each fingertip.

"Hold on, my darling," he begged, his voice a ragged whisper. "Help is coming. Just hold on a little longer. For me, Jonny. Please, for me."

A FORBIDDEN LOVE

He bowed his head over their clasped hands, his shoulders shaking with silent sobs as he prayed for a miracle, for divine intervention, for anything that would keep his heart and soul from being ripped asunder. In that moment, he would have traded places with John in a heartbeat, would have given anything, everything, to see those beloved blue eyes open once more.

The minutes stretched into an eternity as Christian waited, each second an agony of fear and dread. He clung to John's hand like a lifeline, as if by sheer force of will he could anchor him to this world, could keep him from slipping away into the darkness. "I love you," he whispered, over and over, a litany, a prayer. "I love you; I love you; I love you."

Even so, he waited, hope and despair warring in his heart as the night wore on and the shadows lengthened, the spectre of death looming ever closer. Christian knew, with a certainty that cut him to the very core, that if John left this world, he would take Christian's heart with him, leaving behind a hollow, shattered shell of a man.

So, he held on, with every fibre of his being, with every ounce of love and strength and sheer stubborn will he possessed. He held on, and he prayed, and he waited, the silence of the room broken only by the harsh rasp of John's breathing and the pounding of his own breaking heart.

The door burst open, shattering the oppressive silence. Dr. Blackwood rushed in, his face grave, his movements swift and purposeful. Christian reluctantly stepped back, allowing the doctor room to examine John, though he kept a tight grip on his cousin's hand.

"His lips... his fingers... they're blue," Christian said, his voice barely above a whisper, the words catching in his throat. Dr. Blackwood's expression darkened as he listened to John's chest, his brow furrowed in concentration. The earl and Thomas now hovered nearby, their faces etched with worry and fear.

"I'm afraid Lord John's condition is critical," the doctor said, his tone sombre. "The pneumonia has progressed rapidly, and his lungs are failing. There is... there is nothing more I can do."

The words hung in the air, heavy and final, a death knell. Christian felt the room spin, his knees buckling beneath him. He gripped the bedpost for support, his vision blurring with unshed tears.

"No," he whispered, his voice breaking. "No, there must be something, anything..." The earl stepped forward, his face ashen, his eyes haunted.

"How long?" he asked, his voice rough with emotion.

Dr. Blackwood shook his head. "Hours only, if there is no immediate improvement."

Thomas let out a choked sob, his hand flying to his mouth. Christian felt a wave of despair wash over him, threatening to pull him under. He turned back to John, his beautiful, beloved John, lying so still and pale against the pillows.

"My darling," Kip murmured, brushing a strand of blond hair from John's forehead. "Don't leave me. Please, don't leave me."

John's eyelids fluttered, a faint glimmer of blue beneath the lashes. His lips moved, a whisper of sound escaping them. Christian leaned closer, his heart in his throat.

"Kip..." John breathed; his faint voice almost lost in the room's stillness. "Love... you..."

A FORBIDDEN LOVE

Christian felt the tears spill down his cheeks, hot and bitter. He pressed a kiss on John's forehead, his lips lingering on the fevered skin. "I love you," he whispered. "I will always love you."

The earl moved to the other side of the bed, taking John's other hand in his. His eyes were bright with unshed tears, his face etched with a grief so profound it stole Christian's breath. "My son," he said, his voice breaking. "My brave, beautiful boy."

John's breathing grew more laboured, each breath a struggle, a battle. Christian held on, his heart shattering with every ragged gasp, every shuddering exhale. He watched as the light in John's eyes dimmed, as the life drained from his face, as his grip on Christian's hand weakened and faltered.

And then, with a final, shuddering sigh, John slipped away, his head lolling to the side, his eyes sliding closed. Christian let out a keening wail, a sound of such utter despair and anguish that it tore at the very fabric of the room.

"No," he sobbed, gathering John's now lifeless body into his arms. "No, no, no..." In that moment, all the grief and pain Christian had held inside for the last four years found an outlet.

The earl bowed his head, his shoulders shaking with silent sobs. Thomas knelt beside the bed, his face buried in his hands, his body wracked with grief. And Christian clung to John, his heart, his love, his very reason for being, knowing that a part of him had died with his cousin, that he would never be whole again. The world had lost its light, its warmth, its meaning, and all that remained was the bitter cold of a life without John by his side.

The earl leaned forward, pressing a gentle kiss to John's forehead, his tears falling freely onto his son's ashen skin. "Rest now, my boy," he whispered, his voice thick with emotion. "You've fought so bravely, so valiantly. Your mother and I will always be proud of you."

Christian watched, his vision blurred by tears, as the earl stepped back, allowing him a last moment alone with John. He took John's hand in his, the skin already growing cold, and brought it to his lips, kissing each knuckle with a reverence that spoke of a love beyond words.

"I will always love you, John," he murmured, his voice barely above a whisper. "In this life and the next, my heart is yours, forever and always. I promise you, my love, I will never forget, never let go of what we shared."

He pressed a final, lingering kiss to John's lips oblivious to who would witness it, tasting the salt of his own tears, before gently laying John's hand back on the bed. With a shuddering breath, he rose to his feet, his legs unsteady beneath him as he stumbled from the room, unable to bear the sight of John's lifeless form any longer.

In a daze, Christian found himself in his bedroom, the familiar surroundings offering little comfort as he sank onto the edge of the bed, his head in his hands. The grief washed over him in waves, threatening to pull him under, to drown him in its depths.

A soft knock at the door pulled him from his thoughts, and he looked up to see Thomas standing in the doorway, his eyes red-rimmed and swollen. In his hands, he held a bundle of letters, tied together with a navy-blue ribbon.

"Kip," Thomas said softly, his voice hoarse with emotion. "Jonny... he asked me to give you your letters back, and one letter I have held since 1917 which he wrote in the event of his... his passing."

A FORBIDDEN LOVE

Christian reached out, his hands shaking as he took the letters from Thomas. He recognised John's elegant script on the top envelope, his name written with a care and precision that spoke of the depth of John's love.

"Thank you, Thomas," he managed, his voice barely above a whisper. "For everything. For being there for him, for us, through it all."

Thomas bowed his head, his own tears falling silently. "It has been my honour, Kip. Jonny was a genuine friend, and I will miss him deeply."

Christian nodded, unable to speak past the lump in his throat. He clutched the letters to his chest, the weight of them a tangible reminder of the love he and John had shared, a love that would now forever remain unspoken, unfulfilled.

As Thomas left the room, Christian sank back against the pillows, the scent of John's lavender and cedarwood cologne still lingering on the sheets. He closed his eyes, letting the memories wash over him - the stolen glances, the brush of fingers, the whispered promises in the dark.

Before he drifted off into an exhausted, grief-stricken sleep, he opened the letter from 1917 and read it slowly. He could almost feel John's presence beside him, a ghostly whisper of the love that would forever haunt his dreams.

The morning of the funeral dawned grey and overcast, a fitting reflection of the sombre mood that had settled over Langley Hall. The village of Langley itself seemed to hold its breath; the usual bustle of daily life muted in respectful silence. As the funeral procession made its way from the Hall to the ancient stone church at the heart of the village, it appeared the entire community had turned out to pay their respects. Old men doffed their caps, women clutched handkerchiefs to their faces, and children watched with wide, solemn eyes as the coffin passed by, draped in the Langley family colours, topped with John's military cap and medal.

Christian walked at the head of the procession with his uncle, their faces a mask of stoic grief. He could feel the weight of the villagers' gazes upon them, the unspoken understanding of the depth of their loss. Beside him, Thomas maintained a respectful distance, his presence a silent bulwark of support.

As they entered the cool, shadowed interior of the church, the scent of the incense and lilies hanging heavily in the air. The ushers led the earl and Christian to the front pews; sorrow etched their faces. Christian took his place, his eyes fixed on the coffin that held the earthly remains of his beloved Jonny. Throughout the service, Christian struggled to maintain his composure, his hands clenched in his lap. The vicar's words washed over him, speaking of the brevity of life, the promise of eternal rest. But for Christian, there could be no rest, no peace, without John by his side.

As the final hymn echoed through the church, Christian felt a gentle hand on his shoulder. He turned to see Thomas, his hazel eyes filled with understanding and compassion. In that moment, Christian felt a rush of gratitude for the steadfast loyalty and friendship of this man who had been by their side through it all. Together, they followed the coffin out into the churchyard, where the grey skies had given way to a soft, misting rain.

As they lowered the coffin, Christian felt a part of himself buried with it, his once bright, shining future now a distant dream. And, as the mourners dispersed, Christian lingered by the graveside, his hand resting on the damp, freshly turned earth. He could feel Thomas' presence behind him, a silent guardian, ready to catch him should he fall.

"I don't know how to do this, Thomas," Christian whispered, his voice raw with emotion. "How to live in a world without him."

Thomas stepped forward, his hand coming to rest on Christian's shoulder once more. "One day at a time, Kip. One breath, one heartbeat at a time. And I will be here, every step of the way, for as long as you need me."

Christian nodded, drawing strength from the steadfast presence of this man who had become more than just a servant, but a faithful friend. And as they turned to walk back towards the Hall, Christian knew that while the road ahead would be long and painful, he would not have to walk it alone.

The rain continued to fall, soft and gentle, as if the heavens themselves were weeping for the loss of Lord John Langley. In the heart of Langley Village, the community mourned together, united in their grief for the young lord's untimely death and in their love for his family.

The library at Langley Hall seemed to hold its breath, the air heavy with the weight of sorrow and the musty scent of ancient tomes. Dust motes danced in the shafts of sunlight that filtered through the tall windows, casting an ethereal glow over the sombre gathering within. Christian sat in a high-backed leather chair, his posture rigid, his hands clasped in his lap. Beside him, the Earl of Grafton stood, his weathered face etched with lines of grief, his eyes fixed on the family solicitor, Sir Edward Stirling, who sat opposite them.

"...and to my dear cousin, Prince Christian, I leave the residue of my financial interests in cash, bonds and held in trust, as well as my personal journals and correspondence, in the hope that he may find solace and understanding within their pages."

The solicitor's voice was steady, but there was a note of sympathy in his tone as he read the words that John had so carefully chosen. Christian felt his throat tighten, his vision blurring with unshed tears.

"Furthermore," Sir Edward continued, "I wish to gift my faithful valet, Mr. Thomas Cooper, a cottage of his choice in Langley Village and £1000."

A choked sob escaped Christian's lips, and he felt his uncle's hand come to rest on his shoulder, a silent gesture of comfort and support. Christian's head snapped up; his eyes wide with shock. He had never expected this, never dared to dream that John would entrust him with such a responsibility.

"I..." He cleared his throat, struggling to find the words. "I am honoured by John's faith in me, and I will do everything in my power to uphold his legacy and to care for Langley Hall as he would have wished."

The earl nodded, a flicker of pride and gratitude in his eyes. "Thank you, Christian. I know John would be proud of you, and I am grateful to have you by my side in this difficult time."

As the solicitor concluded the reading of the will, he then moved onto other legal matters. "It is a matter of common law in England, that the prince is now entitled to the use of the courtesy title of *Lord Christian Viscount Langley*' as the earl's legal heir. In addition, for the avoidance of any doubt, my advice would be to immediately renounce his German titles and styles and lodge this with the Lord Chamberlain's office," he looked at Christian.

Christian had already seen any lands he had inherited from his father confiscated by the new republic of Germany along with the abolition of all aristocratic titles, "of course, Sir Edward." He glanced at his uncle, who nodded with

approval.
    Sir Edward took a manilla file from his briefcase and leaned over to hand it to Christian, "in here you will find the details of all your current financial assets and holdings, and also a cheque book for your new bank account in London."
    "Thank you, Sir Edward, for your foresight and efficiency," he placed the folder down next to himself. "Perhaps I should arrange a meeting once we are back in London to go through these papers?"
    "Very well my lord. I will look forward to seeing you then," he turned to the earl. "Will there be anything else my lord?"
    "No thank you Stirling, I think you have covered the essentials," the earl took a deep sigh at the finality of the arrangements just outlined. Sir Edward, collected his papers into his briefcase, stood and bowed to the earl and Christian.
    The earl noticed that Christian's gaze had drifted to the window, where he could see Thomas standing quietly on the terrace, his head bowed in silent reflection. A sudden wave of emotion washed over him as he recognised the grief and sadness clear in his late son's two closest friends. "Perhaps," he said to Christian, "you should tell Cooper of my son's bequest to him?"
    "Yes, uncle I shall," rising from his chair, thankful for the opportunity to get some fresh air. Christian made his way out of the library and onto the terrace, his footsteps soft on the stone. Thomas looked up as he approached, his hazel eyes filled with warmth and understanding.
    "Thomas," Christian said, his voice low and earnest. "I cannot begin to express my gratitude for all that you have done, for Jonny and for me. Your loyalty and friendship have been a constant source of strength and comfort, and I..." He paused, taking a deep breath. "I would be honoured if you continued to serve as my valet, but before you decide," he glanced around to check that they were alone, "you should know that Jonny has gifted you a cottage in the village and a thousand pounds."
    A genuine and honest look of surprise appeared on Thomas' face. "I had no idea he had done that."
    "It is clear that he cared a great deal for you and wanted to ensure that you could live the rest of your life comfortably," Christian now noticed a look of gratitude. "So, you need not continue in service with me. You are free to do whatever would make you happy. Which is what I am sure was Jonny's intention." He let the words sink in. Thomas' eyes widened, a flicker of surprise and then profound emotion passing across his face.
    "Your highness, I mean my lord," he said, his voice rough with feeling. "It would be my honour and my privilege to serve you, in whatever capacity you may require. Jonny was more than just my employer or commanding officer; he was my friend, and I will carry his memory and his sentiment with me always."
    Christian nodded, his vision blurring once more as he reached out to clasp Thomas' hand in his own. "Thank you, Thomas. With you by my side, I know that we can face whatever the future may hold, and keep Jonny's memory alive in all that we do."
    And as they stood there, hand in hand, the sun broke through the clouds, casting a warm glow over the terrace and gardens and the two men who had loved Lord John Langley so deeply. That moment offered hope amidst sorrow, promising a future forever changed, yet one they would face together, courageously and lovingly.

A FORBIDDEN LOVE

"Let's walk Thomas," Christian moved towards the steps down to the gardens.

"Of course, what's troubling you?" Thomas took this as an invitation to share problems, as he had done many, many times for Jonny.

"Well," he said with a small smirk, "you can help me with how to use my new chequebook, but before that," he lifted his arm onto Thomas' shoulders to pull him closer, "I was wondering when we could go sailing…."

The earl stood by the open french doors onto the terrace and watched the two younger men turn and stroll into the gardens beyond. He noticed Kip putting his arm over Thomas' shoulders and then heard the sounds of gentle laughter between the two. A thin smile appeared on the earl's face, happy to see the bond between his heir and valet secured.

A FORBIDDEN LOVE

A FORBIDDEN LOVE

CHAPTER SIXTEEN:
INHERITANCE AND DUTY

April 1921

Spring sunlight filtered through a thin veil of cloud above Langley Village, casting pale shadows across the freshly laid cobblestones surrounding the new memorial. Christian stood at the edge of the gathering crowd, his suit pressed and perfect. The soft Norfolk breeze carried the scent of damp earth and fresh-cut grass, a cruel reminder of life's persistence in the face of so much death.

Thomas stood beside him, a half-step behind as befitted his station, though Christian had long abandoned such formalities in private. This morning, the valet's face, carved from stone, revealed nothing of the grief Christian knew he carried. After all, Thomas had been there, with the earl and Christian as they had held John in those final moments.

"Quite the turnout," Christian murmured, surveying the crowd. Villagers in their Sunday best, farm labourers with caps clutched in weathered hands, children unnaturally still under mothers' watchful eyes.

"They loved him," Thomas replied. "All of them."

Christian swallowed the correction that rose instinctively—that they had gathered for all eighteen names, not just John's—but he knew Thomas was right. His cousin had been the village's favourite son, their golden boy, their sacrificial lamb.

The memorial itself stood draped in a large Union Flag, its shape suggesting a simple obelisk of local limestone, broad at the base and tapering toward the heavens. The earl had insisted on its placement—across from the church, and near the entrance to the boatyard where generations of village boys had learned to sail and swim in the gentle waters of the *Chet*. John and Christian had often sailed from the Estate Boatyard onboard the yacht *'Isabella'*.

"His Lordship is arriving," Thomas mumbled.

Christian straightened imperceptibly as his uncle's motorcar pulled to a stop at the edge of the gathering. The Earl of Grafton, now sixty-six, emerged slowly, assisted by his butler. Grief had aged him cruelly. The lines of his face seemed carved with a sharper instrument than mere time, his once commanding frame diminished but not defeated. Christian felt the familiar twist of complicated emotion—sympathy for the man who had lost his only son, discomfort at their shared German connection that had placed them on opposite sides of the conflict.

The vicar stepped forward, his sombre voice carrying across the hushed crowd. "We gather today to remember those who made the ultimate sacrifice..."

Christian let the words wash over him, focusing instead on the faces around him. Old Mrs. Cooper, Thomas' mother, dabbing at her eyes with a handkerchief. The blacksmith, Powell, standing straight despite the wooden leg that replaced the one left behind in France. Three young women in black—war widows, each with a small child clinging to their skirts. This was the true legacy of the war, not the boundaries redrawn on maps or the treaties signed by men who had never seen the trenches.

His uncle approached the memorial with measured steps. The unveiling committee chairman handed him a cord, and with a single, steady pull, the flag fell away to reveal the gleaming stone beneath. Christian's breath caught. There,

A FORBIDDEN LOVE

carved into eternal memory, were eighteen names. Eighteen sons of Langley who would never return.

And there, third from the top:

'CAPT. LORD JOHN LANGLEY DSO, 9TH NORFOLK REGIMENT.'

Christian's hands were numb, but he felt a warmth in his chest, an uncomfortable heat that he recognised as guilt. He should have been there earlier. Instead, he had been aboard *SMS Frankfurt* in *Scapa Flow*, still serving Germany while John's life was ebbing away.

The earl began to read the names, his aristocratic voice steady despite the emotion that threatened to break through. After each name, he offered a brief remembrance—Andrew Simmonds, who had tended the Hall's gardens for ten years and taught his son the same trade; William Fowler, whose skill with horses was unmatched in the county; James Harding, who left behind a young wife and twin daughters born after his death.

When he reached John's name, the earl paused, visibly gathering himself. "Captain Lord John Langley, my son. A talented artist and musician who served with distinction and courage, taken whilst still in the service of the King."

So formal, Christian thought. So inadequate. He wanted to scream that John had been more—had been laughter and secret touches and whispered promises. Had been a boy who collected seashells and played cricket with effortless grace and blushed when praised. Had been everything.

The list continued, eighteen lives reduced to brief summaries, eighteen futures erased. The village postmaster's son. Two brothers from the tenant farm nearest the Hall. The schoolmaster who had enlisted despite being over forty. The butcher's apprentice who had lied about his age and died at sixteen.

After the names came prayers, the vicar's voice rising and falling in familiar cadence. Christian mouthed the words without hearing them, his eyes fixed on John's name etched in stone. Would it last? Would people remember John a hundred years from now, or would he become just another name, weathered by rain and forgotten by all but the history books?

"They shall grow not old, as we that are left grow old..." The poem struck Christian with physical force. He had read it before, of course, but hearing it now, standing before John's name, made the words unbearable in their truth.

The ceremony concluded with the *'Last Post'*, a single bugler standing at attention, the notes hanging in the April air like lost souls. The crowd dispersed, women wiping tears, men shaking hands solemnly, children released from their enforced stillness darting between gravestones in the adjacent churchyard. Christian remained, unable to leave. His uncle approached, standing beside him in silence for a long moment.

"John would have been embarrassed by the fuss I suspect," the earl finally said.

"Yes, I think he would have, but the memorial is beautiful. Dignified."

"Yes." The earl's gaze lingered on his son's name. "We've found some more of John's things. Mostly his art. Some of it..." He paused. "Some of it features you quite prominently."

Christian's heart stuttered. "We were close as boys."

A FORBIDDEN LOVE

"Indeed." The earl's tone was unreadable. "Cooper has been assisting me and he has put it all together for you," the earl placed a friendly hand on Christian's shoulder, "but now we must return to the Hall for the reception."

After his uncle departed, Christian promised to follow him as soon as possible, and found himself alone at the memorial, save for Thomas who waited patiently nearby. He reached out, tracing John's name with his fingertips, feeling the sharp edges of the carved letters.

"I should have been with him sooner at the end," Christian said, knowing Thomas would understand.

"He knew why you couldn't be," Thomas replied, his voice gentle. "If anything, he blamed himself for not being able to get you released sooner."

Christian nodded, unable to speak. Together, they turned from the memorial and walked back toward the waiting car, leaving eighteen names to stand guard over the village that had raised them, loved them, and now remembered them in cold, enduring stone.

August 1923

The telegram arrived as Christian was breakfasting in his room in Langley House, the morning light casting thin rectangles across the faded Persian rug. Thomas placed it beside the marmalade without comment, though something in his posture—a certain tightness around the shoulders—suggested he suspected its contents. Christian unfolded the yellow paper with steady hands, though his heart had already accelerated, as if recognising bad news before his mind could process the words.

'REGRET TO INFORM YOU EARL OF GRAFTON PASSED PEACEFULLY LAST NIGHT STOP SOLICITOR REQUESTS YOUR PRESENCE LANGLEY HALL SOONEST STOP CONDOLENCES STOP'

Christian set the telegram down carefully, as though it might shatter. He stared at the half-eaten toast on his plate, suddenly tasteless.

"My uncle is dead," he said, the words oddly flat in the quiet morning room.

Thomas nodded once. "I'm very sorry, Kip. Shall I pack your things for an immediate departure?"

Christian wanted to tell him not to bother, that they need not rush. But the weight of what this meant was already settling across his shoulders like an ill-fitting coat.

Christian was now the Earl of Grafton. The title that should have been John's had fallen to him, the half-German nephew, the enemy officer who had fought against England while John died for it.

"Yes, we should leave as soon as possible," he said instead. "Thank you, Thomas."

An hour later, they were on the train to Norfolk, the countryside sliding past the window in a blur of spring green. Christian sat rigidly in the first-class compartment, his reflection in the glass showing a face carefully composed into aristocratic neutrality. Inside, his thoughts churned like the North Sea in a gale.

His uncle had never been the same after John's death. The war had aged him a decade in four years, grief adding another decade in the years that followed.

A FORBIDDEN LOVE

Yet he had thrown himself into work with a fervour that bordered on mania—establishing veterans' funds, lobbying Parliament for better care for the wounded, corresponding tirelessly with the families of men who had served under John. Endlessly, he worked on his political memoirs, as if preserving his diplomatic experiences could somehow make up for his perceived failure in 1914 and all that had been lost.

Thomas sat opposite, quietly reading a newspaper, though Christian suspected he wasn't absorbing a word. Their eyes met in the reflection.

"Did you know he was very ill?" Christian asked.

Thomas folded the paper carefully. "I had heard from Mrs. Winters—the housekeeper at the Hall—that his heart had been troubling him. But he forbade anyone to mention it to you."

"Typical," Christian murmured, though without rancour. His uncle had been a proud man, unwilling to show weakness even at the end. Langley Hall appeared on the horizon as their car navigated the lime tree lined approach to the main drive—imposing, eternal, indifferent to the passing of its custodians. The limestone facade glowed amber in the late afternoon sun, windows reflecting the light like dozens of watching eyes.

Christian felt a familiar constriction in his chest, the mixture of longing and dread that the Hall always evoked. John was everywhere here—in the oak tree they had climbed as boys, in the stables where they had learned to ride, in the library where they had discovered poetry together.

Mr. Harrington, the new family solicitor, awaited them in the grand library. He was a thin man with wire-rimmed spectacles and thinning grey hair, the perfect picture of English legal propriety. He rose as Christian entered, extending a hand in formal sympathy.

"Your Grace," he said, the title dropping between them like a stone into still water.

Christian hesitated fractionally before accepting the address. "Mr. Harrington. Thank you for coming."

"Of course. Please accept my deepest condolences. Your uncle was a remarkable man."

They settled into leather chairs before the unlit fireplace. Thomas remained standing near the door, present but unobtrusive.

"The funeral will be on Saturday," Harrington continued. "The vicar has already been consulted. Your uncle left very specific instructions."

He slid a sealed envelope across the polished table surface. "For your eyes only. Regarding personal matters."

Christian took the envelope, feeling the weight of the heavy stationery in his hand. His uncle's bold handwriting spelled out his name—not his title, simply *'Christian.'*

"As to legal matters," Harrington continued, "the succession is, of course, straightforward. As your uncle's nearest male relative—his sister's son—you inherit the title and entailed estates. The earl made certain that your previous German citizenship would not impede this." A pause. "He was most insistent that his sister's son should inherit, regardless of... any political complications.
I recommend wholeheartedly that you confirm your British Naturalisation through your birth here at Langley and your mother."

A FORBIDDEN LOVE

Christian nodded, suddenly unable to speak. His uncle had protected his inheritance, despite everything. Despite Christian serving in the Kaiser's navy while British boys—including his own son—died.

"There are death duties to be addressed," Harrington continued. "Substantial ones, I'm afraid. And while the estate remains land-rich, it is, regrettably, somewhat cash-poor. Your uncle's charitable endeavours, while admirable, were... extensive."

"I understand," Christian said, though he didn't, not really. Estate management had never been part of his education.

After Harrington departed, Christian remained in the library, his uncle's sealed letter untouched on the table beside him. Thomas returned with a decanter of brandy and two glasses, taking the liberty of pouring one for himself without being invited. It was a minor breach of protocol that Christian found immensely comforting.

"To His Lordship," Thomas said, raising his glass slightly.

"To my uncle," Christian agreed, the brandy burning a warm path down his throat.

They sat in companionable silence for a moment, the ticking of the grandfather clock the only sound in the vast room. Finally, Christian broke the seal on the envelope and withdrew a single sheet of heavy paper. His uncle's handwriting, normally so controlled, showed signs of the illness that had claimed him—shaky, the loops of his letters more pronounced than usual.

'Christian,

By the time you read this, I will have joined John and your aunt in whatever awaits us beyond. I trust Harrington has explained the practical matters.

There is something I wish you to know. After the war, I never hesitated when John beseeched me to find a way to bring you home - for Langley has always been your home, just as it was my dear sister's, your mother. Although you were always a beloved nephew, it was your bond with my son that taught me much, even at my late stage in life, about the value and power of friendship and love.

I have left my unfinished memoirs in my desk drawer. Perhaps you will find them of some interest, though I fear they are the ramblings of an old diplomat who lived too long into a world he no longer recognised.

Take care of Langley. It has been in our family since Charles II rewarded the first Viscount for his loyalty. Loyalty matters, Christian. As does love. I believe you understand both, perhaps better than I ever did.

Edward.'

Christian folded the letter and returned it to its envelope. Then he crossed to the massive oak desk in the corner, opening the central drawer to find a stack of leather-bound journals, each filled with his uncle's precise handwriting.

"He worked on these every day apparently," Thomas said quietly. "Often until dawn. The doctors said it was too much strain on his heart, but he wouldn't stop."

Christian closed his eyes briefly. "I'm German, Thomas. I was an officer in the Kaiser's navy. How can I possibly be the Earl of Grafton?"

A FORBIDDEN LOVE

"With respect, sir, you're also Lady Victoria's son. The Earl's nephew. And Lord John's cousin." Thomas' voice softened. "You belong here as much as anyone. The village and estate will come to love you, just as they have every previous occupant of this house."

Christian moved to the window, gazing out at the parkland stretching toward the horizon. Generations of Langleys had stood at this same window, watching the seasons change across their domain. Now it was his turn, however improbable that might have seemed five years ago.

"I know nothing about running an estate," he admitted.

"You'll learn," Thomas said. "And you won't be alone."

Christian turned back to the room, his stare lingering on the portrait of John that hung above the fireplace. His cousin's face—his hair a tangle of blond vines, his lips a perpetually crooked line of disinterest concealing the warmth Christian had known so well—seemed to watch him with familiar intensity.

"No," Christian agreed softly. "I suppose I won't."

May 1925

Almost two years later, Christian sat at a cluttered mahogany desk in his study at Langley House, the low afternoon light catching the worn edges of a letter from an old Eton comrade of John's. Outside, London hummed and rattled—motorcars and omnibuses, street vendors and pedestrians—but here in his study, the only sounds were the gentle rustle of fine parchment ledgers and the occasional clink of Thomas filing metal boxes in the cabinet behind him. The ledgers before him told a story in columns of numbers, one that grew more concerning with each page he turned.

After two years as Earl of Grafton, Christian had developed a methodical approach to estate management. What he lacked in traditional training, he compensated for with the precision and attention to detail drilled into him at the Naval Academy in *Wilhelmshaven*. Each property, each investment, each expenditure received his careful scrutiny, catalogued in his neat, angular handwriting that betrayed his German education.

"The Westfield farm accounts," Thomas said, placing another leather-bound volume on the desk.

"Thank you, Thomas." Christian reached for it, their fingers brushing in the exchange. Both men felt a spark – static from the dry air, but it jolted them nonetheless, a brief reminder of the complex relationship that had evolved between them since John's death. Thomas was no longer merely a servant; he had become confidant, advisor, and perhaps the closest thing to a friend that Christian permitted himself.

Thomas moved away, resuming his organisation of the filing cabinet. He worked with the quiet efficiency that had made him invaluable, first to John and now to Christian. His knowledge of the estate far exceeded Christian's own, accumulated through years of service and careful observation.

"The tenant farmers at Westfield are requesting repairs to the drainage system," Christian noted, scanning the latest correspondence. "Again."

"The Old Earl—your uncle—had approved the work just before his passing," Thomas replied without turning. "But they redirected the funds to settle part of the death duties."

A FORBIDDEN LOVE

Christian sighed, setting the ledger aside to rub his temples. The death duties had been substantial—nearly forty percent of the estate's value—and two years later, they were still struggling to meet the payments while maintaining the properties, even after Christian had placed all the substantial wealth he had inherited from Jonny into the coffers.

His uncle's charitable endeavours, while admirable, had depleted much of the liquid capital. His gaze fell on the letter from Henry Pembroke, John's friend from Eton. It had arrived that morning, ostensibly a social correspondence but containing a thinly veiled inquiry about Christian's interest in selling a parcel of the Norfolk estate that bordered Pembroke's family land. The offer was generous, perhaps overly so.

Christian picked up the letter again, noting the fine quality of the paper, the carefully measured politeness of the language. Pembroke had written of shared memories of John, of cricket matches and school holidays, before casually mentioning his interest in expanding his hunting and shooting grounds. The presumption irked Christian—that he might sell off pieces of Langley for the recreational pursuits of John's schoolmates.

"What do you make of Pembroke's letter?" he asked, holding it up.

Thomas paused in his filing, turning to consider the question. "I believe that Mr. Pembroke is aware of the estate's financial difficulties and hopes to capitalise on them."

"Yes, I gathered that much," Christian replied dryly. "What I mean is, should I consider it? The offer would cover next year's death duty payment with something to spare."

Thomas approached the desk, his expression neutral but his eyes revealing concern. "If I may speak frankly, Kip?"

"When have you ever not, Thomas? Even when it was something that I might not necessarily like or agree with." This sentiment represented the basis of their new relationship. Christian often thought that Thomas acted as his conscience in matters of business and the estate.

A ghost of a smile crossed Thomas' face before he continued. "The sale of any part of the Norfolk estate would have... significant consequences. For the village, for the tenant farmers, for the household staff. The Langley lands have been intact for centuries."

Christian nodded slowly. He had suspected as much. While he had grown up in his early years in Germany, his school years at Eton and summers at Langley had taught him the deep interconnection between the estate, the village, and the people who depended on it. It wasn't simply land; it was an ecosystem of relationships, traditions, and livelihoods.

"Show me the complete financial picture," he said, pushing aside the letter. "No sugar-coating, Thomas. I need to understand exactly where we stand."

Thomas hesitated only briefly before retrieving several more ledgers from the cabinet. Together, they spread the books across the desk, creating a topographical map of the estate's finances. Income from agricultural rents, timber, wool, property income in London and elsewhere and investments. Expenditures for maintenance, salaries, taxes. And the looming shadow of the remaining death duties.

A FORBIDDEN LOVE

"The income is only just covering expenses," Christian said, tapping a column of figures with his index finger. "And that's with minimal maintenance on the properties – including Langley Hall. We're deferring necessary repairs, which will only cost more in the long run."

"Yes," Thomas' voice was quiet. "And the payment schedule for the death duties leaves little margin for any unexpected expenses."

Christian leaned back in his chair, staring at the ceiling where a thin crack traced its way across the plaster—another repair deferred.

The London house was showing its age. He had maintained it because selling seemed an admission of defeat, and because it provided a necessary base for business in the capital. But perhaps it, too, was a luxury they could no longer afford.

"If we sold some of the London properties?" he mused.

"It would help," Thomas acknowledged. "But not enough to address the larger, long-term issue."

"And what is the larger issue, Thomas?" Christian asked, though he knew the answer.

"Langley Hall itself, my lord. It consumes a disproportionate amount of the estate's resources. The maintenance, the staff, the heating..." Thomas trailed off, perhaps sensing he had overstepped. Christian felt no offense. Thomas was right. They built the magnificent Hall for a different era—when large households of servants maintained vast rooms for families who entertained on a scale unimaginable in post-war Britain. Now a beautiful anachronism, draining resources that could preserve the rest of the estate.

"Selling is out of the question," Christian said, surprising himself with the vehemence of his reaction. "Jonny loved that house. I won't be the one to lose it."

Thomas nodded, a flicker of relief crossing his features. "There may be... alternatives, Kip."

"Such as?"

Several large estates now welcome visitors. Charging admission for tours, hosting events." Thomas straightened a stack of papers with precise movements. Some wings have been closed off to save money, while parts of houses have been repurposed.

Christian considered this, turning the idea over in his mind. The thought of strangers wandering through John's childhood home, gawking at family portraits and personal spaces, made him deeply uncomfortable. And yet, if it meant preserving the estate...

"We would need to calculate the potential income against the disruption," he said. "And let's determine which parts of the Hall we could modify without destroying its character."

"Of course, my lord." Thomas gathered the ledgers, returning them to their proper places in the cabinet.

Christian rose from the desk, moving to the window. The street below was busy with evening traffic, Londoners hurrying home or out to dinner, their lives untouched by the weight of centuries of obligation that had unexpectedly fallen on his shoulders. This responsibility was unwanted by him; his training was for the sea, not land management. Yet here he was, the fate of Langley in his hands.

A FORBIDDEN LOVE

"There's something else to consider," Thomas said quietly. "The people."

Christian turned. "The people?"

"The village, the tenant farmers, the staff. Langley isn't just a house and land. It's their livelihood, their home." Thomas met his gaze steadily. "Your uncle understood that, as did Jonny. The relationship between the Hall, estate and the village goes back generations."

Something in Thomas' words struck Christian deeply. He had been thinking of Langley as a burden, a financial millstone. But Thomas was right—it was far more than that. It was a community, one that had welcomed him despite his German background, despite the war. One that had mourned John alongside him.

"You're right," he mumbled. "I've been seeing only the ledgers, not the lives behind them."

Thomas smiled slightly, the expression warming his normally composed features. "Perhaps that's why the estate needs both of us, my lord. You have the head for numbers, and I..." He hesitated.

"You have the heart for Langley," Christian finished. "As Jonny did."

"Yes."

Christian returned to the desk, pushing aside Pembroke's letter. "Write to him. Tell him the land is not for sale—not now, not ever." He pulled a fresh sheet of paper toward him. "Instead, let's draft a plan. For Langley Hall, for the estate, for all of it. We must find a way to preserve what matters without selling what can never be replaced."

As they worked into the evening, the city darkening around them, Christian felt something shift within him—a sense of purpose, of belonging. Langley wasn't just John's legacy; it was becoming his own. And he would find a way to protect it, for the sake of the past and the future alike.

Next day the work continued as Christian occasionally let his eyes linger on the faded photograph of John tucked beside the correspondence, the image stirring quiet memories of shared laughter and loss. It was a simple portrait, taken at Eton in 1912—John in his school uniform, his expression serious for the camera but with that telltale glint in his eye that Christian knew preceded mischief. The photograph had travelled with Christian throughout the war, somehow surviving the damage to *SMS Frankfurt* at Jutland, preserved in a waterproof pouch against his heart like a talisman.

The afternoon light was fading now, casting long shadows across the study. Thomas had lit the lamps, their warm glow creating islands of illumination in the growing darkness. Outside, London settled into its evening rhythm, the distant sounds of traffic and humanity creating a constant, comforting hum.

"We must keep his spirit alive, Tom," Christian said suddenly, the words escaping before he could consider them.

Thomas paused in his organisation of the estate papers, his hands stilling momentarily over the neat stacks. "Yes, my lord," he replied, his voice soft with understanding. "I believe we do that every day, in our own ways."

Their eyes met, an unspoken acknowledgment passing between them—of shared grief, of the thread that bound them together through John's memory. Christian returned his attention to the financial papers spread before him, his methodical mind cataloguing necessary tasks. The quarterly review of investments needed completion. Tenant farmers' requests required responses.

The solicitor needed instructions regarding several expiring leases on London properties. He made precise notes in his leather-bound planner, assigning each task a priority and timeframe, finding comfort in the ordered structure.

"I've been thinking about Langley House," Christian said, referring to the Mayfair townhouse that had been in the family since the 1820s. It represented both an asset and a drain on resources. "It's largely sitting empty, except when we use the drawing room for meetings."

Thomas nodded, waiting for Christian to continue. In the lamplight, his face showed the subtle signs of aging that the war and subsequent years had etched upon him—fine lines at the corners of his eyes, a certain gravity to his expression that had replaced the youthful openness Christian remembered from before.

"What if we were to convert it into apartments?" Christian proposed, the idea taking firmer shape as he spoke it aloud. "Maintain the architectural integrity, of course, but create four or five modern flats that could be leased to suitable tenants. We could keep one for our use when in London."

Thomas considered this; his practical mind evident in his expression as he weighed the suggestion. "It would provide a steady income stream, rather than sitting as an underutilised asset. And the location would command substantial rents."

"Exactly." Christian stood, energised by the potential of the idea. He moved to the window, looking out at the darkened street below. "London property values continue to rise. The conversion costs would be recouped within a few years, I should think."

"The staff would need to be considered," Thomas noted, always mindful of the human elements that Christian sometimes overlooked in his focus on numbers. Christian turned back, his brow furrowing. He hadn't thought about the staff implications immediately, and the oversight bothered him.

"Yes, of course. Could they be relocated to Langley Hall? We're understaffed there since reducing the household."

"Perhaps," Thomas said, though his tone suggested doubt. "Some have family in London and some might choose retirement if we offer a pension I suppose." He hesitated. "There would also be the matter of finding positions for those who couldn't relocate."

Christian nodded, the weight of responsibility settling across his shoulders once more. These were not merely employees; they were people whose livelihoods depended on his decisions. People who had served his family loyally, some for decades. The thought of dismissing them, of disrupting their lives for financial expediency, sat uneasily with him.

"We'll need to speak with each of them," he said. "Understand their circumstances, their preferences. Perhaps some would welcome retirement with a pension, others might prefer reassignment. We must be fair, Thomas."

"Of course, my lord." A hint of approval coloured Thomas' response.

A FORBIDDEN LOVE

    Christian returned to his desk, pulling a fresh sheet of paper toward him. He began sketching a rough floor plan of Langley House —the grand entrance hall with its sweeping staircase, the series of reception rooms on the ground floor, the family apartments above, and the servants' quarters tucked into the attic and basement levels.
    "The main reception rooms could be maintained in the largest apartment," he mused, pencil moving across the paper. "The library, drawing room, and morning room, perhaps. The rest could be divided along logical architectural lines." He glanced up at Thomas. "What do you think?"
    Thomas approached, studying the sketch. "The divisions make sense. And maintaining the principal rooms in one apartment would preserve the historical character where it matters most."
    "Precisely." Christian added notes to his drawing. "We'll need an architect, of course. And a builder experienced with historic properties." His mind raced ahead, calculating, planning. "The conversion could begin this autumn, perhaps be completed by next spring."
    As they continued to discuss the practical aspects of the conversion, Christian thought of John again. His cousin had possessed an artist's eye and would have had strong opinions about how the house should be divided, which architectural features preserved, which modern conveniences added. John had loved Langley House, had created some of his finest sketches and watercolours in its morning room, light streaming through the tall windows that overlooked the private garden square.
    The thought sparked a new idea. "The garden access," Christian said. "We should ensure that all the apartments have some connection to the garden. It was one of John's favourite features."
    Thomas smiled. "He used to sketch there for hours in the summer. Said the light was perfect just before sunset."
    "Yes," Christian agreed, remembering long summer evenings when they had sat together on the wrought iron bench beneath the ancient plane tree, shoulders touching, speaking of everything and nothing as the light faded around them. "He would have wanted others to enjoy it."
    The realisation struck him then—that this was about more than financial pragmatism. It was about honouring the past while securing the future. About maintaining what mattered while adapting to a changed world. John had understood this instinctively; it had taken Christian longer to grasp.
    "I begin to understand what he felt," Christian said, his voice low enough that Thomas had to lean slightly forward to hear. "The binds of duty. The weight of it. He used to complain about his father's expectations, about the path laid out before him that allowed no deviation."
    "Yes, it troubled him deeply."
    "I thought him melodramatic sometimes." Christian smiled. "The burden of the heir. It seemed abstract, theatrical even. Now..." He gestured to the papers spread across the desk, the tangible evidence of the responsibilities he had inherited. "Now I understand what confined him. What he could never escape."
    Thomas was quiet for a moment, his gaze thoughtful. "If I may, Kip. I believe Jonny would be proud of how you've shouldered his burden. How you've honoured his memory through your care for Langley."

A FORBIDDEN LOVE

Christian felt a tightness in his throat, unexpected emotion rising at Thomas' words. "I've tried," he said. "Though I never expected to be the one making these decisions."

"Few of us end up where we expect," Thomas' voice carried the quiet wisdom born of observation and experience. "The war changed everything for all of us."

Christian nodded, unable to disagree. The world before 1914 seemed like a distant dream now—the certainties, the traditions, the clear boundaries of nation and class and expectation. The tide of blood and disillusionment that followed washed all of it away.

He turned his attention back to the conversion plans, finding solace in practical action. They worked together until late in the evening, Christian outlining his vision while Thomas offered insights from his years of service in the household. The conversion of Langley House into apartments would not solve all their financial challenges, but it represented a significant step toward stability—a way to preserve the estate's assets while generating the income needed to maintain them.

As they concluded their planning, Christian tucked John's photograph back into its envelope, a gesture that had become ritual. The past would always be with him, informing his decisions, guiding his path. But tonight, for the first time in years, he saw the future offering something beyond mere survival—a way forward that honoured what had been lost while building something new from the remains.

"I think we've made good progress," he said, gathering the papers into a neat stack. "Draft letters to the architect and solicitor tomorrow, would you? And we should meet with an architect and builder as soon as possible."

"Yes," Thomas began extinguishing the lamps, leaving only the one on the desk illuminated. "Will there be anything else this evening?"

Christian shook his head, suddenly aware of the lateness of the hour and the weariness settling into his bones. "No, thank you, Thomas. That will be all."

As Thomas withdrew, Christian remained at the desk, the single lamp casting a warm circle of light in the darkness. His fingers rested lightly on the envelope containing John's photograph, a physical connection to the past even as his mind turned toward the future. The dual pull of memory and possibility, of preservation and change—this, he was beginning to understand, was what it meant to be the Earl of Grafton in this new and altered world.

A FORBIDDEN LOVE

CHAPTER SEVENTEEN:
THE RETURN OF WAR

The autumn of 1939 hung heavy over Langley Hall, its golden light casting long shadows across the east lawn where Christian stood. Twenty-five years had passed since that fateful summer before the first war, and still he lingered at the spot where he and Jonny had once sprawled beneath the centuries-old oak, dreaming of impossible futures. The wind carried the scent of woodsmoke and apples, but beneath it lay something sharper—the metallic taste of another approaching conflict that would once again demand choices no man should have to make.

Christian pulled his coat tighter around his tall frame. At forty-two, his raven hair had silvered at the temples, though his posture remained as straight as it had been during his naval days. The scar above his right eyebrow—that old relic from a boating accident with Jonny—had faded to a thin white line, a reminder of childhood recklessness and shared secrets.

The estate stretched out before him, two thousand acres that he had come to know as intimately as the deck of his first command. When had Langley Hall become more home than the Germany of his ancestry? Perhaps it had always been so, even before the Great War had forced him to choose sides. Now, with Germany once again marching toward conflict, he found himself rooted in English soil, the caretaker of Jonny's legacy.

"Sir," Thomas' voice called from the terrace. "Tea is served in the library." Christian turned to see Thomas framed in the limestone archway, still trim and proper at forty-five, his sandy hair now flecked with grey.

The years had deepened their connection, transforming the relationship from master and servant to something far more complex—confidants bonded by shared grief and mutual respect.

"Coming, Thomas," Christian replied, taking one last look at the oak tree before turning toward the house.

Inside, the library kept its old character—leather-bound volumes lining the walls, the faint aroma of pipe tobacco clinging to the draperies though no one had smoked there for years. Christian settled into the wing chair by the fire, accepting the cup Thomas handed him.

"The timber agent left his report," Thomas said, placing a folder on the side table. "The south copse is ready for selective harvesting. He estimates it will fetch a fair price, despite the uncertainty in the markets."

Christian nodded. "Schedule it for next month. We should prepare for leaner times ahead."

This was their rhythm—Thomas managing the household staff while Christian oversaw the broader estate concerns. Together they had modernised what needed changing while preserving the soul of Langley Hall. In the almost twenty years since Christian had taken up permanent residence, they had become an efficient partnership.

"Also," Thomas continued, his tone shifting subtly, "there's a gentleman waiting in the small drawing room. He arrived without appointment and refuses to state his business to anyone but you. Government type, by the look of him."

Christian's fingers tightened around the delicate porcelain cup. "Did he give a name?"

"Major Hartington, sir. Though I suspect that's not entirely truthful." Thomas' intuition had been honed by decades of service. Christian had learned to trust it.

"Very well. I'll see him now."

The small drawing room faced west, capturing the waning daylight. The man standing by the window turned as Christian entered—medium height, unremarkable features, wearing a well-cut suit that wasn't quite right for country wear. His eyes, however, were sharp and assessing, missing nothing.

"Prince Christian," the man said, offering his hand. "Thank you for seeing me without notice."

Christian accepted the handshake but corrected him firmly. "I haven't used that title in many years, Major Hartington. The Earl of Grafton will suffice."

The man nodded, unsurprised. "Of course. Old habits. May we sit?"

They settled into facing chairs, Thomas appearing silently with fresh tea before withdrawing to stand by the door.

"Thomas stays," Christian said before the major could object. "He has my complete confidence."

Something in the visitor's expression suggested this was expected as well. "As you wish. I'll be direct, then. I represent a department within the War Office that concerns itself with... specialised intelligence."

"You're MI6," Christian stated flatly.

A slight tilt of the head acknowledged this. "We're interested in your particular set of skills and knowledge, my lord. Your background in the Imperial German Navy, your familiarity with their operational procedures, your understanding of their ports and facilities—all of these make you uniquely valuable."

Christian felt a chill that had nothing to do with the autumn evening. "I served in a different navy in a different war. Much will have changed."

"But not everything," the major countered. "The basic geography of the naval installations at *Wilhelmshaven*, *Kiel*, *Cuxhaven*—these remain constant. And your understanding of German naval culture, their patterns of thought... these evolve more slowly than technology."

His hands were steady as he placed his teacup on the table, but Christian felt a warmth in his chest, an uncomfortable heat that he recognised as conflict. "What exactly are you asking of me, Major?"

"Consultation, primarily. Analysis of information we receive. Occasionally, interpretation of communications. Nothing that would place you in direct danger."

"And yet everything that would mark me as a traitor to my previous country."

"A country that has fallen under the control of a regime I believe you find as abhorrent as we do."

Christian stood and walked to the window. The sun had nearly set, casting the formal gardens in deepening blue shadow. "You've done your research on me."

"Thoroughly," the major admitted. "We know about your opposition to the Nazi Party. Your correspondence with Jewish colleagues from your naval days, helping them relocate to England. Your refusal to return to Germany after Hitler's rise to power."

"Yet you question my loyalties."

"Not questioning, my lord. Confirming. These are desperate times."

Christian turned back to face the room, his gaze meeting Thomas' for a brief, weighted moment. In that look passed two decades of understanding, of shared history.

"I'll need time to consider."

"Of course," the major said, rising. "But not too much time. Events are moving quickly." He placed a plain card on the table with only a telephone number written on it.

"There is one other matter. Langley Hall has been identified as suitable accommodation for officers from the new RAF base being established at *Bungay*."

Christian's jaw tightened. "You want to requisition the hall."

"Not all of it. The east wing and main house, primarily. We understand your position here and your... special relationship to the property. Arrangements could be made for you to retain private quarters."

After the major departed, Christian remained in the darkened room, staring into the unlit fireplace. Thomas moved about, lighting lamps against the gathering gloom.

"They'll take the house whether I agree or not," Christian said at last.

"Yes, sir," Thomas replied. "But your cooperation would ensure better treatment of the property."

Christian sighed. "And what of their other request? Do I become an informant against my own countrymen?"

Thomas placed another lamp on the mantel, its warm glow softening the harsh planes of Christian's face. "If I may speak freely, sir?"

"When have you not?"

A faint smile touched Thomas' lips. "The Germany you knew, the one you loved, is not the same country marching across Europe today. And your true countrymen... perhaps they're the ones you've chosen, not those assigned by ancestry."

Christian reached for the crystal decanter on the side table, pouring two measures of whisky. He handed one to Thomas—a gesture that had become commonplace between them over the years, though only in private.

"What would he have done?" Christian asked quietly. The *'he'* needed no clarification.

Thomas accepted the glass, his fingers briefly brushing Christian's. "Jonny would have done what was right, regardless of the cost to himself. As he always did."

They drank in silence, the memory of Jonny—his gentle determination, his quiet bravery—filling the space between them more substantially than words ever could. Later, as they walked through the great hall toward the east wing to assess what spaces might be converted for military use, Christian made his decision.

"I'll help them, Thomas. Not for England or against Germany, but because there are things in this world worth protecting, regardless of borders or birthright."

Thomas nodded; satisfaction clear in his bearing. "I'll send word tomorrow, then. And I'll begin preparing the *Dowager Wing* for your quarters."

"Our quarters," Christian corrected. "I'll need you close by, especially with strangers filling the house."

A FORBIDDEN LOVE

"As you wish, sir." Thomas' tone remained proper, but a warmth suffused his eyes—the same warmth that had sustained them both through the long years of rebuilding their lives after the losses of the first war. Christian paused at the foot of the grand staircase, its oak banister gleaming with centuries of polish. "They'll change everything," he mumbled.

"Not everything," Thomas replied. "Not what matters most."

As September faded into October, the transformation of Langley Hall began. Furniture was moved, rooms repurposed, modern telephone lines installed. Christian watched it all with resignation, withdrawing each evening to the increasingly cozy confines of the *Dowager Wing*, where Thomas had created a self-contained apartment that preserved some essence of the home they had known.

The military intelligence officer returned twice more, each time with maps and documents that Christian pored over late into the night, marking locations, annotating details, dredging up memories of a life and a homeland that seemed increasingly distant.

When the first RAF officers arrived in early November, Christian greeted them with the perfect courtesy his position demanded, but retreated quickly to his private rooms. There, with Thomas serving dinner at the small table overlooking the north garden, he allowed himself a rare moment of vulnerability.

"I wonder sometimes what became of my former comrades," he murmured. "How many have compromised themselves in service to that madman? How many still believe in honour and duty as we once defined it?"

Thomas, now serving as both valet and confidant, placed a gentle hand on Christian's shoulder. "Some questions have no answers worth seeking, sir. We can only move forward."

Christian covered Thomas' hand with his own, drawing strength from the touch. "Forward, then. Into whatever this new war brings us."

The initial two years of the war, passed in a haze of one set of bad news after another. The retreat from *Dunkirk*, German gains in Europe and north Africa all added to an increasingly dark mood about any hope of victory. However, in December 1941, the Japanese Empire attacked *Pearl Harbour* which brought the United States into the war on the side of the allies. Within months American forces were beginning to move to England in preparation for their fight against the Germans, and Langley Hall was given to the *United States Air Force* to accommodate their new base at *RAF Bungay*.

June sunlight streamed through the tall windows of Langley Hall's entrance hall, illuminating dust motes that danced above stacks of olive-drab footlockers. Christian and Thomas stood at the threshold, momentarily frozen by the spectacle before them. The marble-floored space that had once echoed only with genteel footsteps now boomed with American accents and the sharp report of military boots.

A young lieutenant lounged against the banister of the grand staircase, his uniform cap tipped back on his head and a cigarette dangling from his lips—a posture that would have scandalised the dowagers of pre-war England but seemed perfectly natural in this strange new world of 1942.

"They've certainly made themselves at home," Thomas murmured, his voice pitched low enough that only Christian could hear.

A FORBIDDEN LOVE

Christian nodded; his expression carefully neutral as he surveyed the transformation. The past eighteen months under RAF occupation had been startling enough—polite British officers billeted in the family bedrooms, operations maps spread across the library table, radar equipment humming in what had once been the music room. But this American invasion brought a wholly different energy, brash and unabashed, that seemed to fill every corner of the hall with its vitality.

"Shall we proceed?" Christian asked, straightening his shoulders slightly. At forty-five, he still maintained the bearing of the naval officer he had once been, though he now wore a well-cut civilian suit rather than a uniform.

They moved forward, navigating around a group of enlisted men who were manhandling a large wooden crate toward the east wing. The Americans nodded respectfully but didn't halt their colourful commentary on the weight of their burden or the ornate surroundings.

"Jeez, would you look at this place? My whole neighbourhood in *Brooklyn* could fit in this foyer," one said, his accent thick as molasses.

"Yeah, and every statue probably costs more than my old man makes in a year," his companion replied, shifting his grip on the crate.

Christian pretended not to hear, but Thomas noted the slight tightening around his eyes. This wasn't merely about strangers occupying their home; it was about the collision of worlds—old European aristocracy meeting young American democracy in all its brash glory.

They had subtly militarised the entrance hall. Bulletin boards flanked the grand fireplace, covered with duty rosters and base regulations. A makeshift reception desk now stood where a priceless *Chippendale* console table had once displayed fresh flowers. The ancestral portraits still gazed down from the walls, but they now overlooked stacks of field telephones and typewriters rather than silver calling card trays.

"I believe they've set up their command post in the library," Thomas said, guiding Christian through the chaos. They passed the Music Room, its doors thrown wide to reveal a space now serving as some sort of recreational area. Card tables had been set up where delicate settees once stood, and a gramophone blared with jazz that seemed to vibrate the crystal drops of the chandelier overhead.

An officer emerged from the crowd, standing out in his crisp uniform and regulation haircut. Unlike some of his more casual compatriots, he projected military discipline as he approached them.

"Captain Harris, logistics officer," he introduced himself with a firm handshake. "You must be Earl Grafton. Base commander sends his apologies for not greeting you personally. He's still tied up with the advance team at the airfield."

"Quite understandable," Christian replied with practiced courtesy. "I trust you're finding the accommodations suitable?"

"More than suitable, sir. Palatial compared to our last posting. Though I'm afraid we're still getting organised—bit of a culture shock for some of our boys."

As if to underscore his point, a commotion erupted behind them. A stocky American officer with a shock of ginger hair and a bright red baseball cap—jarring against his olive uniform—had backed into a side table, sending a Ming dynasty vase wobbling toward its edge.

A FORBIDDEN LOVE

Time seemed to slow as the priceless artifact teetered, then plummeted toward the marble floor. There was a collective intake of breath from those who understood the value of what was falling, then a sickening crash as porcelain fragments scattered across the floor like delicate blue and white confetti.

The American's face flushed as red as his cap. "Jesus Christ, I'm so sorry!" he exclaimed, dropping to his knees to gather the pieces. "I'll pay for it, I swear…"

Thomas stepped forward, his expression betraying nothing but calm efficiency. "Please don't trouble yourself, sir. That's quite all right."

"All right? This looks antique!"

"Oh dear, that's another relic of our past gone askew," Thomas said with such dry understatement that Christian had to turn away to hide the twitch of his lips. "We've become quite accustomed to it, I'm afraid."

Christian watched Thomas handle the situation with the diplomatic grace that had always been his gift. There was something almost comical about the juxtaposition—Thomas in his impeccable suit, helping the flustered American officer to his feet with quiet dignity, assuring him that in times of war, porcelain was the least of their concerns.

Later, as they continued their walk through the house, Christian commented, "that vase survived the Boxer Rebellion, two world wars, and three centuries of clumsy footmen. Only to meet its end under an American baseball cap."

"It was rather garish, that cap," Thomas agreed. "Though not as garish as some of the neckties I've spotted this morning."

Christian allowed himself a small smile. "I suspect we'll need to secure anything we truly value. The East Wing gallery, particularly."

"Already done, sir. I've moved the most precious items to our quarters or the secure storeroom in the cellars. Though I left enough to make the place feel inhabited rather than a museum stripped for evacuation."

They paused at the window overlooking the south lawn, where a group of American soldiers had improvised a baseball game. Their shouts and laughter floated up, oddly cheerful against the backdrop of war.

"They're so young," Christian observed.

"As we all were, once," Thomas replied. "Though I don't recall being quite so…"

"Loud?"

"Exuberant was the word I was searching for."

They shared a look weighted with memory. Both had seen enough of war to know that youthful exuberance could disappear in an instant, replaced by something harder and darker. Perhaps that explained their instinctive protectiveness toward these brash newcomers, despite the disruption they brought.

"The RAF officers were easier to accommodate," Christian said as they continued toward his private wing. "They understood the… protocols of a house like this."

"The British have had centuries to perfect the art of imposing upon others while making it seem like they're doing you a favour," Thomas observed with the faintest hint of irony. "These Americans haven't mastered that particular skill."

"No, they impose with enthusiasm and apology in equal measure." Christian's tone softened slightly. "There's something refreshing in their lack of pretence, I suppose."

A FORBIDDEN LOVE

They passed the small anteroom that had once served as a waiting area for visitors to the Dowager Viscountess. Now it functioned as a checkpoint, staffed by a bored-looking corporal who straightened immediately upon seeing them.

"Earl Grafton and Mr. Cooper," Thomas informed him smoothly. "Returning to the private quarters."

The corporal consulted a clipboard. "Yes, sir. You're both on the permanent access list. Go right ahead."

This was new—under the RAF, Christian and Thomas had moved throughout the house freely. The Americans, it seemed, brought with them a more defined sense of security and territory.

Having transformed the *Dowager Wing* into a comfortable, if compact, apartment, Christian safely entered, loosened his tie, and sank into his favourite armchair. The room, with its view of the rose garden, remained largely unchanged—a small sanctuary of pre-war life preserved amid the chaos.

"What do you make of them, Thomas?" he asked as the other man poured two glasses of sherry from a crystal decanter—their customary afternoon ritual. Thomas weighed the question, as he did all things.

"They're different from the British officers. More... democratic in their approach. The distance between their enlisted men and officers seems less formal, though still present."

"Yes, I noticed that as well. And they seem to have a more improvisational attitude toward regulations."

"Which may prove either refreshing or maddening, depending on the day." Thomas handed Christian his glass before taking his own seat—a liberty that would have been unthinkable in the pre-war years but had become natural in their private quarters.

Christian sipped his sherry, savouring the familiar burn. "Do you ever wonder what Jonny would have made of all this? Americans occupying his ancestral home, playing baseball on his croquet lawn?"

A gentle smile softened Thomas' features, "I think he would have joined their game, sir. And probably introduced some incomprehensible British variation of the rules just to confuse them."

The image warmed Christian more than the sherry. "Yes, he would have, wouldn't he? Always finding a way to build bridges while maintaining that quiet mischief of his."

The *Dowager Wing* felt like a different world—a pocket of quiet dignity preserved amid the American invasion. Christian settled behind the desk that had once belonged to the Lady of the house, his elegant fingers tracing the inlaid pattern on its surface. The afternoon light filtered through lace curtains, casting dappled shadows across the ledger books Thomas had laid before him. These moments—these practical discussions of estate matters—had become a comforting ritual over the years, an anchor of normalcy regardless of what war and time had wrought upon Langley Hall.

"The north tenant farm is still behind on their rents," Thomas said, taking his customary chair opposite the desk. In these private quarters, the formalities that governed their public interactions softened into something more companionable. "Though considering that farmer's son is in a prisoner of war camp in Germany, I've taken the liberty of extending them further credit."

Christian nodded his approval. "As you should. What of the harvest projections?"

"Better than last year, despite the labour shortage. The Land Girls assigned to us have proven remarkably capable." Thomas' mouth curved slightly. "Mrs. Perkins in the kitchen continues to complain about their trousered presence, but even she can't deny the results."

This small report—the daily management of an estate fighting to maintain itself during wartime—was their shared responsibility now. Christian had the title and authority, but Thomas possessed the practical knowledge and connections with the local community that made things function. Together, they had kept Langley Hall viable through the Depression and into this second great conflict.

"And our... other matters?" Christian asked, his voice dropping though they were alone.

Thomas understood the reference immediately. For nearly three years now, Christian had been providing intelligence to the British government—careful analyses of German naval capabilities, interpretations of intercepted communications, insights into the psychology of the *German High Command*. It was delicate work, balancing his loyalty to his adopted country against the homeland that still claimed part of his heart.

"The usual courier came yesterday while you were in Norwich. I've placed the documents in the secure box." Thomas tilted his head toward the false-bottomed drawer in the writing desk. "They're particularly interested in your assessment of the new U-boat tactics in the North Atlantic."

Christian sighed, rubbing the bridge of his nose. "I'll review them tonight. Though I wonder if the Americans' arrival will complicate these arrangements."

"I've already spoken with our contact. The arrangement continues, though with added discretion. The Americans need not know the full extent of your... contributions."

There was a gentle protectiveness in Thomas' tone that Christian relied upon. His role as an intelligence asset remained closely guarded—known only to a small circle within British military intelligence. The Americans, with their more straightforward approach to warfare, might not appreciate the nuanced position of a former German aristocrat providing insights against his native country.

"What of the estate staff?" Christian asked, changing the subject. "How are they adjusting to our new guests?"

"Mixed reactions. Cook feels both appalled by American appetites and flattered by their enthusiasm for her cooking. The remaining housemaids are navigating between caution and curiosity."

Thomas' expression turned briefly amused. "Young Sarah was caught arranging to teach one of the radiomen to waltz in the servants' hall after only an hour here."

"And you, Thomas? How are you finding our American cousins?"

Thomas considered the question with his customary thoughtfulness. "Louder than the RAF, certainly. More direct in their manner. But there's an... optimism about them that's rather refreshing after three years of British stoicism in the face of bombing."

A FORBIDDEN LOVE

Christian nodded, understanding perfectly. The Americans brought with them not just their military might but a certain unburdened confidence—the assurance of a country whose cities remained un-bombed, whose civilian population had not endured nightly air raids and strict rationing for years on end.

"I suppose we should be grateful," Christian mused. "Their presence means the tide is turning."

"Indeed, sir. Though I confess I'll be grateful when they learn that doors are meant to be closed gently rather than allowed to slam."

The small joke lightened the mood, and they continued through the estate matters with practiced efficiency—discussing fuel allocations for the coming winter, repairs needed to the tenant cottages, arrangements with the Ministry of Agriculture regarding the fallow fields.

This was the business of survival, of continuity, ensuring that regardless of who occupied the grand rooms of Langley Hall, the estate itself would endure. They were just concluding when a sharp knock came at the door—distinctive in its confidence and rhythm, unmistakably American.

"That will be our new commanding officer," Thomas said, rising to answer it.

Christian straightened almost imperceptibly, adjusting the set of his shoulders and the expression on his face. Over the years, he had perfected this transition—from the private man to the public figure, from Christian to the Earl of Grafton, custodian of the estate. It was a subtle shift, but Thomas recognised it in the slight lifting of his chin, the cooling of his gaze.

"Show him in, please," Christian said, his voice now carrying the polite distance appropriate for meeting a stranger who had, by circumstance of war, become temporary master of much of his domain. Thomas moved to the door with practiced grace, his own manner shifting subtly into the perfect servant—back straight, expression pleasant but reserved.

He opened the door to reveal an American colonel in a crisp uniform, cap tucked under his arm in a gesture of respect. The moment stretched, then shattered. Thomas froze, his hand still on the doorknob, his carefully composed expression cracking into naked shock. The colonel likewise seemed transfixed, his blue eyes widening, his mouth falling open before spreading into a disbelieving smile.

"Tom?" The word emerged as half question, half exclamation.

"Pete?" Thomas' voice was barely above a whisper. Two men, separated by years and countless experiences, felt a shared moment. Then, with a movement that defied all protocol, the American colonel stepped forward and embraced Thomas firmly, clapping him on the back with unrestrained emotion.

"My God, it is you! I had hoped, when I saw an assignment to Langley Hall, so I pulled a few strings, but I wasn't sure if you'd still be here after all this time!"

Thomas remained stiff for only a heartbeat before his arms came up to return the embrace. Their fingers brushed as they pulled apart, and they seemed to feel a spark – static from the dry air, but it jolted them nonetheless. This reunion crackled with shared history, palpable even to Christian.

"Lieutenant Kowalski," Thomas said, his voice regaining some of its composure though his eyes remained bright with emotion. "I had no idea..."

A FORBIDDEN LOVE

"It's Lieutenant Colonel now, but for God's sake, Tom, it's still *'Pete'* to you." The American turned, suddenly remembering they weren't alone, and directed his attention to Christian. "I apologise for the informal greeting, sir. I'm Lieutenant Colonel Piotr Kowalski, United States Army Air Forces, commanding the 391st Bombardment Group."

Christian had risen from behind the desk, watching this unexpected reunion with undisguised interest. "No apology necessary, Colonel. Any friend of Thomas' is welcome at Langley Hall."

"Friend doesn't quite cover it," Pete said, his smile softening with memory. "Thomas and I served together in France, 1918. Well, not together exactly—he was batman to a British officer, I was an American liaison. But we shared some... significant experiences."

Thomas cleared his throat, still visibly affected by the encounter. "Lieutenant Colonel Kowalski knew Lord John Langley during the final months of the war."

Christian's interest sharpened immediately. Any connection to Jonny always captured his full attention. "Indeed? I wasn't aware that Jonny had American connections in his regiment."

"Not in his regiment exactly," Pete clarified. "I was assigned to British HQ as a liaison officer in '18. That's where I met Captain Langley—your cousin, I believe?"

"Yes," Christian confirmed, studying the American with fresh eyes. There was something in the colonel's manner—a certain gentle respect when he mentioned Jonny's name—that suggested more than casual acquaintance. "John was my cousin, though we were raised more as brothers for many years."

An understanding passed between them, unspoken but clear. This man had known Jonny in those final, terrible months of the war.

"Please, Colonel, join us," Christian gestured to the comfortable chairs by the fireplace, moving their meeting from the formality of the desk to a more conversational arrangement. "I believe this calls for something stronger than tea, Thomas?"

"Of course, sir." Thomas moved to the sideboard; his hands only slightly unsteady as he poured three measures of whisky. His composure was returning, but Christian noted the heightened colour in his cheeks, the unusual brightness in his eyes. This reunion had affected him deeply.

Pete accepted the offered glass with a nod of thanks. "I had hoped you might be here, Tom. When I saw the assignment to Langley Hall... well, I requested it specifically as I felt like I already knew the place."

"You came looking for me?" Thomas asked, surprise clear in his voice.

"Among other reasons," Pete admitted. "The strategic location near the coast, the condition of the airfield—those were the official factors. But yes, I remembered you saying you'd return to service here after the war."

There was history here—rich, complex, and clearly significant to both men. Christian took a sip of his whisky, content to let them navigate this unexpected reunion at their own pace.

"I had no idea you'd joined the Air Forces," Thomas said. "Last I knew, you were returning to New York."

"Army first, then Air Forces when they separated in '41," Pete explained. "After the last war... well, civilian life didn't suit me as well as I'd expected."

A FORBIDDEN LOVE

There was something wistful in his expression, quickly masked. "But look at you—still here at Langley Hall after all these years. Still keeping everything running smoothly, I see."

"Thomas has been indispensable," Christian interjected warmly. "Particularly since I took over management of the estate. I doubt Langley Hall would have survived without his dedication."

Pete's gaze shifted between them, assessing their dynamic with intelligent eyes. "You've known each other a long time, then?"

"Since childhood," Thomas explained. "As you know I served as Lord John's valet before the first war, and then as his batman during his service. After Lord John's death, I remained as the earl's valet, and eventually when he inherited the estate, I began to help with its management."

"Thomas is being modest," Christian added. "He's far more than a servant. He is the institutional memory of Langley Hall and my closest advisor." The warmth in his voice conveyed the depth of their connection with no need to articulate the decades of shared experience and mutual respect.

Pete nodded, understanding evident in his expression. "John spoke of you both often. With great affection."

Thomas' composure slipped again, just slightly. "Did he?"

"Oh yes, he said that you and the earl were the only people that truly knew him." Pete's voice softened. "I think he would be pleased to see how you've worked together and kept his home intact through another war."

Christian watched as Thomas absorbed this, saw the flicker of emotion cross his face—pride mingled with old grief. The mention of Jonny always affected them both this way, opening that shared wound that had never fully healed.

"Perhaps, Colonel," Christian suggested gently, "you might join us for dinner tonight? Thomas can arrange for something in our private dining room, away from the hubbub of your officers' mess. I'm sure you have much to catch up on, and I admit I'm curious to hear about your acquaintance with my cousin."

"I'd be honoured," Pete replied, his smile genuine. "And please, both of you, call me Pete. If we're going to be sharing this magnificent pile of stones for the duration, we might as well be comfortable with each other."

"And please, in private it's *'Christian'*, if you like?" the earl offered to an eager nod from Pete.

As they finished their drinks, making arrangements for the evening, Christian observed the subtle changes in Thomas—the animation in his normally composed features, the occasional unguarded smile. Whatever connection existed between Thomas and this American colonel; it clearly ran deep.

Later, as Pete took his leave to attend to his duties, promising to return for dinner, Thomas closed the door behind him and leaned against it for a moment, his expression unreadable.

"You never mentioned him," Christian whispered. It wasn't an accusation, merely an observation.

Thomas straightened, resuming his customary poise. "There were many things from that time that seemed better left in the past."

Christian nodded, understanding perfectly. They all carried private histories, memories too complex or painful to revisit except in the silence of their own thoughts.

"Will it be difficult?" he asked. "Having him here?"

A FORBIDDEN LOVE

Thomas pondered the question. "Not difficult, precisely. Unexpected. Like opening a door to a room, you thought long sealed."

Christian recognised the metaphor. There were many such doors in their shared history—closed but never locked, the rooms behind them still furnished with memories that could still surprise with their vividness.

"Well," Christian said, rising to refill their glasses, "I look forward to hearing more about this connection. Anyone who knew Jonny in those final days... that's a perspective I haven't had before."

"Yes," Thomas agreed, accepting the refreshed drink. "Though I suspect Colonel Kowalski's stories may reveal aspects of Jonny that might surprise even you."

There was something in his tone—a careful neutrality that Christian had learned to recognise as Thomas' way of preparing him for potentially unsettling information. But before he could inquire further, a distant crash and a chorus of American voices raised in good-natured argument reminded them of the transformation taking place throughout the rest of Langley Hall.

"We should prepare for dinner," Thomas said. "The colonel—Pete—will have many questions, I imagine."

"As do I," Christian replied lightly. "Beginning with how our reserved Thomas came to be on first-name terms with an American officer."

Thomas' smile held secrets accumulated over decades of service. "That, sir, is a story best told over a good meal and better whisky."

"Then we shall ensure both are provided in abundance," Christian declared, raising his glass in a small toast. "To unexpected reunions."

"To unexpected reunions," Thomas echoed, his voice steady but his eyes alight with memories stirred back to life.

Thomas departed, leaving Christian alone with his secret papers for an hour. He made the necessary arrangements for dinner with the kitchen and then returned to his rooms. His quarters were modest by the standards of Langley Hall—a small sitting room with a bedroom adjoining—but they reflected his character in every detail. Books lined the shelves, their spines worn with use rather than display. A single landscape hung above the fireplace, depicting the Norfolk coastline in muted greys and blues.

With his immediate duties completed, Pete sought out Thomas' room, guided by the corporal on duty at the desk. He knocked quietly on the door, uncertain now whether this was the right thing to do.

"Enter," said Thomas, assuming it might be someone with a message. He turned slowly from his seat to see Pete stood in the centre of the room, his commanding presence somehow diminished by the intimacy of the space, by the weight of two decades of silence between them. Thomas stood, surprised by Pete's presence.

"I thought we should talk before dinner Tom," he moved towards the mantle when he noticed a familiar picture. His fingers traced the edge of a silver frame containing a faded photograph—three young men in uniform, their faces caught in a moment of wartime camaraderie that had once seemed eternal.

"You kept it," Pete said softly, lifting the frame for a closer look. His thumb brushed across the glass, over the image of a younger self standing between Thomas and Lord John Langley—all of them thin-faced but smiling, arms slung over each other's shoulders.

A FORBIDDEN LOVE

"Of course I kept it," Thomas replied, his voice carefully measured as he closed the door. He moved to the sideboard, busying himself with glasses and a decanter of whisky. "It's one of the few photographs I have of Jonny from that time." The unspoken hung between them, and one of the only memories I have of you.

Pete replaced the frame carefully, accepting the glass Thomas offered him. Their fingers didn't touch this time—Thomas had made sure of that—but the deliberate avoidance was its own form of contact.

"You've done well for yourself, Tom. These are fine quarters for..." Pete paused, uncertain of the proper term.

"For a servant?" Thomas supplied with a hint of wry amusement. "Things evolved over the years. My position here is... somewhat unique."

"I can see that. The way you and Christian interact—there's a trust there. A partnership of sorts."

Thomas gestured toward the modest armchairs flanking the fireplace. "Time and circumstance create unusual bonds," he said, taking his seat with the same quiet dignity he'd always possessed. "Christian found himself responsible for an estate he hadn't been raised to manage. I had the institutional knowledge he needed. We adapted."

Pete settled into the opposite chair, his uniform looking oddly formal in the homey surroundings. For all his military bearing, there was something vulnerable in his expression as he gazed at Thomas across the small space between them.

"Why did you never write, Pete?" The question emerged more bluntly than Thomas had intended, slipping past the careful composure he'd maintained during their earlier reunion.

Pete's eyes dropped to his glass. His hands were steady, but he felt a warmth in his chest, an uncomfortable heat that he recognised as guilt. "I did write. Three letters in the first year after I returned home."

"I never received them."

"I suspected as much when no reply came." Pete took a deep swallow of whisky. "The third one came back marked
'*Return to Sender.*' I thought perhaps... you didn't want to hear from me."

Thomas' expression remained composed, but a slight tension around his mouth betrayed his feelings.

"The postal system immediately after the war was chaotic. And I was traveling with Christian for several months in '19, helping him sort out his affairs between Germany and England."

"I should have tried harder," Pete admitted. "But then life... happened. My father's business was struggling. My mother's health was failing. And there were expectations..."

"Expectations," Thomas echoed, understanding in his tone. The word encompassed so much—family pressures, societal demands, the narrowing of possibilities that came with peacetime conformity.

Pete nodded; relief clear in his expression at being understood without having to articulate every painful detail. "I told myself it was for the best. That whatever happened in France should stay there. That we both needed to move forward without... complications."

"Is that what I was to you? A complication?" There was no bitterness in Thomas' question, only a quiet curiosity.

A FORBIDDEN LOVE

"God, no, Tom," Pete leaned forward, his earnestness breaking through his military reserve. "You were the clearest thing in a muddled time. You and Jonny both—you showed me possibilities I hadn't imagined. But back home, those possibilities didn't exist. Or if they did, the cost was too high."

Thomas nodded slowly. He understood all too well the compromises required to navigate a world that offered such narrow channels for men like them. He had found his own accommodation with reality—his position at Langley Hall, his companionship with Christian, the quiet life he'd built within the parameters available to him.

"When did you marry?" he asked.

Pete's eyebrows rose slightly. "You knew?"

"Your ring," Thomas said simply. "You weren't wearing one in 1918."

Pete twisted the gold band on his left hand. "1922. Eleanor. A family connection through my mother's side. Two children—Matthew and Sarah."

His voice softened with genuine affection when mentioning his children, though Thomas noted the difference in tone when he spoke of his wife. "And you? Did you ever...?"

Thomas shook his head. "My life took a different path."

"With Christian?"

The directness of the question might have offended Thomas from another man, but from Pete—who had known him in those raw, honest days of wartime—it merely prompted a small, enigmatic smile.

"Christian and I have a bond that transcends easy categorisation," he said carefully. "We share a history, a devotion to this place, and... memories of someone we both loved."

Pete nodded, understanding the complexities that couldn't be spoken aloud, even between old friends. "Jonny would be pleased, I think. To know that you both found a way to honour his memory through your care for each other and this place."

Thomas' composure wavered slightly at the mention of Jonny. "You knew him only briefly," he said, not accusingly but with curiosity, "yet you speak as though you understood him well."

"Some people reveal their essence quickly in wartime," Pete replied. "Jonny had a gift for seeing people clearly and accepting them completely. It made him easy to trust, to confide in." A shadow crossed his face. "I often wondered if that openness of his made him more vulnerable at the end."

Thomas stilled. "What do you mean?"

"Only that he seemed to feel things more deeply than most officers allowed themselves to. It made him a better leader, but I worried it came at a personal cost." Pete hesitated. "Did he ever speak to you about me in those final weeks?"

"No," Thomas admitted. "He was always the soul of discretion."

"So, you taught him well then Thomas." A weighted silence fell between them. Both men sipped their whisky, lost in memories of a time that had shaped them in ways they'd never fully articulated, even to themselves.

"We should join Christian," Thomas said, glancing at the small clock on the mantelpiece. "He'll be waiting for us in the drawing room of his apartment."

A FORBIDDEN LOVE

Pete nodded, setting aside his glass and rising. "I'd like that. I have so many questions about this place, about John's childhood here. And about you, Tom—the years between then and now."

They made their way through the corridors of the *Dowager Wing*, their steps falling into synchronised rhythm as they had during walks through war-torn French villages two decades earlier. The familiarity of it—muscle memory preserved across time and distance—added a poignant undercurrent to their otherwise casual conversation about the estate and its history.

Christian's drawing room, when they entered it, offered a welcoming contrast to the militarised atmosphere of the rest of Langley Hall. A naval chart was spread across a side table, anchored by crystal paperweights, evidence of Christian's ongoing intelligence work.

Christian himself greeted them warmly, having changed from his afternoon suit into evening attire—a concession to pre-war formality that seemed to acknowledge the significance of this reunion dinner. He gestured them toward the arrangement of chairs near the fireplace, where crystal decanters and glasses awaited them.

"I hope you don't mind dining in these more intimate surroundings, Colonel," Christian said as he poured drinks with the effortless grace of a man accustomed to entertaining. "The main dining room has been converted to a briefing area for your officers."

"Please, it's Pete," the American reminded him. "And this is perfect. I've seen enough military installations to last a lifetime. It's refreshing to experience something of the real Langley Hall."

"What remains of it," Christian said with a faint smile, though there was no bitterness in his tone. "This wing preserves something of its former character, at least."

As they settled into conversation, the light outside the tall windows faded from golden afternoon to the soft indigo of a summer evening.

Candles were lit, casting the room in a warm glow that softened the faces of the three men as they gradually moved from polite small talk to more substantive exchanges.

One of the few remaining household staff—a simple but elegant meal created despite wartime rationing served dinner. Thomas, though technically dining as a guest, rose several times to assist with service—a habit too deeply ingrained to abandon.

"Please, Tom, sit," Pete urged after the third such instance. "Let someone else play butler tonight."

Christian nodded his agreement. "Indeed, Thomas. You're as much a host here as I am."

This small acknowledgment of Thomas' elevated status within the household spoke volumes about the evolution of relationships at Langley Hall over the decades. Thomas acquiesced with a slight inclination of his head, resuming his seat at the table.

As the meal progressed, the conversation turned increasingly to shared memories—stories of Jonny's childhood relayed by Christian, anecdotes of his military service shared by Thomas, and Pete's own recollections of their time together in France.

A FORBIDDEN LOVE

"So, Tom, when did you first meet Jonny?" asked Christian. Wanting to put this piece of the puzzle in place after many years. "He always told me that he couldn't remember as you had always been there." Thomas, took a deep breath and glanced skywards as he retrieved the memory.

"I think it would have been when he was about four or five as I remember. The late Countess had just bought him a pony to learn to ride on and he was over in the stables, as I remember," he paused to fetch another memory. "So, I was seven or eight and loved horses so was often there too. The Head Groom, a friend of my father, had no objections and would let me lead Jonny around on the pony.

In the end we would go riding together, but just on the lawns," he looked at Christian, "and then you turned up the next summer with your mother, and he insisted I teach you to ride too."

"Oh yes, I remember that – his complete insistence!" Christian smiled, "even though the bloody brutes terrified me."

"Yes, he could be insistent, but he had this way of making everyone feel understood," Pete said, gesturing with his fork as he described a particular incident involving Jonny defusing tension between British and American troops. "Never raising his voice, just quietly redirecting everyone's attention to what they had in common rather than their differences."

"That was Jonny's gift from childhood," Christian agreed, a fond smile softening his aristocratic features. "Even when we were boys, he could navigate conflicts that left me baffled. I was always more direct—a trait my German father encouraged."

"Not unlike American directness," Pete observed. "Perhaps that's why John and I got on so well despite the brevity of our acquaintance."

Thomas, who had been quietly attentive throughout this exchange, offered his own observation. "Jonny appreciated authenticity in others. He found it... restful, I think, after the constant performance required by his position."

The evening deepened, the candles burning lower as they moved from dinner to coffee and brandy served in the comfortable arrangement of chairs by the fireplace. The conversation flowed more freely now, punctuated by occasional laughter and thoughtful pauses—three men discovering the common ground that existed between vastly different life experiences.

"You know," Pete said during one such pause, studying Christian over the rim of his brandy glass, "I can see what Jonny saw in you."

The statement hung in the air, unexpectedly intimate. Christian's expression registered surprise, then curiosity. "Oh? And what was that?"

Pete contemplated his words. "A steadfastness. A quality of being exactly who you are without apology, but also without imposing that self on others." He smiled slightly. "He described you once as *'the most honest man I know, even when he's being diplomatic'.*"

Christian looked momentarily taken aback, then deeply moved by this glimpse into his cousin's perception of him. "He said that? To you?"

"During one of those endless nights in the officers' mess or his quarters," Pete confirmed. "When conversations drift to the things that matter."

A FORBIDDEN LOVE

Thomas watched this exchange with quiet intensity, noting the subtle flush that coloured Christian's cheeks—not from embarrassment but from the profound impact of hearing how Jonny had spoken of him to others.

The conversation shifted then to lighter topics—cultural differences between Britain and America, the challenges of adaptation on both sides.

"You should see my men trying to understand cricket," Pete laughed. "Though I've promised to try to organise a baseball game and invite a local village team to learn our national pastime."

"Speaking of American customs," Christian ventured, "one of your officers mentioned something called *'sliders'* with such longing that one might think they were a religious experience rather than food."

Pete's face lit up with exaggerated enthusiasm. "Miniature hamburgers! Perfect little bites of beef, onions, and cheese on tiny buns. When this war is over, I'm taking you both to *White Castle* in *New York*. You haven't lived until you've had a proper American slider at two in the morning after a night on the town."

"I confess I'm struggling to imagine either Christian or myself at a place called *White Castle* at two in the morning," Thomas remarked dryly.

"That's exactly why you need to experience it," Pete insisted. "Just as I've had to adjust to your English breakfast with its... what do you call them? *Bloaters?*"

"*Kippers*," Christian and Thomas corrected in unison.

"*Kippers*, right. Smoked fish at breakfast—took some getting used to. But now I might miss them when I go home."

The simple mention of going home—an inevitable reality of wartime assignments—cast a momentary shadow over the warmth of the evening. It was a reminder that this reunion, however meaningful, was temporary, subject to the larger movements of the war and the separate paths their lives would resume afterward.

As the evening drew to a close, Pete rose to return to his duties, thanking Christian for his hospitality and exchanging a warm handshake with Thomas that lingered just a moment longer than necessary.

"We have much more to discuss," Pete said, his gaze meeting Thomas' directly. "About the past, and perhaps... other matters."

Thomas nodded; his composure perfect but his eyes revealing more. "There will be time, I hope, before your duties take you elsewhere."

After Pete had departed, Christian remained by the fireplace, swirling the last of his brandy thoughtfully. "An interesting man, your Colonel Kowalski," he observed. "One senses there are depths beneath that American affability."

"Yes," Thomas agreed, beginning to gather the coffee cups with habitual tidiness. "He always had that quality, even as a young lieutenant."

Christian watched him for a moment, then asked quietly, "Was there something between you? During the war?"

Thomas' hands stilled, then resumed their task. "There was... a connection. Brief, intense, and ultimately impossible to maintain across the distance that followed."

Christian nodded, accepting this revelation without judgment. After all these years, they had few secrets from each other, though some truths remained delicately shrouded in careful phrasing.

"And now? With his return?" Christian's question held no jealousy, only genuine concern for Thomas' emotional well-being.

197

A FORBIDDEN LOVE

"Now we are two middle-aged men with established lives and twenty-three years of separate experiences between us," Thomas replied pragmatically. "Whatever existed then belongs to a different time."

Christian rose and crossed to where Thomas stood, placing a gentle hand on his shoulder. "Even so, I'm glad for you that he's here. Connections from that time... they're precious, regardless of what form they take now."

Thomas looked up, meeting Christian's gaze with uncharacteristic openness. "Yes," he agreed softly. "They are indeed precious."

They remained like that for a moment—two men who had weathered decades together, finding in each other the understanding and acceptance that the wider world often denied them. Then, with the practiced ease of long companionship, they moved to extinguish the candles and restore order to the room before retiring for the night, each carrying their own private reflections on the unexpected bridges between past and present that this day had revealed.

Morning light filtered through the tall windows of what had once been the study next to the library, now converted into an improvised strategy office. Maps covered the walls where portraits of Langley ancestors had hung for centuries, their gilt frames replaced by wooden pins and coloured markers tracking the movement of warplanes across the European theatre. Christian stood beside Pete at the central table, his elegant fingers tracing coastlines he knew intimately both from naval charts and personal memory.

The German naval bases—*Wilhelmshaven, Kiel, Cuxhaven*—places that had once been his professional home now transformed into targets for Allied bombers. His face revealed nothing, a mask of professional detachment cultivated through years of walking the narrow line between his German heritage and his English loyalty.

"The primary U-boat pens at *Kiel* will have been reinforced," Christian explained, his voice steady as he indicated a section of the chart.

Pete leaned closer, his American uniform a stark contrast to Christian's carefully tailored civilian clothes. "What about approach vectors? If we can't crack the pens themselves, we can at least disrupt the surrounding infrastructure."

Christian nodded, shifting his attention to another area of the map. "The repair facilities here and here," he said, marking two locations with a red pencil, "are more vulnerable. Targeting them would create bottlenecks in their maintenance schedule. And this channel," his finger traced a narrow waterway, "—is their primary exit route to the *Baltic*. Mining operations could be effective, though dangerous to execute."

Thomas entered silently, bringing fresh coffee on a silver tray. His presence was so unobtrusive that neither man paused their conversation, though Pete's eyes flicked toward him, a momentary softening in his otherwise professional demeanour.

"Thank you, Thomas," Christian acknowledged, taking a cup without looking up from the map. "Colonel Kowalski and I will be occupied for another hour at least."

"Very good, sir." Thomas set the tray down and withdrew, his steps soundless on the carpet that had once cushioned the feet of musicians and dancers in more peaceful times.

A FORBIDDEN LOVE

Pete took a long sip of coffee, then refocused on the chart. "Your knowledge of these installations is remarkably detailed," he observed. "Current, too."

Christian's expression remained neutral, though a slight tension appeared at the corners of his mouth. "I maintain certain... connections. Former colleagues who share my concerns about the current regime."

"That must be difficult for you," Pete said quietly. "Providing intelligence that will be used against your homeland."

Christian straightened, his blue eyes meeting Pete's directly. "Germany as I knew it no longer exists, Colonel. The country of *Goethe* and *Beethoven* has been perverted into something unrecognisable. What loyalty I owe is to that older Germany—and I honour it best by helping to excise the cancer that has taken root there."

Pete nodded, understanding in his expression. "Still, I appreciate the position you're in. Not every man could navigate such divided loyalties with grace." Christian realised now how Jonny had forged an easy bond with Pete.

A ghost of a smile touched Christian's lips. "An accident of birth placed me between two nations. Circumstances forced me to choose. The choice was made long ago—I merely continue to live with its consequences."

They returned to the maps, the conversation shifting to the technical details of flight paths, fuel consumption, anti-aircraft defences, and weather patterns. Christian's knowledge—born of both his naval training and his intelligence work for the British—proved invaluable as they identified potential targets and approaches.

"This information will save American lives," Pete said as they concluded their session, rolling up the annotated charts. "And British ones too. Our combined bombing campaign stands a better chance of success with insights like yours."

Christian began replacing the cover on a detailed model of the *Kiel* harbour. "I take no pleasure in it," he admitted. "Some of the men your bombs will kill were once my colleagues. Perhaps even friends."

"War creates impossible choices," Pete acknowledged. "I've sent men on missions knowing not all would return. You do what you must, then live with it afterward."

The simple statement, delivered without drama or self-pity, reflected a soldier's pragmatism that Christian recognised from his own military days. They shared that burden—the weight of decisions that balanced lives against strategic necessity.

"Will you join Thomas and me for dinner again this evening?" Christian asked as they prepared to leave the improvised strategy room. "I believe cook has managed to secure a brace of pheasants through somewhat mysterious channels."

"I'd be delighted," Pete replied. "But first, if you don't mind, I'd like a word with Thomas. Something personal."

Christian nodded, an understanding passing between them that required no elaboration. "Of course. I believe he's inspecting the conversion of the east wing storerooms. I'll leave you to find him."

They parted ways in the corridor, Christian heading toward his private quarters while Pete made his way through the increasingly military environment of Langley Hall. American soldiers saluted as he passed, radio operators hunched over equipment in what had once been sitting rooms, clerks clacked away at typewriters set up on antique writing desks. The juxtaposition of modern war machine against the backdrop of centuries-old aristocratic splendour created a surreal tableau—two worlds colliding out of necessity rather than natural evolution.

Pete found Thomas exactly where Christian had suggested, overseeing the transformation of a large storeroom into additional quarters for American officers. He stood with clipboard in hand, directing the placement of cots and footlockers with the same attentive precision he might once have applied to arranging flowers for a formal dinner.

"Tom," Pete called softly from the doorway. "Could I borrow you for a few minutes?"

Thomas looked up, his professional mask slipping momentarily to reveal a flicker of pleasure before smoothly returning to its customary composure. "Of course, Colonel. Stevens, please continue with the inventory while I'm gone."

He joined Pete in the corridor, falling naturally into step beside him as Pete led them toward a small courtyard garden that had somehow remained untouched by the military transformation engulfing the rest of Langley Hall.

The garden offered a pocket of tranquillity—roses climbing ancient walls, a small fountain bubbling at its centre, stone benches positioned to catch the best of the summer sun. It might have been a scene from before the first war, let alone the second, preserved as if in amber.

"I thought we might speak privately," Pete said, gesturing toward one of the benches.

Thomas nodded, taking his seat with characteristic grace. Though he now wore the attire of a senior household manager rather than a servant, his posture kept the perfect erectness that had been trained into him since youth. Pete sat beside him, leaving a respectful distance between them. For a moment, he gazed at the roses, gathering his thoughts.

"I've been married for twenty years, Tom," he said, his voice gentle but direct. "Two children—my son is nineteen now, my daughter seventeen."

Thomas' expression remained carefully neutral. "Yes, you mentioned your family yesterday."

"What I didn't mention was why." Pete turned slightly to face Thomas more directly. "After those letters went unanswered, after I thought you wanted nothing more to do with me... I tried to build the life that was expected of me. The only life that seemed possible in America after the war."

"I understand," Thomas mumbled. "Truly, I do."

"Eleanor is a good woman. A family friend. She knew from the beginning that what I offered wasn't... wasn't the kind of love most women expect in marriage. But she was pragmatic. She wanted children, security, a respectable position in society. I could provide those things," Pete continued, his gaze steady on Thomas' face.

"We made a practical arrangement, one that's served us both reasonably well over the years. The children have been our true bond—they're remarkable young people, Tom.
Matthew is in officer training now, likely to be sent to the Pacific Theatre. Sarah is studying mathematics at Barnard College—brilliant girl, reminds me of my mother."

A FORBIDDEN LOVE

Thomas listened quietly, his hands folded in his lap, his eyes never leaving Pete's face. There was no judgment in his expression, only attentive interest that encouraged Pete to continue.

"I won't pretend it's been a perfect life, or even the one I might have chosen if circumstances had been different. But it's been a good life in many ways." Pete paused, then added more softly, "though there have been times—many times—when I've wondered about the road not taken."

"The road that might have included me," Thomas supplied, his voice steady.

"Yes." Pete's admission hung in the air between them, simple and profound.

A gentle breeze stirred the roses, carrying their scent across the small garden. It was a peaceful moment, at odds with both the military bustle just beyond the garden walls and the emotional complexity of their conversation.

"I gave up hope, Tom," Pete continued after a moment. "When those letters went unanswered, when I had no way of reaching you, when the demands of civilian life in America closed around me like a fist... I convinced myself that what happened in France was a wartime anomaly. Something born of extraordinary circumstances that couldn't—shouldn't—survive in ordinary time."

Thomas nodded slowly. "Perhaps you weren't entirely wrong. The war created its own reality—compressed time, intensified emotions, suspended conventional judgments. We were different people then."

"Were we?" Pete's question held genuine curiosity. "Or were we simply more ourselves than society normally permitted?" Thomas considered this, his gaze drifting to the climbing roses whose pattern he had known for decades.

"Both, perhaps. The person I was then contained the seeds of who I am now, but I've grown in directions I couldn't have anticipated."

"And you, Tom? After Jonny died, after you returned here... was there ever someone for you?"

The question was gently asked, but Thomas' expression closed slightly, becoming more guarded. "My life took a different path than yours. My position here, my responsibilities to the estate and to Christian... they became my focus."

"That's not quite an answer," Pete observed, though without pressing.

Thomas' lips curved in a slight smile. "No, it isn't. But it's the one I'm comfortable giving."

Pete accepted this with a nod, understanding the boundaries Thomas was establishing. "Fair enough. I didn't come here expecting... well, I'm not entirely sure what I expected. To apologise, certainly. To explain. Perhaps just to see you again and know that you've been well."

"I have been well," Thomas assured him. "My life here has provided purpose, security, and companionship. Not everyone is fortunate enough to say as much."

There was something in his tone—a quiet dignity, a certainty about the choices he'd made—that both impressed and saddened Pete. He found himself wondering about the nature of Thomas' relationship with Christian, about the private life this reserved Englishman had built within the confines of his position and the constraints of his era.

"And what of you and Christian?" he asked, treading carefully. "You've been together a long time."

A FORBIDDEN LOVE

Thomas' expression revealed nothing, his composure absolute. "Christian and I have a profound bond forged through shared history and mutual respect. The nature of that bond is... personal."

Pete nodded, accepting the gentle rebuff. "Of course. I didn't mean to pry."

"Yes, you did," Thomas replied, unexpected humour warming his voice. "But I appreciate your directness. It was always one of your more appealing qualities."

Pete laughed, the tension between them easing somewhat. "Some things don't change, I suppose. Still the blunt American after all these years."

"Refreshingly so," Thomas agreed. Then, with a slight shift in tone: "I bear you no ill will for the choices you made, Pete. We each navigated the aftermath of the war as best we could, with the options available to us."

"Even my failure to try harder to find you?"

Thomas considered this. "Even that. Perhaps especially that. Had you succeeded... what then? What possibility truly existed for us in 1919, or 1922, or any of the years since? You in *New York*, me in Norfolk, both bound by different duties and expectations."

Pete sighed, running a hand through his hair—a gesture that momentarily stripped away the military officer to reveal the young lieutenant Thomas had known. "You're right, of course. Practical as always." He smiled ruefully. "That doesn't stop me from wondering, though. From imagining alternatives."

"The luxury of middle age," Thomas observed. "Looking back at the branching paths of our lives and contemplating the roads not taken."

They sat in companionable silence for a moment, each lost in private thoughts of what might have been. The fountain's gentle splashing provided a soothing counterpoint to the occasional distant sound of military vehicles or shouted orders.

"I should return to my duties," Thomas said finally, rising from the bench with characteristic grace. "And you to yours, I imagine."

Pete stood as well, automatically straightening his uniform jacket. "Yes. Though I'll see you at dinner tonight?"

"Of course. I've requested that cook prepare a pheasant dish Jonny was particularly fond of. I thought... it seemed appropriate, given our shared connection to him."

The mention of Jonny brought a softening to Pete's expression. "He would have enjoyed seeing us reunited like this, I think. He always had a romantic streak beneath that proper English exterior."

"Indeed, he did," Thomas agreed, a fond smile briefly illuminating his features. "Though he would have been appalled at what you Americans have done to his cricket pitch."

Pete laughed. "Converting it to a baseball diamond, you mean? Cultural exchange, Tom. Broadening horizons."

"As you say, Colonel." Thomas' tone was dry, but his eyes held genuine warmth.

As they walked back toward the house, Pete asked casually, "will you show me the photograph albums Christian mentioned? The ones of Jonny's childhood here?"

A FORBIDDEN LOVE

"If you like. They're kept in Christian's study." Thomas glanced at him curiously. "You were quite fond of him, weren't you? In that short time, you knew him."

Pete's expression grew more serious. "He saved my life, Tom. Not literally, but in other ways... he helped me understand parts of myself I'd been afraid to acknowledge. He had a gift for that—seeing people clearly and accepting them completely."

Thomas nodded, understanding perfectly. "Yes, that was very much his nature. Even as a boy, according to Christian."

They paused at the entrance to the house, the threshold between the peaceful garden and the military operation that now occupied Langley Hall. For a brief moment, standing side by side in the doorway, they might have been their younger selves again—two men brought together by circumstance and war, connected by genuine affection and shared understanding in a world that offered little space for either.

"Tom," Pete said, "regardless of the past or what comes after this war... I'm glad to have found you again. To know that you've built a good life. It matters to me."

Thomas' composure wavered slightly, a rare crack in his perfect self-containment. "It matters to me as well," he admitted. "More than I expected it would."

Their eyes met, a current of unspoken understanding passing between them—acknowledgment of what had been, what might have been, and what was now possible within the constraints of their separate lives. Then, with the practiced ease of men accustomed to compartmentalising their emotions, they stepped back into their respective roles—the American colonel and the English estate manager, each returning to the duties that defined their days.

Later, as Thomas arranged flowers for the dinner table in Christian's private dining room—a small ritual of normalcy amid the military disruption—he found himself humming a tune he hadn't thought of in decades. A popular song from 1918, one that American soldiers had sung in French cafés and that he and Pete had once danced to during a rare evening of leave. The memory, long buried beneath layers of subsequent experience, surfaced with unexpected clarity—the crowded room, the scratchy gramophone, Pete's hand warm against his back as they swayed among other soldiers caught in similar embraces, all of them seeking momentary comfort in a world gone mad with war.

"You seem in good spirits," Christian observed, entering the room quietly.

Thomas looked up, his hands stilling among the roses. "Do I? Perhaps I am."

Christian studied him with the perceptive gaze that missed little. "Your Colonel Kowalski found you, then?"

"He did." Thomas arranged one final bloom, then stepped back to assess the effect. "We had a... clarifying conversation."

"About the past?"

"About the present, primarily. And the choices that led us here." Thomas turned to face Christian. "He has a family in America. A wife, two children nearly grown."

A FORBIDDEN LOVE

Christian nodded, absorbing this information. "And how do you feel about that?"

It was the kind of direct, personal question that would have been unthinkable between them in earlier years, but their relationship had evolved far beyond its original parameters. Thomas considered his answer carefully.

"I feel... at peace with it," he said finally. "His life took its course, as mine did. We've both found our ways to navigate a world that offers limited options for men like us."

Christian moved to the sideboard, pouring them each a small glass of sherry—another of their private rituals. "And now? With his temporary presence here?"

Thomas accepted the offered glass, his expression thoughtful. "Now we have an opportunity for friendship unencumbered by youthful expectations or romantic illusions. There's a certain freedom in that."

"Indeed," Christian agreed, raising his glass in a small toast. "To friendship, then. In all its complex forms."

"To friendship," Thomas echoed, the crystal making a clear, pure sound as their glasses touched.

They drank in companionable silence, two men who had built a life together that defied easy categorisation—not quite master and servant, not quite family, but something unique and precious that had sustained them both through decades of change.

"He asked about my photographs of Jonny," Christian mentioned after a moment. "I thought perhaps after dinner we might share some of the albums."

"He would appreciate that," Thomas agreed. "He holds Lord John in high regard. Apparently, they formed quite a bond during their brief acquaintance."

A soft smile touched Christian's lips. "Jonny had that effect on people. He collected strays and orphans of all sorts—human and otherwise."

"Including German cousins," Thomas observed with gentle humour.

"Precisely." Christian's expression grew more serious. "This reunion... it's good for you, isn't it? A connection to that time that neither of us can provide for each other."

Thomas nodded, touched by Christian's perception and consideration. "Yes. Though not without its complexities."

"The worthwhile things rarely are," Christian replied.

As they finished their sherry and prepared for their American guest's arrival, Thomas felt a curious lightness—as if a weight he hadn't known he was carrying had been partially lifted. Not erased, but redistributed somehow, made more bearable by being acknowledged and understood. Pete's return had reopened old wounds, certainly, but perhaps in doing so had allowed them to finally begin healing properly instead of being buried beneath layers of time and obligation.

And if there was a certain wistfulness in his preparations for the evening ahead, a quiet acknowledgment of paths not taken and possibilities unrealised, it was balanced by genuine appreciation for the life he had built—a life of purpose, dignity, and deep connection, however unconventional its form.

A FORBIDDEN LOVE

September 1945

      Autumn painted Langley Hall in shades of amber and gold, the afternoon sun casting long shadows across the south lawn where American servicemen played their last baseball game.
      Christian and Thomas stood at the window of the library—recently restored to something approaching its pre-war state—watching the casual athleticism of young men who had spent the past three years dropping bombs on German cities and now found themselves celebrating victory with the simple pleasure of a hometown game.
      Pete stood among them, his colonel's insignia catching the light as he demonstrated the proper grip on a baseball bat to a local village boy who had become a regular spectator of these strange American rituals.
      "I shall rather miss the noise," Christian admitted, his reflection in the glass revealing the subtle lines that war years had etched more deeply around his eyes. At forty-eight, his dark hair now bore distinguished streaks of silver at the temples, but his posture remained as straight as it had been during his naval days. "The house has always been too quiet since..."
      He didn't finish the thought. He didn't need to. Thomas, standing beside him with the comfortable proximity of decades-long companionship, nodded in understanding. Since Jonny. The unspoken name that still connected them more profoundly than any other bond.
      "Perhaps we should install a gramophone in every room," Thomas suggested with the dry humour that had become more evident in his manner over the course of the Americans' stay. "With a rotation of Glenn Miller records."
      Christian's lips curved into a smile. "And a supply of those remarkable chewing gum sticks that seem to sustain the average American soldier between meals."
      Their gentle banter was interrupted by a knock at the library door. Pete entered without waiting for a response—another American habit that had initially scandalised the remaining household staff but had gradually become accepted as part of the cultural exchange that Langley Hall had hosted since 1942.
      "Thought I'd find you two hiding from the festivities," Pete said, his grin as boyish as it had been when they first met, though his face, too, showed the weathering of war and responsibility. "The men are asking when you're going to come try batting, Christian. They've got a wager going on whether your naval training translates to a decent swing."
      "I fear they would lose their money," Christian replied, though his expression suggested he was not entirely opposed to the idea. "Germans aren't known for baseball skill, and I, at least in that regard, remain German."
      Over the three years of the American occupation, these three men had forged a connection that transcended their differences in nationality, background, and position. What had begun as an unexpected reunion between Thomas and Pete, shadowed by the complexities of their wartime past, had evolved into a three-sided friendship anchored by their shared memories of Jonny.
      They had fallen into a pattern of weekly dinners in Christian's private quarters, where the formality of rank and station dissolved into the easy camaraderie of men who had each, in their own way, experienced the transformative power of war. Pete brought American whiskey and stories of his bombing missions that

carefully hid the more harrowing details.

Christian contributed his extensive wine cellar and occasional intelligence insights that subtly shaped Pete's strategic thinking. Thomas provided the exquisite meals that somehow materialised despite rationing, and the quiet observations that often cut to the heart of matters the others circled around.

But most importantly, they shared Jonny. Through photographs often spread across Christian's desk—Jonny as a towheaded child clutching a cricket bat, as a solemn Eton student, as a young officer with serious eyes that belied his gentle smile.

Through Thomas' carefully preserved mementoes—the pocket watch Jonny had given him before that final deployment, the letters written in a hand that grew increasingly uncertain as the war progressed.

Through Pete's stories of the American newcomer's perspective—Jonny's kindness to a young lieutenant far from home, his quiet courage during bombardments, his gift for finding humour in the bleakest circumstances.

Each man held a piece of Jonny's story, and in sharing those pieces, they created a more complete picture of the person they had all loved in their different ways.

For Christian, he had been the cousin who became a brother, the emotional anchor in a childhood divided between two countries. For Thomas, he had been the young master whose recognition of his humanity had transformed his understanding of service and connection. For Pete, he had been the officer who saw beyond nationality to the person beneath, offering acceptance when it was most needed.

Now, as the war ended and the Americans prepared to return home, these three men stood in the library that had witnessed their growing friendship, aware that another transition approached.

"The transfer papers are ready for signature," Pete said, producing a folder from inside his uniform jacket. "As of 0800 tomorrow, Langley Hall officially reverts to civilian control." His tone was professional, but his eyes reflected the more personal
significance of this administrative detail. "Three years to the day since we arrived."

"Has it been so long?" Christian mused, accepting the folder. "It seems both an eternity and a moment."

"War has that effect on time," Thomas observed. "Stretching it and compressing it simultaneously."

Pete moved to the window, watching his men play what would likely be their final game on English soil. "Most of the squadron ships out next week. I'll remain with a skeleton crew to oversee the decommissioning of the base and transition of the facilities."

"And then?" Christian asked, though all three knew the answer.

"And then back to America. Back to Eleanor and civilian life." Pete's expression held a complex mixture of anticipation and reluctance. "If the Air Force has its way, I'll be teaching at the academy in *Colorado*. Good posting, safe. No more sending young men to drop bombs on cities."

The relief in his voice was palpable. Despite his commitment to the Allied cause, the burden of commanding bombing missions—of calculating acceptable losses and collateral damage—had weighed heavily on him. Christian, with his own military background, understood this particular cost of leadership better than most.

"You must visit us when you return to England," Christian said, moving to the sideboard to pour three glasses of whisky—a ritual that had become their custom. "Langley Hall will seem quite ordinary without the military communications equipment and young men sleeping in the Long Gallery, but I believe you'll find it has its charms nevertheless."

"I'd like that," Pete replied, accepting his glass. "And you two must visit America. I still owe you that tour of proper American cuisine I've been promising. Hot dogs in *Central Park*, clam chowder in *Boston*, barbecue in *Kansas City*."

Thomas raised an eyebrow, his expression suggesting mild scepticism about these culinary delights, though his eyes held genuine warmth. "A compelling invitation, to be sure."

"I mean it," Pete insisted. "Both of you. My home is open to you anytime. Eleanor would welcome you—she's heard enough about *'my English friends at the grand estate'* to be curious."

The invitation hung in the air, sincere but complicated by unspoken realities. While Pete had shared selected stories of his wartime experiences with his wife, the full nature of his connection to Thomas remained unvoiced, existing in that space of understood but unacknowledged truth that men of their generation had learned to navigate.

"Perhaps in a year or two," Christian suggested, raising his glass. "When travel becomes less complicated and the world has settled into whatever new shape awaits it."

"To future visits, then," Pete said, lifting his own glass. "And to present company, and absent friends."

"To present company," Thomas and Christian echoed, the crystal making a pure, clear sound as their glasses touched, "and absent friends."

They drank in companionable silence, each man privately contemplating the bonds that war had forged between them and the inevitable separation that peace would bring. Outside, the baseball game concluded with cheers and good-natured arguments, the sound drifting through the open window like a reminder of the wider world beyond their private sanctuary.

The following morning brought formal ceremonies and carefully worded speeches as Langley Hall was officially returned to civilian status. Christian, impeccably dressed in a suit that Thomas had pressed to military precision, signed the necessary documents with the fountain pen that had belonged to Jonny's father.

Pete, resplendent in his dress uniform with campaign ribbons arrayed across his chest, offered official thanks for the cooperation and hospitality shown to American forces.

Photographs were taken for local newspapers and military archives—visual evidence of Anglo-American cooperation at its most cordial. In one such image, carefully preserved in later years in Christian's study, the three men stood on the front steps of Langley Hall: Christian in the centre with his aristocratic bearing, Pete to his right with military posture, and Thomas slightly to his left, proper but undeniably part of the central composition rather than relegated to the background as a servant might once have been.

The departure of the Americans occurred in stages over the subsequent weeks—first the majority of the bomber crews, then the support personnel, finally the administrative staff that had managed the complex logistics of an overseas air base. Pete remained until the end, overseeing the removal of military equipment and the restoration of requisitioned spaces to something approaching their pre-war condition.

On his final evening at Langley Hall, they dined together not in Christian's private quarters but in the formal dining room, now restored to its original purpose. Thomas had arranged for the table to be set with the full splendour that peacetime once again permitted—silver candelabra polished to mirror brightness, the finest crystal and china that had spent the war years carefully packed away in the cellars, flowers from the gardens arranged with his characteristic precision.

"A proper English farewell," Pete remarked, taking in the elegant setting with appreciation. "Though I've grown rather fond of our more casual dinners in your apartment."

"As have I," Christian admitted. "But some occasions warrant ceremony. Your departure certainly qualifies."

They spoke of the future that evening—of Christian's plans to gradually restore the estate to its pre-war condition, of Thomas' designs for rehabilitating the formal gardens that had been partially converted to vegetable plots during rationing, of Pete's anticipated return to academic life and his children's burgeoning careers.

"The silver lining of these terrible years," Christian observed. "Old structures breaking down, making space for new possibilities."

As the evening concluded, Pete presented them each with a small gift—for Christian, a finely crafted American compass in a walnut case; for Thomas, a leather-bound volume of *Walt Whitman's* poetry with certain passages discreetly marked. A brief meeting of eyes acknowledged the significance of the latter only between giver and recipient, an exchange that contained decades of understanding.

"Until we meet again," Pete said as his jeep awaited in the circular drive the following morning. "Whether here or across the Atlantic."

"We shall hold you to that invitation," Christian assured him, their handshake firm and lingering.

When Pete turned to Thomas, formality gave way to emotion. Their quick but heartfelt embrace communicated what words could not easily express.

"Take care of each other," Pete said quietly, including both men in his gaze. "As you always have."

They watched his vehicle disappear down the lime tree avenue, standing together on the gravel outside Langley Hall as they had stood when the Americans first arrived three years earlier. Though neither spoke, their shared silence contained the understanding that another chapter had closed, another transition navigated together.

In the years that followed, Langley Hall gradually reclaimed its identity as a private estate rather than a military installation, even if it was a little more worn around the edges. Rooms that had housed officers returned to their original purpose as guest chambers and family spaces.

The library, once cluttered with tactical maps, again became a sanctuary of literature and quiet contemplation. The gardens, under Thomas' patient supervision, bloomed with renewed vigour.

Christian and Thomas continued their partnership in managing the estate, their relationship deepening with each passing year. The rigid boundaries of class and position that had once governed their interactions had eroded during the

A FORBIDDEN LOVE

war years, never to be fully restored. While they maintained certain formalities for the benefit of staff and visitors, in private they operated as equals, their mutual respect and affection clear to anyone who observed them closely.

Pete kept his promise to maintain contact, his letters arriving with pleasing regularity from America. Sometimes they contained photographs—Pete with his growing family, including grandchildren in later years; the academy in *Colorado* with its dramatic mountain backdrop; American landscapes so different from the gentle Norfolk countryside. Occasionally, Pete enclosed newspaper clippings, annotating them thoughtfully to document the social changes sweeping through post-war America.

In 1952, Christian and Thomas finally accepted his long-standing invitation, traveling to the United States for an extended visit that took them from *New York* to *Colorado* and several points between. Photographs from this journey, displayed alongside family portraits in Christian's study, showed them looking somewhat bemused but game as they navigated the *Grand Canyon* on mules, sampled hot dogs at *Coney Island*, and stood before the vastness of the Pacific Ocean.

"Not quite the Norfolk coast, is it?" Thomas remarked in one such image, his customary reserve softened by clear wonder at the California shoreline. Upon their return to England, they brought with them not only souvenirs and stories but also a renewed appreciation for Langley Hall and its place in their lives. The estate had weathered economic challenges in the post-war years, requiring adaptations and compromises, but it remained their anchor and sanctuary.

Pete visited England once more before his death in 1961. During that final visit, he stayed at Langley Hall for nearly a month, the three aging men spending long evenings in the library with the photographic albums spread before them, tracing the connections that had shaped their lives across two world wars and half a century of friendship.

"He would be proud of what you've preserved here," Pete said on his last evening, gesturing to encompass not just the physical estate but the less tangible legacy they had maintained. "Jonny always understood that places like this were about more than land and buildings. They were about continuity, about carrying something worthwhile forward."

Christian, his raven hair now fully silver though his blue eyes remained sharp, nodded in agreement. "We've tried to honour that understanding. Though I suspect he would be amused by some of our more modern compromises."

"The guided tours on weekends?" Thomas suggested with a small smile. "Or the gift shop in the old butler's pantry?"

"Both, I imagine," Christian chuckled. "Though he would appreciate the practical necessity. Tradition must adapt to survive."

After Pete's departure—the final time they would see him, though they didn't know it then—Christian and Thomas continued their quiet life at Langley Hall, increasingly focused on ensuring the estate's survival for future generations. They established a trust, negotiated with the National Heritage, and arranged for limited public access that would provide necessary income while preserving the core of the property as a private residence.

Through all these practical considerations, the memory of Jonny remained their touchstone—the standard against which they measured their stewardship, the presence that had first connected them and continued to unite them through the decades.

A FORBIDDEN LOVE

A FORBIDDEN LOVE

CHAPTER EIGHTEEN:
NORFOLK RECOLLECTIONS

February 1952

    The fire cast long shadows across the Persian carpet, its flames dancing in the gleam of the crystal decanter on the mahogany side table. Christian sat hunched over his leather-bound journal, pen poised but unmoving, as outside the windows of Langley Hall, winter pressed its cold fingers against the glass. Time had greyed his dark hair; however, his eyes held their intense blue, a captivating feature from his younger years. Thomas moved quietly about the room, his footsteps barely audible as he arranged yellowing letters on the table, each one a fragment of a past they shared but seldom spoke of aloud.
    The marble hearth, ornate with carved acanthus leaves, framed the roaring fire that was the room's only concession to the February chill. Christian had always preferred this smaller lounge to the grand drawing room; it held fewer ghosts, fewer echoes of laughter from summer gatherings before the Great War had swept away their certainties like autumn leaves. Amid the 1952 winter, postwar, a new queen's upcoming coronation made the room seem timeless.
    Christian swirled the amber whisky in his glass, watching the firelight refract through the crystal, creating constellations that existed for mere moments before dissolving. His fingers, once so nimble at the helm of destroyers, now showed the first betraying spots of age, the veins more prominent beneath skin that had grown translucent. He set down his pen with a soft sigh.
    "These passages about Norfolk in 1914," he said. "I've written and rewritten them a dozen times. Still, they refuse to come right."
    Thomas paused in his methodical arrangement of the letters, each one carefully removed from its envelope and smoothed flat with fingers that had performed this ritual countless times before.
    At fifty-eight, his movements had slowed a little, but they retained the precision that had made him such an exemplary valet in his youth. His hazel eyes, surrounded now by fine lines that spoke of both laughter and sorrow, lifted to meet Christian's.
    "Perhaps, sir, some memories resist being captured in words."
    Christian nodded, acknowledging the wisdom in Thomas' gentle observation. The '*sir*' now was an occasional formality Thomas used when conversations were serious or intense, a vestige of their original roles that had evolved into something far more complex over the decades. It provided a comforting structure to a relationship that defied easy categorisation.
    "It was the quality of the light," Christian mused, turning a page in his journal. "That August before everything changed. I've never seen it's like anywhere else in the world. Golden, but somehow soft around the edges. The way it fell across the terrace when we'd take our tea."
    Thomas' hands stilled over a letter postmarked 1915. "I remember it well, Jonny, would often sit sketching in that light. Said it made even the ordinary seem worthy of preserving."
    The mention of John's name settled between them like a physical presence. Christian's gaze drifted to the mantelpiece where a small, exquisitely executed watercolour hung in a simple frame—a study of the hall's north terrace with

two figures seated at a distance, their features indistinct but their postures conveying an intimate familiarity. One of the surviving pieces of John's artwork.

"He captured it perfectly there," Christian said, nodding toward the painting. "Though he claimed it was merely a practice sketch. He never did recognise the true value of his own work."

Thomas arranged three more letters chronologically before responding, his movements deliberate, as if ordering the past could somehow make sense of it. "He was always more generous in his assessment of others than of himself."

The scent of beeswax from the polished furniture mingled with the peaty aroma of Christian's whisky and the subtle smokiness from the fire. Outside, the wind had picked up, occasionally rattling the windows in their frames, but inside the room maintained its cocoon of warmth and memory. Christian turned back to his memoirs; the pages filled with his elegant, slanting script. Passages had been crossed out, rewritten, annotated in the margins—a evidence of attempts to render truth from recollection. He had begun the project three years ago, spurred by the realisation that few remained who remembered the world before 1914, fewer still who knew the private truths behind the public history.

"Listen to this," he said, flipping back several pages. "*The summer of 1914 stretched endlessly before us, each day unfurling with the certainty of youth that believed itself immortal. We sailed, we rode, we argued philosophy under the ancient oaks. War was theoretical, death an abstraction. Even as Europe trembled on the precipice, we remained suspended in amber, preserved in that golden Norfolk light.*" He looked up at Thomas. "Too romantic, perhaps?"

"Not for those who were there, Kip," Thomas replied. He held up a letter, its creases deep from repeated folding and unfolding over decades. "This one's from July 1914 to his father. He mentions that exact sailing trip—the one where you nearly collided with a small boat on the Chet junction."

A smile, rare and genuine, transformed Christian's face, softening the aristocratic features that had grown more austere with age. "He exaggerated wildly about that incident. I was a perfectly competent sailor; we missed them by... yards not feet as he would have described."

Thomas' answering smile held the same warmth. "As I recall, there were rather differing accounts of that day." They shared a moment of quiet amusement, a small victory against the gravity of their larger reminiscence. Then Christian's smile faded as he turned another page in his journal.

"Every word I write seems haunted by his absence," he murmured, his tone carrying both longing and resignation. "As if I'm trying to capture smoke between my fingers."

The fire crackled and settled, sending a shower of sparks up the chimney. Thomas set down the letter he was holding and crossed to the sideboard, where he poured a modest measure of whisky for himself—a liberty that would have been unthinkable in their early years but had become part of their evening ritual. He returned to his seat, cradling the glass between his palms.

"Perhaps that's as it should be, Jonny's presence was always most felt in what remained unsaid."

Christian lifted his gaze, studying Thomas with an intensity that momentarily bridged decades. "You understood him better than anyone. Better than I did, at times."

A FORBIDDEN LOVE

Thomas looked down at his whisky, watching the firelight play across its surface. "I merely observed. It was my position to notice things."

"It was more than that," Christian insisted gently. "You saw him clearly, without the complications that... clouded my perspective."

They fell silent again, each lost in private recollections. The grandfather clock in the corner ticked steadily, marking out the rhythm of a present that continued to flow, despite all that had been lost. Christian returned to his writing, the scratch of his pen against paper a counterpoint to the clock's measured cadence.

Thomas turned his attention back to the letters, handling each with reverent care. Many were from John to Christian, sent during the periods when duty had separated them—Christian at the naval academy in *Wilhelmshaven*, later aboard German vessels, John at *Cambridge*, then with his regiment in France. Some were from Piotr Kowalski, the American soldier whose unexpected friendship had altered the trajectory of all their lives. Others were official communications—telegrams announcing wounds, convalescence, transfers. The final ones, arranged at the end of Thomas' careful chronology, were the hardest to read, even now.

"These letters from the front to the late earl," Thomas said, breaking the silence. "How detailed should they be in your memoirs? Some of the content remains... difficult."

Christian set down his pen and reached for his whisky, taking a measured sip before answering. "I've wrestled with that very question. To sanitise them would be dishonest, yet some pain seems too private to share with the world." He traced the rim of his glass with a fingertip. "Though the world has seen enough of war now to understand what we could not articulate then."

Thomas nodded; his expression solemn. "There are passages in these letters that still catch my breath, even after all these years."

"Which ones?" Christian asked, his voice lowering instinctively, as if they might be overheard discussing state secrets.

Thomas hesitated, then selected a letter from near the end of his arrangement. The paper had grown thin at the creases, threatening to tear along lines that had been folded and unfolded countless times. "This one, from April 1917. Where he describes the dawn breaking over no man's land, and how it reminded him of the light on the Broads that summer before the war."

Christian's expression tightened. "I remember. He wrote of beauty persisting amid devastation."

The trajectory of their shared history hung in the air between them—the young lord who had died in the immediate
aftermath of war, the German naval officer who had survived, and the valet who had kept faith with them both.

"Every word I write seems haunted by his absence," Christian repeated, his voice barely audible above the crackling of the fire.

Thomas looked up from the letters, his eyes meeting Christian's across decades of shared grief and understanding. He nodded, a gesture of quiet determination. They had navigated these waters of memory before, though rarely so explicitly.

Tonight, something had shifted—perhaps it was the approach of the new Elizabethan age, perhaps simply the recognition that their own time grew shorter with each passing year.

A FORBIDDEN LOVE

Whatever the reason, Thomas' nod acknowledged they would continue this journey together, bridging the gulf of shared secrets that lay ahead. Christian understood the gesture perfectly. He picked up his pen again, dipped it in the inkwell, and began to write.

Summer 1954

Summer evenings at Langley Hall possessed a quality of light that seemed to suspend time itself. The sun, reluctant to surrender the day, painted the formal gardens in hues of amber and gold, lingering on the rose bushes that had finally, after years of careful tending, regained their pre-war glory.

On the wide stone terrace that stretched along the north face of the hall, Christian and Thomas had established their own tradition—wicker chairs positioned just so, a small table between them bearing tea or, on cooler evenings, a decanter of brandy. Their conversations flowing as naturally as the breeze that rustled through the ancient oaks beyond the lawn.

The Anglo-Dutch gardens, once the pride of Viscountess Isabella Langley, had suffered during both wars—first from neglect when staff departed for the trenches, then from the practical necessity of growing vegetables during rationing. Now, in the early 1950s, the geometric patterns of box hedges had been restored, the gravel paths raked to pristine smoothness, the fountains repaired and flowing once more. It gave Christian particular satisfaction to see the central fountain playing again, its spray catching the evening light in ephemeral rainbows that appeared and vanished like memories.

"The head gardener tells me the new roses by the east wall should bloom next summer," Thomas remarked, pouring tea with the same precision he brought to all his tasks. Though officially retired from his position as butler, he remained John's personal aide, but maintained many of his duties out of habit and inclination. "The ones Lady Isabella favoured, that came from France."

"She would be pleased," Christian replied, accepting the cup. "Though I suspect she would have rearranged half the plantings by now. She never could resist improving upon even the most carefully considered design. I remember the pride with which she toured the gardens with my mother."

They shared a smile at the memory of John's and Christian's mothers, both dead these forty years yet still a presence in their conversations. The teacup warmed Christian's hands, though the evening was mild enough that he didn't truly need the heat. Age had thinned his blood, making him more susceptible to chill than in his youth, when he had dived into the North Sea without hesitation, emerging to John's concerned admonishments about pneumonia.

On such evenings, their talk wandered familiar paths through past and present. Sometimes they spoke of John—his art, his music, his gentle humour that could defuse tension with a single well-placed observation.

They discussed Pete Kowalski, who had returned to America in 1945, but now maintained a faithful correspondence, his letters arriving with reassuring regularity from New York, then later from Washington where he had secured a position in the War Department. Pete's most recent letter had mentioned the possibility of a visit to England in the autumn.

A FORBIDDEN LOVE

"I wonder if he will find the place much changed," Thomas mused, gazing out over the parkland where sheep grazed placidly, maintaining the lawns as they had for centuries.

"Everything changes," Christian replied, "and yet, the essential character remains. Like people, I suppose."

They also discussed the present—the new agricultural methods being implemented on the estate farms, the gradually shifting demographics of the village as younger people drifted toward Norwich or London, the books they were reading or music they had heard on the wireless. Christian had developed a fondness for American jazz that amused Thomas, who preferred the familiar strains of Elgar and Vaughan Williams.

"The *Andrews Sisters* have a certain vivacity that English music often lacks," Christian defended himself after playing a new record that had arrived from Pete.

"If you say so," Thomas replied, his tone dry but his eyes bright with suppressed humour.

These exchanges, seemingly inconsequential, were the fabric of their shared life—a tapestry of small moments that had, over decades, woven something sturdy and sustaining between them. The formal boundaries of master and servant had blurred then faded, replaced by something neither man had vocabulary to properly name. It was simply their own—a connection forged in grief, tempered by war, and refined by the passage of years.

If their hands occasionally brushed as they passed the teapot or reached for the same book, they felt a spark – static from the dry air, but it jolted them nonetheless, a reminder of the deep connection that had sustained them through joy and grief, war and peace, loss and recovery. Such moments were never acknowledged directly, existing in the same liminal space as so much of their shared history—recognised but unspoken, understood but undefined.

Christian and Thomas had remained full time at Langley Hall after the war, and the decision was made to sell the Mayfair property. Neither Christian nor Thomas missed the irony of a German becoming the custodian of this quintessentially English estate, though the village had long since accepted *'the foreign lord,'* as he was sometimes still called despite holding a British passport since 1924.

The estate had weathered the second great conflict better than the first. The ballroom still bore a faint, darkened outline on its ceiling where water damage from a leaking roof had been imperfectly repaired during material shortages. Christian had promised himself that once building restrictions eased, he would commission proper restoration work.

The sun had begun its final descent toward the horizon, casting long shadows across the terrace. The ancient oaks that had witnessed centuries of Langley history stood silhouetted against the burning sky, their massive trunks dark anchors in the golden light.

A wood pigeon called from somewhere in the gardens, its melancholy cooing a counterpoint to the gentle splash of the fountain. Thomas turned to Christian with a contemplative expression, his weathered face holding the kind of peaceful gravity that comes to men who have seen much and reconciled themselves to both joy and sorrow.

A FORBIDDEN LOVE

The years had been kind to him in many ways—his frame was still straight, his mind sharp, his hands steady enough to continue the detailed work of preserving the estate's records and correspondence that had become his particular province.

"Do you ever wonder," he asked quietly, "what might have been? If John had lived, if the wars had never happened?"

The question hung in the air between them, unexpected yet somehow inevitable. They had circled this territory for years, approaching it obliquely through discussions of specific memories or practical matters of estate management. But Thomas had never posed the question so directly before.

Christian's gaze followed the flight of a late swallow as it darted above the gardens, its wings catching the dying light. The golden illumination softened the creases that time had etched around his eyes and mouth, momentarily restoring a glimpse of the young naval officer who had once stood on this same terrace, full of certainty and ambition. But his eyes held the depth of experience that only decades could bestow—loss and survival, grief and unexpected joy.

"Sometimes," Christian admitted, his voice soft but steady. "But then I think—Jonny lived fully, if briefly. He loved and was loved. He created beauty through his art. He served with courage." He paused; his gaze meeting Thomas' with the directness that had always characterised their most significant exchanges. "And through his life, however short, he brought us together. All of us. There's a kind of immortality in that, don't you think?"

Thomas nodded, understanding perfectly as he always did. "A life that continues to matter, long after it's ended."

"Precisely." Christian smiled, the expression softening the aristocratic features that had grown more distinguished with age. "And so, we honour him best not by wondering what might have been, but by appreciating what is. This place. This moment." His hand moved to cover Thomas' briefly where it rested on the arm of the wicker chair. "This friendship."

The touch was deliberate, acknowledging what had developed between them over the long years—a bond that transcended their original roles, a relationship that defied easy categorisation but had become the central pillar of both their lives.

Thomas turned his palm upward, his fingers curling around Christian's in a brief squeeze before they both withdrew, the moment complete in itself, requiring no elaboration.

The night had fully claimed the gardens now, the formal patterns of box hedge and gravel path reduced to abstract shapes of deeper and lesser darkness. The fountain's splashing provided a gentle counterpoint to the rustle of leaves and occasional call of night birds. Inside the hall, lights had been turned on in several windows, creating golden rectangles that punctuated the stone facade.

"We should go in soon," Thomas said, though neither man moved to rise.

Christian hummed in acknowledgment but remained seated, reluctant to break the spell of their shared contemplation. "It occurs to me that Jonny would be pleased with how the estate has evolved. He always believed that tradition must adapt to survive."

Indeed, under Christian's stewardship, Langley Hall had navigated the challenges of the modern era with remarkable success. Parts of the parkland had

A FORBIDDEN LOVE

been opened to the public on selected days, generating income that supported maintenance of the historic buildings.

Several of the home farms had been modernised with the latest agricultural methods, while others maintained traditional practices that preserved the landscape John had so lovingly captured in his art. The village school bore his name, as did a scholarship fund for promising young artists from Norfolk.

"He would be proudest of the art program, I think," Thomas said, seeming to follow Christian's thoughts as he so often did. "Seeing those children display their work in the gallery space last month—some of them had never held a proper paintbrush before the classes began."

Christian nodded, recalling the exhibition of children's artwork that had been held in what had once been the ballroom, now converted to a gallery and event space. "Art was his first love. Before cricket, before music—even, I think, before us."

The admission hung in the air between them, remarkable for its directness. They so rarely spoke openly of what Jony had meant to each of them, of the complex geometry of affection and desire that had connected the three young men in that last golden summer before the war. It was as if naming it directly might somehow diminish it, reducing something profound to mere words.

"You're right, of course," Christian said, his voice rough with emotion he rarely allowed himself to express. "As you so often are."

As if by mutual agreement, they rose from their chairs, Thomas' joints protesting slightly after the long period of stillness. Christian offered his arm, a support that was as much about connection as physical assistance, and together they made their way toward the warm lights of the hall that had sheltered generations of Langleys and now, by the strange workings of fate and affection, sheltered them.

The clock in the great hall struck nine as they returned inside, its sonorous tones reverberating through the ancient corridors of Langley Hall. Christian suggested they stay in the library where the fire still burned, its amber glow a welcome contrast to the blue-black darkness that had enveloped the terrace. Thomas nodded, and closed the french doors to the terrace.

The warmth of the room embraced them as they entered, the scent of woodsmoke and leather-bound books creating a sanctuary of memory and comfort. Christian settled into his leather armchair, reaching for the decanter to pour two modest measures of whisky. Thomas hesitated by the fireplace, before accepting the offered drink, his weathered face transformed by the dancing flames into a landscape of shadow and light, each line and furrow telling its own story of service, of loss, of quiet endurance. For a moment, he seemed to gather himself, as if preparing to ford a river whose depth and current remained uncertain.

"There's something I've never told you, Kip," he said, his voice low but steady. "About Colonel Kowalski. About Pete."

Christian set his own glass down on the side table, giving Thomas his complete attention. In all their years together, through two world wars and the countless private battles of peacetime, Thomas had rarely volunteered personal information. His discretion was so fundamental to his character that this deviation from habit immediately signalled the importance of whatever was to come.

"I'm listening, Thomas," Christian said simply.

A FORBIDDEN LOVE

"On his last evening at GHQ, he asked if I might join him in the American bar in the village." Thomas' voice had taken on a distant quality, as if he were narrating events that had happened to someone else.

"The publican gave us a corner table, away from the others. Pete ordered wine for us both." Thomas turned back from the window; his expression still lost in memory. "The place was hazy with cigarette smoke."

He took another sip of whisky, gathering himself.

"We talked for hours. About his life in *New York*, his Polish parents, his dreams for after the war. About Jonny, of course—stories from their time together in France."

Christian remained silent, allowing Thomas the space to unfold his story at his own pace. Outside, the wind had picked up, occasionally rattling the windows in their frames, adding a counterpoint to the crackling of the fire and the measured cadence of Thomas' voice.

"As the evening wore on, the other patrons left. The publican was wiping glasses, making it clear it was time to go, but Pete ordered another round, passed the man some American bills that ensured we wouldn't be rushed." Thomas' lips curved in a slight smile. "He had that way about him—so confident, so certain the world would bend to accommodate his wishes."

Thomas returned to the fireplace, setting his now-empty glass on the mantelpiece next to a small silver frame containing a faded photograph of John in his cricket whites, his face young and untroubled, caught in that final summer before the world changed.

"The air between us... shifted," Thomas continued, his voice dropping lower. "The way it does when something unspoken suddenly demands acknowledgment."

Christian leaned forward slightly; his curiosity fully engaged now. In all their years of shared confidences, Thomas had never mentioned this encounter in such detail, had never hinted at anything beyond the most casual interaction with the American officer who had been their link to John's final days.

"He reached across the table and put his hand over mine," Thomas said, the words coming more quickly now, as if having begun he needed to complete the telling before courage failed him. "His fingers were calloused, warm. Different from... different from what I'd imagined."

He glanced at Christian, a flash of vulnerability crossing his features before he looked away. "He said he'd noticed how I looked at him."

"I was terrified," Thomas admitted. "Not of him—never that. But of myself. Of what it meant about me. Of what might happen if anyone saw, if anyone knew." He shook his head, as if still puzzling over his younger self's fears. "I pulled my hand away, stood up, said we should return to our quarters before the storm broke. There was no storm coming, but he didn't argue."

Thomas fell silent, his gaze fixed on the fire once more. The clock in the corner ticked steadily, marking the passage of this moment just as it had measured out the decades of their shared life at Langley Hall.

Christian set his whisky glass down, the soft clink of crystal against wood punctuating the confession. "Why tell me now, Thomas?" he asked gently.

Thomas turned to face him fully, his expression more open than Christian had seen it in years, "because, quite simply, I needed someone other than Pete to know that and you deserved the truth."

A FORBIDDEN LOVE

Christian nodded slowly, "but don't you think I had recognised that energy between you two back in '42 when he turned up here?"

"You did?"

"Of course I did," Christian said, "some of the looks you exchanged were exactly the same looks that you recognised between me and Jonny all those years ago."

These revelations cast their shared history in a new light, added another layer to the complex web of affection and obligation that bound the four of them across time and distance. John, Christian, Thomas, Pete—each connected to the others in ways that defied social norms, that challenged the rigid boundaries of class and nationality and expected behaviour.

Christian rose from his chair, crossing the small distance between them to stand before Thomas. In their youth, the difference in their heights had been more pronounced; now, with age bending Christian's formerly straight spine and Thomas standing tall despite his years, they were nearly eye to eye.

"Thomas," he said, his voice gentle but firm, "you have nothing to fear from me knowing this. Nothing has changed in my regard for you."

But even as he spoke the words, Christian recognised their inadequacy. Something had changed—not his affection for Thomas, which remained as steadfast as ever, but his understanding of the man who had been his companion through decades of joy and sorrow. The knowledge that Thomas, too, had experienced the confusion and longing that had marked Christian's own youth created a new bridge between them, a deeper recognition of shared humanity.

Thomas' eyes, warm hazel in the firelight, met Christian's with a directness that belied his traditional reserve. "Hasn't it, though?" he asked softly. "Changed things?"

Christian considered this, his aristocratic features settling into thoughtful lines. "Perhaps it has," he acknowledged. "But not in the way you fear. Knowledge is rarely the enemy, Thomas. Not between people who have shared as much as we have."

A FORBIDDEN LOVE

Prince Christian, St Olave's Priory, July 1914

A FORBIDDEN LOVE

CHAPTER NINETEEN:
THE LAST SPRING

Early May 1963

The winter had been harsh and relentless across Britain, the worst many had seen since 1947. In Norfolk, the snow had finally receded after two months, revealing the green of the lawns from the library's view. Thomas, now sixty-nine and long relieved of formal duties, still lived at Langley Hall, enjoying a close friendship with Christian. His presence was a comfort to both, especially since Christian's health had been fragile through the winter, marked by several bouts of pneumonia.

On this late spring day, the clear blue skies urged Christian to move from his upstairs sitting room to his favourite armchair by the library fire, where he could better appreciate the view. Thomas ensured the room was warm with a roaring fire and gently wrapped thick woollen blankets around Christian's legs.

"Here are the letters you wanted to go through," Thomas said, setting a small wooden chest on the side table.

"Thank you, Thomas," Christian replied weakly, though his eyes had regained some of their usual sparkle in recent days, giving Thomas hope for a full recovery.

"I'll be in the small study reviewing today's estate correspondence," Thomas said, placing a small handbell beside the chest. "If you need me, just ring, and one of the boys," referring to their footman who was in his thirties, "will let me know."

"Yes, corporal," Christian responded hoarsely with a broad smile.

At sixty-six, Christian's fingers trembled as they traced the faded ink of one of John's letters, the paper as thin and fragile as his own skin had become.

The library at Langley Hall remained unchanged since before the war, with its imposing marble fireplace and the scent of dust and forgotten knowledge from leather-bound volumes. Time had altered Christian; his height diminished, he was a mere shadow of his 1916 self when John wrote from Cambridge.

'*My dearest Kip,*' the letter opened, using the childhood nickname that only John—and later Thomas—had ever dared to employ. Christian silently mouthed the words, his lips forming the syllables that had once been exchanged in whispers in these very rooms during cherished summers, long before the world split along national lines.

The fire crackled in the grate, its amber light dancing over the ornate wood panelling. Adjusting the wool blanket draped across his knees, Christian cradled the fragile letter with hands that, though once strong enough to haul rigging on naval vessels, were now marked by age and swollen joints—as if handling a wounded bird.

Christian closed his eyes. It was August 1910. *The Chet.* John had just turned thirteen, and Christian was six months his senior. They had stripped down to their underclothes and plunged into the cool water, their youthful limbs flashing pale beneath the surface. Later, while lying in a sun-warmed meadow to dry, John had traced the fresh scar above Christian's right eyebrow—a souvenir from a sailing mishap the day before—and in that quiet moment, an unspoken understanding passed between them, one that would take years to fathom and even longer to

A FORBIDDEN LOVE

acknowledge.

Shifting in his armchair, the leather creaking in protest, Christian continued to read. The letter recounted his life in *Cambridge*, a life shared with his valet Thomas, but it was always the final paragraph that unravelled him.

'I keep your photograph tucked inside my jacket, pressed against my heart. The edges have softened with time, yet your face remains vivid. When I close my eyes at night, your voice rises above the clamour of the courtyard. This cannot be mistaken, Kip—it feels like the sole truth in a world gone mad. No matter what happens, know that we shall be reunited.'

With practiced care, Christian folded the letter along creases so deep they almost split the paper into four parts. He slid it back into its envelope and then returned it to the rosewood box that held all of John's letters—twenty-three in total, the final one having been written on the eve of battle and entrusted to Thomas.

At that moment, the fire shifted; a log collapsed into a bed of embers, sending a shower of sparks into the air. Christian reached for his glass of brandy on the side table, its amber liquid catching the flickering light. As he lifted the glass to his lips, he sensed a subtle change in the room—a perceived shift in the air or a different quality in the shadows cast by the flames. His hand froze, the glass suspended halfway to his mouth as the brandy trembled, forming rippling concentric rings that caught the light.

"Is anyone there?" he called out, wondering if the footman might be spying on him for Thomas. No answer came, but the sensation grew stronger; the hairs at the nape of his neck stood on end. He set the glass down with a gentle clink against the mahogany table.

And then, he saw it—or rather, him.

In the space where sunlight streamed through the tall windows overlooking the terrace lawn, a figure stood in military dress. Not the field grey of Christian's youth, but the khaki of the British Army circa 1916.

The uniform was pristine: campaign medals gleamed on the breast pocket and the Sam Browne belt shone with a high polish. And the face—God, the face—was unmistakably John's.

It was not the haunted visage captured in those final photographs when he was barely twenty, but as he might have looked if he had reached middle age—with matured yet familiar boyish features that remained resolutely John.

"*Mein Gott,*" Christian whispered, the echoes of his childhood German surfacing in his shock.

The figure offered no reply, but the medals on its chest caught the sunlight and gleamed as if forged from real metal, transcending mere memory or hallucination. Christian's heart skipped erratically, as if warning of organs beginning their subtle mutiny against time's relentless march. Yet he disregarded the omen, his entire focus fixed on the spectre before him.

"Is that really you?" he whispered, the words spilling out unbidden.

The figure offered no reply, but a shift in its stance—a slight softening or a head tilt—hinted at acknowledgement. Those eyes, Jonny's eyes, as blue as the Norfolk sky beyond, regarded Christian with an emotion that defied simple labels. Attempting to stand, Christian gripped the intricately carved wooden arms of his chair, but his legs betrayed him, leaving him to sink back, winded from even the slightest effort.

"You've come back," he said, his voice steadier now. "After all this time."

A FORBIDDEN LOVE

The library itself seemed to hold its breath. Only the delicate shifting of coals in the fireplace and the soft rustle of ancient tapestries between the bookshelves, stirred by drafts sneaking through centuries-old stone, interrupted the silence.

The apparition, or the figure in his dream, stepped forward from the shadows into the edge of the light. Its footfalls were soundless upon the Persian carpet. With another step, Christian discerned more clearly the uniform's details—the regimental insignia of the Norfolk Regiment on the collar tabs, and the captain's pips decorating the cuffs.

"Jonny," Christian breathed, using the intimate name reserved for family—the diminutive John had always pretended to despise yet secretly cherished from those he held dear.

His hands steadied as a peculiar calm overcame him—a resignation that comes with age and the understanding that not every mystery yields to rational explanation. "You've come to fetch me, haven't you?" Christian inquired, a smile tugging at his lips. "Always impatient, even now."

The ghost—if it could be called that—stretched out a hand. The gesture was unmistakably Jonny, so familiar and quintessential that warmth welled in Christian's eyes, threatening tears. How many times had John offered his hand in this very way, his head tilted ever so slightly and one eyebrow raised in gentle defiance?

"I'm not as spry as I once was," Christian remarked, his attempt at humour softened by the tremor in his voice. "Give me a moment, won't you?" The figure's face remained an enigma, offering neither confirmation nor denial of Christian's interpretation of its presence. Yet the outstretched hand lingered—an invitation or perhaps a silent promise. Closing his eyes for a moment, Christian mustered the strength remaining in his aged body. When he reopened them, the ghost still waited, its patience reminiscent of the man John had rarely shown in life.

"Just... let me look at you a while longer," Christian pleaded softly.

Silence stretched between them, laden with unspoken words and years that had gone by unshared. In that quiet, Christian caught echoes of their youth—the laughter on the Broads, the crisp click of a cricket bat meeting ball on the south lawn, and late-night confidences in the dim rooms above during those stolen summer nights of 1914, before the world transformed forever.

The vision of John Langley lingered—medals shining, hand still extended—while the ancient tapestries whispered overhead like distant waves lapping against a ship's hull; a sound that brought Christian back to his naval days, before love, war, and loss had irrevocably altered his course.

Christian rose from the armchair, his joints echoing with an orchestra of minor aches. The ghost of John waited, luminous and patient, by the French doors leading to the terrace.

Whether this was a visitation or a mere delusion, Christian was resolved to follow wherever it led. His elegant walking stick—a piece of polished walnut with a silver handle—leaned against the side table.

With familiar gratitude, his fingers closed around its cool metal. It had once belonged to his uncle before passing on to Christian, another unexpected inheritance.

A FORBIDDEN LOVE

"You'll have to forgive my pace," he murmured to the apparition. "Time has not been as kind to me as it has to you."

John's ghost made no sound, yet its eyes—God, those eyes—appeared to soften with understanding. With a slight nod reminiscent of the living Jonny's characteristic gesture, it indicated the door. That familiar movement made Christian's throat constrict.

The ghost seemingly drifted backward, allowing him to open the door and shuffle forward. His free hand rested on the cool brass handle for a brief moment as he hesitated; crossing that threshold meant accepting the start of a strange journey, while staying meant forever wondering what might have been. Each step downward demanded concentration. His knees, worn from decades of sailing and rowing, protested every movement.

"I'm fine," Christian said, though no one had asked, "just moving slowly. Not all of us can boast the luxury of incorporeality."

At the final step off the terrace, he recognised his destination. The ghost beckoned more insistently now, and Christian nodded before making his way toward a bench under an ancient oak tree.

Before him, the garden unfolded in meticulously arranged, geometric beds of early spring blooms, edged with neatly trimmed box hedges. In its centre, a stone fountain sent water arcing upward; droplets caught the rising sun and transformed into liquid amber.

Beyond it, the venerable oak, standing sentinel for centuries, displayed massive limbs partially clad in the delicate green of new leaves. The gravel crunched beneath his feet as he walked along the winding path through the formal garden toward the oak. Overhead, birds began their morning chorus; thrushes and finches communicated from the tops of topiaries and hedgerows.

A bold, red-breasted robin landed on the path ahead, regarded him inquisitively, and then flitted away, untroubled by either the old man or his spectral companion. The ghost moved steadily forward, occasionally glancing back to ensure Christian still followed. The medals on its chest sparkled in the morning light, glinting with a metallic reality despite the ethereal nature of their bearer.

They soon approached the oak tree, its vast canopy casting dappled shadows across the grass. Beneath it sat a weathered bench, its wood silvered with age and the passage of time. It had been replaced twice in Christian's lifetime—once after the war and again in the 1950s—but each time with an identical design, as if the continuity of the object were more important than the materials used.

The figure halted beside the bench and turned to face him; its expression unreadable in the shifting light beneath the oak. It gestured toward the bench, as if offering an invitation. Christian approached slowly, suddenly aware of his laboured breathing—a reminder of the effort of the journey that had warmed his cheeks against the cool morning air. Carefully, he lowered himself onto the bench and rested his walking stick against the armrest.

The vision stayed upright for a moment before, in a movement almost hesitant and human, settling onto the bench beside Christian. No weight shifted the wooden slats, no cushion yielded underneath, yet the apparition still assumed a seated pose, its hands resting on knees that offered no substance. Christian looked out over the lawn, now bathed in sunlight that evaporated the dew into drifting wisps. The day promised fair weather—a rare blessing this year.

A FORBIDDEN LOVE

"I've missed this," Christian said after a lengthy silence. "Sitting here with you."

The ghost offered no response, though Christian hadn't expected one. In life, John had often embraced silence, feeling that words couldn't capture the complexity of his thoughts. It seemed only natural that in death—or whatever state he now occupied—he retained that quietude.

A blackbird alighted on the path before them, its bright yellow beak a stark contrast against its sleek, dark plumage. It tilted its head, inspecting the unusual pair with one glimmering eye before beginning its task of extracting a worm from the moist
earth, unbothered by the metaphysical implications of its
audience.

Christian felt a strange peace settle over him. The garden carried the scent of damp grass and the subtle fragrance of early blooms—snowdrops and crocuses that painted the lawns in soft white and rich purple hues. From somewhere far off came the gentle murmur of water, perhaps from the fountain or the small stream marking the eastern edge of the formal gardens.

He turned to observe the shape beside him, this echo of the man he had loved before he even understood love. In the clear late morning light, he noticed details he had missed in the library's dimness—the delicate lines around John's eyes hinting he had reached at least his thirties, the slight weathering of his skin that spoke of time spent outdoors, and the familiar way his hair fell across his forehead just as it had in life.

"Is this what you might have become?" Christian asked softly. "Or are you simply the way I've always imagined you?"

The ghost met his gaze, and in its eyes, there was a depth and understanding that made Christian wonder if this was more than mere imagination, more than an old man's longing for what might have been. As the morning light grew stronger, birds called out from the branches of an oak, and the two figures—one substantial, one ethereal—sat together on the garden bench as they had so many times before, sharing a silence that was filled with unspoken stories.

"I never married," Christian suddenly declared, the words coming out almost on their own. "There were opportunities, of course, once I had made my mark in England, and there were women who showed interest." The ghost remained silent, its head tilting slightly in a gesture reminiscent of John's attentive listening.

"But it would have been a lie," Christian continued. "After living one lie during the war—the dutiful naval officer, the patriotic German—I couldn't bring myself to forge another." He smiled, the familiar lines on his weathered face softening as he spoke. "Besides, I made a promise to you, didn't I?"

Decades later, as Christian gazed upon the ghost of what might have been, he felt an absence of bitterness. Time had smoothed out the harsher edges of regret, leaving behind only a bittersweet acceptance of the roads not taken. "I did once consider breaking that promise," he admitted. "Back in '39, when it was clear another war was looming, I thought that a marriage of
convenience might offer protection. As a German in England,
my situation was anything but secure." The ghost's expression shifted, a hint of concern passing over its features.

A FORBIDDEN LOVE

"But in the end, I couldn't do it," Christian said. "It felt like betraying you, betraying what we had."

"Thomas," Christian said, his tone suffused with warmth. "You know, he loved you—not in the same way I did, but with a devotion uniquely his own. He remained at Langley all those years, even when opportunities for higher positions elsewhere were within reach. I believe he stayed first for you, and later for me."

The ghost's lips lifted into a smile—the familiar Jonny smile that always began at the corners of his mouth before slowly spreading, as if amusement were a realm to be conquered with careful persistence. Christian found himself smiling back, a spontaneous response to a memory of joy.

He closed his eyes once more, letting the sun's gentle heat seep into his bones. Age had rendered him perpetually chilly, as if his body could no longer produce enough warmth to counter the damp English climate. Yet now, sitting beside John's ghost in the spring sunlight, he experienced a warmth he hadn't felt in months.

"I've led a good life," he murmured after a pause, still with his eyes closed. "Not the one we once planned, but a good life, nonetheless. I had my boats, my books, and a small circle of friends who truly understood me the way you did. The estate has flourished under my care. I've always aimed to be worthy of your legacy." Opening his eyes, he turned toward the ghost. "But I've missed you every day. Every single day for forty-four years."

Then, quite unexpectedly, the ghost reached out—a gesture so surprising that Christian held his breath. The spectral hand hovered just above his own, never quite touching, perhaps unable to, yet close enough for Christian to imagine a faint connection, a cool hint of presence like a momentary shadow crossing an otherwise sunlit path.

He exhaled slowly, his heartbeat irregular in a way that might alarm a doctor but seemed entirely fitting in a conversation with a ghost. "I'm tired, Jonny. Not at this moment, but in a way that cannot be fixed by sleep."

He had outlived nearly everyone he knew from his youth—witnessing two world wars, the rise and fall of empires, and the transformation of one century into the next. He had seen horseless carriages replaced by jet airplanes, telegrams give way to telephones, monarchies fall and republics emerge from their remnants. Throughout it all, John's memory had been a constant, a fixed point against which he measured the passage of time and his own journey.

Now, in the presence of this impossible visitation, Christian sensed a circle coming full form—whether that circle represented life itself or something even greater, he could not tell. The ghost smiled once again with that crooked, familiar grin that had once made Christian's heart race and his palms sweat. Even now, an echo of that sensation stirred within him—a recognition of something profoundly essential.

Time itself seemed to lose its linear nature, stretching and contracting like an accordion played by unsteady hands. Minutes may have spanned hours, or hours compressed into the intervals between heartbeats. The sun ascended to its zenith, then began its slow descent toward the afternoon, shifting the light from the clear gold of morning to the deeper amber of approaching evening.

And still, there they sat—an old man and a ghost—sharing smiles and silent laughter over cherished memories, communicating in a language beyond words and physical confines. In this suspended moment, the garden transformed

A FORBIDDEN LOVE

into a space outside time, a sanctuary where the past and what might have been coexisted in perfect harmony.

Thomas ambled along the gravel path; his aged hands steady on a silver tray carrying a steaming drink for Christian. He had felt a pang of worry upon discovering the library empty, even though signs of recent use were clear—the dent left in the leather armchair, the partially consumed brandy glass, and the open rosewood box of letters on the side table.

It was the open door leading to the terrace that offered the first clue, and instinctively he knew where Christian would be. As he neared the ancient oak, Thomas let his thoughts drift through a lifetime of memories built on service and friendship.

He remembered having known Jonny and Kip since he was about ten until joining the staff at just fourteen as a hall boy, dutifully clearing chamber pots, hauling coal, and polishing boots. His promotion to footman at nineteen had coincided with John's fifteenth year, and by some twist of fate two years later he had been assigned as the young lord's valet.

He recalled that very first morning in his new uniform, his nerves betraying him as he tried to seem more seasoned while collecting Jonny from *Victoria Station*. '*We'll learn together,*' they had both said at some point—a simple promise that laid the foundation for a bond surpassing the typical master-servant relationship.

Thomas paused by the fountain, shifting the tray to ease the strain on his arthritic wrists. The water shimmered as it rose and fell, reminiscent of the crystal decanters he had spent countless hours polishing. He remembered John's artistic sensitivity, how he had once dedicated an entire afternoon to capture that glimmer in watercolours, growing increasingly frustrated with every unsuccessful attempt.

A smile touched Thomas' face at the memory. Even then, he sensed there was something unique between them, though he lacked the words to define it—a connection that went beyond mere familial ties or school friendships, something intimate that resided in the quiet spaces between their words and the careful way they navigated each other's presence.

The path curved around a cluster of rhododendrons, unveiling the oak tree. There, Thomas spotted Christian seated on a bench beneath its wide-spreading branches, his silver hair a soft halo as his head bowed in what seemed like either quiet contemplation or subtle prayer.

The posture was unexpectedly serene, a striking contrast to the restless energy that had characterised the man well into his eighties.

"Good morning, Kip," Thomas called out in a controlled tone despite the distance. "I've brought you a hot drink."

No reply came—a common occurrence given that Christian's hearing had waned over the years, so he often failed to notice Thomas until he was very nearby. Thomas continued forward with the crunch of gravel under his meticulously polished shoes. As he drew closer, he observed Christian remained utterly still, without even a slight shift or adjustment to ease the burden of aging joints. There was only perfect, complete stillness.

A thrush darted across the path, stirring an involuntary recollection: Lord John, perhaps twelve years old at the time, excitedly pointing out a similar bird and explaining to Prince Christian the difference between a song thrush and a mistle thrush.

A FORBIDDEN LOVE

It was the vivid enthusiasm of youth and the eagerness to share something valuable with someone whose opinion truly mattered. Shaking off the memory, Thomas refocused on the present. Christian sat immobile, his profile defined against the backdrop of fresh foliage, his hands neatly folded in his lap. Now close enough to see clearly, Thomas noticed the old gentleman's eyes were shut and his expression entirely serene.

"Kip?" Thomas said again, softer this time.

There was still no reply. A flutter of worry stirred in Thomas's chest as he quickened his steps, the tea items clinking gently on the tray.

Reaching the bench, he carefully set the tray at its far end, then approached Christian. The elderly man's face wore an expression of such serene calm that Thomas hesitated to disturb him. Yet the eerie stillness—the complete lack of the slightest movement that signified life—confirmed what Thomas had slowly feared.

"Kip?" he said for what felt like the final time, reaching out to rest a gentle hand on Christian's shoulder.

Still nothing. No rhythmic rise and fall of the chest. No soft whisper of breath. Thomas sighed deeply—a sound laden not with shock but with a bittersweet blend of sorrow and resignation. He had known this day would eventually come—indeed, he had suspected it might have come months earlier, given Christian's increasing fragility. That it arrived on such an ideal spring morning, in this cherished place filled with memories, somehow felt apt.

Then Thomas noticed what Christian held in his right hand—a photograph, its edges softened by years of frequent handling. Without even looking, Thomas recognised it: the picture of Jonny in his lieutenant's uniform, taken in the spring of 1917 just before his departure to France. The same photo Christian had kept by his bedside for decades.

With utmost care and respect, Thomas reached out to touch the photograph. Even as Christian's fingers stiffened with the fading warmth of life, they still clutched it firmly. Thomas made no move to dislodge it.

Some bonds, he believed, transcended death. Instead, he gently adjusted Christian's slightly rumpled collar and swept away a stray leaf resting on his lap—small acts of dignity, the final services he could offer the man who had been, in many respects, the centre of his world for over fifty years.

Lowering himself onto the bench beside Lord Christian, Thomas felt the protest of his aging bones. The dappled shade of the oak overhead cast shifting patterns of light and shadow across them with every passing breeze. From this quiet vantage, he took in the full expanse of the formal gardens, where the strict geometries of the flower beds softened under the gentle growth of spring.

His thoughts wandered to John, taken at just twenty-two years old; to Christian, who had returned to England after the war, haunted and altered, finding sanctuary at Langley Hall under the Old Earl's care; to the peaceful life they had slowly built together here—a life constrained by the times yet rich with private joys.

Throughout it all, Thomas had been there—the confidant, the protector, the one who facilitated their discreet happiness. He had intercepted whispers, deflected probing questions, and acted as a buffer between them and a world that could never understand the depth of their connection.

A FORBIDDEN LOVE

Now, as he sat beside the still form of Christian, Thomas experienced an odd sense of completion. His service, which had begun with the young Lord John and extended to his cousin, had come to its natural end. The circle was complete. Reaching into his jacket pocket, he produced the pocket watch that had been his steadfast companion since 1925—a gift from Christian. The time read just past eleven; the household staff wouldn't notice for at least another hour. Thomas closed the watch with a soft click and returned it to his pocket. He resolved to give Lord Christian this final hour of repose in the garden before alerting the authorities. It was the least he could do.

A flicker at the edge of his sight caught Thomas's attention. For just a moment—so fleeting it might have been a trick of the mind—he thought he saw two figures strolling away across the lawn.

One wore an army lieutenant's uniform, and the other was dressed in naval attire. Their postures were upright, their steps light, free from the burdens of age or weakness. As he observed, they seemed to disappear into the day's brightness, like morning mist melting in the sunlight.

Thomas blinked, and the image—if it was indeed an image—was gone. The lawn was empty now, the grass gently swaying in the spring breeze. He turned back to Christian, noticing the gentle smile that lingered on the elderly man's lips. With deliberate care, Thomas retrieved the photograph from Christian's hand and tucked it securely into his breast pocket, placing it directly over his heart.

"There you are, Kip," he whispered. "Right where he belongs."

A FORBIDDEN LOVE

A FORBIDDEN LOVE

CHAPTER TWENTY:
EPILOGUE

Thomas Cooper moved through Lord Christian's study like a shadow detached from time, his footfalls muffled by the thick Persian rug that had witnessed decades of confidences. Three days since the funeral, and the room still held Christian's presence— in the half-finished glass of brandy on the mantelpiece that no one had dared to clear away.

The morning light filtered through tall sash windows, striking dust motes that danced in amber beams, casting long fingers across walls hung with fading tapestries and ancestral portraits that had witnessed everything and told nothing. Thomas ran his hands now along the polished edge of Christian's writing desk, feeling the familiar whorls in the wood grain that he had dusted for nearly fifty years.

"One last service," Thomas murmured to the empty room, his Norfolk lilt still present despite decades in aristocratic households. He straightened his back—butler's posture ingrained even now—and opened the leather portfolio he had brought. Inside lay tissue paper, labels, and twine; the tools for archiving a life.

First came the naval medal, tucked in a drawer beneath stacks of correspondence. The Imperial German Navy Cross for valour at *Jutland*, where Christian had served aboard *SMS Frankfurt*. Thomas turned it over, watching light glide across its surface. The young prince had returned from that battle with more than a medal—the scars on his chest, and something in his eyes had hardened. The medal went into its own wrapping, Thomas' fingers lingering on the ribbon, now fraying at the edges.

He wrote another card, more details—dates, significance, the story of how Christian had dismissed its importance over dinner one evening, claiming that "any fool with the misfortune to be standing in the right place" might have received it.

The silver locket required more delicacy. Thomas found it in Christian's bedside table, where it had lain every night within arm's reach for over forty years. Its chain was worn thin from handling, the silver casing dulled by the oils of skin. Thomas knew without looking what it contained, but he opened it nonetheless—a ritual of confirmation.

Inside, behind glass slightly clouded with age, was a lock of fair hair, bound with silk thread so fine it was nearly invisible. John's hair, cut during his convalescence in 1918 after being wounded in the retreat from *Lateaux Wood*. Thomas remembered Jonny secretly buying the locket for Christian and storing it safely until its discovery in 1919.

"You guarded it well," Thomas said softly to the absent Christian, closing the locket with gentle pressure. He wrapped it separately, making another notation, more detailed than the others—the provenance of the hair, the date it was taken, the circumstances. Some future historians might dismiss such sentimentality, but Thomas knew better. In these small artifacts lay the truth of two lives intertwined despite a world determined to pull them apart.

As he worked, Thomas allowed himself rare moments of recollection. He saw them as young men, laughing on the terrace, their shoulders touching just slightly more than necessary. He remembered how John would brighten at the arrival of letters with German postmarks in *Cambridge*. Thomas arranged the wrapped items in a neat row on the sturdy oak table that dominated the centre of the study.

The table where Christian and Pete had pored over maps, during the second war. He adjusted each package until they were perfectly aligned, a final act of service to the precision Christian had always appreciated. He recalled Lord John's funeral in 1919, how Christian had stood like granite by the grave, his face a careful mask, accepting condolences with perfect aristocratic reserve. Only Thomas had seen him later that night, kneeling by John's empty bed, shoulders heaving in silent agony.

Thomas had quietly withdrawn, leaving grief its privacy, but the next morning, he'd found Christian in the study, composing himself with brandy at an hour when most of the house still slept.

"He always said you were worth your weight in gold, Thomas," Christian had said without turning around. "Said you saw everything and mentioned nothing."

"A good servant observes discretion, my lord," Thomas had replied.

Christian had finally faced him then, eyes red-rimmed but dry. "Not servant. Never that. Witness, perhaps. Custodian." He'd gestured vaguely at the room, at the house, at their shared decades. "Someone must remember truthfully when we're gone."

The morning stretched into afternoon as Thomas meticulously catalogued each item. He fetched a fountain pen from his pocket, uncapping it with practiced ease. The whisper of nib against paper joined the soft ticking of the longcase clock in the corner—a rhythm like heartbeats, counting down the minutes of this final duty.

Outside, gardeners trimmed hedges and raked gravel, life continuing in its measured pace. Inside, time seemed suspended as Thomas created an archive of love disguised as friendship, of devotion masked as loyalty, of a bond that had survived war, social pressure, family obligation, and the steady erosion of years.

His hands were stiff when he finished writing, but he felt a warmth in his chest, a sense of completion that came with honouring his promise. He had been faithful to the trust placed in him, to the confidence of two men who had found in each other what the world would have denied them.

As he gathered his papers and prepared to move to the next task, he paused by the window, looking out over the formal gardens where two young men had once walked, their shadows stretching toward each other in the fading light.

"The story continues," Thomas whispered to himself, knowing that his next discovery would ensure that nothing of value would be lost to time. The small mahogany desk in Christian's dressing room offered more privacy than the study, which servants occasionally entered despite Thomas' instructions.

Thomas settled into the leather chair that still held the impression of Christian's form, adjusting the lamp until its golden circle illuminated just enough of the surface for writing. Beyond the window, darkness gathered prematurely, clouds swelling like bruises against the late afternoon sky. A fitting backdrop, Thomas thought, for the task of recording grief.

He arranged his materials with the precision that had governed his service for six decades: leather-bound journal centred on the blotter, fountain pen uncapped and resting in the silver holder Christian had given him for his fiftieth

A FORBIDDEN LOVE

year at Langley Hall, reference notes aligned to his right, ink bottle secured against accidental tipping. The ritual of preparation steadied his hands, which had begun to tremble after his discoveries in the study.

The journal was new, purchased in Norwich the previous month when Christian's health had begun its final decline.

Thomas had selected it specifically for this purpose—bound in navy calfskin with cream pages of substantial weight that would endure for decades. The first page remained blank, awaiting words that now seemed simultaneously essential and impossible.

Thomas dipped his pen, watching ink cling to the nib in a perfect bead before he touched it to paper. The date came first: '*17 May 1963*'. Then he hesitated, the pen hovering above the pristine surface. Beginning with such deeply personal, significant information: where to start? He saw Christian's decline daily, supporting in ways John couldn't have even if he were alive.

The first drops of rain struck the window, tentative messengers of the approaching storm. Thomas straightened his posture and began to write:

'I undertake this record three days after the passing of Lord Christian Langley, Earl of Grafton, known previously as Prince Christian. As his closest servant for 50 years and personal confidant in his final decades, I alone possess certain knowledge of his last days and private sentiments which must not perish with me.'

Thomas paused, considering his next words carefully. The scratching of his pen resumed:

'The Earl maintained remarkable lucidity until his death, despite increasing physical weakness. His final coherent conversations focused primarily on Lord John Langley, his cousin by blood but companion in spirit, who preceded him in death by forty-four years. Christian spoke often of their shared youth at Langley Hall, of summers spent sailing on the Broads, and of their brief reunion in 1919.'

A gust of wind drove rain against the glass in a sudden fusillade. Thomas glanced up, momentarily distracted, then returned to his writing with renewed purpose:

'On the evening of May 10th, as I adjusted his pillows, Christian confided: "They will call us friends, cousins, bachelors in the official records. But you know better, Thomas. You saw us as we were."'

'When I acknowledged this truth, he continued with surprising vigour: "They lived their love quietly, yet boldly, against all the tides." I believe he spoke of himself and John in the third person as a means of achieving the perspective history would later impose upon them.'

Thomas paused again; the memory of that evening vivid in his mind. Pillows propped up Christian; illness had diminished his once-imposing frame, yet his eyes burned with unusual intensity. The lamp had cast deep shadows across his face, emphasising the sharp cheekbones and the old scar above his right eyebrow—that childhood mark that had somehow never faded.

He resumed writing, his script flowing more freely now:

'Throughout his final week, Christian repeatedly requested items from his desk—specifically letters from the period 1915-1919, when he and John were separated by war. He would read these in private, often closing his eyes afterward as if to better visualise the scenes they described. These letters, the visible record of an invisible bond maintained across enemy lines, seemed to provide more comfort than any medical palliative.'

A FORBIDDEN LOVE

'On May 11th, Christian summoned the family solicitor and made certain amendments to his will. I was not privy to these changes, though I observed that afterward Christian appeared more at peace, as if having secured something of vital importance.'

'That evening, he called me to his bedside and pressed a key into my palm—the key to his desk, though I did not realise its significance at the time. "The truth endures if someone guards it," he told me. "Jonny always said you saw everything and mentioned nothing. Now I ask you to see everything and record it, when the time is right."'

'As Christian's strength failed on May 12th, his German accent—long erased by decades in England—returned prominently. He spoke at times in his native tongue, primarily recounting memories of his naval service and his childhood in Germany before the Great War. Yet even in delirium, he would return to English when speaking of or to John, as if that relationship existed in a linguistic territory of its own.'

'In lucid moments, he expressed concern for his personal effects, extracting from me a promise to personally oversee their disposition. He stated, "Certain things remain outside history's purview, for now."'

'That night, I maintained vigil at his bedside while the doctor slept in an adjoining room. Shortly after midnight, Christian woke suddenly from apparent slumber and grasped my wrist with surprising strength. "I see him, Thomas," he whispered, his gaze fixed on something beyond the foot of the bed. "John is waiting. He looks as he did that summer before everything changed."'

'On his last morning, Christian found strength, choosing the library to view his terrace and gardens. I left him with his chest of letters, but on my return, I found that he had ventured outside to sit under his favourite oak tree. There he passed away, with a serene look of contentment on his face.'

The ink from Thomas' pen mixed with a tear that had fallen unnoticed onto the page, creating a small blur that he did not attempt to blot. Some imperfections deserved preservation. He wiped his eyes with his handkerchief and continued:

'I record these details not merely as historical curiosities but as testament to a bond that defied convention and societal expectations, it transcended the conventional understanding of friendship, family loyalty, or even romantic attachment as commonly perceived. They constructed a private universe within the public one, maintaining appearances required by their position while creating space for authentic connection.'

'I have today taken possession of certain artifacts preserved by Christian —letters, photographs, and personal mementos documenting their relationship from boyhood through to Lord John's final day and his final day. These items reveal aspects of their bond unknown to all except myself and a wartime friend of us all.'

'The careful preservation of these materials suggests Christian's desire that their true relationship not be entirely lost to history, even as he protected it from contemporary scrutiny.'

'As the sole remaining witness to their private life together, I consider it my final duty to ensure these items—and the truth they represent—survive to reach a more understanding age.'

Thomas glanced at the small clock on the mantelpiece. Nearly two hours had passed since he began writing, yet it felt like minutes. The storm continued unabated, but the emotional tempest within him had begun to subside, channelled into purpose through the act of documentation. He turned to a fresh page and wrote with renewed conviction:

A FORBIDDEN LOVE

'John and Christian lived during a period when their love was considered both criminal and pathological. They risked everything—position, reputation, freedom—for a connection society refused to validate. Yet they found ways to look forward to a future together after the Great War.'

'History, with its preference for formal documentation and clear categories, will likely record them as bachelor cousins who shared certain interests and maintained unusually close family ties. This simplification does violence to the truth of their lives together.'

'In recording this, I neither sensationalise nor sanitise. I merely testify to what I witnessed: two men who loved each other completely, consistently, and courageously.'

'They lived their love quietly, yet boldly, against all the tides of their time. Future generations may judge them more fairly than their contemporaries could. Until then, I preserve their story as they lived it: with dignity, discretion, and unwavering devotion.'

As the next day approached, Thomas retrieved an engraved wooden box from the estate office—a document case commissioned by the 5th Earl in the 1840s, crafted from English oak with the Langley crest inlaid in silver on its lid.

The interior, lined with cedar and divided into compartments, provided ideal protection for the packaged materials. Thomas arranged everything with consideration for both preservation and presentation, ensuring that whoever eventually opened this archive would encounter its contents in logical, respectful order.

Once all items were secured in the box, Thomas composed a formal letter on Langley Hall stationery:

'To Messrs. Harrington & Whitby, Solicitors
Lincoln's Inn Fields, London
18th May 1963
Gentlemen,

Enclosed please find personal materials belonging to the late Lord Christian Langley, Earl of Grafton, to be held in your secure storage facilities alongside the existing Langley family papers.

These documents and artifacts are to remain sealed for a period of fifty years from the date of Lord Christian's death (14th May 1963), to be opened on or after 14 May 2013.

Upon that date, these materials shall be made available to qualified historical researchers with appropriate credentials and legitimate scholarly interest in Anglo-German relations, aristocratic life in the twentieth century, or related fields of inquiry.

Should Langley Hall remain in family possession at that time, the current titleholder shall be notified before any materials are accessed. However, family objections may not prevent access after the specified date has passed.

The enclosed journal, written by myself as witness to Lord Christian's final days and his relationship with the late Lord John Langley, provides context for these materials and should be considered an authenticated primary source.

I certify that all enclosed items are genuine and were preserved by Lord Christian himself in a private compartment of his personal desk, discovered by me while executing my duties as executor of his personal effects.

Respectfully submitted,
Thomas Cooper
Personal Aide to the Earl of Grafton, Langley Hall.'

A FORBIDDEN LOVE

Thomas read over the letter twice, ensuring its language was precise yet sufficiently circumspect. Fifty years seemed an appropriate interval—long enough for social attitudes to evolve, for the immediate family to have passed on, for the materials to acquire historical rather than merely personal significance. By 2013, perhaps the world would be ready to understand what these two men had managed to create within the confines of their era's narrow understanding.

Thomas secured the lid with a small brass key, which he would attach to the letter for the solicitors. He ran his palm over the inlaid crest, feeling the slight rise of the silver against the smooth wood. The Langley motto, inscribed in Latin below the shield, caught the strengthening morning light: *'Veritas Fide Dignior'*— Truth Is More Worthy Than Faith.

He rose from the table, lifting the box with both hands. Its weight—the physical heft of memories, of preserved moments, of tangible evidence—felt appropriate. Such a significant relationship should have substance, should register its existence through more than memory alone.

Thomas crossed to the desk and set the box upon its surface, where it would remain until he could personally deliver it to the solicitors in London the following week. He had already arranged for secure transportation, unwilling to entrust this precious cargo to ordinary postal services.

Thomas leaned against the windowsill, suddenly aware of his own advanced age, the slight tremor in his hands, the ache in joints that had served this house and its inhabitants for almost sixty years. He had witnessed so much from his position at the periphery of great events—two world wars, the dissolution of empires, the gradual unwinding of the aristocratic system that had defined his entire existence.

Yet through all those sweeping historical currents, what remained most vivid in his memory were the private moments: Christian sitting close to John as he played on the piano; John sketching Christian's profile while the latter pretended to read, a small smile playing at his lips; the two men walking the estate grounds at sunset, maintaining a proper distance when visible from the house but allowing their shoulders to touch when they thought themselves unobserved.

"It will endure," he said quietly, addressing both the box and the presences he sensed rather than saw. "Your story will endure."

The box remained on the desk, patient as history, waiting for the moment—still a half-century distant—when its contents would speak again of two men who had loved quietly, boldly, against all the tides. A shared forbidden love.

No direct male descendants could be traced and so the title of Earl of Grafton lapsed. Many distant cousins are identified and the estate is divided between them which necessitates the sale of Langley Hall. It becomes a boarding school. To honour the community responsibility felt by Christian and his ancestors, they sold off most of the wider estate at discounted prices to existing tenants.

Local legend holds, that during summer thunderstorms, the laughter and footsteps of two boys can be heard up on the roof of Langley Hall.

THE END

A FORBIDDEN LOVE

A FORBIDDEN LOVE

HISTORICAL NOTES:

Sexuality:
- English law identified anal sex as an offence punishable by hanging as a result of the Buggery Act 1533, which was pioneered by Henry VIII. The Act was the country's first civil sodomy law, such offences having previously been dealt with by the ecclesiastical courts.
- While it was repealed in 1553 on the accession of Mary I, it was re-enacted in 1563 under Elizabeth I.
  James Pratt and John Smith were the last two to be executed for sodomy in 1835.
- Although section 61 of the Offences Against the Person Act 1861 removed the death penalty for homosexuality, male homosexual acts remained illegal and were punishable by imprisonment.
- The Laucher Amendment, section 11 of the Criminal Law Amendment Act 1885, extended the laws regarding homosexuality to include any homosexual act between males, even when there were no witnesses.
- **This meant that people could be convicted for private acts, and often a letter between two people expressing affection was enough evidence to convict.**
- Author and Playwright Oscar Wilde was convicted under this law and sentenced to 2 years of penal labour.
- Conversely, lesbians were never acknowledged or targeted by legislation.
- It was not until 1967 that gay sex was decriminalised for those over 21, it was only in 1998 that the age of consent was equalised at 16.

European and world events:
- **1913:** Treaty of London ended the first Balkan War;
- 28th June, **1914**: Assassination of Franz Ferdinand
  the heir to the throne of the Austro-Hungarian Empire by Serbian separatists;
- 5th July: Austria seeks the support of Germany against Serbia if Russia intervenes;
- 25th July: Austria mobilises against Serbia;
- 31st July: Russian mobilisation in support of Serbia;
- 1st August: German mobilisation and declaration of war against Russia in support of Austria;
- 1st August: France mobilises in support of Russia;
- 2nd August: Germany invades Luxemburg.
- 3rd August: Germany declares war on France;
- 3rd August: Belgium denies Germany permission to pass through its territory;
- 4th August: Germany invades Belgium;
- 4th August 11.00am: Britain demands Germany withdraws from Belgium under the terms of the Treaty of London of 1830;
- 4th August 11.00pm: Britain declares war on Germany;

- 31st May – 1st June **1916**: Battle of Jutland;
- 6th April **1917**: USA declares war on Germany as a result of their U-boat campaign;
- 20th November – 3rd December: Battle of Cambrai;
  8th August **1918**: start of the Hundred Day Offensive;
- 11th November: Germany signs the Armistice of Compiègne, effective from 11.00am;
- December: second wave of Spanish Flu hits Europe. Over 20,000 casualties reported in London in March **1919** alone;
- 21st November: German High Seas Fleet surrenders to Royal navy and is interned at Scapa Flow;
- 21st June **1919**: Scuttling of the High Seas Fleet
- 28th June: Treaty of Versailles signed in France;
- 1st September **1939**: Outbreak of World War Two;
- 7th December **1941**: Entry of USA into the war after Japanese attack on Pearl Harbour;
- 2nd September **1945**: End of WW2 with the surrender of Japan.

About the author

John Williams is a retired teacher of history and published local historian. Check out his other work at:

www.ingramcontent.com/pod-product-compliance
Ingram Content Group UK Ltd.
Pitfield, Milton Keynes, MK11 3LW, UK
UKHW010743190525
5973UKWH00033B/258